"I would rather be here with you than anywhere else in the world," she said.

"I feel the same." He was about to say more, but when he felt the prick of a metal point at the back of his neck, he froze.

Natalia turned her head slightly to see the tip of a spear only a finger's breadth from her face. Her eyes drifted up the wooden shaft to where strong, green hands gripped the weapon. A massive Orc stood staring down at them while his two companions held the spears. He knelt, bringing his face close to Athgar's.

"*He has the grey eyes of the Torkul,*" the Orc announced in the guttural speech of his race.

"*Greetings,*" said Athgar, using the same language. "*I am Athgar, of the Orcs of the Red Hand.*"

A look of surprise erupted on the Orc's face. "*You speak our language! What manner of magic is this?*"

"*It's not magic,*" insisted Athgar. "*I am a member of the tribe. Move your spears, and I shall prove it.*"

The Orc looked at one of his companions. "*This is most unexpected.*"

"*It is a trick, Urughar,*" insisted his comrade. "*A trap set by the Torkul. Do not trust him.*"

The Orc turned his attention to Natalia. "*And what of this female?*" asked Urughar. "*She is not of the Torkul.*"

"*Is she his prisoner?*"

"*No,*" said Athgar, "*she is my bondmate.*"

Urughar turned his attention back to the Therengian. "*You know our culture, I will grant you that, but give me a good reason why I should not kill you both here, right now.*"

"*I know the way of your people,*" the Human replied. "*It is not the Orc custom to kill uninjured prisoners. Take us to your chieftain, and let the tribe decide our fate.*"

The Orc stood, stretching his back while looking around the pine forest. He glanced at the third Orc, a somewhat rotund fellow. "*What think you, Ogda?*"

"*Let Kirak decide,*" he replied. "*It is not for us to make that decision.*"

ALSO BY PAUL J BENNETT

FLAMES

THE FROZEN FLAME: BOOK THREE

PAUL J BENNETT

First Edition: October 2020

ePub ISBN: 978-1-989315-65-1
Mobi ISBN: 978-1-989315-66-8
Apple Books ISBN: 978-1-989315-67-5
Smashwords ISBN: 978-1-989315-68-2
Print ISBN: 978-1-989315-69-9

This book is a work of fiction. Any similarity to any person, living or dead is entirely coincidental.

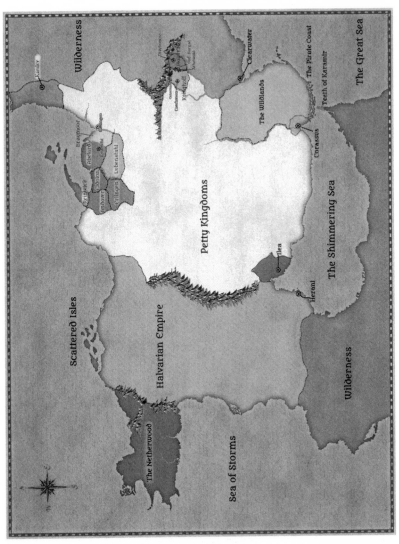

The World of Eiddenwerthe

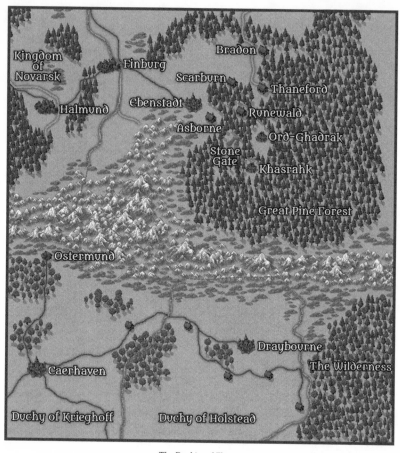

The Duchies of Flames

AROUND THE FIRE

Summer 1104 SR*
(Saints Reckoning)

A thgar stared into the flames, his mind deep in thought.
"A copper for your thoughts?" said Natalia.

He gazed across at her, taking in her black hair and pale features. He had met her less than a year ago, and yet somehow, he felt as though they had known each other their entire lives. He smiled, feeling a warmth at the thought of her embrace.

"Well?" she asked. "Are you going to keep staring, or are you going to come over here and tell me your deepest thoughts?"

"I was thinking of Kargen and Shaluhk," he confessed, "though I will take you up on the offer." He rose, moving closer while she took the blanket from her shoulders, spreading it to encompass them both as he sat beside her on the log.

"They must be well on their way by now," she mused.

"I'm not so sure about that. It's not easy convincing an entire tribe to leave their home."

"They have little choice. You know the Duke of Krieghoff won't take his defeat very well. He'll retaliate. I only hope the Orcs escape in time."

"They will," said Athgar. "The Ancestors watch over them."

"Would that be the same Ancestors who sent us here?" She looked around the forest.

"They work in mysterious ways. We're on our way to Ebenstadt, remember?"

"We spent weeks crossing the mountains. Of course I didn't forget, but why? What do they have in mind for us?"

He shrugged. "I have no idea. Maybe it's better that way? What we don't know can't worry us."

"Do you believe they control us?"

"No, the Orcs are quite clear in their beliefs. The Ancestors guide them, not control them."

"With some exceptions," Natalia added.

"True. I doubt either of us will ever forget the treachery of Khurlig. Her spirit was almost the end of us all."

Natalia nodded her head thoughtfully. It wasn't so long ago that she had, with Shaluhk's help, tried to contact one of the Orc Ancestors with some-what disastrous results. If it hadn't been for the timely intervention of Uhdrig, they both might have ended up dead, or even worse, trapped in the spirit realm forever.

Athgar saw her shudder and put his arm around her shoulder. "It's all right he soothed. "It's all over now."

She glanced around the small clearing, turning skyward to where the majestic pines gazed down on them. "I've never been one for the outdoors, but you make it quite bearable."

A spark from the fire drew their attention. "It appears the hare is almost done," he said as he reached forward, withdrawing the makeshift spear from the ground and examining its slightly burned offering. "I think I cooked it too long."

Natalia laughed, the sound echoing through the trees. "My hero, the mighty hunter. Did no one ever teach you how to cook?"

He offered her the spear. "You're welcome to give it a try?"

"I'm the city girl, remember? I spent my life at the Volstrum." She smiled, lessening the blow. "Don't worry, I'm sure there's enough unburned meat for us to survive."

He pulled forth a knife and began cutting off a thin strip.

Natalia took the tender morsel, popping it into her mouth and chewing. "Not bad," she said, "but it could use some spice."

"I'll give you spice," he said, lowing the spear. He leaned in close, kissing her even as she tried to chew. They both fell back from their makeshift perch into the leaves and pine needles that blanketed the forest floor.

Natalia shrieked out in laughter, Athgar soon joining in the merriment. Eventually, they fell silent, each looking into the other's eyes.

"I would rather be here with you than anywhere else in the world," she said.

"I feel the same." He was about to say more, but when he felt the prick of a metal point at the back of his neck, he froze.

Natalia turned her head slightly to see the tip of a spear only a finger's breadth from her face. Her eyes drifted up the wooden shaft to where strong, green hands gripped the weapon. A massive Orc stood staring down at them while his two companions held the spears. He knelt, bringing his face close to Athgar's.

"*He has the grey eyes of the Torkul,*" the Orc announced in the guttural speech of his race.

"*Greetings,*" said Athgar, using the same language. "*I am Athgar, of the Orcs of the Red Hand.*"

A look of surprise erupted on the Orc's face. "*You speak our language! What manner of magic is this?*"

"*It's not magic,*" insisted Athgar. "*I am a member of the tribe. Move your spears, and I shall prove it.*"

The Orc looked at one of his companions. "*This is most unexpected.*"

"*It is a trick, Urughar,*" insisted his comrade. "*A trap set by the Torkul. Do not trust him.*"

The Orc turned his attention to Natalia. "*And what of this female?*" asked Urughar. "*She is not of the Torkul.*"

"*Is she his prisoner?*"

"*No,*" said Athgar, "*she is my bondmate.*"

Urughar turned his attention back to the Therengian. "*You know our culture, I will grant you that, but give me a good reason why I should not kill you both here, right now.*"

"*I know the way of your people,*" the Human replied. "*It is not the Orc custom to kill uninjured prisoners. Take us to your chieftain, and let the tribe decide our fate.*"

The Orc stood, stretching his back while looking around the pine forest. He glanced at the third Orc, a somewhat rotund fellow. "*What think you, Ogda?*"

"*Let Kirak decide,*" he replied. "*It is not for us to make that decision.*"

Urughar looked back at Athgar. "*It seems my companions wish to take you back to Ord-Ghadrak. If you give us any problems, I shall have you killed on the spot. Is that clear?*"

Athgar turned to Natalia. "They want to take us to a place called Ord-Ghadrak. I'm assuming it's the name of their village."

"And then?" she asked.

"I imagine we'll meet their chieftain."

"Will your torc keep us safe?"

He instinctively put a hand to his neck where the golden necklace lay beneath his clothes. It had been a gift from Kargen to symbolize his close ties with the Orcs of the Red Hand, a sure sign he was held in high esteem. But now, amongst these new Orcs, he wondered if they would recognize it. He and Natalia had been expecting to arrive in a Human city, not an Orc village. So he had hidden it, for such open displays of Orc culture might be seen as provocation amongst Humans.

"Orc tribes have many differences," he announced. "I can't guarantee we'll see the same sort of reception as we had in Ord-Kurgad."

"I wish Kargen and Shaluhk were here," said Natalia. "They'd know what to do."

A spear pressed close, eliciting a wince from Athgar as the point drew blood.

"*Silence!*" the Orc roared. "*Now, get to your feet. We have a long way to travel, and darkness will soon be upon us.*"

ORD-KURGAD

Summer 1104 SR
(In the tongue of the Orcs)

Kargen struggled through the assembled mass to where Shaluhk stood, their son, Agar, by her side, clutching a wooden axe. At nine months of age, he had been walking for some time as was typical of his race. He had already accompanied his father on the hunt, though only as an observer.

"Is all ready?" asked Shaluhk.

Kargen nodded, taking in those around him. "We have enough food for a ten-day of travel, maybe even two if we conserve our strength. The real issue will be water, for we are entering uncharted territory."

"The Ancestors will guide us."

A short, pale-skinned Orc moved closer, the crowd parting to allow him through.

"Master Artoch," said Shaluhk, "are you sure you will not come with us? We would welcome a wielder of flame."

The elderly shaman bowed. "You flatter me, but I can not. Those who have chosen to remain will need my guidance."

"You know the Humans will return," warned Kargen, "and in greater numbers than before. They will not sit idly by allowing us to live in peace after the defeat we have dealt them."

"I know," said Artoch, "and yet what would you have me do? I can not abandon our people in their time of need."

"We are not abandoning them," said Kargen, his emotions threatening to get the better of him. "If they were not so stone-headed, they would realize that. Convince them to join us, Artoch. It is their only hope of survival."

"I have tried, believe me." He reached up, placing his hand on his chieftain's shoulder. "May the Ancestors guide you, Kargen," he said, "and you too, Shaluhk. You are the future of our people."

"I wish you the best of luck," said Kargen, "for you face a difficult time."

"As do we all," noted the master of flame. "Now, I shall return to the village to help those I might. You, on the other hand, must begin the great exodus eastward into the vast wilderness where Humans fear to tread. Farewell, my friends."

They watched him go, soon disappearing from view. Shaluhk reached down, lifting up the wicker basket and frame so she could slip it over her shoulders.

Kargen took a last look at the village, then hefted his own burden, a large basket containing an assortment of weapons, including the precious warbows. Athgar had shown them how to make a bow that would take advantage of the Orc's massive strength, and Kargen was loathe to part with them. He looked around searching the crowd, to no avail.

"Where is he?" he asked.

"He will be here soon enough," explained Shaluhk. "My brother is often late for things. It was true even of his own birth."

Kargen looked at her in surprise. "I thought he was the older?"

"He was, but I could not come forth into the world until he made up his mind to enter it first."

A familiar cry echoed through the crowd. "Where is that sister-son of mine?"

"Laruhk," said Shaluhk. "It is about time you showed up. Where have you been?"

Her brother pushed his way closer, then halted, brandishing a small bow. "I have this," he announced, "for Agar."

The tiny Orc ran towards his uncle, his wooden axe still clutched in his hand.

Laruhk knelt, replacing bow for axe. "You carry this," he said, "and later, once we are underway, I will show you how to use it." He tucked the axe into Agar's weapon belt, the mark of a true huntsman.

Shaluhk placed her hands on her hips, a very Human pose. "He can barely use the axe, Brother. How can you expect him to be able to master a bow?"

"Why not?" said Laruhk. "I was of a similar age when I first used one."

Shaluhk shook her head. "You were almost two. Sometimes I think you forget more than you remember."

"Two years, nine months. What is the difference?"

Kargen held up his hand. "Perhaps it is best if we leave this discussion for another time. We have a migration to begin."

"Very well," said Shaluhk, "but I warn you, the matter is far from settled."

"Take the hunters forward," ordered Kargen. "They are the eyes and ears of the tribe. They know what to do."

Laruhk bowed. "As you wish, my chieftain."

He ran off, calling others to his side as he went.

"He means well," said Kargen.

Shaluhk took Agar's hand. "So he does, but he needs someone to keep his mind occupied. He is far too... what is the Human term?"

"Frivolous?" suggested Kargen.

"Yes, that is precisely what my brother is."

"He needs a bondmate," said Kargen.

Shaluhk scanned the crowd. "He will not find one here. All of our females of age are already bonded."

"Then maybe he will find one in our travels?"

She gave her chieftain a quizzical look. "We are travelling into the wilderness. Orc females do not grow on trees, you know."

Kargen laughed a low, rumbling sound that reverberated through the crowd. "You are beginning to sound like Nat-Alia."

"And is that a bad thing?"

"No, not at all." He lapsed into silence.

She placed her other hand on his arm. "I miss them too, but we must believe we will meet them again."

"Perhaps," he replied, though with little enthusiasm.

The crowd started thinning as the first of them began moving. Soon they were heading eastward through the heavily wooded forest that had been their home for generations.

Kargen and Shaluhk stayed with the centre of the column, helping others, and doing what they could to keep their spirits raised. It was not an easy thing to leave one's home, particularly under the threat of war, but Kargen was determined to see them safely through this ordeal.

By midday, they had topped a rise. Kargen halted, watching the distant smoke drifting up from the village, evidence life still went on amongst those who had chosen to remain.

Shaluhk paused by his side, her hand instinctively finding his. "Something troubles you."

He nodded. "To reach the wilderness, we must cross the width of the Duchy of Holstead. I doubt the duke will take kindly to us doing so."

"But we mean no harm. Can he not see that?"

"We are talking of Humans, a race who has persecuted us for generations."

"And yet it was the Duke of Holstead who allowed us to live in peace."

Kargen nodded. "Yes, but recent events have put even that in jeopardy. He will not be pleased to see the soldiers of his nemesis so close to his lands. For years, we have served to protect his border. Our exodus leaves it dangerously exposed."

"We can not be held hostage by the whims of dukes. We are our own people, not here to be used as some kind of weapon by Human nobles."

"True, and yet, like it or not, we have become essential to their defence."

"Come, my bondmate, such thoughts can only serve to weaken us. Let us not look to the past, but to the future."

Kargen nodded, then turned, releasing her hand to scoop up little Agar. The Orc youngling let out a roar of delight as he was hoisted onto his father's shoulders. His actions complete, he took her hand once more.

"Come, then," he said. "If Athgar and Nat-Alia can do this, so can we. We are a team, you and I, who lead with one heart. Let us guide our people to their destiny, whatever that might be."

THE BLACK AXE

Summer 1104 SR

Athgar and Natalia arrived at Ord-Ghadrak well past midnight. The first sign of the village was when Athgar spotted the distant torches throwing their light off the pine trees. They soon entered the clearing, coming face to face with the large wooden palisade.

The walls were the height of three men, made of thick trunks of spruce roughly hewn and anchored into the soil. Unlike Ord-Kurgad, which had no permanent gate to speak of, here the gate consisted of a great double door of thick, solid planks. When it was thrown open upon their arrival, it revealed an interior much like that of any other tribe with a scattering of rough wooden structures spread around a large central firepit.

Orcs gathered around as they made their way towards the largest building, a great hall with thick wooden walls and a roof to match. Athgar thought the great hall in Ord-Kurgad was impressive, but this structure dwarfed even that grand structure. It also looked ancient as if the wood itself had been carved from the living forest generations ago.

When the group halted, Orcs gathered around in fascination. Urughar prodded Athgar with his spear, forcing him forward as the other villagers watched.

Athgar could discern little beyond the fire, his night vision blinded by the light, but the murmuring quieted as someone made their way towards them.

The crowd parted to reveal an impressive figure, tall even by Orc standards, and fully a head taller than any man Athgar had ever seen. His dark green skin was marked by lighter scars that ran across his face as if he had been clawed by some great creature in years past. The chainmail shirt he wore reflected the light of the fire as he advanced to halt before them.

Athgar quickly glanced over his shoulder to see Natalia, held in place by the threat of a spear. The great Orc bent slightly, peering into Athgar's eyes.

"*What have we here?*" said the Orc, his voice low and menacing. "*Is this a Torkul I see before me?*"

"*I'm a Therengian, if that's what you mean.*"

Athgar's reply elicited a cry of surprise from the crowd.

"*How is it,*" the Orc chieftain continued, "*you speak our language?*"

"*I claim kinship with the Orcs of the Red Hand.*"

"*Ridiculous. No Human has ever earned that honour, let alone a Torkul.*"

"*And yet you have allies who are Human.*"

"*What nonsense is this?*"

Athgar pressed his case. "*It's true. I swear it. Consult with your shamans, and you will see. Ask them about your brethren in the Netherwood.*"

The great Orc turned, looking behind him, searching for a face in the crowd. "*Mortag,*" he beckoned, "*come here. I would seek your wisdom.*"

An Orc, bent with age, stepped forward. He cradled his left arm, which hung, withered and frail. "*You called, mighty Kirak?*"

"*Tell us what you know of the Netherwood.*"

"*It is a land far to the west,*" Mortag replied, "*where dwell a tribe of our people. It is said a Human named Redblade came to their assistance in their time of need. If you wish to know more, you will have to consult with Laghul, for she is the mistress of the spirits, while I am merely a master of flame.*"

Kirak laughed, a deep rumbling sound that reminded Athgar of Kargen. "*Hardly,*" the Orc continued. "*You are the most powerful flame wielder this tribe has ever known.*"

The chieftain turned his attention back to Athgar once more. "*It seems you speak the truth, Human. Tell me, what is your name?*"

"*I am Athgar of Athelwald, master of flame.*"

His statement brought another gasp from the crowd. Mortag moved closer, peering into his eyes. "*I see no sign of deception. Can this be true?*"

"*Free my hands, and I will show you.*"

Kirak ignored the outburst, looking instead at Mortag. "*Is this even possible? Do the Torkul have shamans of their own?*"

"*No, my chieftain, they do not, though it is said their Ancestors did many generations ago.*"

He looked at Urughar. *"Release his bonds. Mortag, watch this Human closely. If he attempts to escape, burn him."*

"Yes, mighty Kirak."

Athgar turned as Urughar pulled a wicked-looking knife. The Orc smiled, then began sawing away at the bindings.

Natalia struggled, but Ogda held her arms in an iron grip.

The Therengian rubbed his wrists, feeling the tingling sensation as the blood returned to his fingers. He slowly raised his hands to his neck and withdrew the torc.

"Here," he said. *"This was a gift from Kargen of the Red Hand. Take it if you must."*

Kirak leaned forward, taking the end of the torc in his massive hand. It was carved of gold made to look like rope, and the ends were capped with miniature Orc heads, red stones set in their mouths.

"Fine work," said the Orc chieftain, releasing the torc, *"and obviously of Orcish origin. You must have been welcome indeed to receive such a gift. How is it one of your race came to live amongst our people?"*

"I lived amongst my own people in the village of Athelwald, in a region to the south of the Grey Spire Mountains. I was a maker of bows and traded with your brethren in Ord-Kurgad. All of that changed when my village was destroyed, and I was left for dead. I was found by Kargen, an Orc hunter, and taken back to his village."

"An interesting tale," noted Mortag, *"and yet it doesn't explain how you came to be a master of flame."*

"I was taught by Artoch," explained Athgar. *"He said I had the spark."*

The shaman turned to his chieftain. *"He speaks the truth, noble leader. I am familiar with Artoch, and I, too, see the spark within him."*

"How can this be?" mused Kirak. *"The Torkul here give us nothing but trouble. How can this individual be so different?"*

"Can not the tribes of Orcs differ?" asked Athgar. *"Humans are no different."*

"You have given me much food for thought," the chieftain continued. *"I must consult with my advisors before we take a vote. You will go with Mortag, Athgar of Athelwald, and he shall test the depths of your knowledge."*

"And what of my companion?"

Kirak's gaze swivelled to Natalia. *"She is of no consequence to us. She may accompany you."*

Athgar was about to protest the Orc's callous disregard for her but thought better of it. Better to not let them know that possibly the most powerful Water Mage on the Continent was amongst them.

They were led to a hut where Urughar untied Natalia. He ordered them to remain, then left with a promise of food.

Athgar looked at Natalia, concern written on his features. "Are you all right?"

"I'm fine," she replied. "I managed to pick up on a little of the conversation, but I'm afraid my Orcish is not very good."

"Their master of flame is going to test me, likely to see how powerful I am."

"And then what?"

"I'm not sure. I also thought it best to not reveal your magical abilities. I hope you don't mind?"

"Not at all, I think it wise. After all, we don't yet know if these Orcs are friend or foe."

"Yes, and they've been having trouble with Therengians, or Torkul, as they call us."

"Do you think they might be survivors from Athelwald?"

He gave it some thought. "Possibly, but my understanding was that only a handful escaped; the rest were sold off as slaves. I doubt a dozen Therengians would prove much of a threat to an entire tribe of Orcs."

"There's something else going on here," noted Natalia. "They are obviously familiar with your people. Could there be another village around here somewhere?"

"I never thought of that, but it would make sense. Athelwald couldn't have been the only village left."

She reached out, touching his arm. "Do you realize the implications of this, Athgar? You may have found your people!"

He smiled at the thought. Ever since the loss of his village, he had searched for them. Now it seemed likely the search was coming to an end. Could they finally settle down and live in peace? He became aware of Natalia's gaze and was left feeling guilty. Was this what she wanted? He was suddenly struck with a sense of melancholy, a look not lost on his companion.

"What's wrong?" she said. "You should be happy."

"What of you?" he asked.

"What of me? Whatever do you mean?"

"What do you want? You were raised in the Volstrum. Would you ever consider settling down in a backwards village?"

"I am content when we are together," she said, "wherever that may take us. I think it is our destiny to live amongst your people. Maybe it's why the Ancestors sent us here."

He shook his head. "It would be nice, but I don't see it that way. Something is wrong here. There shouldn't be such animosity between the Orcs and the Therengians."

"Then perhaps THAT'S why we're here, to heal those wounds."

"Perhaps," he replied, though in his heart he knew it was unlikely.

Urughar soon returned, dropping two wooden bowls before them.

Natalia picked one up, breaking out into a big smile. "Orc porridge, one of my favourites. You know Shaluhk used to give it a hint of maple."

The Orc looked at her in surprise. *"Shaluhk?"*

"Yes, she was the Life Mage. Sorry, I meant Shamaness of the Red Hand. She's also my sister."

"What is she talking about," asked the Orc in his own tongue.

Athgar made the quick switch to Orcish. *"She is a tribe sister to Shaluhk, who was trained by Uhdrig."*

"Uhdrig," said the Orc. *"Now, that is a name I am familiar with. You should talk to Laghul. She would be most interested in your tale."*

"Could you arrange such a thing?"

Urughar broke out in a grin, showing his sharp ivory teeth, then he left the hut, leaving Athgar and Natalia alone once more.

"Did you understand any of that?" he asked.

"A little," she replied. "I take it he's going to bring the shamaness?"

"Yes. Hopefully, she can verify our story. The Orcs can communicate over long distances, can't they? Do you think she can contact Shaluhk?"

"I wouldn't count on it," said Natalia. "The tribe is likely on the move."

"That won't matter."

"It won't? Isn't a moving target harder to find?"

"No," said Athgar. "My understanding is that Spirit Magic works regardless of range or position. It has more to do with how familiar the caster is with the recipient."

"But how would this Laghul be familiar with Shaluhk if they've never met?"

"I have no idea, but they learned of things across the Sea of Storms, so they must have some way of doing it. Unless you're suggesting they can travel great distances by magic?"

"Don't be ridiculous," said Natalia. "You'd need a magic circle for that."

"A magic circle?"

"Yes, aren't you familiar with them as a Fire Mage?"

"I can't say I am. The Orcs don't use them as far as I'm aware."

"Not even circles of stone?"

The blank look on Athgar's face told her all she needed to know. "Never mind. Perhaps it's beyond their understanding."

"They are an intelligent race," said Athgar, growing defensive, "and they've used magic far longer than Humans."

"I meant no offence, but their history is an oral one, isn't it? I would imagine the complexities of using a magic circle would be hard to pass down in such a manner."

"Can you use such powers?"

"No, I was never taught the spell of recall. They reserve those types of things for the more experienced mages in the family."

"I can see why," he mused.

"What's that supposed to mean?"

"Such a spell would be particularly powerful. It could be used to get into all sorts of mischief."

"We're talking about experienced mages here," she added, "not children."

"Is there a difference? We've both seen first-hand how power can corrupt people."

Natalia's features softened. "You're right, of course. Not everyone is capable of protecting such a secret, and it could wreak havoc on a country's ability to defend itself against a magical attack. They are probably better off without it."

"The Orcs have a unique perspective on magic. It is always used with the utmost care. Something most Humans don't seem to worry about."

"I'd have to agree with you there. All of my training taught me to unleash my full power whenever casting. It was only after meeting you that I learned proper control."

"Why do you think that is?" Athgar wondered. "Humans unleashing everything, I mean."

"Ego. It's well known most Fire Mages like to display their prowess. You're the only one I've ever met who controls his magic. It's what sets you apart." She smiled. "It's also one of the things I treasure about you."

"So what do I do when Mortag comes for me? Do I show him my full potential or hold back?"

"I can't make that decision for you. You know the Orcs better than I. Which approach do you think would be better?"

"I'm inclined towards control. It is, after all, their way."

"There, you see? You had the answer all along."

Now it was Athgar's turn to smile. "True, but it took your encouragement to help me see it."

"That's what I'm here for, amongst other things."

"Other things?"

A grin spread across Natalia's face. "Of course. We can't stay locked up as prisoners forever, can we? Do you think we could have a bath?"

He was about to agree when Mortag came through the door. The old Orc's withered left arm was in a sling, his right holding a gnarled staff.

"So," he began, "you claim to be a master of flame. Step outside, and let us see your craft."

"Do you speak the common tongue?" asked Athgar.

"The common tongue? What an insult to the elder races. Only Humans would refer to their own language as common."

"Call it what you like, but my companion speaks limited Orcish."

Mortag shrugged. "I must confess I know a little. It comes in handy when talking to prisoners such as yourself, but I am here today to test you, not her, and as you speak our tongue, I shall remain using it. Now, come outside and bring your companion if you wish. No harm will befall either of you. I promise."

He rose, indicating for Natalia to do likewise. They followed the flame wielder outside to where a small crowd had gathered.

"This," began Mortag, "is where apprentices learn to cast their spells." He pointed at a stone obelisk that stood some fifty paces away. "Can you hit that?"

"Most certainly," he replied. "I assume you wish me to use a streak of fire?"

The old Orc nodded. "You may begin when ready."

Athgar stepped forward, clearing his mind and shaking his hands in an effort to relax. Next, he closed his eyes and began concentrating on his inner spark, letting it grow inside of him. Then his eyes opened, and he thrust his hands to the front, sending a streak of flame heading towards the target. It struck the rock dead centre, splashing fire to either side, then vanished, leaving behind a scorched smell.

Mortag nodded in appreciation. "Good, very good. I see you use our methods well. What else can you do?"

"I can start fires," Athgar replied.

The Orc waved his hand, brushing aside the claim. "That is easy, but can you produce flames on a weapon?"

"I can, on axes, swords, and even arrows."

"Smoke?"

"Yes." He wanted to add he'd even seen battle but thought better of it. Orcs were hunters, not a warrior race, despite their reputation for it.

"What else can you do?" the Orc inquired.

"I can cast warmth, a spell that served us well when we crossed the mountains."

"What of the phoenix?"

"I'm afraid it is beyond my training, though I have seen one in battle."

"You have fought other mages," Mortag declared.

"How did you know?"

"You show no fear in my presence, a most remarkable feat for a Human. Many would tremble at the thought of such power beneath the surface." He glanced at

Natalia. "She, also, is unafraid. I sense you have both been through much since your village was destroyed."

Athgar stared back, unsure of how to answer.

"Now," the Orc continued, *"we have seen the accuracy of your casting. Let us see you demonstrate your full power."*

"Very well, what will you have me do?"

Mortag pointed to where a group of Orcs were stacking wood in preparation for a bonfire. *"We will start with that. They are preparing a fire for the morning meal."* He waved away the Orcs, then waited as they cleared the area, turning to face Athgar. *"You may proceed when ready."*

Athgar looked at Natalia, who merely nodded. He took a step forward, thrusting both hands out in a pushing motion. The air around them seemed to shake, and then a giant fire roared to life from beneath the logs, reaching up high into the night sky. The nearby Orcs were caught off guard and could do little but gape in wonder at the display.

Mortag turned to the Therengian, his features noticeably paler than they had been. *"Most impressive,"* he said. *"You have learned well from Master Artoch."*

Athgar bowed his head. *"Thank you. I strive to do him honour."*

A smile broke out on the face of the master of flame. *"Your coming is fortuitous. The Ancestors must have sent you to help us in our time of need."*

"Why? What is it that ails you?"

"That," said Mortag, *"is for Kirak to explain."*

Urughar led them to the great hut. Though larger in size than that of Ord-Kurgad, it was similar in layout. One end consisted of the chieftain's private rooms, and it was here the Orc hunter led them.

Athgar and Natalia stepped inside to see Kirak seated on a pile of animal skins. Beside him was a female Orc who appeared even taller, though thinner of frame than the great chieftain.

"Come, sit," said Kirak.

Athgar sat, with Natalia beside him.

Kirak offered him a bowl filled with a pale white liquid. *"Will you drink the milk of life?"*

He accepted the bowl, sipping lightly from its rim, then passing it to Natalia. She took her own sip, then passed it, in turn, to Urughar.

"Now," said Kirak, *"let me officially welcome you to the Orcs of the Black Axe. This"*— he indicated the female Orc—*"is Laghul, our shamaness. It is she who has confirmed your story, reaching out to the Ancestors of the Red Hand."*

"Greetings," said Laghul, *"and welcome to our tribe. As a member of the Red*

Hand, you shall be granted all the rights and privileges of our race, including a hut, which you may use at your leisure."

"Thank you," said Athgar. "You do us a great honour."

"Please, tell us of your journey."

"Shaluhk, who is now the Shamaness of the Red Hand, consulted the Ancestors. On their advice, we are travelling north, seeking a city known as Ebenstadt. Do you know of this place?"

Laghul nodded her head. *"We do. It lies some distance to the northwest, past the villages of the Torkul, though to my knowledge no Orc has ever set foot there."*

"Your master of flame indicated you were having trouble with the Torkul. I assume they are like me? People with grey eyes, that is?"

"They are," said Kirak, *"and they have been a thorn in our side of late."*

"Can you be more specific?" asked Athgar. "Maybe there is some way in which we can help?"

Kirak eyed him suspiciously. *"And why would you agree to do that?"*

"It is in both our best interests. I believe these Torkul are my people, though long separated from my own village. When Athelwald was destroyed, its people were carted off into slavery. I have since learned some escaped, and I'm hoping they found refuge amongst their fellow Therengians."

"And how does that serve our interests?"

"My people lived in peace and harmony with the Orcs of the Red Hand. I see no reason why it cannot be so here. Tell me what it is that they have done."

"They encroach on our lands," said Kirak, *"and threaten the very balance of nature. Our Ancestors brought us here to live free of the influence of Humans. And yet now that very same plague has been brought to our homes."*

"When you say they are encroaching, do you mean hunting or settling?"

"The former, but it is only a matter of time until they put down roots. Already they have migrated from the west, pushing them ever closer to our homes."

"Have you tried talking with them?" Athgar asked.

"They are Humans. They will not listen to reason. At the mere sight of us, they attack."

"They are likely fearful," explained Athgar, *"as you are of them. Tell me, do you know why they migrated?"*

"No," Kirak confessed, *"and they are unlikely to explain it to us. It is hard to be reasonable at the point of a spear."*

"Perhaps," offered Natalia, in her broken Orcish, *"we can help."*

"Yes," added Athgar. "Show us how to find them, and we shall try to reason with them. Let's hope we can get to the bottom of this."

Kirak looked at Laghul, who simply nodded her head. *"Very well,"* said the chieftain. *"The Ancestors have seen fit to send you to us. Let us now see if their decision was a wise one."*

CONFRONTATION

Summer 1104 SR

Laruhk sprinted down the column, halting before Kargen to stop and gasp for air.

"What is it?" asked Kargen.

"Humans," the hunter replied. "A large number of them, with weapons."

"The farms we passed must have spread word. They are likely the duke's men."

"What do we do?"

"We must halt," ordered Kargen. "Move the hunters forward, younglings and elderly to the rear. I shall go and talk to the leader of this group. Let us hope he will see reason and allow us safe passage."

"And if not?"

"Then we might have to alter our plans."

"I do not like this, Kargen. It could mean a battle, and we are already weakened."

"I do not like it either, Laruhk, but we must see to the safety of the tribe. We have more than two hundred Orcs to look after. I will not see them fight unless absolutely necessary."

"I shall do as you ask."

Laruhk ran off, calling out names as he went.

Kargen looked around, spotting Shaluhk, who was lifting young Agar to her shoulders. She met his gaze and wandered closer.

"What ails you, bondmate?"

"It is the Humans," he explained. "They have learned of our journey and are seeking to stop us."

Shaluhk looked skyward. "It is easy enough to spot us. The column of dust can be seen for a great distance, but I am at a loss as to where they came from."

"There is likely a town nearby," said Kargen. "That would be why they are so alarmed. What would you do if a large force were closing in on your own village?"

"Fair enough," said Shaluhk, "but can we not reason with them? We are, after all, only interested in travelling east and mean no harm."

"I doubt the duke's men will be as understanding. I fear they will insist we return to Ord-Kurgad."

"That would be a death sentence."

"I see we are of the same opinion."

"What can I do to help?"

"Consult the Ancestors," said Kargen. "They may offer a solution. In the meantime, I must make contact with these Humans and hope they see reason."

The afternoon wore on. The troops of Holstead stood in the sun, sweating, while horsemen galloped back and forth, carrying dispatches.

Commander Harmon, watching from the back of his horse, squinted, looking westward. "What are they doing?"

"It appears nothing, sir," replied his sergeant. "They are just standing there."

"I can see that. I meant, what are they doing here, outside of their lands?"

"I have no idea, sir."

Harmon swore. "Go. Fetch Krasmus, and we will see if he can be of help."

"The mage, sir? Surely not! This is an army matter."

"And what would you have me do, Sergeant? Lead my men into a slaughter?"

"They're only Orcs, sir, no threat to our forces."

"Have you ever seen an Orc close up?"

"No, sir."

"Well, trust me when I say they're large, very large, and not the type of thing you want swinging an axe at you." Harmon shuddered involuntarily. "Besides which, they appear to outnumber us."

"But they are only Orcs!"

"As you've already said, but even savages can inflict casualties. Now go and fetch Krasmus."

The sergeant wheeled, riding off at a gallop.

Harmon cursed his luck. He had risen through the ranks, but the army of Holstead was nothing to brag about. Men like his sergeant were commonplace, and they hadn't fought a real battle for generations.

He watched the greenskins moving about, noticing a thin skirmish line being deployed. Were they seriously thinking of attacking?

"Commander?" came a familiar voice.

Harmon, startled out of his musings, turned to see the Royal Enchanter, Krasmus.

"Your Grace," he said, "as you can see, we have a bit of a situation here."

The mage scanned the west, observing the deployment of Orcs. "So it would seem."

"What can you do about it?"

"I'm afraid I'm an Enchanter, not a battle mage."

"Still," insisted Harmon, "there must be something you can suggest? Do the Orcs fear magic?"

"Not that I'm aware of, no. In fact, they have their own mages, though they call them shamans."

"Do you have any GOOD news for me?"

"I could cast the spell of tongues," replied the Enchanter. "It would allow you to speak their language."

"You expect me to talk to them?"

"Isn't that what you were intending, Commander? To order them back to their lands?"

"But they outnumber us, Krasmus."

The mage sighed. Sometimes it was necessary to point out the obvious to these military leaders. "They may have the numbers here, but you represent the duke, and he can field an army ten times theirs. Invoke his authority. They're bound to back down."

"I suppose, but why are they even here? Do they really think we'd let them rampage through our lands?"

"I have no idea, but THEY do. Why don't you go and ask them yourself?"

"Very well," said Harmon, "cast your spell."

"Yes, Commander." Krasmus closed his eyes, calling on the forces within him. Words of power began to flow from his tongue, and then he snapped his eyes open, pointing to the commander. A slight blue haze descended onto him, soaking into his skin, the Enchanter's own personal touch to the well-established spell.

"It is done."

"Good," said Harmon. "Come with me."

"Me?"

"Yes, you're one of the duke's mages. What better way to project his power."

"If you say so."

Harmon urged his horse forward while Krasmus cast the spell once again, this time on himself. His incantation complete, he galloped forward to catch up.

The greenskins drew closer, and Harmon halted. Two of the creatures walked towards them, their weapons, at least for now, tucked away.

"*I am Commander Harmon, of his dukenesses army.*" He turned to Krasmus in surprise. "Did I say that correctly?"

"More or less. The Orcs lack some of our finesse in their language."

"Why does it sound so bad to my ears?"

"The spell only imparts a rudimentary skill," the mage replied.

"Can't you do something to make it better?"

"I'm afraid not, my lord; it is one of the limitations of magic."

The larger of the two Orcs raised his hand in the air.

"I come in peace," he said in the common tongue of man.

"Saints be, he speaks our language," said Harmon.

"I am Kargen, Chieftain of the Red Hand."

"Greetings, Kargen," said Harmon. "In the name of His Grace, the Duke of Holstead, you are hereby ordered to return to your lands." The commander sat back in his saddle, pleased with the discharge of his duty.

"I am afraid I can not," said Kargen. "My people are heading east, towards the wilderness."

Harmon's face paled as he turned to the Enchanter. "He can't do that! He's heading straight for Althaven!"

"Tell him that," muttered Krasmus.

The commander returned his attention to the greenskin. "I cannot allow it. Return to your lands at once, or my men will be forced to engage."

"We have no wish to fight," replied the Orc.

"There," whispered Harmon, "I've got him now." He raised his voice once more. "Then return to your lands, and let us see an end to this confrontation."

The Orc turned to his companion, muttering something in the ancient language of his race. Harmon strained to hear, but the brute's voice was too low and his speech too fast.

Kargen stepped closer while his companion ran back to the west. "We will go home," he announced, "but we must wait until tomorrow. The sun is too low."

Harmon bowed, trying to appear magnanimous, but inside he was relieved to avoid the confrontation.

"Very well, but you shall begin your return early tomorrow morning."

"Agreed," said Kargen. "By first light, we shall be on our way."

Harmon turned, guiding his horse back towards his own line of troops. "Well, that went much better than I expected."

"So it did," agreed the mage. "It appears you didn't need my services after all."

"They may still double-cross us. I wouldn't put it past them."

"Should we take any precautions?" asked Krasmus.

"Yes, I shall send word for reinforcements, preferably cavalry. I understand they have no horse of their own?"

"Not that I know of."

"Good," said Harmon, "then that should settle it. Now that's done, will you join me for a drink?"

"I should be delighted, Commander."

Kargen poked the fire with a stick. *"Is everything prepared?"*

"It is," said Laruhk. *"They will be surprised come morning when all they find is an empty group of fires."*

"We must take care. Remember, we want them to think we are heading west."

"And so they will. We will leave a trail that even a Human can not miss."

Kargen placed his hand on his friend's shoulder. *"This is no laughing matter, Laruhk. The safety of our people depends on it."*

"I shall lead the hunters myself, and we will draw them westward, then double back and catch up. Are you sure this is what you want?"

"It is," the chieftain replied. *"We can not go east, and the land to the south is too open. We would be easy prey for horsemen. Our only chance is to go north, into the mountains, where their horses can not follow."*

"They will send more soldiers once they have discovered our ruse."

"So they will," Kargen agreed, *"but hopefully by then we will be safe in the foothills."*

"And the Ancestors suggested this?"

"In a roundabout way."

"What does that mean? Did the Ancestors agree or not?"

"They did not disagree."

"You are being stubborn, Kargen. You take after my sister."

"I shall take that as a compliment. Now go, Laruhk, and may the Ancestors watch over you."

All night long, the Orcs moved north, their most skilled hunters bringing up the rear, carefully hiding their tracks. The elderly went first, accompanied by Shaluhk, who led the way, Agar once more on her shoulders. Orcs are a hardy breed, but the pace soon wore on them, and more than one elder had to be helped along the way.

Shaluhk found herself wishing she had mastered her magic, making her able to summon warrior spirits to assist, but it was too late now. Her mistress, Uhdrig, was dead, and with her went any chance of learning new magic.

She paused, watching as Kragor picked up an elder. The hunter placed him across his massive shoulders and moved on, bearing the burden with quiet dignity. The entire escape felt desperate, and she wondered, not for the first time, of the wisdom of this strategy. Would not the Humans see the ruse for what it was? Shaluhk shook her head. No, it would work. She had faith Kargen had made the right choice, the only choice he could, given the circumstances. They would continue their trek northward. It was all that was left to them.

Laruhk looked out over the field, peering from the long grass that hid his position. *"They appear to be taking the bait."*

"So they are," agreed Durgash. He held up his warbow. *"Are you sure Kargen said we could not use these?"*

"Yes, he was very clear on the matter. He does not want to injure any of the enemy. It will only make them madder."

"I can not imagine they will be pleased to find we have led them astray."

"Agreed," said Laruhk, *"but we must do our part. Our job is to delay them long enough for the others to escape."*

"An easy enough task. I see no hunters amongst them."

"You would not know a hunter if one sat on you."

His companion let out a snort, stifling it quickly lest they be heard. *"A good one, my friend."*

"Go," said Laruhk, *"and remember to use the common tongue."*

Durgash grinned, showing his teeth, and then speaking Human. "I will!"

Laruhk watched as the Human soldiers reached the firepits. The flames had long since burned out, now releasing only wisps of smoke into the early morning air. They milled about, unsure of what to do, while other men, their junior leaders, barked out orders.

A group of horsemen appeared, trotting past the Orc's position. He was sure they would spot him, one even going so far as to splash him as it rode past, but the rider's eyes were focused on something in the distance. Laruhk remained hidden.

"Over here," someone yelled. "We've found tracks."

The horsemen spurred on their mounts, disappearing from sight. Not much later, another cry echoed out over the field. "I found something!"

"They are this way," came another voice. Laruhk chuckled to himself, pleased with the ruse. Kargen had planned the diversion, but it was Laruhk who had thought to turn the Human's own language against them. Athgar would be proud.

He waited as the horsemen rode past yet again, seeking out this new voice, then rose to a crouch, putting hand to mouth.

"There they are!" he called out. "To the south!" He dropped back down to his stomach and held his breath. Sure enough, hoofbeats drew closer, and he felt the ground rumble as they rode by.

The game continued, but then the Humans grew tired of the chase. They began to ignore the calls, concentrating instead on moving westward in a methodical manner, looking for a trail to follow. By noon, they were well past Laruhk's position, and he began to grow concerned. He wondered how he might confuse them further, and then a thought struck him.

The Orc crawled forward on his belly, seeking his prey. He soon found a group of horses standing nearby while their riders rested. Remembering the trampling that had so wounded him during the attack on Ord-Kurgad, he flinched but then shrugged. He had survived the injuries, thanks to the efforts of his sister. Obviously, it was not yet time for him to join the Ancestors.

He rose from the ground, moving forward slowly. The riders were all chatting away, deep in conversation. Laruhk drew closer, watching them from the corner of his eye as he approached their horses. His plan was simple enough. Snatch the horses, or release them, and then make his escape.

All that changed when one of the soldiers turned towards the horses. Laruhk froze, but as their eyes met, he knew he had been discovered. He let out a yell as he rushed towards the horses, intending to scare them into running, but the riders had tethered them to a fallen trunk. The Orc was soon amongst them, casting his eyes about, trying to figure out how to untie them.

The warriors called out as they drew their weapons. Laruhk, out of desperation, pulled his knife and began sawing away at a leather lead. Leaping onto the back of a horse, he was ready to speed away to safety, but the beast merely stood there, perhaps frozen with fear.

He tried talking to the animal and then cursed himself for speaking Orc. Next, he tried common, but the stubborn creature was having none of it. Finally, his heart pounding in fear, he slapped the horse's rump, sending it careening off across the field. Laruhk held on for dear life, grasping the mane to steady himself. He felt the wind in his hair, the pulse of the great beast beneath him, and then his head struck a branch as the horse rushed into some trees. One moment he was sitting on the beast's back, the next, he was lying on the ground.

Laruhk shook his throbbing head, trying to stop the world from spinning. His eyes finally came into focus only to stare up into the drawn swords of three soldiers. He smiled, throwing out his arms to his front in supplication. "I am your prisoner," he said, using the common tongue, and then everything went black.

He awoke to a slap. Before him knelt the Human leader, the man who had called himself Commander Harmon.

"Speak, you imbecile," the man was ranting. "I know you understand our language."

Laruhk stared back, unsure of the man's meaning. He tried to speak, but his tongue was swollen, his throat parched.

Harmon looked at his companion. "Is there nothing you can do?"

"He is an Orc, Commander. I doubt torture will loosen his tongue."

Harmon leaned in closer. Laruhk wanted to hit him, but he realized his hands were tied behind his back. He thought back on Kargen's words, then took a deep breath.

"Water," he said, his voice cracking.

"Get him some water," said Harmon. "Maybe that will loosen his tongue."

"Are you sure, sir?"

"Do as I say, man!"

"Yes, sir." His companion held up a cup, tipping the contents down Laruhk's throat.

"Thank you," said the Orc.

"Now speak, you vile creature," said Harmon. "Where have they gone?"

"Back to Ord-Kurgad," said Laruhk, "where you ordered them."

Harmon smiled. "You lie, Orc. We have sent riders ahead. There is no sign of them."

Laruhk's face fell. It appeared the ruse would not work after all. "Very well, I shall tell you, but you must promise not to punish them."

Harmon looked like he wanted to say something but instead took a breath, his face turning red. "Go on," he urged.

"We tried to lure you westward so we could make an escape."

"To where, man?"

Laruhk wanted to laugh, for being called a man was funny to him. Instead, he took a deep breath. "They are going south, to the wilderness."

"I knew it!" said Harmon. "It was a trick all along. These are crafty creatures, these Orcs."

"Your orders, sir?"

"Send the cavalry south. As soon as they've found the trail, we'll send the infantry to follow."

"And what of the prisoner, sir?"

Harmon rose, a smile crossing his features. "He has given us all he can. Dispose of him, Sergeant."

"Yes, Commander." The warrior moved closer, drawing his sword. Laruhk gazed up at him, unable to do anything but watch his own doom approaching.

The commander had moved out of sight, but the sergeant, obviously enjoying himself, made a show of holding the blade before Laruhk's eyes.

"See this, greenskin? This is the instrument of your death. Say your prayers to whatever you believe in."

As he drew back his sword, ready to plunge it into Laruhk's chest, he suddenly halted, a look of surprise on his face as the tip of an arrow blossomed from his chest, splattering Laruhk with blood. The sergeant fell forward to his knees, then flat onto his face, the tail end of the arrow protruding from his back.

Moments later, Durgash was there, warbow in one hand, his knife in the other. *"Can you walk?"*

"No," said Laruhk, *"but I can run!"*

HUNTING GROUNDS

Summer 1104 SR

Urughar slowly brushed aside the weeds, his eyes searching the area. "*I see no sign of them at present, but our hunters marked their presence here only yesterday.*"

"*Then we shall proceed on our own,*" said Athgar. "*I think it best they don't know we're here at your request, at least initially.*"

"*Good luck to you, Therengian, and may your axe stay sharp.*"

"*Thank you, Urughar.*"

The Orc hunter withdrew, leaving Athgar and Natalia in silence, the only sound that of distant songbirds.

"It's very peaceful here," she noted.

"So it is," he agreed. "How do you think we should proceed?"

It took only a moment for Natalia to make up her mind. She rose, stretching her back and luxuriating in the warmth of the sun. "There's no sense in skulking around here; we should walk out in the open."

He soon joined her, though his hand gripped his axe tightly.

"Put that away," she said. "We want to make friends, not intimidate them. Besides which, we might not see them at all."

"They were here yesterday."

"There is no guarantee they are still here. If you were hunting, wouldn't you want to take the kill back to your village?"

"Of course, so Skora could skin it for me."

"She was the old woman who helped look after you and your sister, wasn't she?"

"That's right, I'm surprised you remember. I wouldn't have thought you'd consider it important."

"People are always important, and, aside from your sister, she's probably the closest you have to a family. Hopefully I'll meet her one day."

Athgar frowned. "I doubt you'll get the chance. She was old when I last saw her. She's probably dead by now."

"Why would you say that?"

"Skora always had a streak of rebellion. I doubt she'd take well to a life of slavery. What about you? Do you remember much about your mother?"

"No, but then again, I was young."

"But you were thirteen when you went to the Volstrum, weren't you? Can't you remember something?"

"Ten, actually. I vaguely remember a face, but the academy kept us busy. There was little time for reflection. I'm afraid I've lost most of my childhood memories."

He reached out his hand. "Then we'll just have to make new ones."

Natalia grasped his hand in hers as they stepped into the clearing. Athgar paused as he spotted movement, and then a hare raced across the clearing, a wolf in pursuit.

"I doubt we'll see any hunters yet," he said, pointing. "If they were in the area, the wolves would be scarce."

"Don't they normally hunt in packs?" she asked.

"They do, but this one looks young. Perhaps he's learning?"

"Should we be alarmed?"

"No, they seldom attack Humans."

"Seldom, or never?"

Athgar smiled. "They've been known to attack farm animals from time to time, but only in harsh winters. This place looks to be teeming with wildlife."

She cast her eyes about, then turned to face him. "Are we looking at the same place? I see no signs of life."

He pointed at a nearby tree. "Something's been nibbling at the bark over there, and there are deer prints beneath us, not to mention the hare we just saw."

She looked down in wonderment. "Deer prints?"

Athgar knelt, pointing them out. "Yes, here. Don't you see them? A young buck would be my guess."

"How can you possibly tell that?"

"I'm a hunter, remember? The depth of the print gives a rough idea of the weight."

"This is definitely your world," she said. "You feel at home here, don't you?"

"I feel at home wherever you are," he replied, "but I was raised in a place like this, though there were not so many pine trees in Athelwald."

"And more maple," noted Natalia. "I do so like the taste of it."

"You're thinking of Shaluhk's porridge again."

"I am. I think I've developed a taste for it."

"Come on, let's get moving."

"Which direction?"

Athgar scanned the area. "Kirak said they came from the west. That seems like a good enough place to start."

They started walking, enjoying the warm summer's day, but here, north of the Grey Spires, the land was cooler than Ord-Kurgad, and Athgar found himself shivering slightly. He pulled his tunic closer, warding off the chill wind that blew in from the distant mountains.

"There'll be snow soon," he mused.

"Don't be ridiculous," said Natalia, "it's still summer. You're just not used to this latitude." She saw the look of confusion on his face. "And by that, I mean we're farther north than you're used to."

"I suppose we are. How does this compare to the Volstrum?"

She laughed. "This would be a warm day in Karslev, not that I was allowed out much."

"I much prefer smaller villages," Athgar noted. "Big cities make me uneasy."

"For good reason. We've seen nothing but trouble when we visit one."

"I hadn't thought of that, but you're right. First, there was Draybourne, where I was robbed."

"Yes," she agreed, "but you met me, so it wasn't all bad."

"True, but then we went to Corassus, where the Cunars tried to kill us."

"Yes, but we went there looking for them, remember?"

"Also true, but then there was Caerhaven, where, let me see if I remember correctly. That's right, they tried to kill us again!"

"And we saved the Orcs," she said. "Don't forget that."

"Maybe it's best if we never go to Ebenstadt. Someone's likely going to try and kill us."

"Or," she retorted, "perhaps we'll visit the city, and everything will turn out well. You should try to be more positive."

"I'll give it a try, but I can't promise anything."

"That's all I can ask." Natalia was about to say more, but Athgar halted, his hand still clasping hers, causing her to turn to see what was wrong. He was staring at the ground and then knelt.

"What is it?" she asked.

"Tracks."

"Another deer?"

"No, Human. I suspect from our Therengian friends. It's relatively fresh, likely from today."

"That means we're close. Tell me, what's the tradition of greeting a Therengian?"

"I'm not sure what you mean," Athgar said.

"Do we shake hands? Or is there some sort of ritual we must adhere to?"

"Therengians are much like anyone else. How would you greet your fellow countrymen?"

"My fellow countrymen are trying to kill me, remember?"

"You know what I mean."

"I do," she replied. "Very well, we'll greet them as we would any other Human we happen to find wandering around in the wilderness."

Athgar barked out a laugh. "I suppose there is that. How does one go and explain our presence here without mentioning the Orcs?"

"If anyone asks, we'll tell them we're looking for Ebenstadt. That was our original objective."

"A good idea. Better to stick as close to the truth as possible."

They continued on their way, following the tracks as best they could. The trail took them into the woods, where the scent of pine was strong. Natalia halted, resting her hand on a tree trunk to steady herself.

"Is something wrong?" asked Athgar.

"My back is sore," she said. "Must have been that hut they put us in. I wish Orcs had proper beds."

"You never complained about them in Ord-Kurgad?"

"The beds there were raised off the ground if you remember. Here, the Orcs prefer sleeping on the ground."

"We were on furs," he reminded her.

"Which lay on the ground. It's the same thing." She waved him on. "You go ahead. I'll catch up."

"I don't want to leave you."

"I won't be long. You can search out those footprints; see which way they go. I just need a moment to catch my breath."

He stared at her, undecided.

"Go," she urged.

Athgar turned, searching the ground once more. The trail led him about an arrow's flight west, then turned north into a clearing. He looked across an open field to see a distant trail of smoke, evidence of a camp or village. He began backtracking his way to Natalia.

Natalia sat, feeling a sudden sense of vertigo. She wondered if the Orc food was causing it but quickly put such thoughts from her mind. Could she be ill? She had caught a fever back in Krieghoff. Was it now returning?

The sound of snapping twigs caught her attention, and she stood, expecting Athgar's return. Instead, she found herself staring into the eyes of someone else, a man with grey eyes like her beloved. But where Athgar had brown hair and a thin, scruffy beard, this man had hair the colour of night, with thick facial hair to match.

He stepped forward, his spear held loosely in his hand.

"What have we here?" he called out.

Another voice chorused in. "What is it, Brother?"

A second, taller man emerged from the trees, with an axe in hand and a trio of rabbits slung from his waist.

"It's a skrolling," said the first.

"And a woman," noted the second.

Natalia tried to back away, but the dizziness hit her again.

"Trust you to find a woman in the middle of nowhere, Harwath."

The shorter of the two moved closer, reaching out to touch her face. She fought off the dizziness, trying to summon a spell, but her body would have none of it. She collapsed back to the ground, her legs weak.

"See how she reacts to my presence, Raleth?" said Harwath. "She is destined to be mine."

"I think not," came Athgar's voice from behind them.

They both whirled, Harwath instinctively raising his spear.

"I wouldn't if I were you," said Athgar, his bow trained on the man.

Raleth raised his hands. "We mean you no harm, friend. Is this your woman?"

"She is my wife," he said. "I am Athgar of Athelwald, and this is Natalia."

"Greetings, Athgar. I am Raleth, and this is my younger brother, Harwath. You must excuse his behaviour. We see so few skrollings in Runewald, particularly such pretty ones."

"Skrollings?"

"Outsiders," explained Harwath. He stepped closer, lowering his spear and peering into Athgar's eyes. "You are one of us," he declared.

"I am a Therengian, if that's what you mean. I take it Runewald is your village."

"One of them," answered Harwath. "And yes, that is our home, at least for now."

Athgar lowered his bow and unnocked the arrow. "Then I offer greetings."

Raleth extended his hand. "An offer gladly accepted, friend."

Athgar took it, noting the firm grip. "Is your village far?"

"Not at all. It lies just north of here. Why don't you let us take you there?"

"I-I should be glad to, but I must see to my wife first."

He moved to Natalia, kneeling by her, concern written on his face.

"I'm all right," she stammered. "Just a little dizzy."

He felt her forehead, but all seemed normal. "Come, let me help you up."

She took his arm, rising to her feet. The woods began to sway, and so she closed her eyes, taking a deep breath, then letting it out slowly.

"I'm fine," she announced. "Let us proceed."

Athgar turned to Raleth. "Lead on," he said, "and show us this Runewald of which you speak."

"Is your companion ill?" the hunter replied.

"Just something I ate," said Natalia.

Harwath shook his head. "Skrollings will eat anything. They should know better."

Raleth punched his brother in the arm. "That's no way to show our hospitality. Show them the way, Brother." He fell in beside Athgar and Natalia as the younger man led the way. "You'll have to excuse Harwath. Your woman is the first real skrolling he's ever seen."

"You have no contact with outsiders?" asked Athgar.

"Not generally, and when we do, it usually means a fight."

"You're at war?"

"In a manner of speaking, yes," said Raleth, "but it would be better if our king explains."

"You have a king?"

"We do, King Eadred. The villages are united under his leadership. He resides in Runewald. Would you like to meet him?"

"I would," said Athgar. "I've never met a king before, let alone a Therengian one."

"Did you say you were from Athelwald?" asked Raleth.

"I did. Why?"

"You are not the first person we've met who hails from that distant place."

Athgar's heart skipped a beat, and he felt Natalia's grip on his arm tighten. He tried to sound uncaring, but his voice betrayed his emotions. "Who else have you met?"

"A young woman, about the same age as you, along with an old crone."

"Skora?"

"Yes, do you know her?"

Athgar turned to Natalia. "It looks like you'll get a chance to meet her after all. Who is this other woman? Is her name Ethwyn?"

"No," replied the hunter, "Melwyn. We found them wandering in the woods last fall, nearly dead from starvation. We assumed they had escaped from the knights, but it turns out they were from across the mountains to the south."

"They are from my village," said Athgar.

"Wasn't Melwyn once betrothed to you?" asked Natalia.

"Yes," he replied, then fell silent.

"And you left her for this skrolling?"

"It's a long story," Athgar said, "and Natalia is far more than just an outsider; she is a powerful mage."

Raleth took a step to the side, putting some distance between them. "A mage, you say?"

"Do not fear, we are friendly," said Natalia. "Have you no mages in Runewald?"

"None," said Raleth, easing back into position. "It is forbidden."

"By who?" asked Athgar. "Your king?"

"No, by long tradition. Have you no knowledge of our ancestors?"

"Very little, I'm afraid," said Athgar. "As I'm just now realizing, Athelwald was quite isolated."

"Then you will, no doubt, be interested in meeting our bard, Dunstan."

"You have a bard?" said Natalia. "How marvellous."

"How is it you came to be in these woods?" asked Raleth.

"We are searching for a place called Ebenstadt," she answered. "Do you know it?"

His face darkened. "Indeed I do, but it is a place that is best avoided."

"Why is that?"

"They seek to destroy us."

They emerged from the forest to see the village laid out before them. It was surrounded by a small fence, little more than waist-high, designed to keep animals penned in more than for protection. The houses were all constructed from wooden planks, much different from the wattle and daub Athelwald had used, and yet the thatched roofs were the same, giving the place an eerie familiarity.

Pigs rolled around in the mud, while a couple of scraggly looking sheep bleated. Athgar was reminded of home, and yet the general mood here was unsettling. In his own home, the villagers would have welcomed strangers, but here there were looks of contempt thrown towards Natalia, doubtlessly due to her pale skin and lack of grey eyes.

"Athgar? Is that you?" The voice was unmistakable. He turned to see Melwyn, his betrothed, rushing across the ground. She ran up to him, wrapping her arms around him in a hug.

"By the Gods," she said, "it's good to see you."

He took her arms from around him and held her at a distance, sadness on his features. "It's good to see you too, Melwyn."

"What is it?" she asked. "What's wrong?"

He glanced over at Natalia, but she was staring at the ground.

"I have bad news," he said. "It's about Caladin. I'm afraid he's dead."

The words stunned her. After Athgar's failure in the hunt, Melwyn's father had broken off their engagement, settling on the much more successful Caladin as a match for his daughter, but then the slavers had come. Athgar had found him chained to a sinking ship as a galley slave, and it was his Fire Magic that had ended the young man's life. He would have perished alongside his old rival had it not been for Natalia.

Melwyn straightened. "I feared as much. Still, it is good to see you, Athgar. Fate has brought you to me once more."

"No," he said. "I am bonded now."

"Bonded?"

"Yes, married, to Natalia." He took the Water Mage's hand in his. "I met her in Draybourne."

"She is a skrolling," said Melwyn, her look of distaste easy to read. "And in any event, Athelwald was destroyed. Who conducted the ceremony?"

"The Orcs of Ord-Kurgad."

A look of relief washed over her face. "Then it is of no consequence. We are building a new life here, Athgar. You and I can be a part of that. It is a new beginning for our people."

"Natalia is my future," he insisted, gripping the mage's hand tighter still, "and I will not have you speak ill of her."

"This is not over, Athgar," the woman swore. She moved closer to Natalia until they were face to face. "You have not heard the last of this, skrolling!" Melwyn turned, storming off.

"Well," said Raleth, "it appears she still holds a torch for you."

"That ship has long ago sailed," said Athgar. He saw the look of confusion. "Sorry, it's an expression I picked up in Corassus."

"Never heard of the place."

"Nor should you have."

"Let me take you to my home," said Raleth. "You must be hungry."

"Indeed," said Athgar. "Lead on."

The house of Raleth was a single-room dwelling, with a central fire over which a pig was roasting, tended to by a grey-haired woman with long braids hanging down her back.

"My mother, Anweld."

"Greetings," said Athgar.

"You did not tell me we would have guests, Raleth."

"I did not know we would find them in the woods," he replied.

"Come," the woman said. "Sit and make yourselves comfortable. Shall I fetch you some mead?"

"If you would be so kind," said Athgar. He sat before the fire, waiting as Natalia took her place beside him. She looked pale, and he wondered again what ailed her.

"This is Athgar," said Raleth, "and his wife, Natalia."

The woman examined their faces, but if she was surprised by the presence of an outsider, she hid it well. "You are guests of my son and shall always have a place in this house."

"Are you always so welcoming of outsiders?" asked Natalia.

"Not generally, no, but then again, we encounter them so infrequently." She turned her attention to Athgar. "You, on the other hand, are one of us. From what village do you hail?"

"Athelwald."

Anweld's eyes lit up. "The same as Skora," she said.

"You know her? Is she here?"

"I know her well, but she now serves the king, for no one else would have her. She spends her days in manual labour."

"She is a skilled cook," said Athgar.

"Maybe she once was, but now she is feeble and weak. Her trials have not been kind to her. Shall I send for her?"

"If it wouldn't be an inconvenience?"

"Not at all." She turned to her youngest son. "Harwath, stop staring at that pig and go and fetch the old woman."

"What old woman?"

She cuffed his ear, eliciting a shout. "Skora, the one we were just talking about. Have you no ears?"

He rose, his irritation quite evident. "I don't see why Raleth can't fetch her."

"Because he is their host. Now be about your business; we haven't got all day." Anweld turned to Athgar and Natalia as her son left the hut. "You must excuse him. He can sometimes be a bit thick."

"Sometimes?" said Raleth.

"Hush, now," she warned. "He's still your brother."

She passed out cups filled with mead, the aroma of honey held within its warmth.

Athgar took a sip, then downed the contents, pleased with the taste. Natalia sniffed hers but merely placed it on the floor, untasted.

"Are you not thirsty?" he asked.

She shook her head. "No, you can have it if you wish."

He took the proffered cup, lifting it to his lips.

"What has brought you here?" asked Anweld.

"We are searching for a place called Ebenstadt, but Raleth tells us it is to be avoided?"

"It is indeed. Might I ask the reason for your visit?"

Athgar was caught. Should he reveal he was sent by the Ancestors of the Orcs?

"I saw it in a dream," he lied.

"More of a nightmare, I should think. Still, it is a curious thing. Perhaps it is the will of the Gods. You should meet King Eadred. I'm sure he could help."

"What is King Eadred like?" asked Athgar.

Anweld paused before answering. "Like many kings, he is a busy man, but he's always eager for outside news. I'm sure he would agree to see you if you wish. In fact, I daresay he would insist on it."

"I should very much like to do so."

The door opened, revealing Harwath once more. "I found her." He stood aside, permitting Skora to enter.

The old woman walked with a stoop, looking quite frail, but there was no mistaking the light in her eyes. "Athgar, is that you?"

Athgar rose, going to her and throwing his arms around her. "Skora, it's so good to see you alive and well."

"Alive? Most certainly, but well? Not so much."

"Come, sit," he begged. "Let me introduce you to Natalia."

He led her across the room to where the mage had just risen. She held out her hand, but Skora moved closer, hugging her as well.

Natalia returned the gesture, then the old woman held her at arm's length, looking into her eyes.

"This is Natalia Stormwind," said Athgar. "She's my wife."

"She is more than that," said Skora. "She's carrying your child."

THE PASSES

Summer 1104 SR

(In the tongue of the Orcs)

Kargen stood to the side as his tribe walked by. For days they had travelled with little respite until their feet were blistered and sore. Now he gazed south to where the last few hunters brought up the rear. He spotted Laruhk and waved him over. The hunter broke into a jog, soon closing the distance.

"Where are the Humans?" asked Kargen.

"It is the strangest thing," replied his comrade. "They were hot on our trail only to turn aside for no apparent reason. The last we saw of them, they were heading southwest."

Kargen's face darkened.

"What is it?" asked Laruhk.

"I suspect the Duke of Krieghoff has attacked Ord-Kurgad. The Duke of Holstead is likely reacting to the invasion."

"Then we are safe!"

"Yes, but I fear our fellow villagers may have been lost to us. I must have Shaluhk consult the Ancestors."

Laruhk stared to the southwest as if he could actually see the distant village that had been their home. "There shall never be another place like it."

"Nonsense," said Kargen. "Ord-Kurgad is not a place. It is an idea that lives within the beating heart of this tribe. We shall rebuild, my friend, and the Orcs of the Red Hand will again prosper."

"How can you be so sure?"

"Can you not see? Fate has guided us here. We set out to head east and instead find ourselves fleeing north. It can be no coincidence that we are heading in the same direction as Athgar and Nat-Alia. Our destinies are intertwined. The Ancestors have suggested as much."

"Then we shall see them again?"

"Undoubtedly, providing we can make it through the mountain passes."

Laruhk turned his attention south once more. "At least the Humans are no longer following us."

"It is true that there is no longer danger behind us," said Kargen, "but it is what is before us that worries me. We have many elders and younglings. They represent our tribe's wisdom and our future. Neither can be risked."

"Spoken like a true leader."

Kargen bowed his head. "You honour me, but the truth is, this is a tribal effort. Each one of us plays their part, you included. It is only by working together that we will get through this."

"What do you think we will find north of the mountains?"

"There are fellow Orc tribes north of the range, but it is a wild land. Precisely where they can be found is anyone's guess."

"We will find them," Laruhk assured his chieftain. "And when we do, they will welcome us with open arms."

"I would not be so quick to jump to that conclusion. A tribe must look after its own first, and we may place a strain on the area with our need for food. It may well be that we will not be welcome, or worse, that we shall have to submit to absorption."

"Surely not? The Orcs of the Red Hand have a proud and storied history. We can not give that up to live amongst another tribe!"

"There are some who would gladly give up that honour to live in peace with their fellow Orcs. In any event, it will not be up to you and me to decide. Only the tribe itself can make a decision of that magnitude."

Laruhk gazed north at the distant peaks. "But we must get through the mountains first."

"True," said Kargen, "and then navigate our way out of them into an unknown land."

"If Athgar and Nat-Alia can do it, so can we."

"We have no way of knowing if they made it or not," said Kargen, "though I hope they have been successful."

"Could my sister not contact the Ancestors? Would they not know something?"

"Only if they have passed from this life."

"And yet they offer advice?" said Laruhk. "Was it not the Ancestors who sent our friends north in the first place?"

"It was," said Kargen, unconsciously stroking his chin, a mannerism he had adopted from the Therengian after being told it made him look more distinguished. At first, it had been a mere mockery of his friend, but the act had grown on him, and now it reminded him of his close relationship with the Human.

"It will be dark soon," said Laruhk. "We must call a halt."

"So be it. Send word for the advance scouts to return, and bring the hunters in from the rear. We will rest the night and make for the mountains early tomorrow morning."

Kargen turned, making his way northward. He soon found Shaluhk sitting on a tree stump, watching as hunters cut wood for the fires.

"There you are," she said. "Your son wants you."

Kargen moved closer, kissing his bondmate, then lifting Agar to his shoulders. "Has he been trouble?"

"No more so than usual. He has your sense of adventure."

"Adventure? Me? Why would you say that?"

"You were the one who started trading with Athgar's village all those years ago."

"Not just me," he defended, "Laruhk was there as well."

"We both know it was not my brother's idea. He is a follower, not a leader."

"Do not forget Durgash," Kargen added.

"Yes, the trinity of terror. That is what your mother used to call you three, was it not?"

He grinned. "My mother thought the world of them both."

"That did not stop her from complaining about all of you if I recall."

"You should be glad I spent time with your brother," he said. "It gave me time to be near you."

She smiled. "Ah, now I see. It was all a grand plan to win me over. Well, you succeeded. You, alone, have my heart."

"As you have mine."

Agar roared, swinging his wooden axe. Kargen laughed.

"He's been doing that all day," said Shaluhk. "He thinks we are on a hunt."

"We are, in a sense. A hunt for a new home."

"And where will this hunt take us, do you think?"

"You would know better than I," said Kargen. "You are the one who can talk to the Ancestors."

"I have told you before, my love. The Ancestors only advise. It is up to us to make the decisions, you most of all. You are, after all, our chieftain."

"And you, our shaman," he added. "You know as well as I that we must act as one."

Agar yawned, his last act of defiance for the day.

"Finally," Shaluhk said, lifting him down from her bondmate's shoulders.

Kargen looked down on his son, who was struggling to keep his eyes open. "How is the food situation?"

"There is sufficient for the near term," she replied, "but we shall be hungry by the time we clear the mountains."

Kargen sat beside his bondmate, bearing the weight of the tribe on his shoulders. Shaluhk placed Agar on the ground, covering him with a blanket, then moved behind Kargen, wrapping her hands around his neck and hugging him tightly.

"We shall get through this, bondmate."

"So we shall," he agreed.

Laruhk shivered, feeling the bite of the cold mountain air. He was high up in the foothills, winding his way towards the distant peaks. Turning to Durgash, he raised his voice to be heard over the roar of the wind. "It is no good; the path here ends in a cliff. We must make our way back and find another passage."

"That will be the third time we have done so," said his companion.

"What else can we do, fly?"

Durgash shrugged his shoulders, another Human mannerism the tribe had adopted. Was there no end to Athgar's influence? Laruhk chuckled at the thought.

"If Athgar and Nat-Alia can make it," said Laruhk, "then so can we. There must be a trail here somewhere."

"What makes you so sure they made it?" asked Durgash. He pointed northward, towards the peaks. "They could be up there somewhere, nothing but frozen corpses."

"You really think the Ancestors would guide them to us to allow them to die so easily? Remember, Athgar is a master of flame, and Nat-Alia can control water. What is a mere mountain range to such power?"

"I admire your convictions," said Durgash, "but I still wish we knew the path they took."

"As do I. Perhaps the others have been more successful?" offered Laruhk. "Let us return to our camp and find out."

Back down the mountainside they went, treading carefully lest the rock beneath them give way and send them tumbling to their doom. Three times they had set forth, and every time found naught but a dead end. It was beginning to feel like the very mountains were alive, thwarting their every move.

Shaluhk stared into the flames, deep in concentration. Her arms lay on her legs while she sat cross-legged, chanting the words of power that would call forth the spirits of the Ancestors.

As if in answer the fire crackled, sending sparks high into the cold night air. Agar sat by Kargen, watching her with an intense concentration rare for one so young.

"I call upon the Ancestors," she called out. "Show yourselves that we might seek your wisdom."

Kargen watched her work, knowing full well that only she could hear their answers. When her head tilted, he wondered what voices she heard.

"No!" she cried out. "It can not be." A shadow fell across her face. From across the fire, Kargen sensed her sorrow, a palpable feeling that washed over them both. Even little Agar shuddered as a wave of emotion engulfed them all.

Shaluhk's head fell, tears running down her cheeks. Crossing her hands, she dispelled the magic and then let loose with gut-wrenching sobs.

"What is it, Shaluhk? What has happened?" asked Kargen.

"Ord-Kurgad is no more," she announced, her tear-filled eyes rising to meet his. "They are dead. Every single one of them. An all-out war has come to the Human lands."

Kargen bowed his head. "So it is as we feared. Artoch and the others have met their end. It is indeed a sad day for our people."

"There is more," said Shaluhk, "but I fear such news may break you."

"Speak, my love. As chieftain of this tribe, I must know."

"Their deaths were not quick, my bondmate. They suffered at the hands of the Humans."

A rage began burning inside Kargen.

Shaluhk watched, fearing nothing would dampen that hatred. "I have it from Artoch himself. He walks amongst the Ancestors now." She rose, coming to sit beside him, wrapping her arm around his shoulder. "There is nothing you could have done to prevent it."

Kargen stood quite unexpectedly, taking her by surprise. Looking skyward, he roared out a challenge, his voice echoing off the distant peaks.

She waited until he stopped trembling, then stood beside him, looking into his face. "You honour them," she said, "but we must look to our future now, not our past."

"I can not forget what the Humans have done to us," he swore.

"And yet it was Humans who saved us," Shaluhk reminded him. "Were it not for our friends, we would all have suffered the same fate."

His shoulders slumped. "It is true," he admitted, "but should I ever find those responsible for this atrocity, they will pay with their lives."

"As they should," added Shaluhk.

Laruhk stomped his foot in a vain attempt to dislodge the accumulated snow. They were high up in the mountains, with a sheer precipice before them.

"And you brought me all the way here to show me this?" asked Kargen.

"Look beyond the gorge, Kargen. Do you not see it?"

The chieftain shielded his eyes from the brightness of the snow-capped peaks. "I see it. A path leading up into the hills, but what good is it to us with this in the way?"

"If we can descend the cliff, we can make our way up that distant path. It looks like it reaches all the way to the peak."

Kargen mulled over the situation. He approached the gorge, crouching to peer down. "The drop is great, but we have rope."

"Can it be done?"

The chieftain turned back to his friend. "We must try, for all other options have failed us. Our food dwindles by the day. If we do not cross soon, we shall have to seek game to the south, and that will lead us back into the Human lands, where only sorrow awaits."

"Durgash and I will make the attempt," said Laruhk. "If we can not reach that path by the end of this day, we shall return."

"Bring six hunters to this spot," said Kargen. "They will anchor your line and watch for your signal. If you locate the base of the path, then send forth a flaming arrow."

"And how will I light such a flame? All around us is snow and ice."

"A valid point." He stood, his hand instinctively reaching for his chin. "I have an idea. Come with me."

They made their way back to camp, seeking out Shaluhk. Kargen hugged her, then began rummaging through her wicker basket.

"What are you doing, bondmate?" she asked.

"Looking for something."

"If you would tell me what it is you seek, I might be of assistance."

"Athgar left behind his flint and steel, did he not?"

"Of course," said Shaluhk. "They wished to travel lightly over the mountains, and what need did a Fire Mage have for such tools? Why do you seek it? You know how to make fire already."

"I do," he said, "but where we are going, wood is scarce. Such tools would be beneficial."

"I don't understand."

"I do, Sister," explained Laruhk. "Durgash and I will seek out a path and then signal with a fire. We must take sticks with us for such a task."

"Then why not rub them together to make fire?" asked Shaluhk.

"The wood in these parts is sparse, and what little there is, is covered in snow, making it far too damp," her brother replied. "With Athgar's tools, I think we could make it work."

"Here it is," declared Kargen, lifting the metal ring from the pack. "You strike the flint with it."

"I know how it works," said Laruhk. "I have seen him use it often enough as have you."

"Then gather your kindling, mighty hunter. There is much work to be done."

Laruhk grinned. "Yes, my chieftain."

Kargen stood at the precipice, his eyes gazing north.

"It is getting late," said Shaluhk.

"So it is," he admitted, "and yet there is still much work to be done. If Laruhk is successful, it means we will be crossing the mountain passes for the next few days. It will be hard going, for we will not be able to stop and make fire."

"And once we are through?"

"Hopefully, we will see a hidden wilderness teeming with game."

"And if not?"

"Then we shall go hungry longer. There is no way to tell how far these mountains go. We may be amongst them for some time. Perhaps we should turn back?"

"And return to the Human lands?" said Shaluhk. "You know we can not do that. It would be the end of us all."

"Then our choice is made for us. We must continue."

"Yes, and it is all in the hands of my brother. Do not worry. If there is a way through, he and Durgash will find it."

The sun cast its red rays across the western peaks as it approached the horizon.

"Where is he," said Shaluhk, "and why does he not signal?"

Kargen stared off into the distance. "Wait for the darkness," he said. "He has limited fuel and knows the fire is best seen at night. Stay strong. They will be successful. I know it in my heart."

They stood in the darkness as the daylight fled. The moon soon made its appearance, illuminating the white of the snowy peaks.

"There!" said Kargen, pointing. "Do you see it?"

Shaluhk stared, breaking out in a grin. "I do," she announced. "They have made it! They have found the path!"

"Yes," he agreed. "Now all we have to do is get everyone down this cliff."

Getting the hunters down the steep precipice was easy, but the elderly and young gave them no end of trouble. They finally settled on using a basket for the young, lowering them down one at a time at the end of a rope, then hauling it back up for the next. While this approach proved useful for the wee ones, the elderly were too big to fit. They had to come up with a different solution, so they settled on each elderly Orc being tethered to a hunter. As the hunter descended, their partner would dangle beneath them, watching the cliff wall to avoid hurting themselves.

It was painstaking work, yet by day's end, the entire tribe had made the descent. Laruhk and Durgash returned to lead the way onward, but Kargen insisted they wait until everyone was past this hurdle. Splitting the tribe, he insisted, was not the Orcish way.

That evening they sat around the last of their fires, huddling for warmth. When night fell, they would sleep peacefully beneath the precipice, for once shielded from the harsh mountain winds.

"This is the last of our wood," said Kargen. "Starting tomorrow, we must continue without fire." He turned to Laruhk. "Tell me of the way ahead."

"There are large drifts of snow that will impede us," the hunter replied. "And we would do well to mark the path for those that follow."

Kargen nodded. "Let each hunter unstring his bow. We will then plant them in the snow at regular intervals to mark the path."

"They will be hard to see," noted Shaluhk.

"Then let us tie a cloth to their tops to make them more visible."

"I have a red blanket that might suffice," she offered.

"Excellent, then we shall cut it up and distribute the pieces. As the last of us takes the path, they will collect them for use farther up."

"It will likely ruin the bows," warned Laruhk.

"Better a ruined bow than to die of the cold. If it will lead us all through this, so much the better."

When they began their ascent the very next day, the Ancestors smiled upon them, gracing them with mild weather. The winds died down, allowing them to make satisfactory progress, but on the second day, the mountains decided to impede their progress, sending snow to blind them.

By the third day, bereft of fire, the tribe was struggling. Already there were signs of trouble, with two of the elderly falling into the snow. Kargen had the hunters spread a blanket across two bows, allowing them to carry the frail members of his tribe, but the cold soon claimed them. With no other choice, they were forced to leave the bodies in the frigid mountain air, stopping only to recognize their contributions to the tribe.

More than once, Kargen wished for the presence of Artoch. The fallen master of flame could have saved them, but then the chieftain rebuked himself, lamenting that he should have done more to save them.

Shaluhk comforted him as best she could, telling him such losses were inevitable. "You have done well to save so many," she said, "but you can not save them all."

For two more days they struggled, and then when they crested yet another ridge, Kargen ambled to the front, no longer strong enough to run. He stood beside Laruhk, the two of them staring to the north where the lush green of a distant forest beckoned them.

"We are almost there," said Laruhk through cracked lips and a dry throat.

"And just in time," croaked out Kargen. "For our food is gone and water is scarce. Spread the word. This news shall hearten our people."

KING OF THE THERENGIANS

Summer 1104 SR

"Are you sure?" asked Athgar

Skora kept looking at Natalia. "I have helped in the birthing of many babes. Trust me, I know the signs. Tell me, dear, have you any signs of discomfort?"

"My back has been sore," Natalia replied, "but I thought that was from sleeping on the ground."

"Any dizziness?"

She hesitated. "Yes."

"There, you see? Old Skora is not as useless as she looks."

Natalia looked at Athgar, worry in her eyes, but all she saw was love. "This can't be happening," she said, "not now."

"Children will come when they want," said Skora. "Parents have little choice in the matter."

"It looks like we shall be spending some time here," said Athgar.

"She's pregnant, not invalided," the old woman added. "It will be months before such is the case. There is no reason she cannot travel. Tell me, Athgar, what has befallen you since last we saw each other? I had thought you dead in Athelwald."

"And I was left for such. If it hadn't been for the Orcs, I would have perished."

"The Orcs?"

"Yes, the Orcs of the Red Hand. You remember Kargen and Laruhk? It is they that found me, and their tribe that taught me the magic of fire."

His statement brought the room to silence.

"You mean to say you are also a mage?" asked Raleth.

"Yes," said Athgar.

"This is glorious news, indeed."

"Glorious? I thought you disliked mages?"

"We do, at least those that are skrollings." Raleth cast a glance at Natalia. "Sorry."

"This IS an interesting development," added Harwath, suddenly taking an interest in the conversation. "He must be seen by the king as soon as possible."

"I'm afraid I don't understand," said Athgar.

"It has been generations since there were Therengian mages. We thought all the lines died out decades ago. If you are as you say, then this is a monumental discovery."

In answer, Athgar held out his hand, palm upward as he canted the magical words, calling on his inner spark to produce a small green flame.

Raleth and Harwath both stared, awed by his display.

"Well, mage or not," said Anweld, "he needs some food. Now stop gaping and pass out some of that stew."

Harwath tore his eyes away, going to gather some bowls while his brother kept staring.

"What else can you do?" asked Raleth.

"Nothing without risking burning down your house," said Athgar, "but I can assure you I was taught well."

"Yes," added Natalia, "he was taught by the master of flame."

"Master of flame?"

"Yes, Artoch, the Orc he was talking about earlier."

Raleth's face grew troubled. "Are you saying the Orcs can use this type of magic?"

"The Red Hand could," replied Athgar. "It's how they got their name."

"We've had some problems with the Orcs in this region," Raleth continued. "Could they have the same ability?"

Athgar took a moment to think about his response. It would do little good to admit he had spent time amongst the Black Axe tribe, so he gave a noncommittal answer. "Yes, it's possible."

Raleth rose. "I must warn the king. I fear we may be heading into a conflict that could destroy us."

"We shall be happy to meet him," said Athgar, "should he wish it, of course."

"I'm sure he will," said Raleth. "In the meantime, I suggest you eat. You'll likely need your strength." He left the hut, leaving the rest to consider his words.

"Tell me, Skora," asked Natalia, "what is King Eadred like?"

The old woman sat in silence a while, obviously struggling to answer. "He is a man dedicated to his role as king, but he lacks the decisiveness required of a leader. He is, however, exceptionally knowledgeable about the history of our people."

"A history I'm very interested in learning," said Athgar.

"Naturally," said Skora, "but you have yet to finish your tale. You talk of being saved by the Orcs yet have not told us how you met your wife."

"We met in Draybourne," offered Natalia. "He was trying to save me."

"Trying?"

"I'm a full-fledged Water Mage and had the situation well in hand. Unfortunately, I took him for one of my attackers and injured him."

"Once she realized her mistake," added Athgar, "she looked after me while I healed."

"She sounds like a remarkable woman," said Skora. "And it's nice to see she's someone worthy of you."

"I don't know about worthy," said Natalia.

"Nonsense. It's plain to see you're meant for each other. A much better match than Melwyn."

"We met her earlier," said Natalia. "What can you tell me about her?"

"What's there to tell? We managed to escape the slavers, then wandered in the wilderness: her untrained in the hunt and me too weak from hunger to do anything. We were near death by the time we made it out of the mountains."

"Melwyn was not untrained in the hunt," said Athgar. "She was blooded before I was."

"Is that what her father told you?"

"Are you saying it's not true?"

Skora shook her head. "My dear boy, you were blinded by the passion of youth. Melwyn was no more successful than you were. The difference was that her father looked out for her. It was his spear that brought down the deer, not hers."

"How do you know?"

She tapped her nose. "I know things, but in any event, it's of no consequence. You have found your true love. That is all that matters."

"Skora," said Natalia, "if we are to stay here, will you help me with this child?"

A smile broke out on the old woman's face. "I would be delighted to. I shall gladly become part of your household."

"Household?" said Natalia. "We're not nobility."

"It's a Therengian term," explained Athgar. "It's more of an informal family."

"Like we are with the Orcs?"

"Precisely."

"Very well," Natalia replied, "welcome to the household, Skora of Athelwald."

The old woman cackled. "It is not yet set in stone. I'm afraid the king may still have need of me."

"Then we shall have to see if we can change his mind," the Water Mage insisted.

Raleth opened the door.

"Back already?" said Anweld.

"The king wishes to see the newcomers," he said.

"Excellent," said Harwath. "When?"

"Immediately."

The younger brother looked at their mother.

"Well, don't just stand there," she said. "We mustn't keep the king waiting."

They all made their way to the king's hall, which lay only an arrow's flight away. It was large by Athgar's standards, though not as grand as the great hall of the Orcs. Inside, they found quite a few villagers standing around their king, peppering him with questions.

At their entrance, two guards moved to intercept them. The commotion drew everyone's attention. King Eadred took his seat upon a plain, high-backed chair covered in furs.

"What have we here?" he asked.

"This is Athgar of Athelwald, my king," said Raleth. "The man of whom I spoke earlier."

The king lounged on his throne, scratching his light brown beard. His long hair hung to his shoulders, but he wore it in braids that framed his face. Athgar looked him in the eyes, meeting the man's penetrating stare with one of his own.

Eadred turned his gaze on Natalia. "And who is this skrolling?"

"Natalia Stormwind," she replied, her back straightening.

"She is also a mage," added Raleth.

"What's this now?" said the king. "You spoke of one mage, not two."

"My apologies, my king."

Eadred rose from his seat, moving closer to examine the newcomers. He was a tall man, easily a head taller than Athgar, and yet he didn't command the room the way Kargen did.

"You," the king said at last, "are one of us"—he turned to Natalia—"but you are a filthy skrolling." He spat on her, causing her to flinch."

"My lord," a voice spoke up.

The king turned to see the source, a smile breaking across his face. "Lady Melwyn, you grace us with your presence."

"This man, Athgar," she said, "we were, at one time, betrothed. I beg you let us return to that arrangement."

The king turned his attention back to Athgar. "Is this true? Were you at one time promised to the daughter of a chieftain?"

Athgar found himself at a loss for words. Melwyn's father was no chieftain, just another hunter in the village, no more a man of influence than his own father had been as a simple bowyer.

"That was long ago," he finally managed to squeak out, "and I am now bonded to another."

"Only in the custom of the Orcs," added Melwyn.

"The Orcs?" roared the king. "What treachery is this?"

Athgar had enough. He took a step back, calling forth his arcane power to conjure a flame in his hand. The green fire flickered, drawing everyone's attention, including Eadred, who drew back in fear.

"Natalia is my wife," Athgar declared, "whether you accept her or not. And she carries my child."

A hush fell over the room. Athgar struggled with what to say. He had acted impulsively, and now he regretted his actions. How was he to now end this without bloodshed?

"Why do you hate the Orcs so much?" asked Natalia, finding her voice. "Surely they have done you no wrong?"

"They deny us what is ours," said Eadred.

"I think you'll find the land was theirs long before you arrived."

"What would you know of such things? You are an outsider!"

Natalia felt a rage building within her. "I am a Stormwind!" She let loose with her power, pointing at the firepit. It quickly frosted, extinguishing the flames, and plunging the hut into near darkness, leaving it illuminated by Athgar's flame alone.

As she finished her spell, she felt a coldness enter her stomach, and then a wave of dizziness overcame her. Skora caught her arm as she wavered, steadying her.

Athgar took a step forward, causing the others to back up farther. He turned his attention on the extinguished fire, and the flames leaped to life once more.

"So," said the king, "it is true. The bloodline lives on. Mages have returned to the Therengians."

"Returned?" said Athgar.

Eadred appeared eager to make amends. "Come, let me tell you of our people's history, for they are your people as well."

"What about me?" asked Melwyn, her eyes wide with fear at the magical display.

"Athgar has made his choice known. You shall have to learn to live with it." He looked back at Athgar. "Shall we?"

Athgar nodded, taking Natalia's hand and guiding her to his side. They both sat, Skora adjusting the furs for the expectant mother.

"Tell me," said King Eadred, "what do you know of our people?"

"Very little, I'm afraid," admitted Athgar.

"Our ancestors carved out a kingdom the likes of which has never been seen since. We were mighty warriors then, with a rich culture based on trade. A far cry from our present circumstances."

"What happened?"

"Amongst our rulers were powerful mages much like yourself. They were the glue that held the realm together."

"If that's true," said Athgar, "then why did it fail?"

A sad look crossed the king's face. "Our history tells us it was the skrolling mages that defeated us. As the realm grew, so did its diversity. Soon, these outsiders curried favour with the king and wormed their way into his confidence. This is what led to the corruption of the ruling class. Then the thanes started fighting amongst themselves, weakening the kingdom even more. Once we started down that dark path, we were fair game for our enemies. The skrolling lands picked us apart bit by bit until we finally collapsed."

"These skrolling mages you spoke of," asked Natalia, "were they Elementalists?"

"That would be for the bard to recite."

"Can we call him?" asked Athgar. "I should very much like to hear what he has to say."

"Very well," said King Eadred. "Send for Dunstan."

"I am here, my king," came a soft voice.

"Make way for him," the king commanded. "Come, tell us of the fall of Therengia."

"Of course, sire. Shall I accompany it with music?"

"No," the king added quickly, "just the words if you will." He leaned in close to Athgar. "His singing isn't what it used to be."

The bard began. "It is said that, at its height, there were no warriors more feared or respected than those of Therengia."

"I suspect that was before the widespread use of heavy cavalry," said Natalia.

The king looked at her in surprise. "What would a skrolling know of such things?"

"I was trained as a battle mage," offered Natalia. "And as such, I am familiar with the history of knighthood."

"Gods' teeth," said the king. "Knights are a scourge on us."

The bard interjected. "May I continue, Lord King?"

Eadred waved him on.

"At the height of their power, the alliance covered an area half the size of the Petty Kingdoms."

"Alliance?" said Athgar. "Who were they allied with?"

"Why, the greenskins," noted Dunstan.

"What's this now?" said the king. "I don't remember hearing that before?"

"You never asked, my king."

"I think you're making this up."

"No, my lord, I swear to you the tale is just as written. I have told it many times before. Surely you remember?"

"I do not remember Orcs being mentioned."

"They are not, my lord, at least not directly. The ancient poems speak of the alliance, but there are other, less well-known stories that confirm the role the Orcs played."

"Oh, yes?" said the king. "And what role was that? Slave?"

The bard shook his head. "No, my king. The Orcs were trusted allies. The writings are quite clear on that."

The king sat, dumbfounded.

"Your Majesty," said Natalia. "Perhaps it can be so again?"

"What do you mean?"

"We understand you are under threat from a place called Ebenstadt."

"We are," Eadred admitted. "They have been pushing us eastward for years. Why, the city itself is built on the remains of one of our villages."

"Then maybe instead of confronting the Orcs, it is time you put aside your differences and seek common ground with them. If the skrollings threaten you, how long until the Orcs, likewise, come to their notice?"

"You speak with wisdom, Water Mage. What is it you propose?"

"Let us take an invitation to the Orcs. We can then settle your differences and learn to work together rather than remain at odds."

"An interesting idea," noted the king, "but who here speaks the language of the greenskins."

"I do," said Athgar, "and I have already met Kirak, their leader."

"I shall give it some thought," said Eadred. "In the meantime, you are welcome here, Athgar of Athelwald. Long has it been since a mage of our own has trod this ground. A place shall be found for you."

"And my wife?"

The king cast a quick glance at Natalia. "Of course," he added grudgingly.

"Might I ask a boon, Lord King?"

Eadred roared out a laugh. "So bold! We have only just met, and yet already you ask a boon. Very well, go ahead. What is it you wish?"

"Only the services of Skora to help the mother of my child."

"Skora?"

"Yes, the old woman from my village that serves your household?"

"Oh, THAT old woman. Of course, consider her yours."

"Thank you, Lord King." Athgar turned to Skora, who bowed knowingly.

"Now, you have given me much to think on," the king continued. "I must have my peace."

Eadred stood, prompting his guests to do likewise. Everyone began filing out, save the king and his guards.

Athgar caught Skora's hand as they exited. "You are free to make your own decision, Skora. I would not have you a slave."

"It is kind of you to say," the old woman replied, "but I shall look after your child in any event."

"I like her," said Natalia.

"Of course you do," Skora said. "What's not to like? And wait until you've tasted my porridge."

"With maple?"

"My dear, you can have anything you like with it."

At the king's insistence, they were given a spare hut that had belonged to a hunter who had perished in the continual skirmishing with the skrollings. Having sat empty for almost a year, the structure required some repairs, but Athgar soon had it in good shape.

Once their new home was put to rights, he went out hunting with Raleth and Harwath. Using the skills he had learned from the Orcs, he bagged two deer, making him the talk of the village. Skora soon showed she had not forgotten how to dress a carcass.

Life began to settle down for the pair of them, and yet still, they waited for King Eadred to make a decision. Towards the end of the month, when

Athgar had returned from gathering yet more wood, Natalia sat watching him as he carefully placed it atop the flames.

"I've been thinking," she said.

"Oh? What about? Me, I hope?"

She smiled. "That, too, but no, I was considering what they said about Therengia."

"About its fall, you mean?"

"Yes. There's something about it all that's been nagging at me."

He paused, stick still in hand. "Go on."

"I think it might have been the family," she said. "Or at least what later became the family."

"What makes you say that?"

"It sounds like just the kind of thing the family would do. The Stormwinds and Sartellians have been sending people to courts for generations."

"Yes," Athgar agreed, "but it's only natural, isn't it? That's where the real riches are."

"It's more than that," Natalia said. "I think they do it for power. Imagine the influence an experienced mage could have on a ruler."

"So you think these 'outside mages' were predecessors to the family?"

"I do, though I have no proof."

"And if they were?" asked Athgar. "Why would they wish to collapse the kingdom? Surely they would want to maintain their influence? Destroying them would do just the opposite."

"I think that was unintentional. I think they were trying to use their power and influence without securing their positions first. The whole thing turned on them when they lost control."

"How does that help us now?"

"I don't think it does," Natalia admitted, "but if this is true, they might be the real power behind many of the Petty Kingdoms."

"I'm no expert on the Continent, but aren't the Petty Kingdoms constantly fighting amongst themselves?"

"Yes, and yet, still, I think there might be a connection."

"I suppose it's not outside the realm of possibility," he said. "How would you confirm or deny such an idea?"

"I'd have to travel to the hall of records in the Volstrum." She held up her hands. "Don't worry, I'm not seriously considering it."

"Good," he said, sitting beside her and placing his hand upon her stomach, "because I am not risking you or our child for such a thing."

"Are we doing the right thing, Athgar?"

"What? Having a child? Of course we are."

"I'm happy to hear you say that, but no, I meant taking on this fight between the Orcs and Therengians. Can we really bring peace to them?"

"Yes," he replied, "provided the king makes up his mind sometime in our lifetime."

"He doesn't seem very decisive."

"Skora warned us," Athgar said.

"So she did."

REFUGE

Summer 1104 SR

(In the tongue of the Orcs)

The Orcs of the Red Hand descended into an ancient forest, populated by giant spruce trees that reached far above them. There was little in the way of undergrowth here, save for moss and the ever-present rocks, worn smooth by the passage of time. Kargen finally called a halt, letting the exhausted members of the tribe collapse to the ground.

"We must find water," he said.

"I shall take Durgash and search the area," said Laruhk.

"Be careful. We are in unknown territory. Who knows what dangers may lurk here?"

"Look around, the trees thrive. There must be plenty of water for them to reach such heights."

Kargen looked skyward. "There is certainly no lack of wood in these parts."

Shaluhk looked up from where she sat with Agar. "Is this, then, to be our new home?"

"For now it is merely a resting place," answered her bondmate. "We can not make that decision until we have thoroughly explored the area."

"In any event," added Laruhk, "we have seen no trace of the Humans."

"Not yet," his sister added, "but we have seen little of the area at this time."

"She speaks the truth," said Kargen. "I would not tarry here were it not for our exhaustion."

"This place has its blessings," noted Shaluhk, examining a moss-covered stone. She held it up for his inspection. "Look, warriors moss. It looks like it grows here in abundance."

"And yet the lack of vegetation would suggest there is little in the way of game. I fear we must move farther north before we find sufficient food."

"But first the tribe must rest," cautioned Shaluhk.

"Yes, as long as we discover some water."

"We shall find it," said Laruhk. "The Ancestors would not have guided us here to our death." He trotted off, calling out to Durgash as he went.

"My brother is tired," said Shaluhk.

"As are we all," said Kargen, "but if we are to survive, we must find a way to persevere. Tell me, is any of this moss edible?"

"Yes," she answered. "Over there is elk moss. It can be eaten raw, but some find it unsettling. It is best when boiled until soft."

"And that will sustain us?"

"In the short term, yes, but a tribe of our size requires a lot of it."

"Then locate those who can identify it and gather what you can while I go and seek to comfort the sick and weak."

"That is my burden," said Shaluhk, "for I am the shaman of this tribe and its healer."

"True, and yet your knowledge of moss is more important at this time. Once we have fed them, you shall have your chance to see to their well-being."

It didn't take long for Laruhk and Durgash to find water, for many streams trickled into the area, fed by the snow-capped peaks. In the end, a small pond proved the easiest to reach, and so the weary travellers picked up their meagre belongings and made the trek to this new-found source of life.

Now, their thirst slaked, they partook of boiled moss, a somewhat taste-less concoction that, nonetheless, provided some welcome relief from hunger.

That evening, Kargen felt the tribe had recovered enough to hold a meeting. Lacking any huts, they gathered at the water's edge, campfire providing enough light to stave off the coming darkness.

As Kargen stood, the tribe fell silent. "We have come far," he started, "through the Human lands, that have since fallen into war, and past the mountains. Now we are amongst trees once more, though they are far different from what we are used to. The time has come to make some decisions, decisions I can not make alone."

He began pacing back and forth, occasionally looking at his tribe, but mostly just staring into the fire. "Our Ancestors have led us here, but now we must carve out our own fate. My question to you is whether we stay here or continue farther north?"

An elderly Orc stood, a sign he wanted to address the tribe.

"Yes, Dulok?"

"You have led us here through thick and thin, Kargen, and you have weighed the choices you have set before us this day. Tell us, what can we expect if we stay or if we leave this place?"

"A good question," noted Kargen. He swept his gaze over the tribe, noting all the eyes that were locked onto him. "Here we have water aplenty and much wood to rebuild a village, but there is scant evidence of game in the area. If we stay, I fear it may restrict our diet to nothing but moss and fish"—he looked at the pond—"provided such can be found here. On the other hand, there is no guarantee things will get better as we travel farther north. The truth is we have scant knowledge of this area."

"And what of our shamaness?" asked Dulok. "What does she think?"

Shaluhk rose, passing off Agar to her brother. "We can not survive on moss and water alone. Trying to do so would make us weak and sickly. We know there are other tribes in this area somewhere, and that means sufficient hunting to sustain a village. I propose we continue this trek until we have found a new home."

Dulok nodded his head, then sat, allowing others to speak should they wish.

Kragor stood, his treasured warbow clutched in his hand. "We elected you chieftain, Kargen. You have led us through adversity to this place of relative safety. We can not stay here; Shaluhk has said as much, and so I say we go north, deeper into the forest. Surely, once we are beyond the mountain's feet, game will be found aplenty."

"I thank you for your words," said Kargen, "though I daresay your bow has seen better days."

The Orcs all chuckled, for the snow had not been kind to the warbows of the Red Hand.

"Normally," Kargen said, "we would take a vote, but our stones have been lost, along with our home. Let us then raise hands to indicate our choice."

He sat, leaving Shaluhk to continue. "All those in favour of moving on, raise your hand." She moved amongst them, counting. "Put down your other arm, Durgash. Only the one may be counted."

Her task finished, she resumed her position at the head of the fire. "The tribe has spoken with a clear voice. We shall head north and seek out better hunting grounds."

The Orcs began beating the ground with their fists, their sign of agreement. Kargen waited for it to die down before rising again. "We shall resume our journey in two days. Until then, we must regain our strength and gather what water and food we can. In the meantime, I shall send hunters ahead to seek out a suitable path for us to follow. Unless there are others who wish to speak, this assembly is over."

The tribe rose, drifting off to different parts of the camp. A number of Orcs came forth giving Kargen words of encouragement and support, but his mind was elsewhere. He finally sat, staring at his son as the youngling played with his wooden axe.

"What are you thinking, bondmate?" asked Shaluhk.

"I am wondering what kind of future Agar will have."

"The tribe will prosper," she said, "and one day, he will be a chieftain, like his father."

"How can you be so sure that things will end so well?"

"I have faith," she replied.

"You believe the Ancestors will save us?"

"No, I have faith in you."

The tribe resumed their march with little fanfare. Hunters had already scoured the area, confirming that game was virtually non-existent. Still, at least the travel was easy, for the land was relatively flat and devoid of any major obstacles aside from the massive trees. Several times Kargen sent hunters up into the boughs, their objective to ascertain how far they could see, but the green canopy appeared to stretch on endlessly.

For days they travelled, determined to find a new home. After a ten-day, they found the first signs of game, and Laruhk managed to bring down a deer. It was not enough once split amongst the tribe, but the forest floor promised much more. The undergrowth veritably exploded, providing a source of nuts and berries along with a myriad of plants that could augment their diet.

They grew stronger each day, lifting their spirits immeasurably. Occasionally the forest would open onto a field, allowing the warmth of the sun to make itself felt. At these times, the tribe would halt, sending out hunters to seek food while they rested.

On one such occasion, many days into their march, Kargen felt confident enough to announce a feast, for deer had become much more plentiful, and smaller game, such as hares and birds, were also found in abundance. A large fire was built to roast the deer while others set out to clear away room to sit. For the elderly, they rigged a shelter from the sun while others worked at preparing the skins of their newly fallen prey.

By late afternoon, Durgash pronounced the food ready to be eaten, and the celebration began. The atmosphere was festive, and it looked like the Ancestors had finally guided them to their new home, where food was plentiful and enemies scarce.

All that changed in an instant as Shaluhk sat, crafting the milk of life, grinding her ingredients before adding them to water. Agar, close by, was using his wooden axe to try and cut down a branch. The first sign of trouble was a distant snort. Shaluhk froze, her mother's instincts immediately on the alert. Abandoning her work, she rushed towards her son just as a large creature burst from the woods.

It was easily the biggest living being she had ever seen putting even the horses of the Human knights to shame. Within its massive muzzle, long and tapered like that of a horse, it bore sharp, pointed teeth that looked quite able to tear flesh with ease. Even more strange was its flattened, bony head, giving it the appearance of a boar. It ran on stubby legs, shorter than that of a horse, but stronger, likely built for endurance rather than speed. All of this was covered by coarse hair that tufted along the beast's back.

It raced towards Agar, letting out a terrifying roar. The tiny Orc wheeled about, facing the threat with his axe held ready, screaming out a cry of defiance.

Shaluhk crossed the distance in a flash, scooping him up into her arms just before she threw herself behind a tree. The creature roared past, the ground thundering as it rushed by.

The camp exploded into chaos as others became aware of the danger. The creature, having finished its burst of speed, halted, turning its attention to the firepit. An Orc hunter named Urglan stood his ground, spear held at the ready, yelling at others to get out of the way. The beast turned on him and launched into a gallop, its cloven hooves closing the distance rapidly. The Orc stabbed out with the spear, striking the creature's side, but it merely glanced off the tough skin.

With a shout of warning, Urglan dived to the side, but it was too late. The creature opened its mouth wide, exposing its sharp teeth as the powerful jaws clamped down on Urglan's leg, snapping it like kindling. A tug of its head sent the Orc's body flying, the leg still held tightly in its mouth.

An arrow flew across the fire, sinking deep into its shoulder. Kragor nocked another and let fly, but the shot went wild. The giant boar, if that's what it was, turned in the blink of an eye and raced off, heading towards another group of Orcs.

Kargen rushed into the clearing, calling for other hunters to assist. The beast bowled into a group of three, sending them flying in all directions. Dulok was the next to fall. He stood, spear in hand, calmly planting the end in the ground as those behind him dashed for cover. The creature, however, didn't pause, merely turned quickly and continued its run, striking the spear squarely. The blade scraped along its forehead, leaving a crimson cut, but it ignored the pain, opening its massive mouth to bring its teeth chomping down onto the old Orc. Dulok's head and torso disappeared into the creature's maw as it lifted him, snapping him in two and sending black blood flying everywhere.

Kargen bellowed a challenge but was ignored. Kragor let loose once more, sending an arrow deep into the creature's leg, finally slowing it. Letting out a strange keening, it turned yet again, rushing directly towards the archer.

Durgash pushed Kragor from the creature's path at the last possible moment only to fall beneath the hooves himself. There was a sickening crunch as it passed, and then it whirled to face Kargen.

The great chieftain stood his ground, axe held in two hands. He stared at the beast, watching its eyes as it returned his gaze. There was no malice there, only the watchful eyes of predator and prey, but which was which?

For an instant, time seemed to stand still, and then the creature was moving again, its thunderous approach kicking up dirt and needles of pine.

Kargen was dimly aware of a distant chant, and then the creature inexplicably slowed, giving him time to react. He sidestepped, bringing his axe across in a low swing to the legs. Flesh parted, and then he felt his weapon bite as it dug deep into bone. Down the creature went as surely as a tree being felled. More arrows thudded into its now exposed underbelly, and then hunters rushed forward with spears to finish the job. It thrashed about, knocking two more Orcs off their feet, and then the creature finally stilled.

Kargen wheeled around, seeking out Durgash, but Shaluhk was already there, calling upon arcane forces in an attempt to mend the broken flesh.

Laruhk appeared at his side. "By the Ancestors, what was that thing?"

"I have no idea," Kargen replied. "But if it is any indication of the predators in this area, I think we should keep moving."

"Agreed." Laruhk gazed over at Shaluhk, who was laying hands on the injured Durgash. "How is he, Sister?"

"He will survive," Shaluhk replied. "Your trinity is still complete."

"Trinity?" said Laruhk.

Kargen smiled. "It is a long story."

Other hunters gathered, then the rest of the tribe, assured of its demise, began to approach the carcass.

"Look at those teeth," said Laruhk.

"Indeed," said Kargen. "They snapped poor Dulok in half, not to mention ripping the leg off of Urglan."

Laruhk moved even closer. "This thing's head is the size of my chest," he announced. "And did you see how far its mouth could open? It is a wonder it did not kill more."

"It caught us by surprise," said Kargen. "We should have been better prepared. From now on, we must take greater care in protecting our people. We can not afford to let this happen again."

"Agreed."

Shaluhk rose, taking Agar's hand and leading him across to where the two Orcs were in discussion.

"Durgash will recover," she said, "but he must rest."

"It is a miracle he even survived," noted Laruhk.

"The Ancestors watched over him this day," agreed his sister, "but he has lost much blood. I am afraid his hunting days are over for a while."

"How long is awhile?" asked Kargen.

"A ten-day, at least."

The chieftain turned to Laruhk. "It appears you will have to find a different hunting partner for the time being."

"I shall be pleased to perform that duty," called out Kragor, moving closer to pull his arrow from the body. He tugged hard, only to find it had sunk a hand's depth into the beast. "It was a good thing Shaluhk saved you," he noted, "or else we would have had to elect a new chieftain."

"Shaluhk saved me?" said Kargen. He briefly remembered the chanting, then turned to his bondmate. "What spell did you use?"

"Slumber," she said. "Not enough to put it to sleep, but it slowed its reactions."

Kargen smiled. "A good choice. It saved my life."

"I could not have my bondmate die," she said with a grin. "It would have been no end of trouble to select a new one."

He moved closer, wrapping his arms around her in a hug, still able to feel her trembling. "I thank the Ancestors you were there," he whispered.

"As I shall always be."

. . .

"What shall we call that thing?" asked Laruhk. He was sitting at the fire, roast beast on his dagger.

"I do not know," said Kargen. "It is like nothing I have seen before."

Laruhk took a bite, spitting it out immediately. "Well, it is definitely not a boar. This meat tastes rancid."

Kargen laughed. "Then it is not to be hunted. What of the hide?"

"It is tough," said Shaluhk. "Unsuitable for clothing but perhaps useful on a shield?"

The chieftain smiled. "Shields! An excellent idea."

"I haven't seen a shield for some time," noted Laruhk, "though they were common enough in our youth."

"Then we shall have to learn to use them anew," announced Kargen.

"Why?" asked Kragor. "Surely there is nothing in these woods against which it would prove useful."

Kargen smiled. "While it is true that such a thing would be useless against that"—he pointed at the carcass—"it would certainly be useful against Human horsemen."

"But there are no Humans here!" said Kragor.

"You forget. We are following in the footsteps of Athgar and Nat-Alia."

"And?"

Kargen turned to Shaluhk. "Tell me, bondmate, where it was the Ancestors told them to seek?"

"A Human city," she said, "named Ebenstadt."

"We have no idea where that is," said Laruhk.

"Nor do I," Kargen confessed, "but if the Ancestors are interested in the place, should we not also be?"

"You think we are going into danger?" asked Kragor.

"Life is dangerous, and I might remind you that the creature was defeated only by the combined might of the tribe. If we work together, we will prevail."

"Elk-boar," proclaimed Laruhk.

They all turned to him in surprise. "What?" said Shaluhk.

"Elk-boar. That is what we should name the beast."

Shaluhk rolled her eyes, a mannerism that threw the others into fits of laughter. "That is the worst name I have ever heard!"

PARLEY

Summer 1104 SR

Athgar pushed the branches away from his view. "There's a clearing here," he announced. "The perfect spot to wait for the Orcs."

"And you're sure they will find us?" asked Cenric.

Natalia looked at the king's champion. "You doubt the word of my husband?"

A look of annoyance briefly crossed the man's face, but then he composed himself. "It is not that I doubt his word, but these clearings all look so similar. Could he be mistaken?"

Natalia looked at Athgar. "What do you say to that?"

"There is a large elm tree over yonder split by lightning in the distant past. I doubt every clearing would have such a thing."

Cenric grunted an acknowledgement. Behind him, three warriors waited, each clutching their spears, their fear making them alert.

"The Orcs are willing to negotiate," said Athgar. "I can guarantee you they mean no harm."

"Easy enough for you to say," noted Cenric. "It's not you who has had trouble with them."

"Perhaps you will understand them better when we talk with them."

"Perhaps," the warrior replied, his words lacking conviction, "but I shall still be on my guard."

"As you should be," said Natalia. "Shall I take the lead?"

"By all means," said Athgar.

Cenric reached out, grabbing Athgar's arm. "You would let your woman walk into danger? What kind of a man are you?"

"Natalia is a powerful mage and more than capable of looking after herself. In any event, we are MEETING Orcs, not attacking them."

"They cannot be trusted," Cenric asserted.

Natalia's voice turned frosty. "I have found them to be far more trustworthy than most Humans."

Cenric stared back, unsure of what to make of the statement.

"In any event, we should get moving," pressed Athgar.

They entered the clearing, Natalia taking the lead with a strong stride. Halfway across the field, they heard a call, then a rustle of leaves revealed a trio of Orcs making their way from the other side, led by none other than Urughar.

"*Greetings, Athgar of Athelwald.*"

"*And to you, Urughar.*"

"*I see you have brought the other Torkul. Are they willing to talk?*"

"*That is my hope,*" replied Athgar. "*Allow me to introduce Cenric of Runewald. He comes representing King Eadred of the Therengians.*"

At the mention of his name, Cenric stepped forward. He stood for a moment, examining the Orc in detail, his hands resting on his hips. Urughar adopted a similar pose. Athgar had the uneasy feeling they were sizing each other up.

"Lord Cenric," said Natalia, "have you anything you wish to say on behalf of your king?"

"Yes," the big man replied. "Tell them King Eadred agrees to meet with their chieftain. He should come to our village in two days with no more than three of his followers."

"That is quite unacceptable."

Cenric turned on her, his face growing red. "It is not your place to gainsay my king, skrolling!"

Natalia stood her ground. "And would King Eadred be willing to enter the Orc village with just three men?"

His silence spoke volumes.

"I thought as much. King Eadred must treat the Orc chieftain, Kirak, as an equal. Only then will peace be achieved."

Cenric's lips went tight as he considered the situation. "What would you suggest?" he finally said.

"This is a nice place. Why not have each side send a delegation here?"

"An excellent idea," said Athgar. "Shall we say in two days? That would give each side time to consider what they'd like to say."

"Yes," said Natalia, "and we should limit the numbers on both sides."

"I would agree to that," said Cenric. "Shall we say three advisors per side?"

Athgar turned to Urughar, resorting to the tongue of the Orcs. *"We propose that the leaders meet in two days at this location. Each side will limit their numbers to include only three advisors. Would this be acceptable to Kirak?"*

"I believe it would," answered the Orc. *"Very well, we shall meet again in two days. Farewell, Orc friend."*

Athgar bowed, then turned to Cenric. "He agrees."

"Good," the warrior replied. "Now let us be gone from this place; the air here is foul." He turned around, stomping past his trio of guards to make his way back to the treeline.

Natalia hung back, waiting until he was out of earshot before speaking. "I'm not sure I trust him."

"Nor I," Athgar admitted, "but he will do his duty to his king."

"And Eadred? How will he react?"

"I can only hope he has the best interests of his people in mind. Reaching an understanding with the Orcs will lead to prosperity and peace, something they desperately need."

"And when the soldiers from Ebenstadt come for them?"

"We'll have to cross that bridge when we come to it. We can't fight all their battles at once."

She smiled, warming his heart. "You've become quite the statesman."

"Statesman? That's a word I'm not familiar with."

"Don't worry, it's a compliment. It means you've learned how to help people."

"I like it, though I fear the declaration might be a bit premature. There is still much to discuss before they even begin to trust each other."

"True, but we've made progress today. It gives us something to build on."

The hall of King Eadred was lit well into the night. A great fire burned, while around it gathered the important people of the village. Athgar had to wonder who determined their distinction as such but soon came to the realization it was those who agreed with the king's missives. Athgar was only present because of his knowledge of the Orcs, while Natalia's presence was due to his insistence that, next to him, she was the foremost authority on Orcs in Runewald.

"The real question," the king was saying, "is whether or not we can trust them. How do we know they will keep their word?"

"They are an honourable race," said Athgar.

"And yet their reputation would say otherwise."

"I don't trust them at all," added Cenric.

Natalia bit back her exasperation, electing instead to try a calmer approach. "If I may, Your Majesty? How many Orcs have you actually met?"

"None," relayed the king, "but we have all heard the stories."

"Stories?"

"Yes, of their barbarity."

"You are a Therengian," she continued.

"Yes, what of it?"

"Would it surprise you to know that amongst the Petty Kingdoms, your own people have a reputation for depravity and barbarism?"

"That's a lie!"

"Just as it is for the Orcs," Natalia said. "I have spent time amongst their people, and I can assure you they want the same things that you do."

"Which are?"

"Peace and prosperity."

"They shall have peace," said Cenric, "at the point of a spear!" He roared with laughter, the others soon joining in.

Athgar fumed. This was going nowhere. How could he convince them the Orcs were not their enemies?

Skora, who had been helping serve the assembled group, knelt beside him, whispering in his ear. "Natalia is tired."

Looking over, he saw his bondmate stifling a yawn. He stood, bowing respectfully. "With your permission, Lord King, I shall retire. It appears my wife is fatigued."

"Of course," said Eadred, "and our best wishes go with her."

Athgar saw the scowl on Cenric's face but chose to ignore it, instead reaching out to Natalia. "Come," he said. "It's time you were abed."

She stood, steadying herself on his arm as a wave of dizziness rolled over her. Taking a breath, she nodded, letting him lead her from the room.

Skora held the door for them. "I shall stay here and be your ears," she said quietly.

Athgar nodded his head and then led Natalia from the hall.

"This is going nowhere," he commented as he guided her towards their hut.

"They see nothing of value in the Orcs. What was it like in Athelwald? Did they distrust Kargen's people?"

"Granted, there were some that disliked them, but most saw the wisdom in trade."

She latched on to his words. "Trade? What kind of trade?"

"Primarily finished goods: arrows, pots, cloth, that sort of thing."

"And for this the Orcs traded...?"

"Raw materials, wood, skins, and, of course, meat."

"That might be the answer to all of this," Natalia advised him. "If we can explain the benefits in terms of trade, perhaps they will be more amenable?"

"Where would we start?"

"We need to determine what this village has that the Orcs might like in trade."

"That's easy," said Athgar, "wool. The Red Hand always had a need for it, especially when winter came."

"And we know the Therengians prize meat. There simply aren't enough hunters to supply the entire village."

"The Orcs also have medicinal herbs," he added, warming to the task. "I'm sure their shaman would have plenty to spare."

"Anything else?"

Athgar looked down at his feet and smiled. "Footwear," he said. "These boots Shaluhk made me are the most comfortable I've ever worn."

"So there are things of value on both sides. We should wander the village tomorrow, see what else we can find that might be of use."

"I look forward to it."

"Good, but for now, I need to rest. My back is aching, and I'm feeling light-headed."

Athgar tossed and turned, visions of war flashing through his mind. When a hand shook him awake, he opened his eyes to a familiar face looming above him.

"Skora? What's wrong?"

"I have just now come from the king's hall," she said. "Eadred means to deceive the Orcs."

He sat up, his heart pounding. "Deceive them, how?"

"I overheard him talking with Cenric. He means to attack while their chief is negotiating. He will lead a small party to the rendezvous, but, unnoticed by you, a larger group will follow, armed and armoured for battle. Our king hopes to leave them leaderless and disorganized."

"Then he's a fool!" declared Athgar. "The Orcs elect their leaders. If Kirak were to die, another would simply take his place."

"Eadred is a vain man," said Skora. "He cares only for his own riches, and those of his most trusted men. He seeks to destroy the Orcs and plunder their home."

"He would have a hard time. The village is walled."

"Walled? Truly?"

"Yes," said Athgar, "and I doubt he would have the men to breach it. His plan can only lead to greater death and destruction."

"What can we do?"

Athgar looked at Natalia, but she was deep in slumber. "We must send word to Kirak."

"Would that not cause the very same conflict you seek to avoid?"

"It's the only way. Perhaps if he is given sufficient warning, he can take steps to avoid the trap."

"When shall you go?"

Athgar threw off his covers. "This very moment."

"You cannot," said Skora. "It is far too dark, and you would likely lose your way. You must wait until morning."

"What is the king doing now?"

"He has retired," said Skora. "He would likely be asleep by now."

"Very well," he said, laying his head down once more. "I shall leave first thing in the morning. Thank you, Skora. You may have just saved our people."

"If only the king felt the same way."

Two days later, they stood at the edge of the clearing once more. King Eadred was led by three guards but noticeably missing was his champion, Cenric. Athgar ignored the absence, concentrating instead on the field before them. Across the way, he could make out Urughar bearing the black banner of his tribe; a large rectangle of cloth hanging from the crossbeam of a pole.

King Eadred had no such banner, leading Athgar to wonder why? Did the Therengian people not have a flag?

"They are ready," announced Natalia. "Shall we proceed, Your Majesty?"

They stepped into the clearing, Athgar leading the way. The Orcs, seeing their approach, did likewise, eventually meeting in the middle of the field.

"*Welcome Kirak, Chieftain of the Black Axe,*" said Athgar, effortlessly switching to the Orc language. "*May I present King Eadred of the Therengians.*" He swept his arm, indicating the king.

"This," continued Athgar, in the common tongue of man, "is Chief Kirak of the Orcs of the Black Axe."

The two leaders nodded their heads in greeting. The tension in the air was palpable. Athgar instinctively looked to the woods. It took him a moment to spot Raleth. The hunter was perched at the edge of the trees, acting as Athgar's eyes and ears. He looked briefly at Natalia, who nodded in understanding.

The Water Mage stepped back, distancing herself from the rest of the party, her eyes locked on the treeline.

"Tell the Orc," said the king, "that we are pleased to greet him."

"His name is Kirak," rebuked Athgar. "Would you have him refer to you as 'the Human'?"

He watched as the king's face turned red. His Majesty obviously felt the need to say something, but with the enemy so close, he would not deign to show discord. "Please convey to Chief Kirak my pleasure at making his acquaintance."

Athgar made the translation, and the Orc chieftain bowed his head slightly. Kirak spoke, then Athgar turned to face Eadred. "He invites you to sit, that you might discuss things in detail."

"Here?" said the king. "On the ground?"

"We have little choice, Your Majesty, unless you prefer to stand the entire day."

"Very well." Eadred sat down in a huff, giving the impression of a petulant boy.

Kirak sat opposite, his aides taking seats to the side. Athgar, as translator, sat at one end, separating the groups. He noticed Natalia making her way towards Raleth's position and smiled, knowing her absence would not be detected.

Cenric crouched, waving his men forward. The spearmen moved up quickly, mimicking their leader. To the front, he saw a group of Orcs standing around, leaning on spears, intent on the negotiations that were underway in the field before them.

He hefted his shield, feeling the reassuring weight of it. Orcs were said to be strong, and looking at them now, he could well believe it for their shoulders were much broader than that of Humans. The plan was to advance with thrown spears, using their longer range to inflict damage first, but if they should close, it could well come down to the hefty axes slung on their backs.

Cenric risked a glance left and right, making sure everyone was in place. He had twelve men with him and another twenty no more than ten paces behind. That thought gave him comfort. Gripping his spear, he stood, then began moving forward in a crouch. Once they had drawn closer to the enemy, he straightened, pulling his arm back to heft his weapon.

It must have been a chilling sight to see a line of warriors suddenly emerge from the underbrush, but the Orcs appeared to give little notice. Was this a trap? Cenric was ready to throw, his arm muscles quivering in anticipation, but something nagged at him. He focused on the closest target, and it was as if the vile creature were a ghost. Instead of the dark green skin he expected, they were pale. Slowly, he became aware that they were apparitions, mere ghosts of Orcs.

Lowering his spear, his mind was unable to grasp what his eyes told him was present. The Orcs turned, looking at him in an unworldly fascination, their blank eyes disheartening the great warrior. A rustle off to his left drew his attention, and then a wall of ice erupted before him, filled with whirling blades of death.

Cenric backed up, cursing himself, for surprise was lost, and with it, any hope of carrying out their plans. His men, equally unnerved, looked to him for leadership.

"Withdraw," he managed to say through parched lips. "We cannot fight that which is of the Underworld."

Natalia kept the wall of icy blades in place for as long as she could. Ordinarily, it would be easy, but today she found it taxing. A cold knot in her stomach broke her concentration, and she bent over, worry for her babe of more immediate concern. The spell dissipated, but it had done its job.

The Orc shamaness, Laghul, moved closer. She had called forth the spirits of long-lost hunters to draw the Humans in, but now, her job complete, she was more concerned with Natalia's distress.

"*What is it?*" she asked.

Natalia struggled to understand the words. "*My stomach,*" she said in broken Orc. "*It has gone cold.*"

In answer, Laghul placed an ear to her belly. "*The heartbeat is strong,*" she announced. "*Your youngling is well.*"

Natalia took a deep breath, letting it out slowly. "I must speak to Athgar," she said, forgetting, for the moment, the presence of the Orc.

"*Come,*" the Orc said, "*I will guide you.*"

The shamaness led her into the clearing. Athgar was in the middle of translating when he spotted her, causing him to interrupt the proceedings. Natalia looked pale, even more so than usual, putting him on alert.

"What has happened?" he asked.

King Eadred stared at the Orc shamaness but said nothing.

"You have failed," said Natalia, looking directly at the king. "Your plan to attack the Orcs has been foiled. Now, will you continue your negotiations in earnest, or shall I tell them of your treachery?"

Eadred's face paled. It was one thing to plot against the Orcs, quite another to be exposed for his deceit.

"Very well," the king said. "Let us negotiate in good faith."

    *

They returned to their hut well past sundown. Skora had prepared food, and so they sat, thankful for the respite after the labours of the day.

"I see you are still alive," said the old woman. "I take it that means you were successful this day?"

"We were, thank the Gods," said Athgar, "though it almost ended in failure. If it hadn't been for Natalia, I don't know what would have happened."

"I might remind you it was your plan," noted Natalia.

"Yes, but you're the one who made it all possible."

"And what of the king's treachery?" asked Skora.

"Cenric retreated," said Athgar, "but I still don't know the full story."

Natalia smiled. "The Orc shamaness cast a spell to conjure forth the spirits of hunters. They were used to lure Cenric and his men into their grasp."

"Where you used your magic?"

"Yes, I did"—she cast her eyes down—"but something went wrong."

"Wrong? How so? Surely Cenric retreated?"

"He did, but something happened to me."

A look of worry crossed his face. "What?"

"I felt a cold presence in my stomach as if I'd swallowed a ball of ice."

"Could it be the baby?" he asked. "Think about it. You're a powerful mage. Could you have imparted your magic to it?"

"I don't know. I was never taught such things." Tears formed in her eyes. "What do we do, Athgar? I don't want to endanger our child."

He moved closer, enveloping her in his arms. "I think it best if you don't use your magic for a while."

She nodded, then buried her face into his shoulder. "I'm scared."

"So am I," he admitted. "I wish Shaluhk were here. She'd know what to do."

HOUSE OF STONE

Summer 1104 SR

(In the tongue of the Orcs)

L aruhk gazed up from where he knelt. "There can be no doubt. These are the footprints of Orcs."

Kargen looked around, scanning the distant trees for any signs of activity. "We must be in their tribal area, but I see no sign of them other than those prints. How old are they?"

"Perhaps a day, no more."

"Then this must be their hunting grounds."

"What do we do?" asked Laruhk. "Turn around?"

"No, we will continue, but we must cease hunting. At least until we make contact with our fellow tribe."

"We have no idea which tribe that might be. Could my sister not give us some guidance? Would not the Ancestors know?"

"We can not keep pestering the Ancestors," said Kargen, "or they will refuse to answer the call when we need them most. It is up to us to find our brothers and sisters."

"And if they should prove hostile?"

"When have Orcs ever been hostile to each other? We have enough trouble with Humans. We do not need to find fault with each other."

"Wise words, my friend," said Laruhk, "but should we, at least, take precautions?"

"What would you suggest?"

"Let me put hunters to the front and sides. That way, it will lessen the likelihood of being surprised."

"You are thinking like a leader, Laruhk. Perhaps one day you shall be chieftain?"

"I am content to be a hunter," his friend replied.

Kargen grinned. "So be it. Now, be off with you, hunter, and get your people into place."

"Yes, my chieftain." Laruhk ran off at a sprint, eager to begin his new task.

"He is enthusiastic," noted Shaluhk.

"What is this now? Praise for your brother? Are you feeling well?"

"I am fine. I am just trying to be more thankful for what we have."

"And what has brought forth these feelings?"

"Simply the situation we find ourselves in."

"How so?" Kargen asked.

"It is clear that very shortly, we shall be encountering another tribe. The question, of course, is what that means. Will we continue to be the Orcs of the Red Hand? Or will we be absorbed into another?"

"Why would you think that?"

"I have taken stock of our situation these past few ten-days," she said, "as I know you have. The truth is the very tradition that has named our tribe is dead."

"I am not sure I follow."

"Our tribe dyes their hands red for battle to signify the magic of fire, and yet we no longer have a master of flame."

"It is a development I have not given much thought to," said Kargen, "but now that you mention it, I see what you mean. The loss of Artoch is felt deeply."

"So what do we do?"

"That is for the tribe to decide." He fell silent, but then a smile crept over his face.

"Tell me, bondmate," said Shaluhk, "what is it that pleases you so?"

"You."

"I am flattered, of course, but I know how your mind works. You are thinking of something else."

"I am," he admitted. "It occurs to me Artoch passed on his knowledge before his untimely death."

Shaluhk cast her gaze at the tribe as they walked past. "To whom?"

"To Athgar!"

"But he is a Human."

"True, yet he is also a member of this tribe. As such, who is to say that he could not train others?"

"Very true," agreed Shaluhk, "but he is not with us at present."

"Also true. Still, I am confident we will soon be reunited. We did not come all this way for nothing."

Agar rushed past them, his wooden axe held high, a primal scream erupting from his mouth.

"He is eager," said Kargen.

"Yes," agreed Shaluhk. "He takes after my brother."

"Is that such a bad thing?"

"No, I suppose not. There are worse Orcs he could imitate."

A call from the north drew their attention, then Durgash appeared, pushing his way past the advancing tribe.

"What is it, Durgash?" asked Kargen.

"We have encountered another tribe," the hunter revealed. "You must come at once."

"Very well. Lead the way."

Kargen and Shaluhk followed him northward. Upon contact, the rest of the tribe had halted and were now sitting at rest while their chieftain sought permission to cross tribal lands.

Laruhk waited for them, staring northward to where an unknown Orc stood with shield and spear, dried mud smeared on his face, no doubt to mark him as a hunter.

"I do not recognize the tribe," said Kargen.

"I do," said Shaluhk. "He is a member of the Stone Crushers. The shield identifies him as such."

Kargen focused on the lone Orc. The shield was rounded, as was the custom amongst their race, its front displaying a picture of a stone spear tip.

"Come, bondmate. It is time we talked with our cousins."

"Take care of Agar," said Shaluhk, turning to her brother. "He is around here somewhere."

They approached cautiously, not through fear, but through respect. Kargen bowed his head. "Greetings, Cousin. I am Kargen, Chieftain of the Orcs of the Red Hand."

"Greetings, Kargen of the Red Hand," the Orc replied. "I am Karag, hunter of the Stone Crushers. Do you come in peace?"

"Yes. We have fled our home due to danger."

"What type of danger?"

"The worst of all, Humans."

"I understand your plight. Our people came here for the same reason, though that was generations ago. What is it you wish?"

"Only to live in peace and harmony with our fellow Orcs."

"You have the gift of speech," said Karag, "but it is my chieftain, Zahruhl, with whom you must speak. Only he can allow passage through our lands."

"Then lead the way, Karag, and we shall lay our case before him."

Karag bowed, then turned, leading them deeper into the woods.

The village of Khasrahk was similar in layout to Ord-Kurgad but with one big difference; the walls here were made of solid stone as were the buildings therein.

"Their shamans wield the magic of the earth," noted Shaluhk as they passed the entrance.

"Yes," agreed Kargen. "It reminds me of the legends of the ancient Orc cities. It is said that they, too, were made of stone."

"Despite the stone, they are still our cousins."

A small crowd had gathered to witness their arrival. An elderly Orc, wearing cloth of grey, moved closer. "Welcome," he said. "I am Rugg, master of earth."

"Greetings to you, Rugg. I am Kargen, chieftain of my tribe, and this is Shaluhk, shamaness and healer."

"Honour be to you both," said Rugg. "I assume you have come to see our chieftain, Zahruhl?"

"We have. We wish to seek his permission to cross your lands."

"Then come with me. I will take you to him."

He turned, guiding them towards an immense stone structure. "This is our great hall. No doubt it will look familiar to you."

Kargen was impressed, for like the village wall, it appeared to be made of a single piece of stone.

Rugg noticed the look. "We have used our magic to fuse the stones. It took many years."

"It is quite impressive," said Kargen, "and reminds me of the legends."

"And so it should. The technique has been passed down for generations."

"An enemy would be hard-pressed to break those walls."

The statement gave Rugg pause. He turned, a look of curiosity on his face. "An interesting thing to say. We have never been attacked and are on friendly terms with our neighbours, but it seems changes are coming or so says our shaman." He waved his hand in what Kargen thought was a very Human manner. "But let us not speak of such things just yet. Come, I will introduce you to our chieftain, Zahruhl."

The great hall, with the exception of the stone walls, was of a similar layout as was typical amongst the green race. A large room held enough space for the tribe to gather, while one end was separated by a wall to allow the chieftain and his family some privacy. A wooden door connected the two, on which Rugg rapped three times.

"Come," came the answer.

The master of earth opened the door, ushering Kargen and Shaluhk inside.

"Greetings," said Rugg, "I have brought you guests. This is Kargen, Chieftain of the Red Hand, and this is their shaman, Shaluhk."

"Greetings to you both," the leader of the Stone Crushers replied. "Have a seat, and we shall share the milk of life."

They took their places around the modest fire. A female Orc entered, carrying a bowl filled with the milky-white liquid.

"This is Voruhn," said the chieftain, "my bondmate."

"Honour to your Ancestors," said Shaluhk.

"And to yours," came the reply.

Zahruhl took a sip of the milk, passing it to Kargen. The chieftain of the Red Hand raised the drink to his lips, partaking of only the smallest of sips, then gave it to Shaluhk. In this way, it made its way around the circle, finally coming to rest in the hands of Voruhn. The ritual complete, the bowl was set aside.

"Tell me," said Zahruhl, "why have you come here?"

"We come seeking a new home," Kargen replied. "Our last was devastated by war."

"The Humans?"

Kargen nodded. "Yes, though we defeated them once, we knew it was inevitable that they would return in greater numbers. It was a difficult decision to move on, but we knew we had little choice."

"And so you crossed the mountains."

"How did you know that?" asked Kargen.

"Where else would you have encountered Humans?"

"Will you allow us to pass through your lands?"

"I will," said Zahruhl, "under one condition."

Kargen braced himself. "Go on."

"You must talk to your people. Those that wish it may settle amongst us, adopting our ways."

"Absorption?"

"Only for those who choose it."

"I shall consider your offer." Kargen thought a moment before continuing. "If we do decide to cross your lands, what can we expect?"

"Northeast of here lies the hunting grounds of our cousins, the Black Axe. Beyond them are said to be Humans."

"Anything else?"

"Yes, to the north lies the ancient gateway."

"That sounds intriguing," said Shaluhk. "What manner of gateway is this you speak of?"

"It is an ancient stone construction," said Zahruhl, "but Rugg is better suited to speak of such things." He looked to his master of earth.

"The gateway's origin is lost to history," stated Rugg, "its true use long forgotten in the past, and yet it still possesses great power."

"In what way?" asked Shaluhk.

"It enhances the effectiveness of any spell cast in its vicinity."

"Any magic?"

"Well, that of the earth, certainly. The others we are not sure of."

"Is it of Orcish construction?"

"It certainly appears to be," the master of earth continued. "There are inscriptions on the stone in the ancient language of our race, though none can read it these days."

"If you can not read it," asked Kargen, "how do you know it is in Orcish?"

"It bears symbols that are similar to those used by our shamans, including myself."

"Fascinating," noted Shaluhk. "I have often wondered what our Ancestors were capable of."

"Are there dangers aside from the Humans?" asked Kargen.

"Only from the tuskers, and fortunately, they are few."

"Tuskers?"

"Yes," added Zahruhl, "vicious beasts larger than deer, with tusks and sharp teeth."

"I think we encountered one of those," said Kargen. "It had cloven feet and moved quickly."

"That sounds like a Tusker. Tell me, how did you defeat it? Their hides are said to be impenetrable."

"We used a combination of things," explained Kargen, "including magic, my axe, and a warbow."

"A warbow?"

"Yes, a bow crafted to take advantage of our broad shoulders. It was developed by a member of our tribe, a Human named Athgar."

"A Human?" Zahruhl recoiled in horror. "You let them travel amongst you?"

"I wish it were so, but no, he and his bondmate, Nat-Alia, preceded us. I am surprised you have not met them."

The chieftain waved away the remark. "The forest is thick, and we can not be everywhere at once. Perhaps they have already made contact with our cousins of the Black Axe?"

"One can always hope," noted Shaluhk.

Zahruhl rose. "I will let you return to your people, Kargen. You have much to consider. Once again, I extend the invitation to your tribe. Let them be joined to us as one. It is best for all."

"I appreciate the offer, but the choice is not mine to make. We shall hold a meeting and give you your answer in the morning."

"Very well. Rugg will show you the way out."

They were led back outside, through the great hall, and into the village itself.

"He means well," said the master of earth, "and the addition of your tribe would certainly make us stronger."

"He is generous," said Shaluhk, "but our Ancestors have sent us here for a reason. I can not believe it is to join your tribe." She bowed her head slightly. "I intend no offence."

"And I have taken none. You must do what you think is best for your people, just as Zahruhl does."

They reached the gate to the village where Karag waited.

"Are you ready to return to your people?" the hunter asked.

"We are."

"Then let us go. I would have you there before dark."

They took the vote that very evening. There was much discussion, for the exodus had taken its toll, and many wanted nothing more than to settle down and resume a semblance of normality. Long into the night it went, Kargen taking care that everyone had a chance to say their piece. The motion for the entire tribe to be absorbed into the Stone Crushers was easily defeated, but the next decision proved more difficult. After much discussion, it was decided that each Orc would decide for themselves whether to follow Kargen and the Red Hand or to remain behind under the leadership of Zahruhl.

With a heavy heart, Kargen led seventeen Orcs to the village of Khasrahk the next morning. Rugg met them at the entrance, ready to embrace the new members of his tribe.

"I shall look after them," the master of earth promised.

Kargen said his farewells. The parting was not an easy one. He had known them all for his entire life, but some were old and feared they would never see the final destination of the Red Hand, while others worried about their younglings' futures.

"The village is well defended," said Gralun, an ancient warrior, "and we can live out the rest of our lives here in peace."

Kargen put on a brave face. "I wish you only the best, old friend. Take care of yourself."

Shaluhk hugged Gralun. "May the Ancestors look over you and keep you safe."

"And you," the old Orc replied.

They started back to their camp, their footsteps weighed heavy by responsibility.

"Our tribe is diminished," noted Kargen.

"Yes," Shaluhk agreed, "but not defeated. It shall rise again, Kargen, with you at its head."

He looked at her as they walked. "You are always looking forward rather than back. A trait I greatly admire."

She smiled at the compliment. "It is my duty, as shamaness, to look to the future. You, as our leader, must look to the present."

"And the past?"

"Is behind us," she added, "where it belongs."

"And so we are on the move once more. Will this journey never stop?"

"Have faith, bondmate. The summer is ending. Let us hope the autumn will bring our tribe the rewards it seeks."

They walked in silence awhile, and then Shaluhk saw the look on Kargen's face that she recognized so well.

"What are you thinking about?" she asked.

"What makes you say I am thinking?"

"I know that look; you have knit your brows."

"I do not knit my brows."

"If you say so, but you know I am right. Now, what is it you are thinking about?"

"The tusker," Kargen replied.

"What of it?"

"It would make a terrifying weapon, would it not? Imagine if we could break it to the saddle?"

"We do not use saddles nor ride beasts," said Shaluhk.

"WE might not, but the Humans do. I wonder if our Ancestors ever rode?"

"It is said that young Orcs of the Black Arrow would ride large wolves."

"Black Arrow? I do not recall that tribe."

"Nor would I expect you to. They live far to the west."

"Is this the same west that has Human allies?"

"It is," said Shaluhk. "They are led by a chieftain named Urgon. He, like you, saw the wisdom in working with the Humans."

"And did his tribe prosper?"

"It has, and it continues to do so."

"Then he is lucky. The relationship between Humans and Orcs here has been one of near-constant strife."

"Athgar has shown us another way," Shaluhk reminded him.

"Yes, but his village was destroyed, its people scattered to the ends of the Continent."

"Much like our own, generations ago."

Kargen looked at her, deep in thought. "That is true. I had not considered it. Perhaps this journey is a trial of sorts."

"Trial?"

"Yes, to test our resolve. If that is so, then we will emerge all the stronger for it."

"Now that sounds more like the Orc I love," said Shaluhk. "Tell me, my bondmate, where will we settle?"

"That remains to be seen. For the moment, we will content ourselves with travelling north until we contact the Orcs of the Black Axe. From them, we will learn more of this area, allowing us to finally locate a place to call home."

"And we shall have other Orcs to trade with. Something our tribe has not done for generations."

Kargen turned his gaze south. The village of Khasrahk was far too distant to see, yet in his mind, it was clear. "Our fellow tribe has much to offer. I see the wisdom in Gralun's choice, but it is not for me."

"Nor me," said Shaluhk, "though I do wonder if the bonds we have forged this day may bear fruit in the future?"

"In what way?"

"Imagine if Ord-Kurgad had been protected by walls of stone. The attack would never have been attempted."

"I think you discredit the Humans too much. They would have still attacked but would have required much larger numbers. Still, your observation gives me thought. Maybe, once we settle, we will ask for help securing our new village."

Shaluhk warmed to the idea. "We could exchange shamans."

"You are my bondmate," said Kargen. "I would not send you to another."

"Then they can send their people to us, to be trained in the healing arts."

"Yes, and we shall send Orcs to them to learn the secrets of the earth."

"It seems our future is bright with possibilities."

"It is," said Kargen, his smile lighting up his face. "Now, if only we could find our new home!"

AN ILL WIND

Autumn 1104 SR

As the heat of summer finally gave way to the colder winds of autumn,
Athgar settled into village life with ease, occasionally hunting when
he wasn't busy making bows. The villagers easily grew accustomed to this
strange pair, and Natalia, even as a skrolling, was soon sought out for her
wisdom.

The negotiations with the tribes had continued, but the first signs of real
progress were when Athgar led a group of Orcs into Runewald bearing
goods for trade.

Eadred's displeasure was evident to all, but the rest of the village was
ecstatic, particularly over the herbs and medicines they brought. In
exchange, the Orcs received wool and cloth along with the arrows Athgar
had made.

On a particularly chilly day, Athgar was sitting before the hut carving a
bow of his own design. As he sat, whittling away the wood, a shadow
loomed over him. He looked up to see Melwyn.

"Hello, Athgar," she said.

"Good morning, Melwyn. Is there something I can do for you?"

"May I sit?"

"Of course. Can I offer you something to drink?"

"No, thank you."

She sat opposite him, silently watching as he worked.

"Did you come seeking a bow?" he asked.

"I am no hunter."

"Then what is it?"

"I was curious what had happened to you after Athelwald," she said. "I took you for dead when I didn't spot you amongst the survivors."

"And so I would have been if it hadn't been for the Orcs. Kargen and Laruhk pulled me from the ashes of my hut."

"And now you are a Fire Mage. How did that come about?"

"I was taught by the Orcs."

"It changed you."

"For the better, I hope?"

Melwyn avoided his gaze. "I'm still undecided on that."

"Are you happy, here in Runewald?" asked Athgar.

"I am not unhappy."

"That's a guarded reply."

"I'm very careful with my words," she admitted. "It has served me well here."

"Why have you come?" he asked. "To visit me, I mean."

"I'm trying to understand the hold this skrolling has over you."

Athgar set down his bow, pointing the knife at her as he spoke. "I will not have you talk that way of Natalia. She is my bondmate, and I love her deeply."

"Only because you have never been with another. What could a woman like her offer that you cannot find with me?"

"Compassion, for one thing."

Her face turned crimson, and she opened her mouth in anger, but he cut her off.

"You see only the worst in people, Melwyn. You were happy to be rid of me, but now you see me as a way to advance your station. Imagine, Melwyn, wife to a Fire Mage!"

"And what's wrong with that? Surely it's not too much to ask that a Therengian breeds with his own?"

"It's precisely that attitude that led to the downfall of our people," said Athgar. "It's not us and them; it's about all of us, together, living in harmony."

"That's not the way of the world, and you know it."

"Do I? Who's to say it cannot be so?"

"History," she said, "or did you forget we were conquered?"

"I've forgotten nothing, but things will never change if no one has the courage to try. Remember, I've lived amongst the Orcs, and know they are little different from us."

"They are brutes," insisted Melwyn.

"They might say the same of you," he replied, his voice rising. "If you give them half a chance, I think you'll see friendship has its advantages."

"Your woman has corrupted you."

"We are partners, Natalia and I, not possessions. It might be different in Runewald, but don't you remember Athelwald? Men and women were treated with respect there. What does one have to do to be received the same here?"

"That is simple," said Melwyn. "Get rid of the skrolling."

Athgar rose to his feet. "Whatever we had between us is long dead, Melwyn. You must come to grips with it. Whether you like it or not, Natalia is my wife. Now begone, I have little time for such talk."

She rose, calming herself as she straightened her dress. "You will live to regret this, Athgar."

"No, I am at peace with it, as you should be."

Melwyn turned, walking away without a single glance backward. Athgar sat once more, trying to calm his temper.

"Was that Melwyn?" asked Natalia, coming out the door.

"It was, though I would have preferred otherwise."

"She still loves you."

"No. She craves power and influence and thinks she would gain status as the wife of a Fire Mage."

Natalia displayed a hint of a smile. "How do you know that isn't what I want?"

"You're far more powerful than I. It would be a step down."

"Hardly that," she said, taking a seat.

"How are you feeling?"

"Uncomfortable. You?"

"I was doing well until Melwyn showed up," Athgar admitted. "Now I don't know what I am."

"Do you still care for her?"

"Only as a fellow villager." He looked her in the eyes. "We grew up together and were childhood friends. It wounds me to see the contempt in which she holds you."

"There are only a few in this village that are so inclined," she said. "The rest have come around."

"I understand you've been particularly useful of late."

"Yes, purifying water for ale."

Athgar looked at her in alarm. "I thought we decided not to use your magic?"

"It is little effort, and I am careful to limit my power: a technique I learned from the master." Natalia leaned forward, kissing him.

"Very well," he said as gruffly as he could manage.

"I've noticed you seldom meet with the king anymore."

"He still uses me to translate, but it appears I am no longer part of his inner circle."

She laughed. "Were you ever?"

"No, I suppose not."

"We should visit the other villages," she said. "You know there are five of them in total."

"Five Therengian villages," said Athgar. "Who would have thought? Are they all as big as Runewald?"

"They say Thaneford is even larger. Should we relocate there?"

"Perhaps, in time, but I don't think it's a good idea just now with a baby on the way, do you?"

Her hands went to her belly. "I suppose not."

"In any event, I've plenty to keep me busy here. My arrows have been very popular with the Orcs, and even some of our own villagers have put in an order for bows."

"You know, I like it here," said Natalia. "Aside from the whole 'skrolling' thing, of course."

"That will die off in time."

"Will it? I have my doubts."

"Nonsense," he soothed. "You're already popular with the women of Runewald. It won't take long for the men to come around."

They spotted Raleth. The hunter had only just returned, his boots still covered in mud.

"We haven't seen you in a while," called out Athgar. "Where have you been?"

Raleth turned, making his way towards them. "Ebenstadt," he replied.

Natalia's ears pricked up at the name. "To the city?"

"Only to the outskirts. The king wanted to know what the skrollings were up to." He looked at Natalia and blushed. "Sorry, the outsiders."

"And what did you discover?" she asked.

"They are massing an army. I fear another attack is imminent."

Natalia was struck by a thought. "The Crusades," she said.

"What of them?" asked Athgar.

"The Crusades are a series of military campaigns carried on by the Church to suppress worshippers of death. At least that's what they tell everyone."

"I don't understand?"

"Don't you see?" she said. "Look around you. It's not death worshippers they're trying to destroy, it's Therengians! They're coming for us, all of us."

"Why? What could we possibly have that the Church would want?"

"Who knows? Plunder, or maybe it's just an excuse to get their warriors ready for battle?"

"How long would it take them to assemble their army?" asked Athgar.

"Who knows?" she replied, looking around at the distant trees. "No, that's not right. Let me think this through. The terrain here is harsh, and that presents all manner of difficulties."

"Harsh?"

"Yes, difficult to traverse for an army. They would have to bring their own supply wagons. Not easy for an army that primarily lives off the land."

"And even more difficult to move in these woods," noted Athgar. He noticed Raleth staring at them both. "Natalia was trained as a battle mage," he explained.

"I remember," said Raleth, "though in truth, I have no idea what that means."

"I am trained to use magic in battle," explained Natalia, "but it's more than that. We learned all about the tactics of the Petty Kingdoms."

"The attack will be led by the skrollings' church," said Raleth.

"Are you sure?" asked Athgar.

"It has always been so in the past."

"Then it is definitely a crusade," said Natalia. "That means they will be eager to fight."

"We defeated them once," added Athgar, "and can do so again."

Raleth's eyes went wide. "You beat the army of the Church?"

"We did, though we had some help," said Athgar.

"From who?"

"The Sisters of Saint Agnes," explained Natalia.

"I don't know who that is."

Natalia's eyes bore into the young hunter. "They are a fighting order of the same Church you condemn."

"So they fight amongst themselves? I find that difficult to believe."

"It's true," said Athgar. "The Church is widespread, with its members scattered across the Continent. There's bound to be dissension in such a thing. Look at our own village; is there not disagreement here?"

Raleth nodded. "There are many who disagree with our king, but our voices are silenced."

"You said this not the first time they have attacked," noted Athgar. "Tell me what happened last time?"

"We fled our homes, coming east. We have been doing so for years. Now our enemy masses in the village of our ancestors, Ebenstadt."

"An unusual name for a Therengian village, isn't it?" asked Natalia.

"It is the skrollings' name for it. We used to call it Dunmere."

"When was it lost?" asked Athgar.

"Many years ago, long before I was born."

"And how many times have they attacked since?"

"Twice," said Raleth. "The last time was only five years ago. They razed Ashborne, the village of my birth. I still remember fleeing the flames. Each time we have moved farther east, hoping to escape their grasp."

"Surprising," said Natalia. "I would have thought Runewald older than that."

"It is, but it used to be on the eastern border of our land. Now it is the very frontier. Ebenstadt lies only about fifty miles from here. It will not take long for their armies to arrive once they start moving."

"Do they know the location of Runewald?" asked Natalia.

"I can't say for certain. We have seen naught of their troops in this area, but many of our people have been captured in past campaigns. Someone must have revealed its location by now."

"What will Eadred do?" asked Athgar.

"He will do what he's always done, flee eastward once more."

"That won't dissuade the Church," said Natalia. "They'll be eager to bring about your defeat. I suspect they won't settle for anything less than your total annihilation. The only way to prevent that is to stand and fight."

"Would you have us slaughtered?" asked Raleth.

"You have the advantage. Maybe not in numbers, but your people know the forest, and the Holy Army will have a vulnerable supply line. Proper planning can mitigate their numerical superiority."

Raleth stared at her. "You are wise, Natalia Stormwind, but it is King Eadred who must be convinced, not me."

"Then let us accompany you to his hall. You were about to go there yourself, weren't you?"

"I was," he said. "As soon as I washed the stench from my clothes."

"Then go and wash, Raleth. Athgar and I shall await your return, and then we'll all go there together."

"Very well," the young man responded. He left them quickly, eager to prepare for his report.

"Are you serious about fighting?" asked Athgar. "That doesn't seem like you."

"Perhaps I have been jaded by the recent battle for Ord-Kurgad, but I've come to realize the only way to negotiate with these people is from a position of strength."

"Are you talking about the Church or King Eadred?"

She smiled. "Does it matter?"

The king's hall was relatively quiet when they arrived. King Eadred sat, conferring with Cenric, but other than the presence of two guards, the room was empty.

"My king," said Raleth, "I bring news."

"Let him pass," the king commanded. The guards moved aside, allowing them entry. Athgar noticed Eadred's look of distaste as he spotted the additional members of the party.

"I have come from Ebenstadt," began Raleth.

"And?"

"It is as you feared, Lord King. The skrollings are massing for another attack."

Eadred placed his hand to his temple, looking down in disappointment. "I feared as much."

Those in the room remained silent, allowing him time to absorb the news. When he raised his head, he looked once more at Raleth. "Tell me all you have seen."

"Their army is large," the hunter replied. "Easily twice our number. Many mercenaries have joined them, swelling their ranks. Even as we speak, their army has expanded past the confines of the town."

"And what is the nature of these mercenaries?"

"Mostly foot, my king, though archers were in evidence, along with more knights."

"Temple Knights?"

"No, they remain within the confines of their fortress. These are men of the Petty Kingdoms."

"They are likely not mercenaries," interjected Natalia, "but rather nobles of the land, coming to make a name for themselves."

King Eadred stared daggers at her. "And what would you know of such things?"

"I am a battle mage."

"So you have said in the past, but of what use is that to us now? Are you saying you can defeat their army with your magic?"

"No, but I know their tactics. We can defeat them, Lord King, but we must show courage."

"Courage? Do not speak to me of courage, skrolling! You know nothing of our suffering at the hands of these people, YOUR people."

"They are not my people," countered Natalia. "This is my home now, and I will do everything in my power to protect it."

"Then you are a fool! We cannot withstand the might of the Church. We must withdraw eastward once more."

"We cannot," said Athgar. "That would move us into the Orcs' lands."

"Better to fight the Orcs than this army that so overwhelms us," said the king.

"We can use the terrain to our advantage," insisted Natalia, "and attack their supply wagons."

"No, it is too dangerous. We must withdraw eastward. My decision is final."

Raleth nodded. "Of course, my king."

"Now be gone," Eadred commanded. "I have much to consider before the evacuation begins."

Raleth led Athgar and Natalia from the hut.

"So is that it?" asked Athgar. "We're to run at the first sign of trouble?"

"What else can we do? You heard the king. The enemy outnumbers us. We have little choice."

"You DO have a choice," said Natalia. "You can stand and fight. Retreating now will only delay the inevitable. If you don't stand up to them, they shall return."

"And if we do fight?" said Raleth. "A loss could mean the death of us all."

"Better to die fighting than live a constant life of flight," said Athgar.

"I understand how you feel, Raleth," said Natalia, "but running is not the answer. Trust me, I know. I've spent the best part of a year running from my past, but it keeps catching up to me. The only way out of this mess is to make a stand. Defeat them once and for all, and they will think twice about returning."

"I saw the size of their army, and they were still gathering more."

"Their size works against them," Natalia continued. "Nobles are loathe to follow the commands of others. True, the Temple Knights are a threat, but without a coordinated army behind them, they are useless." She swept her arms out in a grand gesture. "Look at these woods. Do you really think their knights could charge in such terrain?"

"You make a good argument," said Raleth, "but the king has made his decision."

"Then maybe it's time for a new king."

The hunter laughed. "You cannot make a new king. It is hereditary."

"Nonsense," said Natalia. "If a king cannot serve his people, he does not deserve his throne."

"What you speak of is treason."

"No, what we speak of is survival. Which will it be, Raleth? Scurry away whenever danger threatens, or stand and fight?"

"You have given me much to think on."

"Go back to your hut," said Athgar, "and discuss this with your family. Then maybe you will see the wisdom in our words."

"I shall do as you suggest," the young hunter responded.

They walked the rest of the way in silence. Raleth bid them a good day as they arrived at their hut, then ran off seeking his brother.

"Do you really think King Eadred deserves to be removed?" asked Athgar.

"It is now apparent that he only cares for himself, not his people."

"Still, to replace him feels like a big step."

"Do the Orcs not replace a chieftain who cannot lead?"

"I suppose they do, but these are not Orcs. They are Humans, and as such, are used to doing things their own way."

"And what has it brought them?" Natalia asked. "Only misery and death." She leaned in close, placing her hand upon his arm. "I mean no disrespect to your people, Athgar, but look around you. All they want is to live out their lives free from the heartache of war. They deserve more than flight. They need a reason to live, and you can give it to them."

Athgar's eyes went wide. "Me? I don't want to be king!"

"It's that very thing that would make you a good leader."

"But I'm only a bowyer."

"No," said Natalia, "you are much more than that. You are a master of flame, and just like Artoch, you know, deep in your heart, that you have the best interests of your people in mind. We've only been here a short time, my love, but already you have gained the trust and respect of all."

"I doubt the king feels so," said Athgar.

"And that is his folly. You know how to listen to others, and most of all, how to inspire them."

"Since when have I been a leader?" he asked.

"Since Ord-Kurgad. The Orcs of the Red Hand saw you as one of their own, much as the villagers in Runewald do."

"Perhaps you're right."

She smiled. "I know I am."

WELCOME

Autumn 1104 SR

(In the tongue of the Orcs)

L aruhk halted, raising his hand to signal Durgash to do likewise. "I sense someone ahead," he said.

"Humans?" asked his companion.

"No, more Orcs."

"Ah," said Durgash, "the Orcs of the Black Axe, as Kargen predicted. Shall I fetch him?"

"Yes," said Laruhk, "and my sister as well."

"And in the meantime, what will you do here?"

"I shall wait."

Laruhk crouched, listening carefully to the sounds of the forest. Birds chirped in the trees, a sure sign danger was not at hand. He relaxed, letting out his breath. He was in the same position when Kargen and Shaluhk found him.

"You have news?" said Kargen.

"Orcs are nearby," he replied, "likely beyond that twisted tree."

"Then it is time we introduced ourselves," said Kargen. He took a step forward, revealing himself with Shaluhk by his side. "I am Kargen, Chieftain of the Red Hand," he called out, "and this is Shaluhk, our shamaness."

"And I am Urughar of the Black Axe," a voice drifted back. "Come forward so we may see you mean no harm."

They moved closer, soon detecting the carefully hidden hunter. "We come in peace," announced Kargen.

Urughar stood, then came forward, his hands held palms up in front of him to show he was unarmed. "Honour be to you, Kargen and Shaluhk. My chieftain, Kirak, will be pleased for you to visit him. I understand you have come far?"

Kargen looked at Shaluhk, whispering, "How would he know that? The Ancestors?"

"I have no idea," she replied. "And we shall never find out unless we take him up on his offer."

"You are right, of course." He raised his voice once again. "Very well, Urughar. Take us to your chieftain that we may greet him."

They entered the village of Ord-Ghadrak with little fanfare. Word of their arrival spread quickly, and by the time they arrived at the great hut, the chieftain of the tribe was standing before them.

"Greetings, Kirak," said Kargen.

The immense Orc stepped closer, his scarred visage a mere finger's width from Kargen's face.

"Welcome, Kargen of the Red Hand," he finally said. "Welcome to Ord-Ghadrak." He embraced Kargen, a move that surprised everyone.

Kirak looked towards Shaluhk, bowing his head. "And honour to you, Shamaness." Returning his attention back to Kargen, he continued. "Come, let us share the milk of life to celebrate this meeting."

"I would prefer some drink," said Kargen, "for my throat is parched."

Kirak let out a chuckle, leading his followers to relax the grips on their axes. "Well said, my friend. So be it. Come and sample the hospitality of the tribe."

They soon found themselves inside the great hut, sitting around the central fire that dominated the place. Other Orcs had drifted in and now sat nearby, listening intently to the discussion.

"Tell me," began Kirak, "what is it you desire for your people?"

"A place to live," said Kargen, "nothing more. Surely there is room in these parts for another tribe?"

"Ordinarily, I would have said yes, but recent events have changed everything. We have had to deal with the Torkul, you see."

"Torkul? You mean the Humans?"

"They are more than mere Humans," noted Kirak, "for they have the grey eyes of their ancestors."

"Athgar's people," said Shaluhk.

"Yes," Kirak agreed. "It was Athgar that helped broker the peace."

"Athgar is here?" said Kargen.

"He was," the chief replied.

"What of Nat-Alia?" asked Shaluhk. "Was my sister with him?"

"If you are referring to the Human female with pale skin, then yes, even now they live amongst the Torkul in Runewald."

"Is that the village of the Therengians?" asked Shaluhk.

"It is."

"Then it appears our journey is almost done."

Mortag, the master of flame leaned forward, intent on the conversation. "Why would you say that?"

Shaluhk smiled. "From the beginning, Athgar's arrival in Ord-Kurgad portended great change. After we defeated our enemies, we sought to move east, but fate placed an army in our way. As a result, we were forced north, following in his footsteps. It soon became clear our Ancestors were guiding us closer, perhaps to a shared destiny."

"Then it could be that the fate of both our races is tied up in this 'Therengian,'" noted Kirak, "though I must admit Torkul is easier on the tongue."

"Torkul is the name for an enemy," said Shaluhk, "but I believe the Therengians might be our allies. The Ancestors have indicated it was thus in the distant past."

Kirak nodded his head, turning to his master of flame. "What do you think of that, Mortag?"

"We have seen Athgar represent the interests of our tribe," the old Orc remarked. "I think it a reasonable supposition."

"That is his way of agreeing," said Kirak. "And what of you, Laghul? You are our shamaness. Do the Ancestors tell you any different?"

"I would agree with Shaluhk," she replied. "Our race is at a critical time as the Humans spread into our lands. The arrival of our cousins gives us the strength to resist them."

"War with the Therengians is to be avoided," insisted Kargen.

"I agree," said Kirak, "but their king is difficult to deal with."

"Difficult in what way?"

"He pretends to want peace but secretly prepares for war."

"How do you know this?" asked Shaluhk.

"Our hunters keep their eyes open when they visit Runewald."

"How far is this village?" asked Kargen.

"Two days' travel," said Kirak. "I can have Urughar take you there if you wish."

"I should very much appreciate it, though I would have to make arrangements for my tribe first."

"We would be happy to assist," said Laghul.

"Yes," agreed Mortag. "How many travel with you?"

"One hundred and ninety-two," said Shaluhk. "Many of them younglings or the elderly."

"We shall find room," said Kirak, "if only for the short term. We will, of course, expect your hunters to contribute to the stores."

"Of course," said Kargen. "I would have it no other way."

"If you are to travel to Runewald, with whom would I speak to in your absence?"

"Laruhk. He is Shaluhk's brother and a trusted friend."

"Are you sure he is up to it?" asked Shaluhk.

"I would trust him with my life."

"Yes, but would you trust him with your tribe?"

"You trust him with our son," Kargen reminded her.

"So I do," she relented.

"You obviously hold him in high esteem," said Kirak, chuckling.

"I do," said Kargen. "He has been a friend since we were younglings."

"I understand completely," said Kirak, "for many of my closest advisors are the same. Do not fear. Your tribe will be welcome amongst us, and once you return, we shall seek out a new place for you to call home."

"You do me honour," said Kargen.

"No," said Kirak, "it is you who honours me. It is seldom that we meet members of another tribe, and while we get along with the Stone Crushers now, it has not always been so."

"Are you saying that you fight?" asked Kargen.

"There have been skirmishes, but that was many years ago. Now we tend to keep to ourselves, while our neighbours do likewise."

"And if the Humans come, would they assist you?"

"It is a hard question to answer," noted Kirak. "Do you expect trouble from the Humans?"

"Not the Therengians," said Kargen, "but Athgar and Natalia sought out a place called Ebenstadt, and that may be a greater threat."

"Yes," said Kirak. "I remember him asking after it. As I told them, however, we know little of the place. Do you truly think it a threat?"

"Shaluhk would know better than I," said Kargen, looking at his bondmate.

"The Ancestors sent our friends there," she added, "but told us little of why."

"It is ever the way with the Ancestors," noted Laghul. "They always seem to talk in riddles."

"In any event," said Kirak, "I shall make arrangements for Urughar to take you to Runewald. How long will it take you to settle in?"

"Three days," said Kargen, "maybe less."

"Then you shall leave for the Therengian village in three days. Now, let us partake of some food to celebrate the meeting of our tribes."

By the time they exited the great hut, darkness had fallen. Kirak, however, had sent word to Laruhk, and as Kargen and Shaluhk emerged, the first of their tribe was already arriving. Orcs of the Black Axe stood ready to welcome the newcomers, each being guided to a place of rest and food. The overall atmosphere was one of camaraderie as if distant family members had arrived for a visit.

Kargen was grateful for the kind reception. He saw hope on the faces of his people, filling him with a sense of gratitude. Kirak has assured him absorption was not a consideration. He promised the Red Hand would be given a new home. The only thing standing in the way was the Therengians, something that weighed heavily on Kargen's mind.

It was only much later, when he had time alone with Shaluhk, that he managed to express his worry.

"What do you make of our situation?" he asked.

Shaluhk had just finished putting Agar to bed. She looked up from the small Orc to her bondmate, a smile still on her lips. "I like it here. Those in this tribe are nice."

"I was referring to the situation with the Therengians."

"Athgar is the only Therengian I have met," she replied, "and so it is very difficult to form an opinion."

"I have met more in the village of Athelwald, but I can not say Runewald will be the same. We know so little of Athgar's people."

"We must have faith in Athgar and Nat-Alia. They would do nothing to threaten the Orcs."

"On that, we can agree, but we know naught of their present circumstance."

"We shall know soon enough," Shaluhk said. "In three days, Urughar will take us to their village, and then we shall be reunited with our friends."

"And if their king is hostile?"

"Our friends will not fail us."

"What if they have no choice?"

"You worry too much," said Shaluhk. "You must trust in the Ancestors."

"I remember well the words of my father," said Kargen, grinning. "Trust in the Ancestors and carry a sharp axe."

Kargen's group settled in quickly, for the Orcs of the Black Axe were eager to help. The tribe had been prosperous for years, resulting in an increase in population. Consequently, new huts were under construction, with an expansion to the outer walls of the village already underway. The Orcs of the Red Hand responded with enthusiasm, helping to speed the work.

Kargen spent his time wandering the village, lending a hand where he could while Shaluhk sat with Laghul, for her training had not yet been considered complete when her mentor, Uhdrig, had died. The Shamaness of the Black Axe proved a fountain of knowledge, and Shaluhk's understanding of the spirit realm grew by leaps and bounds.

One day soon turned into three, and then a ten-day. More days went by, and the responsibilities of being chieftain kept Kargen busy. It wasn't until nearly two ten-days later that they finally found time to undertake the journey to Runewald.

With assurances from Laruhk that all would be well, they set off, Urughar leading. The terrain here was more open, the trees less dense. Pine trees made way for maple and elm, their colours changing as the weather turned cooler. The trip was pleasant, and as they made their way northwest, Kargen could feel the weight of his responsibilities lifting.

"Tell me, Urughar, how long has your tribe lived in these parts?"

"Generations," the hunter replied.

"And have the Humans always been so close?"

"Yes, but in my youth, they hunted to the west. As I reached my maturity, they had begun to move eastward, seeking food and founding new settlements in the area to the north."

"New? Do you mean to say that Runewald is not the only one?"

"There are, indeed," said Urughar. "To our knowledge, there are five Human villages within a ten-day's travel, though Runewald is the closest."

"And when did they become aggressive?"

"They moved into our hunting grounds, creating conflict. We feared war was inevitable, but then Athgar of Athelwald arrived and showed us the way to peace. You are lucky to have him as a member of your tribe."

"Yes," said Kargen. "He is a good friend and a powerful ally."

"As is Nat-Alia," added Shaluhk, "for she is also a powerful mage."

"It was she who saved the talks," noted Urughar, "by using her magic to keep the Therengian warriors at bay."

"And that brought peace?"

"Not entirely, but it did lead to more negotiations. It has been an uneasy truce, but we have recently begun trading with the Humans. It offers hope for a better future."

"We traded with the Therengians for years," said Kargen, "though only in small quantities. That is how I met Athgar."

"Through trade?"

"Yes. In my youth, my father told me of the Humans, but theirs was a place to be avoided."

"If you avoided it, then how did you meet Athgar?"

"That is a longer story," said Kargen. "When I became a hunter, I had difficulty in the making of arrows."

"He is all thumbs when it comes to such things," added Shaluhk.

Urughar chuckled. "It is often so with our most gifted hunters. I, too, find such fine work hard to master. But tell me, what made you decide to approach the Humans?"

"I found one of their arrows in the woods protruding from a tree. A hunter had likely missed their mark and lost it amongst the greenery. For years I had been taught the Humans were savages, and yet here was this arrow that showed care in its construction."

"What did you do?"

"I located the Humans' trail and followed it back to their village. We all knew of Athelwald but kept our distance, not wishing to antagonize them. Now, as a young hunter, I took it upon myself to investigate and learn more."

Urughar was so intrigued by the story that he stumbled on a fallen branch. He quickly recovered, chuckling as he righted himself. "Go on," he urged, "this is most interesting."

"Where was I?" asked Kargen.

"You were learning more of Athelwald," offered Shaluhk.

"Yes, that is correct. It soon became clear the Humans were poor hunters, still relying on old techniques to acquire game."

"Yes," added Shaluhk, "they used spears if you can believe it."

"We still use spears," said Urughar.

"Yes, as do we," agreed Kargen, "but only for hunting boar. They were using them for everything even though they had bows."

"Why is that?"

"It had something to do with their rituals of becoming adults. Athgar tried to explain it to me, but I found the entire concept difficult to understand."

"And so these Therengians made bows but didn't use them?"

"In their minds, they were weapons of war. I doubt Athgar's father would have been as successful had I not started trading with him. His arrows soon became a common sight amongst our tribe."

"It must have been difficult to approach them that first time."

Kargen smiled. "It was. I watched them for days waiting for an opportunity, and then, one day, Athgar's father, Rothgar, went into the forest alone to gather wood for his craft."

"And that is when you approached him?"

"Yes, though I must admit our first encounter did little to calm his fears. In those days, neither of us spoke the language of the other. It took a long time to convince him I wanted to trade, but in the end, it was worth it. Eventually, he learned our language and I, some of his."

"Yes," added Shaluhk, "and then he actually walked right into Athelwald."

"The Humans must have been alarmed," said Urughar.

"Indeed they were," Kargen agreed. "There were three of us that day, but Laruhk and Durgash chose to remain in the trees. Rothgar managed to calm the village, and from then on, I would visit Athelwald once a ten-day, trading meat and skins for arrows, bows and other assorted things. Rothgar had two offspring, of which Athgar was the eldest. When he was old enough, he took up his father's profession and continued the trade."

"Remarkable," said Urughar. "To think Humans could be so civilized."

"It has been my observation," said Shaluhk, "that Humans, once you get to know them, are not so different from us. Obviously, their physical form is smaller, and I can not even begin to describe how weak their younglings appear to be, but inside, where it counts, we are very similar."

"Their offspring? You have seen them?"

"No," she admitted, "but I have heard stories. Athgar tells us they spend much time in their mother's womb. Far longer than our younglings do."

"Yes," added Kargen, "and they take forever to become adults. Would you believe Athgar was not considered an adult until he was twenty?"

"Twenty?" laughed Urughar. "We mature at fourteen. How did the Humans come to dominate the land under such circumstances?"

Kargen shrugged. "It is beyond my understanding."

"The Humans are fascinating," said Shaluhk. "I look forward to spending time in one of their villages."

"I would not put much hope in that," warned Urughar. "We are only allowed short visits, and none has ever stayed past nightfall."

"Then you do not know Athgar and Nat-Alia," said Shaluhk. "Many times, we have spent the best part of the darkness talking."

"It is not Athgar who limits us so, but his king. Each time we visit, his warriors watch us."

"He does not trust you," said Kargen.

"I think it more than that," said Shaluhk. "I think it is Athgar who he does not trust."

"What nonsense is this? Athgar is a staunch ally. He would never betray his friends."

"All that is true," she replied, "but the Therengian king likely sees Athgar as a threat to his power."

"Then perhaps Athgar should seek to become chieftain," suggested Kargen.

"The Humans do not work that way," said Urughar. "Their position of king is hereditary."

"You mean to say he is not elected?"

"No. Was it not so in Athelwald?"

"Athelwald had no king," said Kargen. "They were run by a leader chosen by their village, much as we are."

"How curious," said Urughar. "I wonder why they differ here?"

"You said they had five villages," said Shaluhk. "That is likely why."

"It is a valid point," added Kargen. "In Orc society, when a tribe gets too big, part of it breaks off, forming a new tribe, but from what you are describing, the Humans do not follow this practice."

"Is that not obvious?" asked Shaluhk. "We passed through the Duchy of Holstead. What better example to us?"

"I had always thought the Therengians were different," said Kargen, "but it appears it is a trait all Humans have in common."

"It is good that we do not follow the same path," said Urughar. "Can you imagine how difficult it would be for a chieftain to care for so many of our people?"

"Agreed," said Kargen. "It is hard enough looking after the Red Hand. I can only imagine what it would be like being responsible for five villages."

"In any event," said Urughar, "you shall see for yourself once we reach Runewald."

REUNITED

Autumn 1104 SR

Athgar shaved off another sliver of wood, then held the bow to his eye, peering down the shaft of yew to examine the finish. Pleased with the result, he set it down, picking up the next in line.

Natalia sat beside him, watching him work. "How many of those are you going to make?" she asked.

"As many as we need. These two are for Raleth and Harwath."

"And the rest?"

He smiled. "Hunferth and Wulfrid both want one."

"That accounts for four, and yet I see six."

"There may be others who have expressed an interest."

"Your reputation is growing," she said. "Now I suppose people will travel from all the nearby villages just to have one of your bows."

"We can always hope."

"And yet we lack for little," said Natalia, sweeping her gaze over their hut.

"Athgar is always thinking of the good of the village," offered Skora. "He would always offer a low price to his friends even though I said he shouldn't."

Natalia nestled into the pile of furs. "You must tell me more, Skora. I know so little of his youth. Was he a troublemaker?"

"No," the old woman replied, "that was more the domain of his sister, Ethwyn. Athgar was the quiet one."

"I can easily believe that. Does he take after his father?"

"To a certain extent, yes. Rothgar was a master bowyer, and Athgar always looked up to him."

"And what of his mother?"

"She died of a fever when he was quite young."

"It's a shame the Orcs couldn't have helped her," said Natalia.

"That was before Rothgar met the Orcs. We knew they were in the area, of course, but were not aware of their customs or the fact they had Life Magic."

"Did Rothgar die in the attack on Athelwald?"

"No," said Skora. "He was gored by a boar when Athgar was sixteen. After that, it was only Athgar and his sister."

"How old was Ethwyn at the time?"

"Fifteen."

"That must have been difficult."

"It was," admitted Athgar, "but Ethwyn was surrounded by friends. I tended to keep to myself."

"And yet you managed to survive, some might even say prosper," said Natalia.

"I kept my eye on them," said Skora.

"Well, I, for one, am grateful for that."

"What of your own childhood?"

"Mine?" said Natalia. "Why would that interest you?"

"You're having a child. It's only natural that one day they ask after your family."

"I have no family to speak of. My mother died when I was ten, murdered by agents of the Volstrum."

"The Volstrum?"

"The magical academy where I was taught."

"Had you no friends, dear?"

"Very few. Stanislav Voronsky was the closest thing to family I can recall. He was the mage hunter who brought me to the Volstrum."

"And he killed your mother?"

"No, that was someone else, a man named Nikolai. You know, I haven't thought about him for months. Does that make me a bad friend?"

"No," assured Skora, "it merely means you have been busy."

"What about you? Did you have a family?"

Skora carefully placed another log on the fire, then sat. "I was married, years ago, but he died. It seems the Gods did not look kindly upon us."

"I'm so sorry."

"It's all in the past now."

"And you never remarried?"

"It is not the Therengian way," Skora replied. "And by the time of his passing, I was beyond the age of childbearing."

"Well," said Natalia, "we are your family now."

Outside, voices shouted out a challenge, interrupting their conversation.

"That sounds like Cenric's men," Athgar remarked. "I'd better have a look."

"Take care," warned Skora. "They are looking for an excuse."

"An excuse for what?"

"To arrest you," said the old woman.

"I doubt even King Eadred would stoop that low."

"Be careful," warned Natalia. "I shouldn't like to have anything happen to you."

He rose from his seat, setting down his knife and bow. "I will, don't worry."

Making his way to the door, he peered outside. Three warriors, armed with shields and spears, had their backs to him, talking to someone out of his view.

"Go back," one of them was saying. "You are not welcome here."

Athgar stepped outside. "What's going on here?"

Their leader, a man named Frithwald, turned his head. "It is the command of the king that no Orc shall be within the walls of Runewald without an escort."

"We have no walls," said Athgar in reply. He moved closer until his view of the Orcs was unobstructed, and then his face immediately broke into a grin.

"Natalia," he called out. "You'd better come and see this."

"What is it?" she asked as she opened the door.

"It appears we have visitors."

She was only three paces past the door when she saw them. "Shaluhk, Kargen, so good to see you!" She closed the distance quickly, her discomfort soon forgotten. Shaluhk was the first to feel her embrace, while Athgar welcomed Kargen.

"Sister," said Shaluhk. "It is so good to see you again."

"And you," said Natalia, "but I don't understand. Weren't you travelling east?"

"We were," the shamaness replied, "but fate has sent us to your door."

"The tribe?" asked Athgar.

"Safely within the village of Ord-Ghadrak, guests of the Black Axe," replied Kargen.

Athgar took note of the third member of their party. "Urughar, good to see you again."

"And you, my friend."

The Therengian turned to the warriors. "It's all right, Frithwald. These are my guests. This is Kargen, Chieftain of the Red Hand, and their shamaness, Shaluhk."

Cenric's man stared back, his face growing red. He clearly wanted to say something, but the sight of the Orcs was intimidating, not to mention the thought of Athgar's Fire Magic. Instead, he simply nodded, then led his men away.

"I hope we have not caused trouble," said Kargen as Natalia embraced him.

"Nothing we can't handle," said Athgar.

"You have done well for yourself," said Shaluhk. "Is this your hut?"

"It is," said Natalia. "Now come inside, and I'll introduce you to Skora."

"The old woman?" said Kargen. "I thought her dead."

"You know her?"

"Of course," the Orc replied. "Who do you think used to prepare your bondmate's skins?"

"Come," said Urughar, "it is this way." He took them through the door, the hunter nodding to Skora as he entered.

"Greetings, Kargen," the old woman said. "It has been a long time since last we met."

Kargen bowed his head. "Skora, you honour us with your presence. It is good to see a familiar face."

"Sit," said Natalia. "I shall fetch us something to drink."

"Let me," said Skora. "A person in your condition has better things to do."

Shaluhk looked closely at her tribe-sister. "Nat-Alia, are you carrying?"

"I am."

"This is glorious news."

"Yes," agreed Kargen. "It means Agar will have a sister to play with."

Natalia beamed. "I'm glad you're here, Shaluhk. There's something I need to ask you about."

"Go on," urged the shamaness.

"Something happened to me while casting, and I'm not sure what to make of it."

"How long ago was this?"

"Some weeks ago. I was casting a spell, and I felt a coldness in my belly as if it was turning to ice."

A look of concern crossed the Orc's face. "Did you feel any pain?"

"No, but I have taken care to limit the use of my power since."

"Natalia's been restricting her magic to purifying water," explained Athgar, "and only in small amounts. We thought it best."

"A wise precaution under the circumstances. May I examine you?"

Natalia nodded as Shaluhk moved closer, placing her hands on the Water Mage's stomach. She pressed gently on several places, then looked into Natalia's eyes. "I can not speak for Humans, but if you were an Orc, I would say that all is well. But to be safe, I'd like to cast a spell."

"Go ahead," said Natalia. "I trust you."

"I shall detect life." Shaluhk sat back, sitting cross-legged, facing Natalia. Placing her hands on her lap, she began uttering words of power. A familiar buzz tingled throughout the hut, then Shaluhk's eyes glowed slightly. She gazed upon Natalia's stomach once more, nodding her head. "All is well," she finally said. "The young one's life force is strong and healthy."

"And the cold I felt?"

"I am afraid that is beyond my experience, but I shall consult with Laghul upon my return to Ord-Ghadrak. She is more experienced than I."

Natalia reached out, grasping Shaluhk's hand. "Thank you. It's nice to be reassured."

"Only the best for my sister-child."

"Can you tell if it is a boy or girl?" asked Athgar.

"No," replied Shaluhk. "It is far too early to tell."

"When is the youngling due?" asked Kargen.

"Some time in late winter, maybe early spring if we're lucky," said Natalia.

Shaluhk looked around the hut, taking in the entire contents. "You appear to have done well for yourselves. You have a home now, and a family on the way. What more could you ask for?"

"It's not all good news," said Athgar. "It appears the Church has reared its head again."

"Tell me more," said Kargen.

"At the Ancestors' urging, we travelled north, seeking a city called Ebenstadt."

"I remember it well, my friend."

"It now appears the Church is raising an army to wipe out my fellow countrymen."

"Yes," added Urughar, "and if the Therengians fall, how long do you suppose they will wait to come after us Orcs?"

"Precisely my thinking," said Athgar.

"What can be done about it?" asked Kargen.

It was Natalia that answered. "We suggested to King Eadred it was time to fight, but he was unwilling to take the risk."

"If the Orcs joined in the fight, he might change his mind," suggested Urughar.

"A good idea," said Athgar, "but before we fight, we must learn more about the enemy."

"What are you proposing?"

"Natalia and I will go to Ebenstadt and try to learn what we can about the situation there. If nothing else, it will let us determine their strength."

"Are you sure that is wise," said Kargen, "considering Nat-Alia's condition?"

Shaluhk waved him off. "You forget, Human younglings take a long time to gestate. Nat-Alia will be fine."

"Very well," said Kargen. "And in the meantime, we shall return to Ord-Ghadrak and, with Urughar's help, convince Kirak to support us. Naturally, the Red Hand shall stand with you."

"Do you think we could convince the Stone Crushers to join us?" said Shaluhk.

Athgar's ears pricked up. "Stone Crushers?"

"Another tribe that lies to the south of us. Their mages employ Earth Magic, something which would benefit us greatly in the upcoming fight."

"Are you sure it will come to that?" asked Urughar. "Is it possible this 'Church' will see reason and stay their hand?"

"I'm afraid our experience indicates otherwise," said Natalia.

"You must have had quite the adventure," said Athgar, "bringing the entire tribe across the mountains."

Kargen grinned. "It was, as you would say, quite something. It all started when we finally left Ord-Kurgad..."

By the time each of them finished telling what had befallen them over the last few months, it was quite late. Urughar was the first to notice it had grown dark.

"I fear we have overstayed our welcome," he said. "Your king will not like us within the village confines for so long."

"It's too late to go now," said Athgar. "You'll have to stay the night."

"Are you sure that is wise? It could mean trouble for you."

"Nonsense, you're my guests." He turned to Skora. "Have we room for them?"

"We have furs enough," the old woman replied, "and plenty to eat."

"There. It's settled; you're all staying."

"I must say," noted Natalia, "your common is coming along nicely, Urughar."

The Orc blushed, turning a darker shade of green. "It comes from attending all these negotiations. Your bondmate is a good teacher."

"It certainly helps having other translators," said Athgar. "And now that Kargen and Shaluhk are here, we can start making real progress."

"Not to mention Laruhk and Durgash," added Kargen.

"Don't forget Kragor," said Shaluhk. "He, too, speaks your tongue."

"So many of us," noted Urughar. "The Therengians will not know what to do with us all."

A voice interrupted their discussion. "Athgar, come out!"

"Who's that?" asked Natalia.

"It sounds like that fool, Frithwald," said Skora. "Likely back to do the bidding of his master."

"I'll deal with this," said Athgar. He stood, making his way to the door.

Shaluhk looked at Kargen, who nodded, rising to his feet to follow his friend. Athgar threw open the door to see Frithwald. This time he was backed up by five men, all armed with spears and shields.

"Does he expect to fight us with spears?" said Kargen.

"You are in violation of the king's orders," the warrior announced, ignoring the Orc's comment.

"And?" pressed Athgar.

The warrior sputtered. He had clearly been expecting Athgar to comply with King Eadred's decree, but now, facing the Fire Mage, he was clearly out of his depth.

"You must send them away," Frithwald finally spat out.

Athgar stared back. Beyond the warriors, a small crowd was starting to gather. "And if I don't?"

"Then I shall have to arrest you."

Athgar crossed his arms. "What does that mean, precisely?"

"It means you will be taken into custody."

"Where? We have no jail!" He noticed the onlookers growing uneasy at the confrontation. None of them appeared happy about the presence of Frithwald and his men. "Go back to your hut," he continued, "and tell Cenric he has no power here."

"You would defy the orders of your king?"

Athgar smiled. "He is not my king. I have sworn no oath to him."

"And yet you live within this village."

"Athgar is one of us!" someone from the crowd yelled out. "Go back, and tell your master to leave him alone."

"We are causing you trouble," said Kargen, his voice low. "Perhaps it would be better if we leave."

"No," said Athgar. "Eadred has had his way for far too long. A king must protect his people, not use them to his own advantage."

"Will you submit?" demanded Frithwald.

"I hold no animosity towards you, and yet I will not submit to an unjust law. This is your home, too, Frithwald. I invite you to help defend it, rather than slink away as your king does." He felt sorry for the young warrior. It was not easy to be caught between loyalties.

The villagers started calling out to Frithwald, telling him to join them. For his part, Athgar kept silent, letting Frithwald consider his options. Finally, the man lowered his spear and turned to the warriors behind him.

"Each of you must make your own decision on whether to fight or stay. The king has commanded us to arrest Athgar, but I cannot, in good conscience, carry out that order. I have taken an oath of obedience, and yet I now find myself conflicted. As a result, I shall return to King Eadred and plead to be released from his service."

"He will not like it," warned Athgar.

"No, nor will I, but I must, regardless. To do otherwise is dishonourable."

Frithwald left them, marching off with his head low, feeling the burden of what lay before him.

"This king will cause trouble," said Kargen.

"Yes," said Athgar. "He likely will."

Kargen took in the mood of the crowd. They were growing more vocal, calling out to the king's warriors to throw down their weapons. "The village respects you, as they should, but I sense your popularity will work against you."

"How so?" asked Athgar.

"The king will see you as a threat."

"He already does, but there is little I can do about that."

"You must try to win him over. If you do not, it will divide the loyalties of Runewald, and that could prove disastrous in the long run."

"You make a good point," said Athgar. "We need the people united if we are to make a stand. I'll visit the king tomorrow and see if I can't make him see reason."

Kargen nodded. "A wise choice. Now, shall we return inside? There is still much to catch up on, and my stomach yearns for more of that venison."

Athgar looked over those gathered one final time. One of the soldiers threw down his spear, and the crowd surged forward, patting the man on his back. It didn't take long for the others to follow his lead.

From across the way, Raleth met Athgar's gaze, and the young hunter nodded in support. It appeared the villagers had the upper hand this night, but Athgar couldn't help but wonder what the ramifications might be of such an encounter.

They returned to the inside of the hut, where Shaluhk and Natalia were deep in conversation.

"...and he carries it everywhere," Shaluhk was saying.

"I hope he can't hurt himself on it," said Natalia.

"It is a wooden axe. It can not do much damage. My brother, on the other hand, made him a bow."

"Is he old enough to use it?"

"No," said Shaluhk, "but Laruhk will not believe me. It was a nice sentiment, even if he can not use it for at least another year."

"A Human child would have to be much older to use a bow. When do Orcs learn such things?"

"Laruhk started when he was two, though I must admit he had a gift for it. Most are a little older, three being more common."

"They can use weapons at three years old?"

"Of course," said Shaluhk, "though they can not fight if that is what you mean. It takes years to master the use of it."

"Humans can barely speak at that age," said Athgar, "let alone carry an axe." He took his seat, settling into the furs to Natalia's right.

Natalia looked at him in surprise. "Are you an expert in children now?"

Athgar blushed. "I might have been talking to some of the villagers of late. Isn't that normal for a new father?"

Natalia smiled. "Father. I like the sound of that."

"I suppose that makes Kargen his uncle," said Athgar.

"Yes," agreed Shaluhk, "and I, his aunt." She looked at Natalia. "That is how you say it, is it not? Aunt?"

"It is," said Natalia, "it is indeed."

THE TRAP

Autumn 1104 SR

They gathered in the king's hall. Eadred had called an assembly to address the village. A rare occurrence, and as a result, they packed the place to overflowing. Indeed, as Athgar and Natalia arrived, they had to push their way through the door, helped by the bulk of Kargen, Shaluhk, and Urughar. The arrival of the Orcs brought silence to the room, a silence soon noted by the king.

"What is this?" he called out, his face a mask of distaste.

"I am Kargen, Chieftain of the Orcs of the Red Hand," the great Orc began. "I come this day to offer the support of my people. Stay to fight the intruders, and we shall fight by your side."

Urughar moved up beside him. "My people, the Black Axe, will fight as well," he said. "Come, let us stand shoulder to shoulder as it was in days of old."

The room exploded into a cacophony of chatter. The sight of Orcs had become more common in the last few weeks but to hear the offer of help was a stirring vision.

"And where were you when the skrollings took Dunmere?" demanded the king.

"They would have fought beside you then," said Athgar, "had you but asked. Instead, you moved onto their lands, calling it your own. Now you are caught between the Orcs and the skrollings. However, there is a solution, Your Majesty. You can join with the Orcs and repel these invaders."

"Don't be ridiculous," said King Eadred. "The enemy outnumbers us, and no one can defeat their Temple Knights. They are the scourge of the Continent."

"You are wrong," said Kargen, placing his hand on Athgar's shoulder, "for this man has done precisely that. It was he and Nat-Alia who helped defend my village against the forces of the Church. We knew not what to expect then, and yet, still, we defeated them. We have learned their tactics. Let us now take that advantage and apply it to your own defence."

King Eadred leaned forward. "If what you said is true, then why have you left your land? You are new to this area, are you not?"

"My people had to leave, for we are not numerous. Unlike you, we had only a single village, but you have five."

"And where would I find the warriors to oppose the Church?" asked the king.

"You have them," said Athgar, "or have you forgotten the fyrd?"

"The fyrd? Don't make me laugh. We cannot take farmers and make them warriors."

"Then why train them?"

"It is a diversion for them, nothing more. No one in the fyrd seriously thinks they can fight."

Athgar looked around the room. Everyone's eyes were locked on him. This was the moment where he would succeed or fail. He felt sweat beading on his brow as he began walking around the room, meeting each person's gaze. "Therengians have always been a people prepared to fight for what they believe in. In my village of Athelwald, fighting in a shield wall was a skill taught from an early age. Is it not so here, amongst my brothers and sisters?"

People began nodding, giving him hope.

"The tradition amongst my people was that the fyrd would gather once a week to practice such skills as the thane thought necessary. You may have a king rather than a thane, but the result is the same. We train in battle so that we can stand up for what is ours."

Murmurs of agreement began to circulate amongst those gathered in the king's hall.

"If we allow the Church to overrun our lands, we shall be scattered, or worse, enslaved. My own village was destroyed by such men. I will not stand by and watch yours suffer a similar fate. I say we stand and fight!"

Those watching erupted into howls of agreement. Athgar paused, his eyes locking with those of the king. Eadred did not look pleased.

Cenric leaned in close to his lord, whispering something in his ear. A smile came over the king, but Athgar knew it was all an act.

"Your words make sense," said Eadred, "and yet I see no plan before us. If we are to make a stand, then where? How many warriors would we deploy? How would they be arranged, and what of the Orcs? Will they stand by on our flanks and watch the slaughter? Or will they join in battle, and suffer as do we? You have no plan, Athgar. The Church destroyed your own village, and now they're coming to destroy us."

"You forget," came Natalia's voice. "You have magic to deploy, where Athelwald had none."

"And of what consequence is that?" asked the king. "Can magic defeat the enemy?"

"It can help," said Kargen. "When my village, Ord-Kurgad, was attacked, our shamans fought alongside Athgar and Nat-Alia. Our hunters fought bravely, but it was their magic that turned the tide. Without it, we would have failed."

"And who's to say you won't fail this time?"

"This is different," said Kargen, "for you can field an army backed up by three tribes."

"THREE tribes? What is this nonsense you speak of?"

"If you agree to make a stand, I shall travel south seeking aid from the Stone Crushers. With their help, we can prepare defences to defeat the enemy horsemen."

Eadred sneered. "Even without their horsemen, they are a formidable force. Their foot soldiers wear armour, whereas we have none. We cannot defeat such a foe."

"You're wrong," said Natalia. "It has been done many times in the past." She moved forward, the crowd parting to give her room to speak. "I am a battle mage, and as such, I have been trained in the history of warfare. The past is filled with tales of small groups defeating larger opponents. You have the advantage here. You know the territory, and the enemy will have to bring food and supplies with them; that makes them vulnerable."

"We cannot kill them all!" shouted Eadred. "There are simply too many of them."

"Defeating an enemy is not about killing more people, it is about destroying their will to fight on. Convince them they cannot win, and they will back down."

"Nat-Alia speaks the truth," said Kargen. "And the skrollings, as you call them, have another weakness: their leaders. Eliminate them, and the rest of the army will fall."

"And how would we do that?" asked the king.

"First," said Athgar, "we gather information. We need to know as much about the enemy as possible. I propose Natalia and I travel to Ebenstadt and do precisely that. We shall discover who is in charge and get a more accurate assessment of their troop types."

Cenric whispered in the king's ear once more. Eadred smiled, then rubbed his beard, deep in thought.

"Very well," he finally announced. "Go to Ebenstadt. See what you can discover. We shall make a stand if the fates allow it, but in the meantime, we must prepare for the worst." He turned his attention to Kargen. "Gather your people, Kargen of the Red Hand. If you can find enough of them, we will make a stand here, at Runewald."

"I shall do as you suggest," said Kargen.

"I do not wish my people to suffer," said the king, "but it is obvious to me that many wish to remain, despite the risk. We will, therefore, prepare for war. I shall send word to all the villages to call out the fyrd and march here. In the meantime, Athgar and his woman will discover what they can about the enemy."

"That is all I ask," said Athgar, bowing.

"Now," said King Eadred, "there are many plans to be made. Be off with you all, and sharpen your axes; they will be needed."

Those assembled began to file out. The overall mood was exuberant, many slapping their friends on the back and talking of the coming battle.

"If only they knew the truth," said Shaluhk, using the Orcish tongue. *"I fear many of them will not live to see better days."*

Kargen nodded his head. *"Your words are wise, my bondmate, but we as a people must stand up to aggression, or it will destroy us all."*

King Eadred waited until the hall had emptied before turning to Cenric. "Athgar is a problem for us."

"He is, my king. He has turned the village against you."

"He has indeed. We cannot allow him to get away with it, else he will soon sit upon my throne."

"Give me the word, and I shall see him banished. I will do it myself if needs be."

"No," said Eadred. "There is a better way. Athgar is going to Ebenstadt, and it provides us with a unique opportunity. While he is away, I shall reclaim my power."

"And when he returns?"

"That's just it," said the king. "You will see to it he does not. Athgar of Athelwald must die."

"And the woman?"

"Her, too. I shall not suffer a skrolling amongst us. Her words have helped turn my own people against me."

"I will do as you say," said Cenric. "When shall I strike?"

"Wait until after they have left Runewald, then none shall know of their deaths. The villagers will, in time, make their own conclusion that they have been abandoned by these troublemakers."

"An excellent plan, my king."

"That went much better than I had anticipated," said Kargen.

"Too much so," said Natalia, taking her seat by the fire once more. "He's up to something."

"Who?" said the Orc. "The king? Surely not?"

"I spent a lot of time at the Volstrum learning how things work at court. I can tell when someone is lying."

"What would Eadred hope to gain by lying?" asked Athgar.

"He wants to maintain his power," she explained.

"What of it? Our plan doesn't take it from him."

"That's where you're wrong. He has lost the confidence of his people. He will seek to regain it."

"And so he can, by defeating the Church."

"King Eadred is only interested in himself," said Natalia. "I doubt he really wants to fight. Why would he? By moving farther eastward, he can still live as a king, while at the same time avoiding conflict."

"No, he can't," said Athgar. "He'd have to fight the Orcs for space."

"It is true," said Kargen. "He is obviously more afraid of the outsiders. He would prefer to fight us than have to deal with knights."

"Let's suppose that's true," said Athgar. "What would be his next move?"

"He talked of raising the fyrd," said Shaluhk. "What is that?"

"It's a local army," said Natalia, "consisting of trained villagers. At the Volstrum, we would refer to it as a levy."

Shaluhk thought a moment before continuing. "If he is calling them from the other villages, do you think he means to subjugate Runewald by occupying it?"

"It is possible," said Kargen, "but I suspect he has more direct action in mind."

"Such as?" asked Athgar.

"I think he means to kill you," offered Kargen.

"That would inflame the villagers even more," said Natalia.

"Only if they knew of your death," the Orc chieftain continued.

"Remember, he approved of your plan to travel to Ebenstadt. I think he intends to kill you on your way there."

"That being the case," said Shaluhk, "you should take precautions."

"We shall remain vigilant," said Natalia, "but we cannot change our plans. Without detailed knowledge of their numbers, we can't devise a defence."

"I have an idea," said Kargen, "but it will require some careful timing."

"In that case," said Natalia, "perhaps Skora can fetch us some mead?"

"I shall be delighted," the old woman replied.

Cenric crouched at the edge of the woods, hidden from view as he observed Athgar's hut. The three Orcs had just emerged, bidding the Therengian bowyer goodbye, and the great warrior smiled, knowing his prey would soon be on the way themselves.

His men shuffled nervously, and Cenric turned to calm them. "The time is nigh," he said. "We shall shadow them until they are far beyond the confines of Runewald."

"And then?" asked Ardhelm.

"We shall slit their throats as they sleep," the big man replied, "and that will be the end of it."

"We must ensure they are far enough from the village that their bodies are not found," the younger man replied.

"Do not worry," said Cenric. "We will bury their bodies deep in the woods. Even the crows will not find them."

Athgar watched as the Orcs disappeared into the forest.

"I wish they were going with us," said Natalia.

"So do I," he replied, "but a city is not the place for Orcs."

"I have your things packed," called out a familiar voice.

Natalia turned in surprise. "Already? You are far too efficient, Skora, and we are quite capable of packing ourselves."

"I have looked out for Athgar ever since the death of his father, and I shall continue to do so now. In any event, I can't have you two rushing off without everything you need. You've got a child to look forward to."

Athgar moved to the bag, hefting it to test its weight. "What have you got in here?"

"A week's worth of dried meat, along with some extra furs. The weather will turn soon, and we can't have you two freezing to death."

"Athgar can keep us warm," said Natalia.

"I'm sure he can," said Skora, "but the wild is hardly the place for such things."

Natalia blushed at the implication. "No, I mean he can use his Fire Magic to keep us warm. It worked well when we crossed the mountains."

"Oh yes, I keep forgetting he's a mage now."

"Not just a mage," said Natalia, "a master of flame."

"Titles mean little to me."

"As is only proper," said Athgar. "Now, let me fetch my bow and quiver, and we shall be on our way."

"Don't forget to drink lots of water," said Skora. "You don't want the baby to suffer."

"She's worse than you," said Natalia.

"As I should be," the old woman added. "Someone has to look out for her."

Athgar laughed. "How do you know it's not a boy?"

The old woman smiled. "I have my ways. Now get going before you lose the sun."

Natalia lifted a waterskin, slinging it over her shoulder while Athgar hung a quiver on the left-hand side of his belt. His trusty axe was tucked into his right, his bow, unstrung, forming a handy walking stick. He grasped the sack of supplies and slung it over his shoulder, taking a moment to adjust its weight, then smiled at Natalia. "Ready?"

"Let us be off," she said. "Goodbye, Skora. Keep an eye on things while we are away."

"I shall," the woman replied. "And you two take care. I want to see you back here, safe and sound."

"As do we," said Athgar. "We didn't trek across half the Continent to die in the woods."

It took them some time to clear the village, for the local inhabitants kept stopping them to wish them luck. It was nearly noon by the time the village disappeared from their view.

"Raleth tells me the first part of the trip is the toughest," Athgar advised her, "on account of the forest. Once we clear it, though, it's relatively flat country till the city comes into sight."

"And then?" asked Natalia.

"The city sits in the foothills of the mountains. Apparently, it can get quite rocky. We'll be going in the front gates, so we won't have to trouble ourselves with that."

Natalia looked down at her dress. "It's a good thing we still have our clothes from Corassus. We'll be able to pass for locals much easier."

"Agreed. I'd hate to think what they'd do if we wore the plain garb of the Therengians."

"There's still the matter of your eyes," warned Natalia. "You'll have to avoid looking directly at people."

"I can manage that."

"How long did Raleth say the trip was?"

"Three days. Two and a half if we're lucky."

"Well then," said Natalia, "we should put the time to good use."

"Doing what, precisely?"

"I thought you might help me improve my Orcish."

Off to the west, the sun was getting low in the sky, stretching the shadows of the trees into the distance. The Fire Mage had halted, and now he and his skrolling wife were spreading furs in anticipation of sleep.

Cenric waved his men forward. There were six of them, including the king's champion—more than enough to handle the likes of these two outsiders.

"We shall wait until they are asleep, then advance," he said. "Ardhelm, you take two and work your way over to the other side of their camp, but don't get too close."

"And once we're in position?"

"We'll wait until nightfall. At least one of them will sleep, maybe even both. That's when we'll make our move."

Ardhelm grinned. "Glory to King Eadred."

"Glory indeed," replied Cenric. "There'll be plenty of it to go around once we're done."

"Do you think they'll have anything of value?"

"I hadn't considered it, but now you mention it, Athgar's woman wears a ring that stands out. We shall award it to the person who slays her!"

They all grinned, for such a piece was considered quite the prize.

"Now, you must get a move on," said Cenric. "You'll need to get into place while you can still make out a way through the trees."

Ardhelm chose his two men and then scurried off.

Cenric risked a glance. Darkness had fallen, but the tiny clearing was well lit by Athgar's fire. The man had taken the time to gather sticks, using them to start a fire. Cenric thought this strange: he was a Fire Mage after all. What use did he have for such methods?

He waited, watching as his target tended the fire. Athgar yawned, and

Cenric's pulse started to quicken. The time to strike was nigh! He rose to a crouch, his men following suit. Cenric's blade came free from the scabbard as he crept forward.

On the other side of the clearing, Ardhelm advanced, axe in one hand, shield in the other. He knew it was scant protection against the magic of the skrolling, but it gave him something to cling to in order to calm his shaking hands.

Closer he drew until he could see the gentle rise and fall of the woman's chest as she slept. He raised the axe for a killing blow.

The first arrow tore into Ardhelm's neck with such force, the bulk of it stuck out from the other side. Ardhelm had scarcely felt the blow when another struck, this one hitting his back and punching clean through his chest. The last thing he saw was the Human woman rolling out of the way as he fell.

Natalia threw out her hands, channelling a small part of her power. Ice shards flew across the camp, striking a man who had raised a spear. They hit him in the face, causing him to fall backwards, his weapon forgotten as his fingers clutched at the wounds. He fell to the ground with a scream.

Cenric watched as Athgar suddenly came alive, his surprise complete. The Therengian's hand thrust out, sending a sheet of flame at the last of Ardhelm's men, striking his foe's arm and igniting his tunic. The man ran into the woods, screaming in pain and terror, his attack forgotten.

Cenric charged forward, but a large green figure appeared right in front of him. He only had a moment to recognize Shaluhk's features before a long knife was plunged deep into his chest. He died instantly, falling to lie amongst the pine needles.

Two men were left, but at the sight of their leader going down, they both turned, running for their lives.

"Do not let them get away," called out Kargen. He drew back his warbow, letting loose with another arrow. It sank into one man's leg, causing him to fall. Moments later, Shaluhk was upon him, her dagger finishing him off with an efficient slash to the throat.

Urughar took out the last man, running him down, and then his axe took his foe in the back of the head.

The only sounds that remained were that of the crackling of a fire and the screams of the man set aflame.

"I've got him," called out Athgar, disappearing into the gloom of the woods. A deep thud echoed back to the camp, and then the screaming stopped. Shortly thereafter, Athgar returned, his face dour. "That's the last of them."

"What now?" asked Natalia.

"You two will continue to Ebenstadt," said Kargen. "We three shall see to the bodies."

"Are you sure they all had to die?" she asked.

"We had no choice. Were they to return, the king would doubtless send more. This way, all he knows is that they disappeared. He will have no idea whether they were successful or not."

"Kargen is right," said Shaluhk. "It was the only way. You should head out as soon as possible. Once we are done here, we will continue with our objective to unite the Orc tribes."

INTERIM

Autumn 1104 SR

Stanislav Voronsky sat back in his chair, putting his boots up onto the table. The smell of stale beer drifted up from the common room below. He winced, thinking of the mayhem that lay only one floor below him.

He had come to Ebenstadt at the bidding of the Grand Matriarch, Illiana Stormwind, but now he wondered if that choice had been wise. Natalia was known to have been in the company of a Fire Mage, a Therengian by the name of Athgar, and the Matriarch had thought it likely they would seek refuge amongst his people. It was a reasonable thought, but Stanislav had to question if the east was worth hiding out in when a Holy Crusade was about to commence. Surely Natalia knew the area was embroiled in war?

He sighed, reaching into his tunic to pull forth the letter from Illiana. The head of the Stormwind family had asked for his help, revealing that Natalia was her granddaughter, but now he had to ask himself if she weren't playing some game of power.

As a mage hunter, he was used to such things, for finding students for the Volstrum was, in and of itself, a bit of a game. Now that he was older, however, he began to wonder if his choice of profession was as honourable as he had once thought. Was Natalia the illegitimate daughter of Illiana's son, or was he being used? He tucked the letter away, unread, and lowered his feet. It mattered little whether or not she had lied. The important thing was finding Natalia and keeping her safe. And who better to do that than the very man who had originally found her?

He rose, throwing on a cape to ward off the cold of autumn, then made his way downstairs to get something to eat. The Crow and Sickle was a noisy place, filled with mercenaries and warriors seeking fame and fortune. The promise of a new crusade burned bright in the hearts of these men. Many of them lived on the edge, enjoying life while they could.

At the bottom of the stairs he halted as a drunken warrior squeezed past him, his hands around the waist of a young woman. He was reminded of days past when he had tried to settle down and raise a family, but it was not to be. Now he was an old man, and the closest he had ever come to a real friendship was Natalia, a thought that sobered him. He must find her before the family did!

Carefully, he threaded his way through the room only to spot a familiar grey tabard. Altering his course, he steered towards its occupant, taking a seat opposite.

"Brother Diomedes," he began, "so good to see you again. Can I offer you a drink?"

The Cunar Knight stared back, his face, at first, stern, but it soon cracked a smile as he recognized his associate. "Stanislav, so good to see you again. I'd heard you were in town, but to actually see you is quite another matter."

"And you, Brother." He raised his hand, signalling the waitress for a couple of ales. "Tell me, how have things been going?"

"Well enough, I suppose." The Temple Knight leaned closer, lowering his voice. "Things are starting to move. The campaign will begin soon enough."

Stanislav's eyes swept the room. "I assume these are some of your recruits?"

"Not the order's," said the knight, "but certainly auxiliaries to the Holy Army. This lot falls under the command of the Duke of Braymoor."

"Is that a good thing?"

The Temple Knight smiled. "Some might think so, but to tell the truth, the man has little experience. Still, they're only here to augment my own order."

"Any word on when the campaign might begin?"

"Likely not till the end of the month. Why? Interested in joining?"

"Me? I'm far too old for that."

"Oh, I don't know. You should see some of the knights who have shown up."

"Knights?"

"Yes, from all over the Petty Kingdoms. They come seeking fame and fortune, and not necessarily in that order." He chuckled to himself.

A maid deposited two tankards on the table, scooping up the coins that Stanislav tossed.

Brother Diomedes took a sip. "Are you here looking for mages?"

"I am always on the lookout for new talent," he replied. "Why? Have you heard of anyone?"

The Temple Knight laughed. "By the Saints, I think you would sell your own mother for a crack at a new mage!"

"What can I say?" said Stanislav. "It pays well."

"I doubt you'll find one here. There are far too many soldiers hereabouts."

"What's that got to do with anything?"

"This is a Holy Army, Stanislav, not that of a king or duke. Mages don't hire on as mercenaries. If they did, we'd have them all under our employ."

"None at all?"

"No, not yet, at any rate. There's still a week left, so I suppose it's possible one might show up, but I doubt it. In any case, if they did, they'd be fully trained, no use to you."

Stanislav took a sip of his drink. "I only ask out of professional courtesy. It matters little in the grand scheme of things."

They sat in silence awhile, nursing their tankards.

"This group has been here awhile," noted Stanislav. "The landlord seems to know them all by name."

"So they have," agreed Brother Diomedes. "In fact, they've likely over-stayed their welcome, if the bartender is any indication."

"Why haven't they marched? I would have thought summer more fitting to the campaign season than autumn."

"So would I, but it can't be helped. The enemy has withdrawn deeper into the forest."

"And that stopped you because...?"

"It forces us to stockpile food. We can't very well live off the land if there are no farms to raid."

"Hence the delay," said Stanislav.

"Exactly. Mind you, we're still waiting on the arrival of the local master of the Order. He has to give Father General Hargild permission to begin."

"Ah yes, the famous Temple Knight discipline. Tell me, will this lot last that long, or will they ransack the town before you can march?"

Brother Diomedes' eyes searched around the room. "It's hard to tell at this moment, but I think if we don't march soon, it will be the latter." He chuckled at his own remarks, then took another tip of his ale, this time in greater quantity than before.

"You still haven't told me why you're here," the Temple Knight continued.

"Yes I have. I'm looking for prospects."

"No you're not. You never go anywhere without a plan, even if it's just rumours." He smiled, pleased he had found a hole in Stanislav's story. "Don't worry," he added, "I know it's the business of the family. I won't interfere, nor will any of my order. You shall have free rein in Ebenstadt."

"Thank you," said Stanislav. "That is most welcome news." He drained his cup dry. "Now, if you will excuse me, I have some business to attend to."

"Will I see you again?" asked Brother Diomedes.

"Of course! Shall I order you another drink?"

"No, I think I've had enough, thank you."

"Very well, then I shall bid you a good day. May your order prosper."

The Temple Knight held up his cup. "And your mages be found."

Stanislav made his way into the street, unaware of the cloaked figure that followed him.

EBENSTADT

Autumn 1104 SR

Athgar stepped aside, pulling Natalia with him as a passing carriage rolled through a rain-filled rut and splashed them both with filth. Natalia shook her hands, trying in vain to dislodge the clumps of mud but to little effect.

"This is just like Draybourne," she said, looking down at her feet, "but at least I have decent boots this time."

"Draybourne?"

"Yes, when I first arrived there, I stepped out of the carriage to sink into the mud. I can still remember my shoe getting stuck."

"Not surprising when you think of it. That was only about a year ago."

She looked at him in surprise. "I suppose it was. Sometimes it feels like we've been on the run forever, but it hasn't been that long, has it?"

"A lot has happened in that time," he mused.

She rubbed her stomach, breaking out into a smile. "It certainly has."

"You know you're not showing yet. You don't even look like you're pregnant."

"I know," she replied, "but just the thought of carrying our child makes me so happy."

"You might think differently when you're further along."

"Perhaps, but for now, I am content, and that's the important thing."

The road they were on twisted around a group of trees, and then Ebenstadt came into view.

"There it is," said Athgar. "The whole reason for us coming north."

"It looks so tranquil from here. You'd think the land was at peace."

"I suppose it is, at least for the moment. The crusade won't begin until the troops march."

"Let's hope they're not in a hurry to begin," said Natalia. "We need time to assess their strength. Once they start moving, it'll be hard to get close to them."

"I've been thinking about that."

"Oh? What in particular?"

"I was thinking," Athgar explained, "it might prove beneficial to join their army."

"You can't be serious?"

"Where better to assess your enemy than by walking amongst them?"

"The idea has merit," said Natalia, "but it's a big risk. Supposing they recognize you as a Therengian? Or worse, if they realize who I am?"

"Look around you," he said, indicating the people approaching the city. "We're miles from anywhere of interest to the family. They like power, and this place is literally in the middle of nowhere."

"The Church doesn't think so," she chided.

"That's different. They're zealots, and they fight for a cause."

"They're not all bad. I'm sure there are many members of the Church who follow its teachings properly."

"A Holy War attracts the fiercest believers," said Athgar. "I doubt we'll find any moderates here."

Another horse trotted by ridden by a warrior.

"There's a lot more traffic than I had anticipated," said Natalia.

"We're coming from the east, the same direction the war will take them. I would imagine the locals are all travelling to the city to avoid getting caught up in the fighting."

"Good for us, we'll be able to slip into town with little notice. You remember what to do?"

"Don't worry," he said, removing his sling bag, "I have my helmet in here somewhere." He rummaged around in the bag, finally producing the conical helm. It had a metal frame into which a leather cap had been sewn. With the nose guard in place, it made him look like any other warrior seeking employment. They had already worked up a story to account for their presence here, but as the gate loomed, it proved unnecessary, for the guards simply waved everyone through, taking little interest in people's identities.

They passed under the raised portcullis and into the cobblestone streets, a welcome change from the mud of the road.

"I thought this used to be a Therengian town?" said Natalia.

"It was," Athgar replied. "Why do you ask?"

"Isn't it strange that it has cobblestone streets?"

He looked down, letting the image soak in. "So it is, now that you mention it."

"That's not all. This road looks old, far older than I would have expected. Didn't Raleth say they lost it five years ago?"

"He did, but he didn't say how long it had been held by the Therengians. Do you think it dates back to the original kingdom?"

"That would make it over five hundred years old," she said. "Though, now that you mention it, some of these buildings look ancient."

Athgar nodded his head. "Yes, the wooden buildings are all new, but those of stone are a whole other story."

"Dunmere was burned if I remember correctly."

"It was, though I doubt the whole city was torched. They couldn't have rebuilt all of this in only five years."

"If my supposition is correct, this is likely the last true city of the Therengians, Athgar. It's a part of your heritage."

"Possibly, but it means little to me. I have an aversion to large cities, remember?"

"Maybe Ebenstadt will be different?"

"We can only hope. In the meantime, let's find some decent lodgings. We'll need to establish a base from which we can conduct our enquiries."

"You're beginning to sound like a real diplomat. Are you sure you haven't had court training?"

He noted the look of mirth on her face. "Very funny."

"I thought so."

They proceeded down the street, passing by a number of shops and homes crowded together, making the entire area look like one long building.

"This place feels very constricting," he noted. "Have you noticed any alleyways?"

"No, but then again, we've only gone a few blocks. On the other hand, the streets are easy to navigate. I think I'd have a hard time getting lost here."

"That's because the streets are laid out similar to Runewald, though not so dispersed."

"More evidence of its history, no doubt."

"So it would seem." Natalia paused at an apple cart, handing over a coin and selecting a ripe fruit. A quick enquiry soon sent them on their way to a modest inn.

"There it is," she said, "The Wolf of Adenburg."

Athgar began laughing.

"What's so funny?"

"Don't you remember Caerhaven? I had that wolf costume when we went to the ball. You're the one who told me the folk tale."

"Oh yes," she said, "I remember now. How strange, it must be some kind of sign. After all, the Ancestors wanted us to come here."

He held out his arm. "Shall we?"

She made an exaggerated bow. "Of course, my lord."

They stepped into a relatively large establishment that was packed with mostly warriors, by the looks of them. Athgar steered Natalia towards the kegs that lined the wall, where an older woman, somewhere in her fifties, was filing two tankards. She looked up at their approach.

"I'll be with you in a moment," she said. "Meg!" The last comment was directed at a young, red-headed woman who made her way through the crowd. "These two are for the fancy man over by the window." She nodded her head, indicating a well-dressed gentleman and his companion, a youth several years his junior.

The woman turned to Athgar. "Something I can get you?"

"We are looking for a room," he replied.

"How long do you want it?" she asked, giving Natalia the once-over.

"My wife and I will be staying in Ebenstadt for a few days."

Her eyes lit up. "Your wife, eh? You should have said so. I took her for a companion."

He looked at Natalia for an explanation, but she shook her head. "Have you a room?" Athgar asked again.

"We do, as a matter of fact."

"How much?"

"Do you have a horse?"

"No, we came on foot."

"Then it'll be three silver a night," the older woman said, "and another two if you want your meals."

"We'll take it," said Natalia.

"Come with me, then. I'll show you to your room."

She led them up some rickety stairs with a well-worn banister, then down a hall past some considerably rough-looking doors.

"These are the shared rooms," she said, bypassing the doors and heading up a second set of stairs.

The hallway here at least had a rug on the floor, tattered though it was.

At some time, this must have been considered nice lodgings, but now everything was faded and the paint peeling. The woman halted, producing a ring of keys from around her neck and unlocked the door in front of her.

"There you go," she said.

They stepped inside a solitary room, with little more than a bed and a large wardrobe standing against one wall. Light seeped in through a small window, its shutters open to let in a fresh breeze.

"I'll send up someone with some blankets," the woman said, passing over the key. "Now I must be off. I've got a lot of customers today."

"Is it always this busy?" asked Natalia.

"No. It's the army, you see. They've come from all over the Continent to chase down those villains. I don't care two coppers for the war, but it's good for business." She turned, disappearing quickly.

"The villains?" said Athgar.

"She likely means the Therengians."

"Why do they hate us so much?"

"This isn't about your people," said Natalia. "It's about power."

"What do you mean by that?"

"I don't think the Church cares who they're fighting. It's the chance to flex their muscles, don't you see?"

"No," said Athgar, "I don't. Explain it to me."

"This is probably the only place on the Continent where so many Temple Knights are gathered. I think they see it as an opportunity to hone their craft."

"By killing? Isn't that against their beliefs?"

"People can justify anything if they set their minds to it. The Therengians are seen as outsiders. Think back to Runewald. Everyone there hates the idea of the skrollings. It's no different here, except the roles are reversed."

"I suppose that's true."

"It is," said Natalia, "but it's also sad. People fear what they don't understand. You and I have experienced life amongst the Orcs. To us, they are our friends, but to outsiders, they are barbarians. They likely see the Therengians the same way."

"Except that Therengia was once a great kingdom."

"I think that makes them even more fearful. To be honest, I doubt the locals even know it's the Therengians who are out there."

"They must know they're fighting someone," insisted Athgar.

"True, but I doubt they know the full story. Whoever leads this army wants the populace behind him. I imagine they will have painted the enemy as vicious cutthroats, eager to kill and ravage. It's all part of the politics of war."

"You seem to know a lot about such things."

"I do," said Natalia. "It was part of our training. As a court mage, you're expected to be well educated in all the techniques of war."

"Even politics?"

"Especially politics. It's only when such things fail that war becomes inevitable."

Athgar sat on the edge of the bed, thinking things over. "Where should we start?"

"We'll eat first, then wander around the town. I'd like to get used to the layout of the streets. It'll also give us an idea of how many soldiers there are in Ebenstadt."

"What about the Temple Knights?"

"We likely won't see much of them," Natalia said. "They'll have a commandery here somewhere, but I doubt we'll be able to get inside it."

"A commandery?"

"Yes, like the sisters had in Caerhaven."

"That place was large," he said. "Do you think it will be similar here?"

"If anything, I'd say larger. This is a crusade, and that means the Holy Army is involved. There's likely to be lots of Cunar Knights to lead it."

Athgar frowned. "If that's true, then probably a Cunar will be in charge. It seems like everywhere we go, they're causing trouble."

"We don't know that's the case here," soothed Natalia. "Maybe they're simply misinformed?"

Athgar shook his head. "No, they're involved. I can feel it in my bones."

"You're just overwhelmed. What can we do to help you relax?"

"A bath?"

She laughed. "Maybe when we get back from our walk. Now let's go, my love. We have work to do."

The streets of Ebenstadt were a wellspring of information. Athgar noticed many warriors roaming about, but Natalia saw so much more, pointing out the armour and weapons of each and identifying their use on the battle-field. It soon became apparent there were a significant number of soldiers ready to fight.

"Who's paying for all of this?" asked Athgar. "It must cost a fortune."

"I would imagine a lot of them are here at their own expense, seeking to make a name for themselves."

"Is that something people really do?"

"You'd be surprised what people do to seek fame."

"How would someone prove their story when they return home?"

"Many don't," replied Natalia. "There are even some who make up their entire history. It serves them well until a foreign noble shows up and exposes them."

"And their reputation is that important to them?"

"Oh yes, fortune often follows fame. A well-seasoned warrior is a valuable asset. Many poorer knights seek service with a wealthy lord, and experience in battle helps them find such positions."

"And there are few battles," said Athgar, "hence the turnout for this crusade."

"Precisely."

"But these men we have seen, they're not Church soldiers, are they?"

"No," explained Natalia, "they're referred to as auxiliaries. The Church has Temple Knights, of course, but relies on others to supply archers and foot soldiers."

"And the Church commands them?"

"Not directly. A father general will command the army, but all of these auxiliaries fall under junior commanders, probably nobles who have committed to the crusade."

"Like who?" he asked.

"That, we have yet to discover."

Athgar halted quite suddenly, urging her to do the same. A well-dressed man had just turned down a side street, not an unusual occurrence, but in his wake followed two men, both clutching daggers. "That doesn't bode well."

"Come on," said Natalia, "let's see if we can be of assistance."

They turned down the side street quickening their pace. The two men were closing in on their target, who looked a little worse for wear. They came to within five feet, and then the well-dressed man turned, entirely unexpectedly, drawing his sword.

"Hand over your coins," demanded one of the dagger men.

In answer, their target lunged forward, stabbing with his sword. The tip of the blade nicked the fellow's arm, eliciting a cry of pain.

"Get 'im," the bleeding man commanded.

Athgar reacted quickly, pulling his axe, but Natalia was faster, pointing her finger and uttering a slew of words that sent ice shards flying through the air. They struck the second thief in the back, knocking him to the ground, his dagger skidding across the cobblestones.

The swordsman stepped forward, his blade held steady, but his attackers decided they'd had enough. Bleeding from the arm, the first man helped his companion to his feet, and then they fled.

Athgar raised his hands to cast, but the victim waved them off. "Let them go," he said. "They can do no harm now." He moved closer. "I must thank you, friends, though I think I could have handled them on my own. I'm Sir Raynald, and you are?"

"Athgar, and this is my wife, Natalia." The words came out of his mouth before he realized he had used their real names. He looked at Natalia, but all she did was shrug; it was too late now.

Sir Raynald looked at the ground, where the remains of the ice shards were melting. "Was that you, sir?"

"No, my wife. She's a Water Mage."

"Then, much to my chagrin, I am indebted to you, ma'am. How can I ever repay such kindness? Could I purchase you both a meal?"

"Certainly," said Athgar. "We should be delighted."

"You said your name was Sir Raynald," said Natalia. "From whence do you hail, Sir Knight?"

"A place called Andover. Are you familiar with it?"

"It's one of the northern kingdoms, isn't it?"

The knight smiled. "It is indeed. May I ask where you are both from?"

"My family is from Karslev, but I was raised in Draybourne. That's where I met my husband."

"I must confess I'm not familiar with the place. Is it close?"

"No," she continued. "It's some distance to the south, across the mountains."

"Ah, I see. I take it you're here for the crusade?"

"We are, in fact. We're both mages, come to make a name for ourselves."

"Well, you've come to the right place." He paused, looking around the area. "There's a nice tavern just up the street that serves a delicious stew. Shall we?"

"By all means," said Natalia.

The Hungry Fox was popular amongst the nobility. As soon as they entered, Sir Raynald's name was called out. It appeared the knight knew everyone here. He guided them to a seat, exchanging pleasantries with the other guests.

"You'll have to excuse them," he said. "We're a close-knit group."

"Group?" said Athgar.

"Yes, the duke's knights. Not his personal knights, you understand, but we fall under his command."

Natalia looked around the room. "Just how many of you are there?"

"This is only a small sampling. We actually number fifty-two."

"Fifty-three," called out a balding man. "He hired another this morning."

"There, you see? Even I cannot keep up with such things."

"Can anyone?" said Natalia.

"I can tell you are a woman of refinement," said Sir Raynald, "but you"—he looked at Athgar—"you're a bit of a puzzle."

"He's a Fire Mage," said Natalia, declining to provide further information.

"Ah, I see," said the knight. He soon turned his attention to a server, who was hovering nearby. "Bring us your best," he said. "It's on the duke's tab."

"Is that wise?" asked Athgar.

"My dear fellow, it's how things are done here."

"Might I ask who hired you on?" asked Natalia. "That is to say, who do we go and see about joining the army?"

"I suppose that depends on who you're going to serve. Ordinarily, I would tell you to go to the temple commandery, but they won't deal with women."

"They won't?" said Athgar. "Why's that?"

"I don't know. Something to do with their oath of celibacy, I should think. No, you want to report to the duke directly. I can take you to him if you wish?"

"Would you?" said Natalia. "We'd be grateful for the help."

"I'm more than happy to be of assistance, but it'll have to be tomorrow as he'll be up at the father general's this time of day."

"At the commandery?"

"No, at his estate. He's not from the local chapter, you see. He also brought staff officers with him, so he needs the extra space. I tell you what, where are you staying?"

"At the Wolf of Adenburg," said Athgar.

"I know it. I'll meet you there tomorrow morning, right after sunrise, if you like. We can walk up to the duke's together, and I'll introduce you. He'll be tickled pink to get a couple of mages into his employ."

THE TRIBES

Autumn 1104 SR
(In the tongue of the Orcs)

Agar ran into his father's arms, bringing a smile to the great chieftain's face.

"He has missed you," said Laruhk. "You have been gone for some time."

"So we have," answered Kargen, "but we have news we must share. Fetch Durgash and Kragor, and then I shall tell what we have learned."

Laruhk rushed off, eager to find his compatriots. Shaluhk smiled as her bondmate lowered their son to the ground. Agar ran off, his wooden axe in hand, hunting for something to do.

Kargen watched him closely, taking pride in his actions. "I remember when I was young," he said. "How simple things were back then."

"Too simple," said Shaluhk.

"Why do you say that?"

"I was not part of your life."

He grinned. "That is true, and I would not change a thing if it meant losing you, but I speak of the responsibility of being chieftain. I think life would have been simpler if I had not taken on that burden."

"You know as well as I that it was your destiny. Without you as their leader, the entire tribe would have been wiped out at Ord-Kurgad. You have shown us the way to a brighter future for our people."

"And yet, still we have to fight. Will there be no end to it?"

"We can not surrender to fear, my bondmate. If we do not fight now, then we will do so later, when the Humans have grown stronger still."

"And supposing we beat them? What then? Will they simply return in greater numbers like they did at Ord-Kurgad?"

"No," said Shaluhk. "We shall not let them. Instead, we will negotiate peace."

"You think Athgar capable of that?"

"No, but Nat-Alia is. She is the voice of reason in all of this. It is her words that will bring us peace in the long run."

Kargen gazed into her eyes. "You are worried; I can see it in your face. Tell me what it is that has distressed you so."

"I worry for Nat-Alia. I fear that in saving us, she will reveal herself to her enemies."

"The Stormwinds?"

"Yes, even if we negotiate peace, word will get out, and she is quite distinctive in her appearance, is she not?"

"She is," he admitted, "and yet the family would have a hard time getting close to her amongst Athgar's people."

"I would suggest we remain close once they return."

"We think along similar lines, but how would we do such a thing? Are you suggesting I give up my position of chieftain?"

"No," she said, "I have a more radical idea."

"I am listening."

"What if our people lived side by side?"

"In the same village?" asked Kargen. "How would that work?"

"It is not as difficult as you might imagine. The Therengians are not so different from us, and the more we traded with them, the more accepting of us they have become."

"That is a far cry from living amongst them."

"I admit it would require a lot of planning."

"Yes," he agreed, "but they are not yet ready for such a move, and neither are we."

"True, but there will come a day when both will see the wisdom in it. Changes must start with ideas."

"You are wise, Shaluhk. I am glad you are my bondmate."

"I would hope there is more to your love than just my wisdom?"

He moved closer, reaching out to caress her, but Agar chose that moment to rush into his leg, eliciting a curse from the chieftain.

Shaluhk laughed. "He takes after his father."

"So he does," said Kargen through a wince.

Laruhk soon returned, Durgash and Kragor with him. They settled in around the fire, eager to hear the words of their leader.

"Now that we are here," said Laruhk, "tell us what has transpired."

"The king of the Therengians sent his men to murder Athgar and Nat-Alia."

"I assume they failed?" said Durgash.

"They did," said Kargen, "for Shaluhk and Urughar were there, along with myself."

"And what became of the men he sent?"

"They shall never breathe again," said Shaluhk.

"They got what they deserved," said Kragor, "but you did not call us here just to tell us that."

Kargen smiled, showing his teeth. "I can see you are observant. I have called you here to seek your counsel. I have in mind a course of action, but I need to know if the tribe will follow me."

"Go on," prompted Laruhk, "speak your mind. There will be no judgement."

"We came here seeking a land of peace where the tribe could prosper," Kargen began, "but it appears there is still a threat to us. The Humans are intent on invading the land of the Therengians."

"You mean the people they call the skrollings?" asked Laruhk.

"Yes."

"What of it?" said Durgash. "Let the Humans fight amongst themselves."

"Should the skrollings be successful, they will likely move farther east, into Orc territory and thus threaten us."

"Better to fight them now, when they are unprepared," declared Kragor.

"My thoughts exactly," said Kargen, "but the Red Hand can not do it alone. If the tribe agrees, I will try to forge an alliance with the Black Axe and the Stone Crushers. Individually, our tribes can not withstand the advances of the Humans, but combined, I believe we can defeat them."

"I understand the idea," said Laruhk, "but I do not understand your reluctance. You do not need the tribe's permission for such a thing."

"I would also ally ourselves with the Therengians."

All three Orcs stared at him with unspoken words.

Kargen continued. "I know King Eadred has not been friendly towards us, but he is acting out of fear. If we can show him we are willing to fight alongside his men, perhaps he will change his mind."

"And if he does not?" asked Durgash.

"Then we will still need to fight. Whether we like it or not, the Humans will eventually spread eastward. The only way to prevent that is by gaining a victory."

Laruhk leaned forward. "But if we defeat them, will they not come back with more men?"

"Shaluhk is of the opinion Nat-Alia might be able to broker a peace treaty with the Church, and I am inclined to agree with her."

"I agree with your reasoning," said Durgash.

"And I," added Kragor.

They both looked at Laruhk.

"Do not look at me. I am the last person who would consider disagreeing with my sister."

"Then it is decided," said Kargen. "I shall invite Kirak and Laghul to visit our hut and lay out our plan before them."

"What can we do to help?" asked Durgash.

"Go amongst our tribe," said Shaluhk. "Seek out their opinions, and gather support for what we must do. If a majority dissents, we shall call a vote. Until then, I will continue with my desire to unite the tribes."

"I do not envy you your task," said Kragor. "I have never heard of such a thing before."

"You forget," said Shaluhk, "to the west, our people have all united in defence of the Humans who live there."

"I wish it were so here," said Laruhk.

"Then we shall make it so, Brother. Great things can be accomplished when we work together."

Laruhk smiled. "She is the smart one, but I have the looks."

Kirak stooped, pushing aside the hides to enter the hut. Laghul, Shamaness of the Black Axe, followed closely behind, her face breaking out into a smile at the sight of Agar sitting there, chewing on the blade of his wooden axe.

"I see he is teething," she said.

"Indeed," said Shaluhk. "Notice how the blade is notched? He has been at it for days."

"Come, sit," said Kargen. "Shall we partake of the milk of life?"

"Such formality is unnecessary, Kargen. We are friends, are we not?"

"Then maybe just drinks?"

Kirak nodded his approval and waited as wooden cups were passed around. He nodded at Agar. "He is growing quickly. Before you know it, he will be going on the hunt."

"I think it will be some time yet," said Shaluhk. "He has yet to grow all of his teeth."

"Do you have younglings, Kirak?" asked Kargen.

"We do: two, in fact. Our eldest is a full-blown hunter, while his younger sister still struggles with the bow."

"Having a youngling makes me think of the future."

"As it does for us," said Kirak. "I would like them to live in peace if it were possible. That is why you invited us here, is it not? To discuss the future?"

"I can see you are on to me. I must confess I was loathe to broach the subject with you."

"As I said earlier, we are friends. Let us talk of such things without repercussions. What is it that weighs so heavily upon you?"

"I wish to unite the tribes," began Kargen, "and then offer help to the Therengians against their oppressors."

"What of King Eadred? Is he aware of this plan?"

"Kargen broached the idea," said Shaluhk, "but I fear he is not to be trusted."

"If he is not to be trusted, why are we helping him?"

"We are not helping HIM," said Kargen, "but rather his people. THEY will accept us, even if HE will not."

"And where will that leave King Eadred?"

"Without his throne," said Shaluhk, "hopefully."

"Then who would lead his people?"

"Athgar," said Shaluhk. "I believe he will see the wisdom of it. It is for the good of his people after all."

"It is dangerous to play such a game," said Kirak, "but I see the reason behind it. War is coming to our land, whether we want it or not. Better to rally against a common enemy than fight amongst ourselves."

"Then you agree?" asked Kargen.

"I am not opposed to the idea, but you must seek counsel with the Stone Crushers. Their participation would give us a great advantage. Bring their chieftain, Zahruhl, into the fold, and I will agree."

"Then I shall travel to Khasrahk and convince him to join us."

"I fear you will have your work cut out for you," said Laghul.

"Why is that?"

"Zahruhl is stubborn. In many ways, he reminds me of King Eadred."

"In what way?" asked Shaluhk.

"For years, he has been trying to make his tribe the strongest."

"Is that what led to the animosity with the Black Axe?" asked Kargen.

Laghul looked at Kirak, who merely nodded. "He has been difficult for years," she said.

"Meaning?"

"He has actively tried to recruit our hunters to his tribe."

"Yes," added Kirak, "despite our insistence that he cease. He seeks to dominate us, perhaps even eventually absorb us, but he plans a long hunt."

"He managed to convince seventeen of the Red Hand to join him," said Kargen.

"The Stone Crushers are not evil," said Laghul, "but they are easily swayed by their chieftain."

"Agreed," said Kirak. "If only my own tribe were so easy to convince." He laughed at his jest, spilling some of his drink. He looked at Kargen in shock. "My apologies."

"It is of no consequence," said Shaluhk, "and it would not be the first time such a drink was spilled." She looked at her bondmate, who blushed, turning a darker shade of green.

"I see we have something else in common," said Laghul, "aside from having younglings, that is."

"You and I enjoy the popular support of our tribes," said Kargen. "Is it not so with Zahruhl?"

"I can not speak for his tribe," said Kirak, "but he has been their chieftain for as long as I can remember. I do not recall ever hearing of an election."

"And yet he must have been chosen. That is our way."

"I suspect he has some form of control over them. The master of earth and his apprentices hold considerable sway over their people. Could they be the power that stands in his shadow?"

"I am still resolved to try negotiating with him," said Kargen. "Is there anything you might be able to suggest that would be of use?"

"Yes," said Kirak. "Get Rugg on your side. He may be able to sway Zahruhl to see reason."

"What does Rugg want?" asked Shaluhk.

"That is difficult to say. I barely know him, but Laghul knows him better than I." He turned to his bondmate.

"It is true," she said. "I have met him a number of times. I have always found him to be reasonable enough. I believe he wants what he thinks is best for the Stone Crushers."

"Which is?"

"That is hard to say with any certainty."

"You will have to tread carefully," warned Kirak. "Zahruhl is quick to take offence."

"I found him to be reasonable enough," said Kargen, "but then again, our meeting was brief."

"Yes," said Shaluhk, "but he did end up gaining some of our tribe, a loss we felt keenly."

"They joined of their own free will," said Kargen. "We can not fault them for their choice."

"I think there is a greater danger," said Laghul.

"What is that?"

"If you fail to convince Zahruhl of the wisdom of your plan, he may take more direct action."

"Such as?"

"There is a very real possibility he might kill you."

"Surely not," said Shaluhk. "He is a chieftain!"

"He has nothing to fear from you," Laghul continued, "or from either of us, in fact. His village is walled in stone. We have no means to breach it, even if we had the will."

"That is not true," said Shaluhk. "We saw how the Humans attacked our palisades. Such tactics are not beyond us."

"Perhaps, but he will have no knowledge of such things. In his mind, his people are safe and secure behind his walls. He will see it no differently."

"I see I will have to be careful," said Kargen.

"No," said Shaluhk. "WE shall have to careful. I can not let you go there alone."

"Do you think that wise?"

"Even Zahruhl would think twice about killing a shamaness!"

"Shaluhk speaks with wisdom," said Laghul. "In any event, the task before you will be difficult. There is the very real possibility he will simply deny your request. That would allow us to decimate our own forces fighting the Humans. He could then sweep in and swallow up what remains of our tribes."

"Let us hope he sees reason," said Shaluhk.

"He will," said Kargen. "He has to."

"I wish you well," said Kirak, "but I do not begrudge you your task."

The next morning found Kargen and Shaluhk once again bidding farewell to Laruhk. Agar ran around the hut, unaware of the seriousness of their trip. Shaluhk found it difficult to part with him so soon. Even after they left, she thought of him, her silence leading Kargen to worry.

"Something is wrong," he said. "You are not yourself."

"I sense we are travelling into danger," she said, "and I can not reconcile it."

"It is not the first time we have travelled under such a threat, nor do I think it will be the last."

"True, but something is different this time."

"Should you have consulted the Ancestors?"

"We can not expect the dead to know the living. Zahruhl is dangerous; that much we know, but what worries me is that our failure may well doom our tribe."

"The tribe will continue without us if necessary," said Kargen. "It has always been so, and will continue to in the future."

"And if we die, what will happen to Agar?"

"He will be raised by his uncle," said Kargen. He laughed. "Then only the Ancestors will be able to help them."

"You jest, but I am serious."

He mellowed his tone. "I am sorry, Shaluhk, but we must be strong. We are on a dangerous mission, you and I, and I do not mean to make light of it, but we are always stronger when together. That is our strength. Just as Athgar and Nat-Alia have their task to complete, so, too, do we. And if we should die, then at least we are together at the end."

"You speak with heart, bondmate mine. So be it. Let us seize our fate with both hands."

"Spoken like a true Orc," he said.

They walked on in silence, the only sound the crunching of pine needles.

"It is peaceful here," noted Shaluhk. "It reminds me of the day we first met."

"It does? I thought we met at your parents' hut. I came to visit Laruhk, and you were smitten by me."

"That is not the first time we met," she said, "and I was hardly smitten. No, the first time we met was when you were out hunting with Durgash and Laruhk. I was sent to find my brother because he was late for his dinner."

"Oh yes, I remember now. You were such a tiny thing back then."

"Was I indeed? And now?"

"Now you are the very model of the perfect Orc."

"Good answer," she replied.

"Tell me, what DID you think of me when first we met?"

"I must admit to some attraction, but you were still young at the time. It was only later when you fully matured that you began to make my heart flutter."

"I am glad you waited. I doubt I would have been a good bondmate back then. Tell me, do I still make your heart flutter?"

She smiled. "Only whenever you enter the room."

PREPARATIONS

Autumn 1104 SR

The headquarters of Lord Deiter Heinrich, the Duke of Erlingen, was a busy place. At some point in the past, the structure had likely housed a great hall, but someone had extended the original building by adding wings to either side, giving the place a more grandiose appearance. Sir Raynald led them into one such wing now, passing through a long corridor where warriors scuttled back and forth, each in a hurry, though, for what purpose, Athgar couldn't say.

When they finally arrived at a door, the knight halted. "This is the waiting room," he announced, "but we'll go straight in to see His Grace." He opened the door, revealing a packed room.

Sir Raynald elbowed his way past a group of burly axemen, ignoring their complaints. "Right through here."

They halted before another door, guarded by a warrior lazily leaning against the wall.

"Ah, Janik, is His Grace in?"

"Are these the two mages?" the warrior asked as he leaned forward slightly and looked them over. "They don't appear very impressive."

"We are in our travelling clothes," explained Natalia, "and have had scant time to unpack much of anything. Is His Grace interested in our magic or not?"

Janik straightened. "My pardon, lady. He is within." Opening the door, he stepped aside to allow them entry. Once through, he followed, closing the door behind him.

Lord Deiter Henrich was an imposing fellow, standing a head taller than Athgar and with a full grey beard. He turned his weathered countenance upon the newcomers with an intense gaze.

"Who is this, Raynald?" he asked.

"These are the two mages I was telling you about last night, Your Grace. Allow me to introduce Natalia and Athgar."

"Greetings," said the duke in his deep baritone. "I trust Sir Raynald has filled you in on the campaign?"

"Not really," said Athgar.

"What my husband means," added Natalia, "is while we are fully aware of the crusade, we are short on details."

"Ah, well, I can provide those." He moved across to the wall, where a crude map had been hung. "This is a map of the area, as far as I can ascertain." Deiter shrugged. "It's not very good, admittedly, but then again, we are in the armpit of the Continent."

"My lord?" said Athgar.

"He means we are in the middle of nowhere," explained Sir Raynald.

"Yes," said the duke, "precisely. It's difficult to find maps of the area, so I commissioned this one myself. Terrible waste of coins if you ask me. I mean, look at it." He scowled, then picked up a tankard, taking a sip. "Tell me, are you familiar with the area?"

"Only in the most rudimentary capacity," said Natalia. "Why do you ask?"

He frowned. "I was looking for someone to lead us."

"These are mages," said Sir Raynald, "not scouts, Your Grace."

"Couldn't they be both?" The duke sighed. "Never mind, I shall have to do without. I'm told the Church is familiar with the area. We'll simply have to trust in them. Now tell me, what kind of mages are you?"

"I am a Water Mage," said Natalia, "and my husband is a Pyromancer."

Lord Henrich rubbed his hands. "A Fire Mage, just what we needed. I should think you'll prove quite valuable, young man."

"Perhaps," piped in Janik, "a demonstration of their power might be in order?"

"Yes, my aide has a good point. What do you say, Athgar? Care to show us what you can do?"

In answer, the Therengian looked around the room. His eyes came to rest on the fireplace, which sat unlit. He pointed. "May I?"

"By all means," said the duke.

Athgar took some logs from where they sat beside the fire and tossed them into the fireplace, stepping back once complete.

"You will note the logs," he said, then closed his eyes, concentrating on his inner spark. Moments later, the fire came to life, bringing a smile to the old man's face.

"Marvellous," he announced. "How about you, my dear. Care to give us a little example of what you can do?"

Natalia concentrated, taking her time to form the words of power. Moments later, the flames died, smothered by frost.

"Impressive," said Lord Deiter. "I can't wait to see what Hargild will make of you."

"Hargild?" said Athgar.

"Yes, Father General Hargild. He commands the army."

"It's not you, then?"

"Ah, I see the confusion. I command the auxiliaries. That is to say, the warriors who do not fall under the Church's direct control."

"His Grace is a seasoned veteran," added Sir Raynald. "He comes to us from his palatial home in Erlingen."

"Where is that if I might ask?" said Athgar.

"It's one of the northern states," said Natalia, "close to Andover if I'm not mistaken."

"You're quite right," enthused the duke. "They are, in fact, our neighbour."

"Well, Your Grace?" said Sir Raynald. "You think them suitable?"

"By all means," the duke replied. "I shall be happy to add them to the list."

"Perchance," suggested Janik, "you might introduce them to the father general this evening?"

"What an excellent idea." The duke turned his attention back to Athgar and Natalia. "We're having a little get-together tonight at the father general's house. I'd like you to be there if that's all right with you?"

"Of course," said Natalia, "we'd be delighted."

"Good. I'll send a carriage for you this evening, shall I? See to the arrangements, Janik."

"By all means, Your Grace."

"Might I ask the reason for our presence this evening?" asked Athgar.

The duke laughed. "I want to rub the father general's nose in the fact that I have not one, but two mages, where he has none."

"Are you sure that's wise, Your Grace?" asked Natalia. "We do not wish to insult him."

"Insult him? Don't be silly; he's a member of the Church. He'll be over the moon to think we have people of your capabilities in the army. No, your presence will merely confirm I am better at raising an army."

. . .

That afternoon found the pair of them sitting in their room.

"What did you make of the duke?" asked Natalia.

"He was a reasonable man. Is that what you mean?"

"Not precisely. I wanted to know what you make of him as a leader. Sir Raynald seemed to think he is quite experienced. That doesn't bode well for the Therengians."

"No," said Athgar, "I suppose it doesn't. Did you see the number of men waiting to meet him?"

"I did," she replied. "It's as if everyone this side of the Grey Spires wants in on the fighting. You'd think the villages were rolling in gold or something."

"Tell me," said Athgar, "do these people really believe they're doing the Saint's will?"

"Some undoubtedly do, but the rest are likely only looking for wealth. After all, soldiers have to make a living too."

"I suppose that's true."

"Listen," said Natalia, "I've been thinking about this evening."

"And?"

"And we need to get our story straight. We've already blurted out our first names. We don't want it to get out that I'm a Stormwind. We need to come up with a false name."

"How about Runell? He was the captain of the *Swift*."

"Good idea," she said. "It'll be easy to remember."

"I would also suggest you hide that," he said, pointing at her ring. It had been a present from Illiana Stormwind and was incredibly expensive, but what was worse was that it held magerite, a gem that indicated the wearer's power, turning darker on those of sufficient skill. Every member of the family had one, though not always worn as a ring. Right now, sitting on Natalia's finger, it was almost black, displaying her power to any that knew how to read it.

"I hadn't thought of that," she admitted. "I'll tuck it away, shall I?"

"That would probably be for the best."

"What did you make of his soldiers?"

"There were lots of foot," said Athgar, "but I didn't see much horse, did you?"

"No, thank the Saints, but he still has fifty-odd knights. That's more than enough to cause problems."

"Yes," Athgar agreed, "and that's not including the knights from the Church. This is not shaping up very well for Runewald."

"We shall have to find a way to offset their advantage."

"How do we do that?"

"By fighting in a place of our own choosing," said Natalia, "somewhere that will neutralize their horsemen. Maybe we could draw them deeper into the woods?"

"How? Won't they go after the villages?"

"Not if the army tempts them," she said, warming to the task. "It would take some careful planning, but if they see us formed up for battle, their priorities will shift. How many men do you think Eadred can raise?"

"I have no idea. I can't imagine Runewald could field more than a hundred."

"Let's assume the other villages are similar, giving us an army of say, five hundred."

"Plus the Orcs," added Athgar.

"Yes," said Natalia, "but they'll have to leave some of their hunters to guard their own villages. How many do you think that leaves them?"

"Well, assuming all three tribes cooperate, I would say somewhere in the vicinity of another two hundred, maybe three if we're lucky."

"That's seven or eight hundred in total. I think that would be more than sufficient to garner some attention, wouldn't you? We can use that to lure them away from the villages."

"Yes, but is it enough to defeat them? We still don't know their numbers yet."

"True," said Natalia, "but now we have a better idea of what we can field. The Orcs of the Red Hand had those warbows of yours. Do the other tribes have them?"

"No," said Athgar, "nor do the Therengians. They favour spear and shield."

"Do they have any armour?"

"I imagine King Eadred does, and so did Cenric. Some of his personal guards might have some chainmail shirts, I suppose."

"That's not very encouraging. We need something that will defeat plate armour."

"The warbows will work well," said Athgar, "but there aren't enough of them. Our best hope is that the Stone Crushers help. At least they have Earth Mages."

"Yes," said Natalia, "I can work with that. We learned all about the power of the earth. It's perfect for creating defensive works."

"Providing we can lure this Holy Army to the right spot," added Athgar.

"Our biggest weakness is the lack of horsemen. That makes it difficult to keep tabs on the enemy."

"Not necessarily," noted Athgar. "We don't know how well organized this army of theirs is. The duke appeared to take great delight in showing up the father general. Do you think it's a weakness we might exploit?"

"And here I thought I was the tactician. What have you got in mind?"

"We try to sow distrust amongst the leaders, maybe cause them to believe that the other seeks to take all the credit for their success."

"That's not a bad idea," said Natalia. "We'll keep our ears open tonight for anything we might be able to exploit. If nothing else, we should be able to get a better idea of their numbers."

Athgar nodded. "It sounds like we have the beginnings of a plan. Now all we have to do is spy on the enemy while avoiding getting killed ourselves." He chuckled.

"What's so funny?"

"I was just thinking about what will happen if they discover our secret."

"Which is?"

"They'll try to kill us. I told you coming to the city wasn't a good idea!"

The estate occupied by Father General Hargild was situated on the edge of town, close to the western gate upon a large plot of land. The carefully manicured lawns encircled a house that formed a solid block of two floors. From the exterior, there was little to mark it as the property of the Church, but once they drew closer, they saw the guards, their distinctive grey tabards easily identifying them as Temple Knights of Saint Cunar.

When the carriage came to a halt, Athgar immediately climbed down. Natalia, however, lingered for a moment at the top of the single step, using the height advantage to see over the other guests.

"Coming?" he asked.

She stepped from the carriage. "Yes, I was just looking for the duke."

"And did you find him?"

"I did, as a matter of fact. He's over to our left, along with a group of knights."

"In that case," said Athgar, "we'd better seek him out. If we want to learn more about the army, that's the best place to start." He took her hand, guiding her through the crowd. There were soldiers here in the livery of the duke, but the rest of the guests favoured less military-styled clothing, preferring instead to dress in their finest clothes.

"I feel a little underdressed," noted Natalia.

"As do I, but there's little we can do about it. We'll simply have to make the best of it. Who are all these people?"

"Likely his knights, though he might have a baron or two who serves under him as well."

"I suppose it only makes sense. He can't command an army all by himself."

They passed by a group of Temple Knights, resplendent in their plate armour.

"How many of those do you think they have?" asked Athgar.

"I don't know," she confessed, "but the night is early yet. Tongues are bound to loosen once the drink starts flowing."

"You think the Temple Knights will get drunk?"

"No, but the duke's men might. With any luck, we'll be able to pry some information from them."

Natalia halted, leading Athgar to almost run into her. "Something wrong?"

"I've lost sight of the duke. I could have sworn he was just over that way."

"You must be the mages Sir Raynald was talking about?" came an unfamiliar voice.

Athgar turned, coming face to face with a man wearing brown robes, the axe of Mathew firmly emblazoned on his chest.

"And you are?" asked Natalia.

"Brother Rickard," the man replied, "lay brother of the Temple of Saint Mathew."

"Not a Temple Knight, then?" asked Athgar.

"Alas, no. I am here to treat the wounded, not fight."

"We have wounded?"

"Saints, no," said Brother Rickard. "I meant with the army."

"I thought this get-together was for the warriors," said Athgar, "though I mean no offence."

"I have taken none," the Mathewite responded. "The fact is I doubt I would even be here, but the father general wanted it known our order is here to give support where needed."

"So I take it you'll be marching with the army?"

"I will, though it pains me to do so."

"Pains you?" said Natalia. "That's a strange thing to say."

"It is," the man continued, "but I must confess I see the entire crusade as being antithetical to the teachings of the Church."

"Then why travel here at all? Surely your superiors didn't send you?"

"That is correct. I volunteered, and before you ask me why, let me explain. It is my calling to look after the sick and wounded. Though I disagree with this crusade, I cannot, in all consciousness, sit by and ignore the suffering that often results from such conflict."

"I admire your convictions," said Athgar. "Are there others who share your views?"

The Mathewite smiled. "I imagine there are, but I am not here to answer for such things."

"Tell me," said Natalia, "you say you disagree with the crusade. I'm curious as to why?"

"The Church was built on acceptance, and yet here we are attacking others because of their beliefs. Mind you, the enemy deserves what's coming against them."

"Why would you say that?" she asked.

The brother displayed a stunned expression. "Has no one told you?"

"No, I'm afraid not."

"They are worshippers of Death Magic."

"Where did you hear that?"

"It's true," he continued. "They pray to their goddess of death, Rikasi."

Natalia was about to ask another question, but she was interrupted by a man in brown robes calling from across the room.

"You must excuse me," said Brother Rickard. "My captain calls. Perhaps I'll see you again later? If not, I'm sure we'll see each other once we march."

"Certainly," said Athgar.

Natalia turned to her husband. "Tell me about Rikasi. I'm not familiar with her."

"Neither is he if he thinks she's the goddess of death."

"What is she the goddess of, then? And is she really worshipped by the Therengians?"

"Rikasi is not the goddess of death," insisted Athgar, "at least not in the traditional sense. She guards the gates to the Underworld, making sure only those of bad character pass. Should a Therengian find himself there by mistake, they can rest assured Rikasi will send them on to the Afterlife. She is a guardian of the dead and certainly not worshipped by Necromancers."

"Interesting," said Natalia. "It appears the entire crusade is built upon a lie."

"You think explaining this will make it any better?"

"Most certainly not. They're using it as an excuse. The real question is, why?"

"You don't suppose there's godstone here," asked Athgar, "like back in Ord-Kurgad?"

"No, that would be stretching chance a little too far for my liking. There's something else. I'm sure of it."

Sir Raynald appeared through the crowd. "There you are. I've been looking for you two. Come and meet the father general, won't you?"

"By all means," said Natalia, "lead on."

Lord Dieter's voice boomed across the room. "There they are!"

As they drew closer, they saw him and his companions. Beside him was a short man, with a carefully cropped beard that was greying around the edges. "This is Father General Hargild," the duke said. "I've been telling him all about you two."

"Greetings," said the father general. He indicated the man next to him, who was similarly dressed in the dark grey of his order. "May I introduce his excellency, Master Talivardas. He is the regional master of our order."

The man was tall, with a long grey beard that stretched past the middle of his chest. His closely cropped hair gave him an imposing appearance, commanding attention from all those around him.

"Pleased to meet you," the Cunar master said, extending his hand.

Athgar reached out, looking down at Master Talivardas' extended hand, but strangely, the palm was downward, forcing the Therengian to acknowledge the ring that stared back at him. He paused, not quite believing his eyes, for here, on the hand of the Cunar master, was a ring set with dark blue magerite. There could be no doubt, this man was a Stormwind!

JUDGEMENT

Autumn 1104 SR

(In the tongue of the Orcs)

Kargen paused, looking at the ground. "We are close," he said. "There are signs of frequent foot traffic."

Shaluhk listened. "We are indeed. I hear the distant sound of a village at work."

Kargen looked at his bondmate. "You did not have to accompany me," he said, "but I am glad we are together."

"As we should be. We are a team, you and I."

"Do you still worry?" he asked.

She nodded. "I can not shake this feeling."

"Then let us return to Ord-Ghadrak. I would not put you in danger."

"No, we can not. Without the help of the Stone Crushers, victory would be in doubt. You know as well as I that we must do all we can to ensure the safety of our people."

"Even at risk to yourself?"

"Yes," said Shaluhk, "and you?"

"I am the Chieftain of the Red Hand," said Kargen. "I can not expect my tribe to risk their lives if I am unwilling to do the same."

"Spoken like a true leader."

"What makes you think that danger awaits?"

"I do not know. I just have a feeling something will go wrong."

"Will the Ancestors not guide us?"

"In their own way, yes. They are the accumulated wisdom of our race. The mistakes of the past are not forgotten, thus allowing us to avoid making them in the future."

"I wonder what they might make of our present plight?"

"We are trying to unite three tribes to help one group of Humans against another. I doubt such a thing has happened before."

"What of the west?"

"That is unfolding even as we speak," said Shaluhk. "And while our kin help the Humans there, insufficient time has passed to tell if it will be to the overall benefit of our people."

"What does your gut tell you?"

Shaluhk laughed. "You sound like Athgar."

"I shall take that as a compliment, but you are avoiding an answer. I would know your thoughts, for I value your opinion."

"There is danger ahead, of that I have no doubt. Kirak warned us about Zahruhl's treachery."

"You think he will not help?"

"I think he WILL, but the price he asks may be too high."

"Perhaps," mused Kargen, "but if he refuses, we are in no worse a position than we are now."

"Not so," suggested Shaluhk, "for his tribe is stronger than us. He has only to wait until we have weakened ourselves against the Humans to move in and absorb what remains of us."

"I think that unlikely. Our people will not submit so easily."

"I think you are wrong, bondmate. Without your guardianship, the tribe will fall into disarray. Say what you like about Zahruhl, but he knows how to lead his people. Khasrahk offers safety and security. Can you say with certainty that our people would refuse such an offer?"

"Would not another rise to take my place if I fell?"

"Who?" said Shaluhk. "Laruhk? You know he would die by your side rather than flee, and the same goes for Durgash. But no, I am afraid your death would spell an end to the Red Hand."

Kargen grimaced. "Then I shall do my best to remain amongst the living."

"As will I," she added. "Now, let us put aside these gloomy thoughts. We have a chieftain to visit."

. . .

The aroma of smoke drifted through the woods, indicating the proximity of the village. Kargen kept a close eye on the path ahead as it twisted through the trees, and then the stone entrance of Khasrahk came into view.

Two Orcs stood watch, the butts of their spears resting on the ground. They gave little notice of their new visitors, not even deigning to welcome them. Shaluhk thought it strange but held her tongue, for complaining would do little to put them in a positive light.

Through the entrance they walked, taking in the village beyond. Much like Ord-Kurgad, the wall ran the perimeter of the place, with an opening through which one could enter. There was no gate to speak of, though in times of war, one could be created relatively easily. Kargen found himself wondering if the dreaded tuskers ever ventured into town, but on closer reflection, he thought it unlikely.

The space beyond the entrance was open, with huts to either side and a clear area that stretched eastward, culminating in the great hut Zahruhl called home.

Kargen slowed, a feeling of caution gripping him. He looked at Shaluhk to see that she, too, had slackened her pace. Villagers watched them warily but none spoke. It was as if every eye in the place was fixed firmly upon them.

At last, a familiar face appeared. Rugg, the master of earth, had exited the great hut and was now walking towards them at a steady pace. Kargen and Shaluhk halted, waiting for the elderly Orc to come closer.

"Greetings, Rugg," said Kargen.

"Honour to your Ancestors," added Shaluhk.

"Kargen, Shaluhk," said Rugg, "what brings you to Khasrahk?"

"We seek an audience with your chieftain, Zahruhl," said Kargen.

Rugg looked around. "And yet you brought no hunters with you?"

"We did not think it necessary," said Kargen. "We have come to discuss matters of great import to our respective tribes."

"Then come," said Rugg, "and I shall take you to Zahruhl."

He turned around, making his way back to the great hut, leaving Kargen and Shaluhk to quicken their pace in order to keep up.

"He is quick for such an old Orc," whispered Shaluhk.

"So he is," Kargen agreed. "I see there is more to the master of earth than first appears."

An Orc hunter stood by the leather flap that hung, curtain-like, across the opening. He pulled it aside as they drew closer, allowing them entrance into the great structure.

Inside the stone building, they halted, and Kargen let his eyes adjust to the gloom. The interior was barren of occupants, making it appear even larger. He couldn't help but once again admire the work that had gone into the construction of the place, for the walls and roof lacked seams, their stone blocks fused together by the power of magic.

"Come and sit," bid Rugg. "I shall see if Zahruhl has time to see you."

Shaluhk recognized the insult, for Kargen was a chieftain; to make him wait was showing disrespect. She opened her mouth to say something, but Kargen's hand calmed her. Rugg disappeared into the chieftain's quarters, leaving the two visitors alone.

"Does he not respect tradition?" said Shaluhk.

"We are in someone else's hut," said Kargen. "We must respect their customs."

"They were friendlier than this the last time we visited."

"True, but we were only passing through."

"What does he hope to achieve by making us wait?"

"He is demonstrating his own importance," said Kargen.

"But you are his equal. Does he not see that?"

"This is not the place to argue such things. We must wait and see how this plays out."

"This is not a game, Kargen. The fate of our tribe hangs in the balance."

"It IS a game; do you not see? Zahruhl wishes to appear strong. If we can make him feel more so, then we have a greater chance of being successful. We must play by his rules, or we shall not achieve our objective."

"Very well," said Shaluhk, "though I like not this treatment."

They sat in silence. Shaluhk closed her eyes, the better to think, but Kargen kept his on the exit. He had heard sounds outside, sounds of feet moving, and he was struck by the idea they might have to fight their way out of Khasrahk. He loosened the axe in his belt.

Rugg emerged from his chieftain's quarters. "Zahruhl has deigned to speak with you."

Kargen and Shaluhk rose, showing their respect.

Moments later, Zahruhl came through the doorway, Voruhn at his side.

"So," said the chieftain of the Stone Crushers, "you have returned to us, Kargen of the Red Hand."

"I have," replied Kargen.

The two chieftains stood there, their eyes locked, each taking the measure of the other.

Zahruhl whispered something to Rugg, who promptly left the great hut by the front door. "Come, let us sit," offered their host, "and you can tell me why you have returned."

Kargen and Shaluhk resumed their seats, waiting until Zahruhl and

Voruhn sat before beginning. "We have come seeking your aid," said Shaluhk.

"For what?" said Zahruhl.

"A great army threatens us all," said Kargen.

"I doubt that. You speak of a great army, no doubt you mean the Humans, but the Black Axe is more than sufficient to deal with the Torkul villagers."

"It is not the Torkul who threaten, but rather the Humans that live to the west. They are preparing to invade our lands with a large army."

"And how do you know this?" asked Zahruhl.

"The Humans of Runewald have seen it. Even as we speak, they prepare to march from Ebenstadt."

"Ebenstadt? You speak to me of other Humans? Let them fight amongst themselves. It is of no concern to us."

"It will grow to be so," said Kargen. "If we do not stand with the Therengians, then we shall be forced to stand alone at a later date."

"You do not know that for certain," said Zahruhl. "And in any event, even THEY could not penetrate the walls of Khasrahk."

"You feel secure behind stone walls," said Kargen, "but the Humans can penetrate even those."

"And how would they do such a thing?"

"They have engines of war that can make short work of your walls."

Zahruhl leaned forward. "How could you possibly know of this?"

"We were taught," offered Shaluhk, "by Nat-Alia of the Red Hand."

"You lie. The Humans do not teach such things to their females."

"You are wrong," said Shaluhk. "She is a battle mage, a wielder of great power."

"Then let her defend your tribe, or does she refuse?"

"Even magic has its limits."

"You speak of magic," said Voruhn, "and yet you yourself are barely trained in such things."

"I am the Shamaness of the Red Hand," countered Shaluhk.

"And yet still," insisted Voruhn, "my words ring true. Leave talk of magic to those who are educated in such things."

"Let us return to your original topic," said Zahruhl. "You asked us to help the other tribes. What manner of assistance do you envision?"

"I propose each tribe sends what hunters it can spare. We shall lure the enemy to a place of our choosing and destroy them."

"I see," said Zahruhl. "And what, might I ask, would be the price you would be willing to pay for such help?"

"Price?" said Kargen.

"You can not expect me to send my tribemates to their death without a cause."

"I am talking about the survival of our people."

"And yet, as I explained, my own tribe is safely within the walls of Khasrahk."

"You would have your kin pay you in exchange for your support?"

"Certainly," said Zahruhl. "I have taken an oath to do what is best for my tribe. Have you not taken the same sacred oath?"

Kargen felt defeated. "I have. What is your price?"

"I do not seek material wealth, but rather the enrichment of my people."

"Which means?" asked Shaluhk.

"I will consider your proposal, but I must have more hunters. You must force a vote of your tribe, and convince them to join the Stone Crushers."

"I shall do no such thing," said Kargen, his temper rising.

"And yet you already have," said Zahruhl, "or did you forget the seventeen of your tribe who already chose to join us."

"I have forgotten nothing, but I will not surrender the entire tribe to you."

Shaluhk heard the door open. Hunters flooded into the room, led by Rugg, but Kargen appeared to take no notice.

"You must do what you think is best," said Zahruhl, "but I wonder what your tribe would do if their leader was no longer amongst them."

Kargen leaped to his feet. "You dare to threaten an Orc chieftain?"

Zahruhl rose in response. "This is my village," he declared, "and I shall do as I please."

"Seize them!" shouted Voruhn.

Kargen pulled his axe, ready to leap across the firepit, but a motion to his side caught his attention. Three hunters stood, their spears levelled at Shaluhk.

"Go ahead," said Zahruhl, "kill me if you can, but know this, before you can cross that firepit, your precious bondmate will fall to my spears."

Kargen fought hard to control his impulses. He looked at Shaluhk, seeing the defiance in her eyes but knew he couldn't do it. He dropped his weapon, then his arms were seized, along with those of Shaluhk as more hunters crowded into the hut.

Rugg looked at his chieftain. "Your orders, Zahruhl?"

In answer, the great Orc turned to his shamaness. "Your thoughts?"

Voruhn gave careful thought before replying. "Let them suffer the fate of Garok."

A smile crept over the face of Zahruhl. "An excellent idea," he said. "Take them away and prepare the punishment. We shall see how much favour the Ancestors show them."

Kargen sat in silence, his hands bound behind his back. Across from him, Shaluhk was calm despite the unknown punishment that awaited them. They were under guard in a small hut while the sound of axes on wood echoed outside.

"What are they doing?" demanded Kargen.

His guard answered with a blow to the head. Kargen spat blood but said no more. The axes fell silent and then the door opened to reveal Voruhn.

"It is time," she announced.

The guard prodded Kargen with the tip of his spear. "Get up," he commanded.

Shaluhk, seeing her bondmate's look of refusal, stood. "Let us show courage in the face of adversity," she declared.

He nodded, mimicking her actions, and then they were led outside to where the tribe had gathered to witness their punishment. Zahruhl stood nearby, between two frames of wood, each constructed in the shape of an X.

"I can not order the death of a chieftain," the Orc proclaimed, "and so I commit them to the Ancestors. Kargen and Shaluhk shall be bound to these frames and allowed no food or water. It will be the elements that kill them, not I."

"Perhaps," offered Voruhn, "the Ancestors will see fit to preserve them."

Zahruhl chuckled. "Perhaps," he agreed, "but I doubt it. Your journey here has been in vain, Kargen. I shall see you dead within a ten-day, and then I shall invite your people to take shelter within these very walls."

"My tribe will not submit," proclaimed Kargen. "They would rather die than give up their freedom."

"We shall see," said Voruhn. "Thirst and starvation can curb the enthusiasm of even the strongest."

Hunters seized their arms, pinning them by their sides, while Voruhn severed their bonds. They were then pushed into place, their arms and legs tied to the posts, leaving them facing one another.

"There," said Voruhn. "Now you can watch each other as you slowly succumb to the elements. Tell me, how does it feel to know your bondmate will die?"

Kargen stared back, pure hatred on his face.

"We shall leave them," announced Zahruhl, "for they are now in the hands of the Ancestors."

"You are making a big mistake," warned Kargen.

"Strong words for one in your position," said Voruhn, "or did you forget it is you who are suffering, not me?"

Zahruhl appeared indecisive, possibly regretting his decision, but Voruhn quickly intervened. "Pay no attention to him. It is an empty threat."

Kargen watched as the whole tribe turned their backs, walking away from the scene. Only a pair of hunters remained, standing at a distance to watch over their plight.

They hung thus for some time, struggling in vain to lessen their bindings.

"You should have killed him," said Shaluhk, "when you had the chance."

"I could not bear the thought of your death," he admitted.

"And yet now we are both doomed."

"It changes nothing. Even if I had managed to kill him, there was still the matter of all those hunters. We would have been dead either way."

"At least our deaths would have been quick," she said.

"Would they? I doubt that very much. If anything, we would have suffered the same fate, but instead of just standing here, we would be bleeding to death. Maybe this is better after all."

"Better? It will take a long time for us to pass to the Afterlife. How can you possibly think it better to end like this?"

"Tell me. You are the healer. What can we expect?"

"The initial thirst will come first, but once we get past that, it will be bearable. The bindings are likely to grow increasingly uncomfortable, and once we weaken, they will grow worse as they have to support our weight."

Kargen frowned. "Stop. I think it better if I do not know. We must face this with dignity."

"It will be difficult, my love, for our strength will slowly wane. Death may take time to claim us."

"How much time?"

"A ten-day at least, but no more than two. Do you still think this is better than dying in the hut?"

"I do," he replied, "but not for the reason you might think."

"Go on," she urged.

"Had you died in there, I would have taken vengeance, but Zahruhl, or Voruhn, would not allow me a clean death, that much is clear."

"And how is that better?"

"I could not let you journey to the Afterlife alone. I would be by your side, even in death."

She smiled despite the discomfort. "Then we shall take this last trip together, as it should be."

THE MASTER

Autumn 1104 SR

A thgar sipped his drink, taking in the occupants of the room.
"Nervous?" asked Natalia.

"With all these Cunars about? You'd better believe it. And what about Master Talivardas? How in the Continent did he end up in charge of the order?"

"He's the regional master, not the grand master."

"What's the difference?"

"The grand master oversees the entire order," she said, "whereas a regional master only looks after one region. In this case, the North East area of the Continent. In rank, he's still only a commander."

"That doesn't make me feel any better," said Athgar. "Do you think he's the one who called for the crusade?"

"No, he doesn't have the authority."

"Then who does?"

Natalia gave it some thought before answering. "The Primus is the usual culprit."

"And he is?"

"Do you know nothing of the Church?"

Athgar pointed at himself. "Old Gods, remember?"

She smiled. "Each of the six orders sends a representative to something called the Council of Peers. From their number, they elect a single representative to lead them, and he's referred to as the Primus. He's also the ultimate power behind the Church."

"And no one else could order a crusade?"

"I suppose the grand master of the order could."

"Which do you think is more likely in this case?"

She looked around the room. "I'd say the grand master. Look around you. Aside from Brother Rickard, we have seen little of any orders other than the Cunars. If the Primus had ordered it, we'd see a more noticeable presence of the others."

Athgar glanced around, ensuring no one could overhear. "How long do you suppose the master's been a Stormwind?"

"You saw his ring; he's powerful. He would have been trained at the Volstrum long before he took service with the order."

"How long does it take to rise to the position of a regional master?"

"Decades," Natalia replied, "but I doubt he did it without help."

"Meaning?"

"The family is not above using murder. We know that from first-hand experience. I imagine other candidates either died or withdrew from consideration, likely the result of applied pressure."

"What kind of pressure could you exert against a Temple Knight?"

"Remember Corassus?" she said. "Brother Cyric indicated many of the Cunar knights didn't follow the rules regarding celibacy. That kind of information could prove harmful when it came to promotions."

"And so Talivardas fought his way to the top," mused Athgar.

"Not quite. He still has a grand master to contend with."

"Do you think the grand master is a member of the family as well?"

"I doubt it, but then again, I wouldn't have thought it possible for a regional master of the order to be one."

"So where does that leave us?"

"It doesn't change our priorities," she replied. "We came here to find out more about the army—that still stands. This extra information complicates matters, but we must put it aside for the time being. We have more important work to do."

"Agreed. Let's see if we can't find an office to break into. It worked in Caerhaven; maybe it'll work here?"

"It's worth a try."

Making their way through the crowd, they stopped from time to time to listen in on conversations, trying hard not to be noticed. They picked a route that would take them to the stairs, believing anything of interest might lie on the top floor, but as they were about to take the first step, Athgar suddenly stopped.

"What is it?" asked Natalia.

"That guard," he said, "he's a Therengian. Look at his eyes."

Natalia noticed the man in question. He was dressed in the livery of Duke Heinrich, a common foot soldier by the look of him. He was wearing a conical helm, complete with a nose guard, but there was no mistaking the colour of his eyes.

"Can others not have grey eyes?" she asked.

"It is the mark of my people," said Athgar. "A dominant trait handed down through succeeding generations, and yet he is not dressed like a Therengian. How can this be?"

"Your people were subjugated, likely many chose to live amongst their conquerors. That man looks to be a descendant of your forbearers."

"Is such a thing even possible?"

"You forget, Therengia was a large realm, taking up almost a third of the area of the Petty Kingdoms. That many people don't simply disappear."

"I suppose that makes sense, but I always thought they were relegated to villages like Athelwald. It appears the Continent is full of surprises."

He turned his attention back to the stairs, but a pair of Temple Knights had moved to block them.

"Is there a problem?" asked Natalia.

"Guests are not allowed," the knight responded.

"Very well," she replied, taking Athgar's arm and pulling him back into the crowd. She lowered her voice. "It appears we have garnered some interest. Those guards are watching us."

"Then we shall avoid doing anything to bring further attention to ourselves."

Natalia squeezed his arm. "See that man over there? The one in the green surcoat?"

"What of him?"

"He's a Ragnarite," she said, "a Temple Knight of Saint Ragnar."

"Remind me what that means?"

"They hunt Necromancers."

"It makes sense," said Athgar, "doesn't it? Brother Rickard indicated the Church believes we're all death worshippers."

"Yes," she agreed, "and that makes our Ragnarite the most dangerous man in the room."

"I'm not sure I follow."

"Ragnarites often work alone. As such, they are the most proficient warriors when it comes to one-on-one combat. Not only that, but he has complete control over the search for Death Mages. If he makes a discovery, people will act."

"We must convince him this entire campaign is flawed."

"No," she said, "not yet, at least."

"Why not?"

"Merely approaching him would bring unwanted attention. He's more likely to arrest us, and then where would we be? No, we must give him no reason to suspect our true purpose here."

Natalia led him away from the Ragnarite, steering him towards a distant door. "With all these Cunars about, it's beginning to get a little uncomfortable."

"Perhaps we'd better leave?" Athgar suggested.

"How many Temple Knights do you reckon are here?"

"You mean on guard, or as guests?"

"Both."

"Well," he said, "I've seen at least two dozen standing at doors and whatnot, and I'd say there's at least thirty more wandering around. Any way you look at it, there's a significant number."

"Yes, and a fair number would have stayed behind in their commandery."

"What makes you say that? Wouldn't they all be here, where the master of their order is?"

"You forget," Natalia said, "they took vows. They tend not to congregate where women gather. They believe it helps them avoid temptation."

"And yet there are plenty of women here," noted Athgar. "Does that mean the guards have broken their vows?"

"No, they're here on duty."

"That's true for the guards, but what about the others?"

"Temple Knights of Saint Cunar are not known to socialize, at least not the common rank and file. I suspect the people wandering around are senior officials, officers subordinate to the father general."

"That would indicate something big is in the works."

"My thoughts exactly," said Natalia. "I should very much like to work our way back to the duke. If plans are being made, we should be present."

"Fair enough..." He was about to say more, but something caught Natalia's attention. "Something wrong?" he asked.

She stood on the tips of her toes, peering through the crowd. "I thought I saw someone," she said.

"Who?"

"I'm not sure."

"You're not sure if you saw someone?"

"No, I'm not sure who I saw. His face was familiar, but I couldn't place him."

Athgar cast his eyes about. "Where?"

"Over that way, but he disappeared into the crowd."

"Should we be worried?"

"Not yet, but if he shows up again, I'll point him out. In the meantime, let's find the duke, shall we?"

They wandered around, finally finding Lord Deiter Heinrich in the company of Sir Raynald.

"There you are," greeted the knight. "I was wondering where you'd gotten to."

"Enjoying the place?" asked Lord Deiter.

"It's quite impressive," said Natalia. "Tell me, who lived here before the father general?"

"I understand it was owned by the rulers of this city. A nasty bunch, I'm told. We kicked them out in the last crusade."

"When was that?"

"About five years ago. To my knowledge, it was the last independent city in the north."

"Meaning?" asked Athgar.

"An independent city has its own leaders, much like Corassus."

"I thought Corassus was a city-state?"

"It is," said the duke. "The two are essentially the same thing. Mind you, Corassus is run by a group of merchants. Here, the leader was a barbarian, or so I'm told."

Athgar scowled. "Why is it we label those that don't conform to our beliefs as barbarians?"

"It's not their beliefs that set them apart," said Lord Deiter, "but their culture. They're a primitive race."

"Then how is it they had a city?" asked Athgar, his face growing red.

"I'm sure I can't say. Possibly they conquered it? It wouldn't be the first time a city fell to a group of outsiders. Mind you, if the architecture of the city is any indication, Ebenstadt is very old."

"Do you think it was part of Therengia?" suggested Sir Raynald.

"Maybe," mused the duke. "I wish I'd learned more history when I was younger. Wasn't their last stand somewhere around here?"

"I believe that was closer to Draybourne," said Athgar. "They had a statue there commemorating it."

"Maybe this was a regional capital?" suggested Natalia. "It was a large kingdom after all."

The duke looked around the room. "That would certainly explain the presence of a place like this. Still, that would have been what, five hundred years ago?"

"Closer to six," said Sir Raynald. "The last of the successor states was captured in 603."

They all looked at him in surprise.

"It's a particular interest of mine," he explained.

"What could possibly interest you about an ancient kingdom?" asked the duke.

"Most of our armies are modelled after them," the knight explained, "and they're the ones who standardized their military organization. Of course, they didn't have the cavalry we have these days, but their footmen were said to be invincible."

The duke barked out a laugh. "Well, that's obviously not true, or they wouldn't have fallen."

"Still," Sir Raynald persisted, "we owe much to them in terms of tactics."

"Nonsense," said the duke. "They are a conquered people. The very tactics they developed led to their inevitable defeat."

"I understood they collapsed through internal strife," said Athgar. "Is that not true?"

"There is always speculation," said Sir Raynald, "but the truth is we shall never really know for sure. Most of their records were lost to history. Even so, what little we do know is often studied by those interested in the art of war."

"War is not an art," said the duke, "but rather a bloodbath. It is numbers that tell in the end, not fancy manoeuvres."

"You must tell me more of these Therengians," said Athgar. "They sound like a fascinating people. Do you know much about their culture?"

"No," replied the knight. "Only their military history, and even that information is often contradictory. How about you? What have you heard?"

"I know very little," said Athgar, "though maybe Natalia might be able to tell you more."

"Therengia was not studied during my training," she confessed. "But I have since learned a few things here and there."

"Such as?" pressed the knight.

Natalia briefly looked at Athgar, unsure of how much to reveal. "They had a standing militia, didn't they?"

"Yes, that's right, the fyrd," said Sir Raynald. "Though I doubt it was very effective. Therengia's strength lay in its professional army. Some say it was the first on the Continent."

"Surely not," said the duke. "Professional soldiers have been around since the dawn of time, haven't they?"

"They have," admitted the knight, "but not in such numbers. Therengia was the first kingdom to create a permanent standing army. Its warriors were said to be the best trained anywhere."

"It's all a myth if you ask me," said the duke. "I'll put my faith in the modern knight. There's no footmen in the world who could stand against them."

"Knights cannot fight alone," said Sir Raynald. "You still need footmen and archers to win battles."

"I'm not denying that, but it's the knights who give us the decisive edge. Ask the father general; he'll tell you." The duke tore his eyes away, scanning the crowd. "Where in the Continent did he get to?"

A Temple Knight approached, bowing his head. "Your Grace, Master Talivardas asks you to come with me. The meeting is about to commence."

"Very well," said the duke. "Lead on."

He began following the man but then paused, looking back at the assembled group. "You'd best come as well. We'll need your advice."

"Ours?" said Athgar.

"Yes, you're the spell casters. You can give us an idea of what to expect."

"What makes you say that?" asked Natalia.

The duke gave them a puzzled look. "We're fighting Necromancers, remember? Who better than a pair of mages to tell us what to expect?"

"Wouldn't a Ragnarite be better?" suggested Sir Raynald.

"Don't be absurd," said the duke. "Ragnarites don't use magic. Come along, we haven't all day."

He led them towards the stairs, the same place they had been turned aside earlier on. This time, however, the guards parted, allowing them to ascend.

They followed some other knights who made their way into a decent-sized dining room where the table had been removed, leaving an ample open area. On the far wall, someone had pinned a large map, though even Athgar, with his limited knowledge of the area, could see how inaccurate it was.

Master Talivardas entered once everyone else was settled, commanding the room's attention. He took his place by the map, producing a rolled parchment.

"I have here instructions from the grand master," he announced. "It authorizes a new crusade to wipe out the evil that has for so long infested this area." He gazed around the room, locking eyes with several others. Athgar could feel the excitement building as if the entire room was ready to spring into action.

"As to the actual campaign, I shall leave its conduct in the capable hands of Father General Hargild." He nodded to the father general, who now moved front and centre.

"As you know," the man began, "we have received troubling reports of death worshippers to the east. Our mission is to seek out these nests of evil and eradicate them. To that end, we have assembled an army the likes of which has never been seen in this part of the Continent." He paused, drawing everyone in. "I am pleased to announce that as of this morning, our total forces exceed two thousand men."

He waited for the noise to die down. "Now I know what you're thinking: two thousand is small in comparison to some of the armies of the northern states, but here, this close to the wilderness, it is unprecedented. And it's also the largest Holy Army to be raised in more than two centuries."

"Might I ask the breakdown of the army?" said the duke.

The father general smiled. "You certainly may. As you know, this is a Church operation, and to that end, we have assembled more than five hundred Temple Knights. This represents a significant investment from the Church. We have even had to strip away some of our garrisons from nearby cities in order to assemble it. This force will constitute the heavy contingent of our army and will be the sword by which the wrath of the Saints is delivered."

"And the rest?" asked the duke.

"Your auxiliaries will be used to screen the advance of the Temple Knights. Your task, Your Grace, will be to locate the enemy, and then pin them in place so we can bring them to battle. To that end, you will have a multitude of footmen and archers at your command, in addition, of course, to your own knights. We are also marching into extremely rough terrain, forcing us to bring our own supplies. That means you'll have to detail troops to escort them."

"Anything else?" asked the duke.

In answer, the father general turned to the map. "This is the area we are marching into. It mostly consists of dense forests with a few open spaces. Our plan is to strike eastward, rolling up the enemy as we find them."

"Rolling them up?" said the duke.

"Yes, pushing them back. Make no mistake, sooner or later they'll decide to make a stand, and when they do, we shall hammer them!"

There were nods of agreement all around, but Athgar couldn't help thinking the plan was lacking some important details. He was about to say something to Natalia, then reconsidered. If the campaign were to be poorly planned, all the better for the Therengians.

"Now, gentlemen," continued the father general, "return to your men and prepare them. We march in two days."

He turned, following Master Talivardas through the door. Immediately after they left, those in the room erupted into a myriad of discussions.

"Fascinating," said the duke.

"I think it was a little light on details," said Sir Raynald.

"Nonsense. It gives us more leeway."

"What happens now?" asked Athgar.

"Now," said the duke, "I can return home and begin planning. What will you two do?"

"Probably go home and sleep," said Natalia. "All this excitement has made me tired."

They drifted from the room, following in the wake of all the knights. As they descended the stairs, Natalia stopped, grabbing Athgar's forearm.

"There's that man again," she said, pointing. "Do you see him?"

Athgar gazed across the room to see a man of average height, with short brown hair and a scruffy beard, making his way to the exit. Every so often, he would pause and look around as if scanning the crowd for someone.

"Let's follow," said Athgar, "but keep back. We don't want to spook him."

They kept their distance, watching as he left the building, heading out into the streets of Ebenstadt.

"Do you remember who he is?" Athgar asked.

"No, but it's someone from my past. He looks much older than I remember him. Maybe someone from before I went to the Volstrum?"

"It's not Stanislav, is it?"

"Saints, no," she said. "I'd know him in an instant. No, this is someone else." She paused. "Wait, now I remember; his name's Nikolai. Stanislav warned me about him, said he was the man who murdered my mother."

"Oh?"

"Yes, he's a mage hunter who used to work for Stanislav. He attacked us when I was first brought to the Volstrum."

"Then we'd best take care. He's likely not changed. What do you think he's doing here? Looking for mages?"

"Not at the father general's place," said Natalia. "However, he does work for the family."

ANCESTORS

Autumn 1104 SR

(In the tongue of the Orcs)

K argen awoke to the sun on his face, warming his skin. They had hung there for days, and he could feel the hunger gnawing at his stomach. Looking across at Shaluhk, he saw that she was just stirring. He tried to call out to her, but his voice had left him. When she finally raised her head, they stared into each other's eyes, the wisp of a smile on her face.

"Can you hear me, my love?" asked Shaluhk.

He nodded.

"We must be strong," she said.

Kargen turned his head, looking at their guards, but the Orc hunters paid them no attention. Villagers were going about their business with little thought to the fate of their prisoners.

Out of the corner of his eye he spotted movement, but his present situation prevented him from getting a better look. Soft voices were exchanged, and then one of the guards left his post. Kargen suddenly felt a chill; was someone coming to finish the job? Had Zahruhl decided to end them now rather than let them linger?

A younger Orc, no more than eighteen summers, came into view, his face covered in grey mud. He also wore grey cloth, marking him as a master of earth, or, considering his age, more likely an apprentice. Walking straight up to the second guard, he spoke in low tones that Kargen couldn't make out, but his words had an immediate effect. The guard nodded, then left his post, leaving the two prisoners alone with the newcomer.

Kargen glanced at Shaluhk. It was clear she had seen the exchange for she, too, was watching with interest as the young Orc drew close. The stranger paused, taking a moment to look Kargen in the eyes, then turn his attention to Shaluhk.

"You are a shamaness," he said.

"I am Shaluhk," she replied, "bondmate to Kargen, Chieftain of the Red Hand."

"I am Urumar, apprentice to Rugg. I have been sent to speak with you."

Shaluhk cast her eyes around before settling them back on the visitor. "And to do that, you must dismiss the guards?"

Urumar turned to Kargen. "We need your help."

"He can not speak," said Shaluhk, "for his voice is gone. A victim of his thirst."

Urumar hesitated, unsure of what to do, indecision on his face.

"We speak with one voice," said Shaluhk. "Tell him what you wish, and I will answer for him."

Urumar looked around the village, waiting as someone ambled by before continuing. "Some time ago, Voruhn caught the eye of Zahruhl."

"What has this to do with us?"

"Let me finish. Voruhn was little more than an apprentice at the time, learning the ways of a shamaness under the tutelage of Glurdash."

"And where is this Glurdash now?"

"Dead," said Urumar. "Killed in an ambush in the forest. It was blamed on the Torkul at the time, but my master has his doubts."

"And?"

"Since Glurdash's death, Voruhn has become powerful. Much more so than could be expected in so short a time."

"Go on."

"My master, Rugg, believes she has delved into dark arts."

"How long ago was this?"

"Only a few ten-days ago, just before your first visit here. However, her influence over Zahruhl has grown stronger, to the point where he can no longer think for himself."

"Has her manner changed?"

"Yes," admitted Urumar. "Her former self is barely recognizable."

"It is not the dark arts," declared Shaluhk.

"Then what is it?"

"I believe she has called on the Ancestors to feed her quest for power. She is possessed, and I think I know by whom."

Urumar stared back at her. "Tell me."

"No," she replied. "If we are to die here, then that secret will die with us."

The young Orc glanced around one more time, then lifted his hands, cupping them before him as he uttered words of power. The area around them echoed with the sound of splintering wood. Moments later, Shaluhk's frame collapsed, dropping her to the ground. Urumar didn't hesitate, turning his attention to Kargen and repeating the spell.

Shaluhk rose, rubbing her wrists and tugging the loosened bonds free. She rushed forward, catching Kargen right as his frame snapped in two. He fell heavily, leaning into her, then steadied himself. Urumar tossed her a knife, and she made short work of the remaining rope.

"Come," the apprentice said. "We haven't much time. Rugg awaits."

He led them through the village and into a small stone hut. Inside were two Orcs, one of which they recognized as the master of earth.

"This is Gahruhl," said Rugg, "sister to Zahruhl. She is a master of earth, like me."

Urumar selected an earthenware jug, passing it to Kargen, who drank thirstily.

"We haven't much time," said Rugg.

"Shaluhk thinks Voruhn is possessed," said Urumar.

"It would explain much," said Gahruhl. "For she has not been herself for some time."

"Has she ever contacted the Ancestors?" asked Shaluhk.

"I can not say for sure," said Gahruhl, "but it would have been part of her training, would it not?"

"I believe she was swayed by the words of Khurlig," said Shaluhk. "An ancient Ancestor who longs to return to the mortal realm. She tried to possess me back in Ord-Kurgad. Were it not for the intervention of my mentor, I would have succumbed."

"And what makes you think it is her?" asked Rugg.

"The hatred for Kargen and myself. She blames me for preventing her return."

"But why would Voruhn allow such a thing?"

"She likely desired power above all else, and Khurlig's words proved persuasive. No doubt she was convinced the knowledge would be hers to use, but instead, she is now a prisoner, trapped within the realm of spirits."

"How can we be sure?" asked Rugg.

"I can journey to the spirit realm," said Shaluhk. "If Voruhn is trapped there, I can find her."

"Then you can bring her back?"

"No, to do that I would have to battle Khurlig."

"I have a plan," interrupted Kargen.

"Go on," urged Gahruhl.

"Your tribe will come for me. When they do, I will challenge Zahruhl to trial by combat. You will have to back my claim, Rugg, or else Shaluhk and I will find ourselves at the mercy of the elements once more."

"I will do as you ask."

"By tradition, the fight will be in several days. It is important that this is enforced, for I must have time to recover. Zahruhl is a great warrior, and I can not defeat him as I am now."

"You can not kill my brother," said Gahruhl.

"Nor do I wish to, for my fight with him is only a diversion."

"For what?" said Rugg.

In answer, Kargen turned to Shaluhk.

She smiled. "While the fight is underway, everyone's attention will be on the combat. I shall use the opportunity to attack the spirit of Khurlig."

"She is powerful," warned Kargen. "Are you sure you are up to it?"

"It will take a lot of attention to control Zahruhl, particularly if he is fighting. She will be weakened."

"Assuming this Khurlig is indeed the cause of the problem," said Rugg.

"We shall know soon enough," said Shaluhk, "for I can consult the Ancestors once I have regained my strength. They will know if Khurlig still treads the spirit realm."

"How is it," said Urumar, "you are untouched by your ordeal when your bondmate is so weakened?"

"You forget," said Shaluhk, "I am a shamaness. I placed myself into a healing trance."

"I did not know you could do that?" said Kargen.

"Nor did I until the need was there."

A yell outside drew their attention.

"It appears your absence has been discovered," said Rugg. "It is time to put your plan into operation."

They waited patiently, the shouts growing louder as more took up the call. Rugg moved to the door, throwing aside the flap of leather to peer outside. "They are over here," he called out.

Hunters came rushing, pushing their way into the small hut, their spears unusable in the close confines.

"I challenge Zahruhl to trial by combat," said Kargen, his voice booming.

"You are under arrest," said a guard.

"It is his right," said Rugg.

"He is not of this tribe," came the protest.

"True, but he is a chieftain, and all chieftains are considered family."

"He is correct," said Gahruhl, "and as my brother is fond of saying, 'It is not our place to determine their fate. Rather it is that of our Ancestors.' Tell Zahruhl the Ancestors will judge them all in three days."

"Are you nervous?" asked Shaluhk.

"Yes," admitted Kargen, "but if you tell anyone else, I shall deny it."

"You are a mighty hunter."

"As is he, and he is significantly larger than I am. I also have to prolong the fight to give you time to deal with Khurlig."

"You will win."

"Will I? You seem so confident."

"I know what we do is best for the tribe."

"You are the one facing the unknown," said Kargen. "How can you be so calm?"

"I merely look calm, but inside I am as nervous as you."

"Then let us sit awhile in calm contemplation. It will steady us both."

"I can not, for I still have to contact the Ancestors. There is yet the chance it is not Khurlig we face."

"Very well. I shall stand watch as you cast if it does not disturb you."

"You could never disturb me," she replied, "and your presence is most welcome." She closed her eyes, taking a deep breath and letting it out slowly.

Kargen watched her begin her incantation, the words of magic flowing from her lips effortlessly. Moments later, she opened her eyes, seemingly taking in the room around her.

It was clear from his point of view she could see someone with them, and he wondered who. She muttered a word of greeting and then cast again, this time at Kargen. He sat still, feeling a slight tingling, and then a ghostly shape took form before his eyes.

"Artoch!" he called out.

"It is I," the old spirit replied. "As I was in life, so I am in death. Tell me, my old friend, does the tribe prosper?"

"In a manner," said Kargen, "but it is Shaluhk who must explain."

The spirit turned to Shaluhk, a smile on his face. "Speak, Shaluhk, for I would hear your words."

"We are in the village of Khasrahk," she said. "Prisoners of their chieftain, Zahruhl."

"Prisoners?" said Artoch. "How can this be? The Orcs of the Stone Crusher Tribe should be friendly."

"We believe," explained Shaluhk, "that their shaman may be possessed by the spirit of Khurlig."

Artoch nodded his head. "She has sought long and hard to return to the realm of the living. Who does she occupy?"

"Voruhn, Shamaness of the Stone Crushers."

"This is terrible news," said Artoch, "for Khurlig is said to have mastered life and death before she passed into the spirit realm."

"If she mastered death, how did she die?" asked Kargen.

"She could bring back the dead, but passed before she could impart the skill to another."

"That is against the most solemn vows of a shaman," said Shaluhk.

"So it is, but Khurlig was driven by a lust for power that could not be satiated. In the end, it was her undoing."

"How did she die?" asked Kargen.

"She was caught attempting to raise an army of the dead."

"But all shamans can call upon the spirits, can they not?"

"This is different," said Artoch. "You can learn to call forth spirit warriors for a short duration, but what she did was Blood Magic, conjuring the dead and binding them to her will for all eternity."

"Do you think she would attempt such a thing here?"

"I am sure of it," said Artoch. "Such magic is powerful, and the dead are fearless."

"How can we defeat her?" asked Shaluhk.

"It will not be easy. You must fight her in spirit form."

"But she occupies the body of Voruhn. How do I compel her to enter the spirit realm?"

"I can not say," said Artoch, "for I am a master of flame, not a master of spirits."

"That is little help," pondered Kargen.

"You can do it, Shaluhk," Artoch assured her. "You have faced her once and come out on top. You can do so again."

"But it was Uhdrig who saved me," she replied, "and it cost her her life. Am I now to sacrifice mine?"

"I do not know," said Artoch, "but the answer lies within you. Dig deep, Shaluhk, and know that we watch over you."

The room fell silent as Artoch began to fade. Shaluhk wanted to ask more, but by the time she had sorted out her questions, it was too late; he had gone.

"That was less helpful than I would have wished," she said.

"At least we know for sure it is Khurlig who is to blame."

"Am I to be forever plagued by her spirit?"

"It is not your fault," said Kargen. "She has been searching for an opportunity to return, and Voruhn provided that."

"Yes, but why, out of all the Orc tribes, did it have to be the one we need
help from?"

"She occupied your body once. Maybe she is drawn to you somehow?"

"I know so little of such things."

"Do you think Laghul could offer more insight?"

"Perhaps," said Shaluhk, "but she is not here, and I must soon face
Khurlig. What shall I do?"

"You must follow the advice of Master Artoch. Look inside yourself, and
find the answer you seek."

"How? I need something that can affect her while in spirit form."

"What would happen if Voruhn were to die?"

"I assume Khurlig would return to the spirit realm."

"Are spirits weak when first they die?" asked Kargen.

"Yes, it takes time for them to coalesce."

"Coalesce?"

"It is the name we give to the forming of their spirits. When someone
dies, their spirit lingers awhile in the physical world. Over time, their physical image begins to fade as their spirit strengthens."

"And this happens whenever someone dies?"

"It does, though sometimes a spirit will linger for a much longer time as
if trapped between worlds."

"A true ghost," said Kargen.

"So I am told, but I have not experienced it for myself."

"Does a shaman coalesce faster?"

"Magical ability has no effect on such a thing," said Shaluhk.
"Why?"

"It occurs to me that Khurlig is a powerful shamaness. She will want to
retain her power, would you not say?"

"I would agree with your statement."

"She is currently within the body of Voruhn. I am guessing if her physical body dies, it would be like dying all over again."

"How does that help us? We are trying to keep Voruhn alive."

"True, but Khurlig does not know that. If we can convince her that her
host is dying, I think she will abandon the body. She will think it better to
be strong in the spirit realm, rather than weak from death."

"I see your reasoning, but that still does not help me. I can not see how to convince Khurlig that Voruhn is dying."

"A spell?"

"She is more experienced in magic than I," said Shaluhk. "She would be able to counter whatever I threw at her."

"Then magic is not the answer."

"I am not sure what you mean."

"Think like a hunter, rather than a shaman, Shaluhk. If I were faced with such a foe, how would I deal with it?"

"You would kill Voruhn," she replied. "But is that not what we are trying to avoid?"

"When I was badly burned, you brought me back from the brink of death. Had it not been for your healing, I would not be standing here today. You can bring people back from the edge of the abyss. You have done so before."

"That is a dangerous game," said Shaluhk. "Placing someone near death without actually killing them would be very difficult."

"I imagine it would," said Kargen, "but I think we are looking at this all wrong."

"In what way?"

"What do we know?"

"We know Khurlig is within Voruhn's body and that Voruhn is trapped in the spirit realm."

"And what does Khurlig know?"

"Presumably anything Voruhn does," said Shaluhk.

"Which means she is unaware we know her true nature. Would you not agree?"

"I would. That gives us the element of surprise."

"We also suspect her attention will be split. She will still have to keep control over Zahruhl during the fight."

"Yes."

"Maybe it is not what we do that counts; rather it is what she thinks we do."

Shaluhk smiled. "Are you suggesting a ruse?"

"You are the expert when it comes to plants. Can we convince her she has been poisoned?"

"Difficult. She is much more experienced than I in such things."

"Then we need to mimic the behaviour of a poison."

"And how do you propose we do that?"

"I have no idea," said Kargen, "but perhaps Rugg does."

"Rugg? What would he know of such things?"

"He is a master of earth, remember? The world of the forest is his domain. Is nature not full of such things?"

"Would that not be seen as interference? There are strict rules concerning trial by combat."

"I am sure Zahruhl, once freed of his domination, would be more than willing to forgive our actions."

"And if he does not?"

"Then we are banished from the Stone Crushers. So you see, we have nothing to lose."

"You forget, bondmate, there is a very real possibility he might kill you. Then where would we be?"

Kargen thought it through. "If I am to die, then I will linger in the physical world until you are ready to join me."

"That is not your decision to make," she replied.

"In that case, I shall do my best not to die."

BAIT

Autumn 1104 SR

Athgar watched as Nikolai entered a run-down building, circular in shape, with a grand entrance supported by two immense wooden pillars. At first, he took it for a house, but the longer he stared, the more he thought otherwise.

"What do you make of that?" he asked.

"It's an old theatre," Natalia replied.

"Surely not! It's round."

"That used to be a popular design, with a central stage and benches arranged in a circle."

"The Majestic back in Caerhaven wasn't like that," he retorted.

"Circular buildings are more common in the north. Even Karslev had such things. They are referred to as theatres in the round and are said to provide a more immersive experience."

She was met with a blank stare.

"That means it feels more like you're truly there," she explained.

"But you are there, aren't you? Watching the play, I mean."

She laughed. "No, what I meant to say is it makes you feel like you're part of what's happening onstage."

"Does it?" Athgar asked. "Make you feel that way, I mean?"

"I must confess I don't know. I've never actually made it to one, but I heard they were quite popular amongst the graduates of the Volstrum."

"So why has Nikolai come here?"

"I'm not sure," Natalia replied. "There must be something about the place that suits his purpose."

"Could it be because the place is abandoned?"

"Abandoned? Why would you say that?"

"Look at the entrance," said Athgar. "The paint on those pillars is flaking, while the wood beneath is cracking, indicating it's been exposed to the elements for some time. It's also the middle of the afternoon. Wouldn't the place be open for rehearsals if someone were using it?"

"You're very observant. I didn't notice any of that."

He shrugged. "It's all part of being a hunter, I suppose. But the real issue, in this case, is still why Nikolai came here, of all places?"

"Do you think he came to meet someone?" said Natalia.

"Possibly, but who? If he's working for the family, the father general's place would have been more convenient."

"That's a good point. We need to get closer, and see what we can discover."

"What are we likely to see inside? You mentioned a circular stage. Anything else?"

"Yes," she said, warming to the task. "Usually there's an outer ring forming a hallway, with doors leading into the central area. It allows patrons to get to their seats more efficiently."

"They have enough customers that they have to worry about such things?"

"Oh yes, a theatre like this can hold far more than the conventional design. Of course the downside is it's much harder to fill. That's likely the reason this place went out of business."

Natalia moved closer, pausing across the street and making it look like she was interested in a nearby shop. Athgar glanced up and down the street, noting the lack of any real traffic. He wandered up beside her, taking his time while trying to draw as little attention to himself as possible.

"It definitely looks deserted," she said, glancing over her shoulder. "How do you want to proceed?"

"We can't just go in the front door; it would draw too much attention. I suggest we work our way around back."

"Good idea," agreed Natalia. "There appears to be an alleyway off to the right."

"Unusual, isn't it?" said Athgar.

"Why would you say that?"

"There are very few alleys in Ebenstadt, and yet there's one here?"

"You're overthinking things," she said. "It's a circular building. It's only logical that it should have a small alley to either side. After all, look at its neighbours; they're rectangular. How would they fit together without an alley?"

"I suppose that makes sense." He glanced up and down the street once more, but no one appeared to be paying them any mind. "I'll go first."

Athgar crossed the street, taking his time as he wandered over to the building next door, a bootmaker by the looks of it. Lingering by its entrance, he once more cast a glance at the theatre, wondering if this could be a trap. He shook off the thought. They had been careful while following this Nikolai fellow. He was confident they had remained hidden.

Moving to the alleyway in the shadow of the building, his hand rested tentatively on his axe. Once he was sure the alleyway was clear, he waved Natalia over.

She took the same path, lingering for a moment by the storefront before disappearing into the alley, halting by his side at the narrowest part of the gap.

"Any sign of a way in?" Natalia asked.

"There's a window over here." Athgar moved towards a warped shutter, then grasped it, giving it a tug. "This looks loose," he said as it fell into his hands, and he now stared into the space beyond. "It seems we have a way in."

Poking his head inside, he looked left and right. "You were right about the design. There's a circular corridor running to either side."

"And ahead?"

"A series of doors set at regular intervals."

"That's what we're looking for."

Athgar pulled the other shutter from its hinges, then climbed in, keeping an eye out for trouble.

"It's clear, so far," he whispered.

Natalia began climbing in, and he lent her a hand. Off in the distance somewhere, he heard the sound of feet as if someone were walking on a wooden floor. He motioned Natalia over and made his way to the nearest door, pressing his ear to the wood.

"I hear something," he whispered.

"Talking?"

"No, pacing."

"Open it, and let's see what's inside."

Athgar yanked on the door a couple times to open it, until it finally swung towards them, revealing a darkened room beyond. Letting his eyes adjust, he then poked his head through. The chamber beyond was quite large, with benches arranged around a circular stage lit by a single lantern. He moved into the room, treading as quietly as he could.

Natalia followed, closing the door quietly behind her. "I don't hear anything," she whispered.

"Nor do I. Let's hope whoever it was has left."

Her eyes were drawn to the lantern, which illuminated a lump on the stage. "What's that?"

"Let's go find out, shall we?"

They moved towards their target, taking care to avoid bumping into the benches. As they drew nearer, the lump soon took shape as a person. Now that they were up close, they could make out chains. It appeared that someone had manacled some poor fellow to the floor, the ends tied off to a ring of metal sunk into the base of the stage.

They strained to hear any sound that might indicate danger. Finally, assured they were alone, they mounted the stage, climbing over its edge to view the body curled up and turned away from them. Its face was hidden from view, but there could be little doubt it was a man. Something about his clothing caught Natalia's breath.

"No!" she shouted. "It can't be!" She rushed forward, heedless of the noise she made.

"Who is it?" Athgar called out.

In answer, she turned the man onto his back, shock on her face.

"It's Stanislav!"

"How can that be? You left him in Karslev, didn't you?"

The doors burst open, flooding the room with lantern light. Athgar could make out numerous men, the glint of steel off their swords quite evident. Their leader soon emerged from the shadows, the same man they had followed.

"At last," he said. "You have no idea how long I've waited for this moment, Natalia Stormwind."

Natalia stood, turning to face this new foe. "Nikolai. I knew it was you."

He smiled. "It's been so long since we last met. My, how you've grown."

"I don't understand," said Athgar.

"How unforgivably rude of me. Allow me to introduce myself. My name is Nikolai Ratislav. I'm a mage hunter, though I must admit I'm here today in a completely different capacity."

"What do you want?"

"It's quite simple, really. There's a bounty on young Natalia's head, and I aim to collect it."

"You won't take us alive," said Natalia.

He shook his head. "I'm afraid you mistake my meaning. I'm not here to capture you, I'm here to kill you!"

He stepped closer, and Athgar raised his hands, ready to cast. "I warn you, we're both mages. We shall not hesitate to fight back."

"Of course," said Nikolai, "I would expect no less."

He turned to his men. "Kill them!"

Athgar noticed movement to his left. Turning quickly, he thrust out his hands and sent a streak of fire across the room.

Natalia raised her hands as well, seeking out a target. She spied a small knot of men advancing towards her and called forth her power, but instead of unleashing her magic, she felt an icy chill in her stomach. Doubling over in pain, she collapsed to the stage floor.

Athgar's flame lit the room for a moment, revealing dozens of men rushing towards him. He abandoned his magic, seeking his axe even as his eyes searched for Natalia. Her plight gave him cause for alarm, delaying his actions just long enough for the point of a sword to prick his left arm. He swore, twisting aside as his foe followed through with the attack, and then his axe came down, hacking into his enemy's shoulder. The man's blade flew from his grip, scattering across the room.

"Save yourself," shouted Natalia through gritted teeth. She tried to concentrate on her magic, but pain lanced through her again. A sword suddenly appeared in front of her eyes, and she looked up to see it held steady by the sure hand of Nikolai.

A pair of crossbow bolts whizzed past Athgar, one narrowly missing his head. He pointed again, loosing off more fire, banishing the darkness if only for an instant. Someone screamed in agony and fell to the floor in flames.

Athgar moved towards Natalia, but Nikolai was there, his sword held to her throat.

"I wouldn't if I were you," the mage hunter taunted.

Athgar was wracked with indecision, for as he took a step towards Natalia, the tip of Nikolai's sword pricked flesh, and blood appeared.

"Give me any more trouble," said Nikolai, "and I'll make sure she suffers a painful death."

"Please, Athgar," called out Natalia, "if you stay, you'll surely die. I couldn't bear that."

"Listen to her," added Nikolai. "She knows you cannot defeat me."

Another bolt shot forth, scraping along Athgar's thigh. He winced at the pain, feeling blood flow, but fought back, picking out a lantern someone had placed on the floor. He concentrated, once more calling on his inner spark. Thick black smoke began billowing from the light source, quickly filling the room.

He staggered forward, seeking Natalia, only to be blocked by three men. His axe descended on one, but then others called out, and suddenly bolts were flying once more. One whizzed past his ear, and he tried to dive to the side in desperation, but his foot slipped on some blood, and his leg shot out from under him, driving him to his knees with a resounding thud. Another bolt sang out, whistling over his head in the smoke. Now the enemy was firing blindly, desperate to take down the Therengian.

Athgar, his lungs burning as he fought for breath, cast about, no longer sure of his bearings. Feeling a slight breeze, likely an open door, he made for it, his eyes stinging, his breath now coming in ragged gasps. Staggering into the hallway, he was desperate to breathe, while behind him came the sound of coughing and yet more crossbows firing off their bolts.

Fresh men appeared down the hallway, crossbows in hand, their eyes squinting against the smoke. Something hit his boot, and he dove through a window to his left, desperate to be free of the danger.

He could hear yelling now, coming from within the theatre. Doors opened, and men flooded out into the street. By Athgar's reckoning, there were close to a dozen of them, far more than he could fight by himself. He cursed his feeling of helplessness and then turned, fleeing down the alleyway.

Nikolai stared down at Natalia, a cloth held over his face. Finally, the yelling subsided, and the smoke began to dissipate.

"Well, well," he said. "What have we here? The mighty Natalia Stormwind, helpless and weak. This is an unexpected delight."

Natalia clutched her stomach and stared up at him, an icy fury on her face.

Nikolai knelt, looking her in the eyes. He waved a hand, and three crossbowmen moved closer, their bolts ready to let loose. He smiled. "Now, let's kill you and get this over with, shall we?"

"What will you do with Stanislav?" she asked.

"I must admit to some unfinished business in that regard. Don't worry, though, I shan't kill him. Not yet, at least."

Nikolai stood, looking on with interest as Natalia tried to stare down the crossbowmen. He raised his hand, ready to signal that they should fire.

"No, wait," said Natalia. "You can't."

"Of course I can," he replied. "You have a big bounty on your head, Natalia. It's nothing personal." He paused a moment. "No, that's not right. It IS personal. Tell me, do you still remember freezing my arm?"

"You were trying to kill me," she responded.

"Not true. It was Stanislav I was trying to kill. You were merely in the way. If truth be told, I wanted you alive. How better for me to retrieve your bounty?"

"And now?"

"Now, I shall take your head and deliver it to the Volstrum. I hear there's a nice prize for proof of your death. Do you have any final words for your former mistresses?"

"No," she spat out.

"Then let's proceed, shall we?"

"No, wait, I'm carrying a child."

"You're lying," said Nikolai. "You'll say anything to stay alive."

"No, it's true. I swear it."

Nikolai lowered his hand. "A child, eh?"

"Yes," she said. "The child of a powerful caster. Worth a hefty reward, I should warrant."

"You have me intrigued at the possibility. The bounty on you was the largest ever issued for an initiate. I wonder what they'd make of you now, crawling on the ground and begging for your life?"

"Do we kill her, my lord?" asked one of the crossbowmen.

"No," replied Nikolai. "If what she says is true, her child will be worth a fortune. Let's take her back to our hideout. We shouldn't wait around here for her barbarian friend to return."

He reached into his sleeve, pulling forth a small vial of liquid. "I wasn't sure if I'd need this, but I see now it has some use." He unstoppered the vial. "Don't worry, I'm not poisoning you. I had this specially prepared, just in case. It's magebane, and a strong dose at that. I've been warned how resistant you are to its effects."

He moved closer, forcing her mouth open and pouring the contents down her throat. "Make sure you swallow it all," he warned.

Natalia felt the liquid as it made its way through her body. She couldn't help but think of the irony, for she couldn't cast a spell even if she had wanted to.

Nikolai drew his sword, and for a moment, she wondered if he had changed his mind. That notion was soon put to rest as he brought the hilt of it down on her head, sending her into darkness.

Athgar stumbled down the street, his mind in turmoil. No matter what might happen to him, he couldn't leave Natalia to face Nikolai alone. Turning around, he was determined to return to the theatre, but then his leg nearly gave out beneath him. He looked down to see blood soaking his thigh. Cursing his luck, he fell to the ground, examining his injury as best he could. He tore off a sleeve, bundling up the material, and held it against the wound.

Looking around, he tried to get his bearings, but when he saw the trail of blood he was leaving, his heart turned cold. He must either find somewhere close to hide or do something before they discovered him. He looked down at the blood-soaked rag and winced, for he knew he could run no more.

Closing his eyes, he took a deep breath as he held the rag in place with his left hand and raised his right, calling forth words of power. A small green flame leaped to life in his palm, and he stared at it a moment, contemplating his next move. He took one more deep breath, then acted. Removing the rag, he placed his right hand on the wound and immediately felt an intense burning as the magical flame took hold. The smell of searing flesh was overwhelming.

It was all over in a moment, and then the world spun. Athgar fought to keep his wits about him, but there was little he could do as darkness claimed him.

Athgar awoke with a start. He saw the moon peering out from behind the clouds, lighting the street with an eerie glow. He had fled the theatre in a mad dash; now he needed to get his bearings. The streets of Ebenstadt were difficult to navigate at the best of times, but now, given his present circumstances, he was utterly lost.

He took a breath and pushed himself to his feet, staggering from the pain of it. In the wilderness, he could have oriented himself using the stars, but here, the buildings hampered that task, making it all but impossible.

Athgar took a step, testing his legs. They were weak but functional, allowing him to make his way farther along the street. He reached a crossroads and found himself looking up towards a familiar sight: The Wolf of Adenburg. Perhaps the Gods were looking out for him after all? Gritting his teeth, he forced himself onwards.

As the inn drew closer, sounds of merriment drifted out into the street. Finally reaching the door, Athgar pushed it open to be met with a wave of warm air. Staggering through, he sought somewhere to sit in the crowded room but found no open seat. Slowly he moved forward, using the wall to steady himself, intent on making his way upstairs to his room.

He was ready to ascend, lifting his foot for the first step when a sudden rush of pain coursed through his leg. Looking down, he was dismayed to see blood flowing freely once more, his wound reopened. In his haste to cauterize the injury, he had obviously failed to ensure the entire gash was sealed. His leg, now refusing to hold his weight, crumpled beneath him, and he fell heavily to the floor, eliciting a groan of pain.

A voice called out from behind him. The next thing Athgar knew, people were crowding around him, faces peering down at his leg in fascination. He was quickly helped to his feet while someone produced a chair, and he dropped into the seat, his head spinning.

"Are you all right?" he was asked.

Athgar grasped an arm. "The Hungry Fox, do you know it?"

"Aye," the man replied.

"Go there," said Athgar. "I beg of you. Find a man called Sir Raynald and bring him here."

The man ran off, though whether he heeded Athgar's words was anybody's guess. Someone placed a tankard before the Therengian, and he gulped it down, eager to dull the pain. He heard a call out for a healer, but he found it difficult to concentrate.

Athgar tried to focus on the pain, desperate to remain conscious. When people began to drift back to their own business, he tilted his head back, taking deep breaths while trying to think things through. Closing his eyes, he concentrated on his breathing, but then his leg started to throb. After what felt like forever, a familiar face loomed over him.

"Athgar? Are you all right? It's me, Brother Rickard. Can you hear me?"

Athgar tried to speak, but the words came out mumbled. Lowering his head, he felt the room spin, and then his head fell to his chest, and all was darkness.

THE DUEL

Autumn 1104 SR

(In the tongue of the Orcs)

K argen hefted the shield, testing its weight.

"Are you sure about this?" asked Shaluhk. "You do not normally fight with a shield."

"True, but Athgar gave me some tips before he left Ord-Kurgad."

"And you think that will be enough?"

"The Stone Crushers do not use shields these days. Rugg had to search high and low to find an elder who had one."

"I fail to see the advantage of using it," said Shaluhk.

Kargen grinned. "Zahruhl has never faced one in combat. He will be hard-pressed to adapt, and that will work to my advantage."

"Will it allow you to defeat him?"

"I am not fighting to win, remember? I must keep him occupied while you deal with Voruhn." He moved closer, reaching out to touch her face. "And what of you? Are you prepared?"

"I am," she replied, fingering the handle of her knife. "Though whether it will be enough, I can not say."

Kargen held out his hand. "Then come. Let us face this together."

She took his hand, and they stepped from the hut. The village was empty save for a few tending to fires. Most were outside the gates of Khasrahk, waiting for the duel to begin.

They walked in silence, stepping through the village gates to see the assembled crowd sitting around the circle. Kargen's mind wandered, remembering Athgar's brush with death at the hands of Gorlag. It, too, had been a duel. A duel that had ended in Gorlag's banishment and Kargen's own elevation to chieftain. The Ancestors had smiled on the Therengian that day. Would they now favour the Chieftain of the Red Hand?

As they drew nearer the circle, fists began thumping the ground. Kargen smiled, for it appeared Zahruhl was not the only one with support this day. He gave Shaluhk's hand a final squeeze, then released it and drew his axe, stepping towards the circle. The crowd parted to make way.

When Athgar had fought, the ring had been marked using ash, as was the custom for a tribe that venerated the magic of fire. Here, the circle was marked by small grey stones, most likely the product of a master of earth.

Zahruhl waited on the other edge of the circle, Voruhn by his side. For a brief moment, Kargen wished Shaluhk was with him to give him strength, but in his heart, he knew she had a far more important task. When Voruhn moved to the centre of the circle, the villagers fell silent.

"In accordance with our ancient customs," she began, "we are gathered here today to witness the judgement of our Ancestors." She pointed at Zahruhl. "On one side, we have the mighty Zahruhl, Chieftain of the Stone Crushers." She paused, letting the thumping subside, then pointed to Kargen. "On the other side stands Kargen, Chieftain of the Red Hand, who has challenged our chieftain's right to rule." Again the thumping, though this time more subdued.

"The rules are simple: combat will continue until one warrior submits, dies, or is driven from the ring." Voruhn paused, letting the words sink in. "Are all in agreement?" She looked at each combatant in turn, noting their nods. "Then let the battle commence!"

She walked from the circle, taking up a position at its edge. As she did so, the crowd stood, ready to back away should the fight come their way.

Kargen moved into the circle, swinging his axe left and right to loosen his muscles, his shield still held low. On the opposite side, Zahruhl held out his hand, and someone handed him his chosen weapon, a massive two-handed axe. It was a terrifying weapon, capable of splitting an Orc in two. Kargen had no doubt his opponent was skilled in its use.

The Chieftain of the Stone Crushers stepped into the ring, his axe held ready for a strike. They began the contest by circling, each taking the measure of the other.

Kargen raised his shield, wary of a sudden rush. His caution was well rewarded, for Zahruhl suddenly darted forward, bellowing as he ran, his axe crashing down towards his opponent. Kargen jumped back, and the great axe bit into the ground with a loud thump, knocking loose a sizable chunk of dirt which flew into the air.

Zahruhl recovered quickly and pressed forward, catching Kargen by surprise. A two-handed axe was slow to wield, yet Zahruhl handled it as though it were a much lighter weapon. Swinging it from the left, he guided the head around in a wide arc towards his enemy.

Kargen threw up his shield at the last moment, a manoeuvre that undoubtedly saved his life as splinters of wood flaked off the rim of the shield when the axe smashed against it. Zahruhl backed up, smiling despite his lack of progress.

"You will not last long, Kargen," he taunted. "And then your bones will bleach in the sun."

Kargen launched a flurry of blows, driving his opponent back. The Stone Crusher soon recovered, planting his feet and using his own weapon to fend off the attack. The effort left them both panting as they separated. Once more, they began circling each other, their eyes locked.

"Impressive," continued Zahruhl. "I must give you credit for your speed, but it will not be enough to save you."

"You talk far too much, Zahruhl. You should save your strength for fighting." As Kargen finished his words, he leaped forward, striking out with his axe. In answer, his foe used the neck of his great axe to block the attack. Kargen's axe dug into the wood, but only a small divot gave any evidence of his success.

The Stone Crusher Chieftain feinted to the left, then shifted his weight as if about to strike. Kargen raised his shield in defence, but at the last moment, Zahruhl jumped to the right, bringing his axe down at an impossible angle to strike the inside of Kargen's shield, narrowly missing his hand. The force of the impact sent a shudder up his arm, driving him backwards.

Kargen saw the opportunity to strike a deathblow, for his opponent had left himself exposed. He was about to swing but then hesitated, remembering his mission.

Shaluhk forced herself to look away. It would do no good for her to watch the fight, for its very success would depend on her own actions this day.

Looking around, she could tell the villagers were all entranced by the battle unfolding before them.

She stepped back from the crowd, raising her hands in preparation. Words of power dripped from her lips, and she felt the familiar release of magic as the spell was completed, revealing the spirit realm to her eyes.

The shamaness glanced around, seeing those watching the combat in muted tones. Unlike travelling to the spirit realm, this spell allowed her to see the ghostlike presence of those who wandered the mortal realm. She moved back amongst the villagers, making her way around the edge of the circle.

There was a sudden gasp, and then she was jostled as the crowd shifted, caught up in the excitement of the spectacle before them. Closer she drew to her goal, pausing only when her target finally came into view.

Voruhn stood watching the fight, but her features blurred, and Shaluhk struggled to focus her eyes. There could be no doubt that the spirit of Khurlig controlled the shamaness, for when she shifted feet, there was a blurring motion. A momentary delay as the possessing spirit caught up with the physical motion of its host.

Shaluhk steeled herself, moving in to strike.

Kargen shifted to this right, watching his foe's response, then he rushed forward in a crouch, his shield held high. Zahruhl's axe came down, deflecting off the centre of the wooden construct and digging into the ground. The manoeuvre threw him off balance, allowing Kargen to strike, driving his own axe into the Stone Crusher's boot, narrowly missing flesh.

Zahruhl regained his balance quickly, shouldering into his opponent and knocking him to the ground. He loomed over his target, raising his axe for the killing blow.

In answer, Kargen pushed forward with the edge of his shield, directly into his foe's stomach, driving the air from his lungs. Zahruhl staggered back, fighting for breath. Kargen rolled to the side, coming to his feet, his axe ready to strike again.

The attention of the villagers was riveted on the battle, but Shaluhk forced herself to ignore what her bondmate was doing. When she was within three paces of her target, she slowly drew her knife, sliding it from her belt carefully to avoid the sickly blue liquid dripping from its blade.

Easing up behind Voruhn, Shaluhk reached down, slicing lightly across the back of the shamaness's calf. The cut was not deep, just enough to draw blood, but the black liquid that poured forth was stained with blue.

Voruhn turned with a start, her eyes seeking her attacker.

"I see you, Khurlig," announced Shaluhk.

In answer, Voruhn pulled a knife of her own. "What have you done?"

All around them, Orcs backed up, their focus on the battle interrupted by this new altercation.

Shaluhk smiled, holding her own blade before her, displaying the mix of black and blue that glistened on the blade. "See how you bleed, Khurlig?"

Voruhn looked at her wound, noting the discolouration. "Dragons-breath? Impossible. It does not grow in these parts!"

"True," said Shaluhk, "and yet it was quite common in Ord-Kurgad."

Voruhn's eyes widened. "You are a fool, Shaluhk. I can simply neutralize the toxins with a spell."

"Go ahead," replied Shaluhk. "For when you start to cast your spell, I shall drive a dagger through your heart. You have two choices, Khurlig. You can release your grip on Voruhn or die with her body, making your spirit that much weaker. Which shall it be?"

Voruhn backed up, cursing. All of a sudden, she shuddered, and then the ghostly form of Khurlig emerged, releasing her hold on the shamaness. The body of Voruhn dropped to the ground, motionless.

Now it was Shaluhk's turn to step back as words of power tumbled from her lips. Moments later, she heard a snap, and her own body fell to the ground. However, in the spirit realm, she advanced towards Khurlig, her hands already preparing for another spell.

The ancient Orc rushed forward, arms extended, ready to throttle the upstart shamaness, but it was too late; her spell had been cast. The ghostly image of a boar took shape and charged right at the Ancestor, tearing into her legs. Khurlig fell, cursing and swearing.

Hunters rushed to the two prone bodies, unaware of the battle raging between the two spirits.

Khurlig beat on the boar in frustration as the manifestation of her will began to fade. Desperate to hold on to what little of the physical realm she could, she thrust out her hands, calling forth words of power that had not been uttered for centuries.

Shaluhk felt her skin crawl, unaware of the reason. Moments later, two spectators fell to the dirt, strange twisted ghosts emerging from their bodies. They rushed towards the younger shamaness, striking out with clawed hands.

She had been a silent observer of the fight between Uhdrig and Khurlig back in Ord-Kurgad that had resulted in the death of her beloved mentor. Now the truth of the matter came rushing into Shaluhk's mind, overwhelming her with the ramifications. She was a shamaness, that was true, but her training was incomplete. How could she ever have thought to defeat such a foe?

A claw raked across her forearm. There was no blood, for they were both spirits, but the pain of the wound lanced up her arm, causing her to scream out in agony. She backed up, trying to put distance between herself and her attackers. Khurlig was still struggling with the spirit boar, the noise of the ancient one's encounter echoing around them.

Shaluhk's thoughts raced, desperate to find a solution as another claw struck out, cutting across her abdomen. She fought back against the pain, using the only weapons she had, her fists. Knuckles struck the strange creature in the face, and she unexpectedly felt the resistance of flesh.

The entire battle felt like a dream, almost as if this were happening to someone else. Her first opponent fell, but in her own desperate struggle for survival, she had forgotten the other one until she felt him leap onto her back and pain as teeth dug into her shoulder. Shaluhk twisted, throwing herself onto the ground to be rewarded with a grunt as her opponent let go of his grip upon her.

Casting her eyes around, she caught a glimpse of Khurlig. The ancient shamaness was back on her feet, the boar having dissipated into nothingness, but the fight had taken its toll.

Even as their eyes met, Khurlig began to fade. A final shriek escaped her lips, deafening to Shaluhk's ears, then Khurlig was no more, banished once again to wander the spirit realm. Her summoned ghosts vanished in an instant.

Kargen struck out with the head of his axe, thrusting it towards Zahruhl's eyes. The mighty Orc pulled his head back to avoid the blow and then stumbled, shaking his head. Kargen watched as his opponent's eyes went wide, taking in his surroundings.

"What is this?" asked Zahruhl. "What is going on here?"

Kargen lowered his weapon. "You have not been yourself, Mighty Chieftain. Forbidden magic was used to control you."

"I do not understand."

"Look to your left," said Kargen. "Even as we speak, Khurlig battles for control of Voruhn."

Zahruhl turned his gaze to see the bodies of Voruhn and Shaluhk lying motionless.

"What magic is this?" he demanded.

"It is an ancient spirit, one who, in life, was one of our most powerful shamans. Her lust for immortality led her to Voruhn. It is not the first time she has attempted such a thing."

The villagers had gathered around the two fallen Orcs, unaware of the cause.

"Voruhn!" called Zahruhl, rushing towards her.

Kargen followed, watching as Shaluhk rose, shaking her head, trying to reorient herself to the physical world. Everyone was shaken to the core as a distant scream echoed off the trees.

Kargen ran to Shaluhk, and they embraced. Zahruhl knelt down beside Voruhn, lifting her head and staring down into her face.

Her eyes fluttered open. "Zahruhl, is that you?"

"I am here," replied the chieftain. "Tell me what has happened."

"It is all my fault. I was too eager for power, too consumed by my quest for knowledge. I called on the Ancestors for help, and Khurlig answered my request."

Shaluhk released her bondmate, moving closer to kneel beside Voruhn. "You were not the only one to be swayed by her words," she said.

"Initially, she simply advised me, but it soon became clear I was not ready for such things. She offered me a solution, a way for me to find mastery in a short period of time."

"She wanted to inhabit your body," suggested Shaluhk.

Voruhn nodded. "Yes, at first it was just for a moment, but the more comfortable I became with it, the longer her spirit lingered. She convinced me that we could both inhabit one body, allowing us to combine her ancient power with my youth, but soon it became a prison for me." Tears ran down her face. "I had to watch, helpless, as she took control of you, Zahruhl. It broke my heart."

The great chieftain looked at Shaluhk. "And this Khurlig, is she gone now?"

"For the present. She has been sent back to wander in the Afterlife until the opportunity arises for her to again walk the spirit realm."

"I thought the Ancestors lived in the spirit realm?" said Kargen.

"That which we know as the spirit realm is a border between the living and the dead," replied Shaluhk. "Some spirits are strong enough that they can linger there, but others can only make the trip if they are summoned. There is always the risk Khurlig will attempt to return. We must be ever vigilant."

Voruhn winced, causing her to look down at her leg. The blood was still dripping, discoloured by the blue ichor.

"I am done," she said, "for I have been poisoned by dragonsbreath."

"No," said Shaluhk, "it is not dragonsbreath. Rather it is crushed blueseed."

"Blueseed?" said Zahruhl. "But that is an aphrodisiac, is it not?"

"It is."

"But you have placed it in her wounds?"

"I have indeed."

"What will be the effect of such a thing?"

Shaluhk simply smiled. "Well, you are bondmates, are you not?"

Zahruhl took a sip from the bowl before passing it to Kargen. "Tell me," said the Stone Crusher Chieftain, "why did you enter the spirit realm to do battle? Surely she could not harm you were you to remain amongst the living?"

"It was imperative I distract her," Shaluhk replied, "or else she might have caught onto my ruse."

"If she was so powerful, how did you defeat her?"

"I unleashed a spirit animal to drain her of her essence."

"Her essence?"

"Yes, just as the living have their limits, so, too, do spirits. We call it stamina, but it is a physical manifestation. In the world of spirits, we call it essence."

"You know so much," said Voruhn. "Uhdrig taught you well."

"Even so, there is much we, the living, do not know," replied Shaluhk.

"You have done our tribe a great service," said Zahruhl. "How can we ever repay you?"

"Stand with us," said Kargen, "and let us put our differences aside. Together, the three tribes can face anything the Humans send against us."

"Your words are wise," said Zahruhl, "and yet I know little of these Therengians of which you speak."

"They are a scattered people, much like our own race. Once, many generations ago, they were a powerful kingdom that ruled much of this Continent."

"What happened to them?" asked Voruhn.

"They were destroyed from within," said Kargen.

"As we nearly were," added Zahruhl. "It seems the Humans are not the only ones who must beware such things."

"Indeed," said Shaluhk. "There is much to learn from the fate of the Therengians."

Kargen passed the bowl to Shaluhk, who drank of the milk of life. The ritual complete, she handed it back to Voruhn, who carefully set it aside.

"How can we help?" asked Zahruhl.

"Your tribe is strong," said Kargen, "particularly in the realm of magic. Your master of earth can help us prepare for battle."

"We can do more than that," said Zahruhl, "for we can also provide the perfect place for battle."

"Tell me of this place," said Kargen.

"It is the ancient gateway we spoke of on your first visit."

"Would that not be dangerous? If we were to lose the battle, it would fall into the hands of our enemies."

"True," said Zahruhl, "and yet the benefit to our shamans would be substantial. Not only that, but the terrain can be used to our advantage."

"Is Kirak aware of its location?"

"He is," said Zahruhl, "for we have used it as a meeting place for many years."

Kargen thought for a moment before continuing. "Might I ask how many hunters can you field?"

"Two hundred, half of them archers."

"An impressive number."

"Will it be enough?" asked Voruhn.

"That largely depends on how many warriors the Humans send against us. I expect the army will be larger than the one that attacked Ord-Kurgad."

"What of these Therengians?" asked Zahruhl. "How many warriors can they provide?"

"I do not know," said Kargen, "but they have five villages, and they train their warriors regularly."

"Just how big are these villages of theirs?"

"I have only seen Runewald, but if it is any indication, I would say we could expect a few hundred at best."

"So there is the distinct possibility we may, in fact, outnumber our allies?"

"Quite possibly," said Kargen.

"And who will command?"

"Each chieftain will command their own people, but I would suggest we plan the battle under the eyes of Nat-Alia."

"The Human female?"

"Yes," said Shaluhk. "She is a battle mage, trained for such things. Her expertise could well make the difference between defeat and victory."

"And you would trust our people under her command?"

"I would," said Shaluhk. "She is my tribe-sister."

"What of this Therengian Fire Mage, Athgar?"

"He will command his people," said Kargen.

"And has he experience in such things?"

"He fought beside us at Ord-Kurgad."

"Yes, but from what you told me, that was a siege, not a battle. The fight we must face is a far different thing than any of us has seen in the past."

"The Ancestors favour him," added Shaluhk. "It was their words that sent him and Nat-Alia here."

"Then we must trust in their judgement," said Voruhn.

"My bondmate speaks with wisdom," said Zahruhl. "Very well, we shall make our preparations. When shall we march?"

"I can not say," said Kargen, "for we have yet to learn details of the enemy's plan. Do not fear, as soon as we hear, I shall send word. In the meantime, make your arrows, and sharpen your axes."

Zahruhl stood, reaching out to Kargen. In answer, the Chieftain of the Red Hand did likewise.

"We shall stand or fall together, Kargen of the Red Hand."

"You honour us, Zahruhl of the Stone Crushers. Now, we must be on our way. Kirak will be awaiting word."

PRISONER

Autumn 1104 SR

Natalia awoke to the sound of dripping water. Shifting, she felt the heavy chains that bound her ankles. Her head pounded from the effects of a high dose of magebane, and she wondered how long she had been unconscious.

Opening her eyes to complete darkness, her first instinct was to panic, but then her intellect took hold, calming her. She was still alive, and Nikolai was likely to keep her so for the potential reward. Taking a deep breath, she tried to stand, but the familiar ice in her stomach caused her to double over once more, the pain excruciating.

Natalia willed herself to relax, only to hear the rattle of chains. It appeared she was not alone! She thought back to her capture and suddenly remembered the body that had lain upon the stage.

"Stanislav?" she called out.

"I'm here," the old mage hunter called back. "Is that you, Natalia?"

She moved towards him, reaching the end of her chain. "I'm here."

He shuffled closer, then a moment later, she felt a hand on her arm. "I'm so sorry," he said. "Nikolai used me to capture you."

"How is it that you find yourself in Ebenstadt?" she asked.

"It's a long story," he replied.

"It appears we have a lot of time."

He sighed. "So be it. After your escape, I was taken to the dungeons beneath the Volstrum. There, I rotted until Illiana Stormwind showed up to visit me."

"Let me guess," said Natalia, "she wanted me dead."

"No," he said. "Quite the reverse. She wanted me to find you and keep you safe."

"Safe? From whom? She's the matriarch of the family, for Saint's sake."

"It is, in fact, the family that she fears. She's an old woman who wants only the best for her granddaughter."

Natalia sat in stunned silence, the words slowly sinking in. "Granddaughter? Are you sure?"

"She had a son, Antonov Sartellian, an extremely powerful Fire Mage that fell into disgrace after visiting the estate of Baron Rozinsky. Do you remember that name?"

"I can't say I do, why?"

"It was on his lands that I found your mother."

"But my mother wasn't a mage, was she?"

"Not as far as I could tell, but if what Illiana told me was true, then your father passed on his power through her."

"That makes no sense," said Natalia. "If that were the case, I would be a master of Fire Magic, not water."

Stanislav shrugged, though the action was hidden by the darkness. "I would have thought so, too, and yet your own awakening was anything but normal. Could he have had some kind of latent Water Magic?"

"That would be contrary to our teachings," she said. "Water and fire are opposites; they cannot exist in one person."

"That has always been the accepted theory," said Stanislav, "but the truth is, no one really knows. Your own family breeds fire and water. According to everything we think we know, that shouldn't work, and yet they've produced some of the most powerful casters on the Continent."

"This is overwhelming," said Natalia, "but it still doesn't explain how you came to be here, in Ebenstadt. Assuming that's where we still are, of course."

"I was told you were in the company of a Fire Mage, a man named Athgar. Illiana gave me access to the family's records. He had become a person of great interest to them after your escapades in Corassus. I thought that tracking him down would prove more successful than searching for you."

"And that brought you here?"

"Not at first," he confessed, "but once we realized he was a Therengian, this seemed like the logical place. Illiana came up with the idea. She thought it the best place for you to hide, amongst his people."

"Then the family knows about Runewald?"

"They've known for some time," said Stanislav, "though it was news to me."

Natalia felt a cold grip on her heart. "They organized the crusade!" she said. "Don't tell me they did that just to find me?"

"They didn't," he replied. "Only Illiana and I were privy to that information. The old woman knew all sorts of things she kept to herself."

"But aren't they here to conquer the Therengians?"

"I suspect so, but the truth is I simply don't know. What about you? I've heard of your fight in Corassus, but little more."

"Athgar and I fled north," she said, "to the Grey Spire Mountains, but fate had something else in store for us."

"Why? What happened?"

"There was a plot by the family to destroy a tribe of Orcs. Someone had discovered godstone in the area."

"And so you helped Orcs?" he asked. "Hardly a way to stay out of sight."

"They were friends of Athgar's. They took him in when his own village was destroyed. I'm surprised you didn't hear tell of it?"

"How long ago was this?"

"Last spring."

"Ah," he said, "that explains it. I was on the road by then. Tell me, this Athgar fellow, what's he like?"

"We met in Draybourne when he tried to save my life, while in response, I almost killed him. After nursing him back to health, we decided to travel together."

"That tells me how you met, but nothing of him as a person."

"He is the most caring person I've ever met," Natalia replied.

"You love him," stated Stanislav. "I can hear it in your voice."

"I do. There's a deep connection between the two of us. It's like nothing I've ever experienced before."

"That's natural when you're in love."

"No," she insisted, "it's more than merely a physical connection. When we fought at Ord-Kurgad, I used my magic to save his life. He had expended too much energy and was starting to immolate. I managed to quench that fire."

"I've never heard of such a thing."

"Nor I, and yet it happened. Kargen once told us we were even more powerful when we were together."

"Wise words," said the mage hunter. "Who's Kargen?"

"An Orc. The Chieftain of the Red Hand. It was his village that we defended."

"I doubt that garnered any sympathy from the family."

"Indeed not," said Natalia. "Nikolai even told me they wanted me dead."

"Dead? The last I heard, they wanted you alive. You must have really annoyed them to convince them otherwise. But tell me, if they wanted you dead, why did Nikolai not kill you?"

"I carry Athgar's child," she said.

Stanislav fell silent as he pondered the ramifications. "From what I've heard, Athgar is a reasonably skilled Fire Mage."

"He's more than that," she retorted. "He's disciplined, and that's what makes him dangerous to the family."

"Disciplined? In what way?"

"It was the Orcs who made him a master of flame. They taught him to control fire and use it sparingly."

"That doesn't sound like the Sartellian way," said Stanislav.

"It's not. Like the Stormwinds, they teach their students to let loose with everything they have. Control, to them, is something undesirable."

"And now you carry the child of a Fire Mage, the very thing they had planned for you."

"I didn't choose to fall in love with Athgar," she argued. "It just happened."

"I'm happy for you, but why don't you use your magic to escape your chains? If you froze them, wouldn't they shatter?"

"I wish I could, but my powers won't work. When Nikolai sprang his trap, I tried to cast, only to double over in pain. I'm scared, Stanislav. Scared that my child has been injured somehow. Then, on top of that, he dosed me with magebane. What will that do to an unborn child?"

"I have no idea what effect that might have," he said, "but it's not uncommon for a mage to lose her powers during pregnancy. It simply means the child has magical potential."

"How long does it last? Will it be over in time to escape?"

"I doubt it. Typically it takes a few weeks for the unborn child to acclimatize. The more powerful the child, the longer it takes."

"You're saying my child will have magic?"

"Don't be so surprised. It's why the Volstrum wanted to breed you, remember?"

"It's one thing to hear it, quite another to experience it first-hand. Does that mean it'll have Water Magic?"

"I would assume so, given your own power level, but I can't say for sure. Would you say Athgar is as powerful as you?"

"No, but I've seldom seen him use the full force of his magic."

"Your loss of magic is only temporary; I'm sure of it, but it does mean we can't rely on it coming back anytime soon. We'll have to come up with another way of escaping."

"We're chained in a dungeon," she said. "How can we even think of such things when we don't even know where we are?"

"It's not a dungeon," said Stanislav, "it's a cellar. When Nikolai brought me here, I managed to get a peek. We're under some sort of mansion."

Natalia's ears pricked up. "A mansion, you say? I think I know where we are."

"Go on," he prompted.

"During our stay in Ebenstadt, we learned that a Stormwind had infiltrated the Order of Saint Cunar. This is likely the house he uses as his headquarters."

"That's good to know should we reach the grounds, but we still have to get out of these chains."

"I'm afraid there's little I can do," said Natalia. "I can barely stand."

"Wait a moment," said Stanislav. "You said that Nikolai knows you're pregnant, yes?"

She nodded, then remembered they were still in darkness. "Yes, what of it?"

"I know a way we can use that to our advantage."

"Go on."

"The first thing we have to do is see how much leeway we have with these chains..."

Nikolai stared at the pale-blue gem set in the ornately crafted silver band. The metal that held the gem in place protruded to either side, giving it a curious shape.

"Something wrong, Boss?" asked Federov.

"It's this ring," the mage hunter replied. "It has an unusual shape."

Federov leaned forward to get a better view. "I've seen something like that before," he said, "though not quite as grand looking."

"And?"

"It's a key."

"A key?"

"Yes," said Federov, "at least I think it is. If I'm right, it'll unlock something."

"Like what, a padlock?"

"No. Likely something smaller, like a jewellery chest."

"How interesting," noted Nikolai. "It seems there's more to this Natalia than I had first thought." He held the ring before him, catching the light off of the gem. "This is blue magerite. Its colour denotes the power of the person wearing it. I'm told when Natalia wears it, it's almost black. That's an indication of very strong power, and yet she wasn't wearing it when I captured her."

"Where was it?"

"In a pouch, worn around her neck."

"Why do you think she kept it concealed?" asked Federov.

"To hide it, no doubt. She must have realized there were people about that might recognize it. That means she may be onto the family's plans in these parts. Still, it matters little now that we have her."

"Providing she didn't pass on word to an accomplice. And there's still that fellow of hers on the loose."

"We shall have him soon enough, then there will be an end to it all. They will both become a thing of the past, and we shall be able to live out our lives in splendour."

"How much do you think this child of hers is worth?"

Nikolai smiled. "Far more than Natalia was, unless I miss my guess."

"And the ring?"

"I think I shall hang on to that for a while. You never know what secrets it may unlock."

"We should toast our good fortune," suggested Federov.

"An excellent idea, my friend. Pour us some wine, and let us give thanks."

Federov rose, walked over to a collection of bottles, and searched through them, finally lifting one for his master's approval. Nikolai nodded in appreciation, and his aide returned to his seat, pulling the cork. He was about to pour the wine when a scream echoed up from below. They both rose, a look of horror on their faces, the ring now forgotten.

"The child!" shouted Nikolai.

They rushed out of the room, taking the wooden steps two at a time down into the cellar. At the bottom stood a door, behind which the prisoners were being held. Pressing his ear to the wood, Nikolai was desperate to hear what had transpired. To his horror, Natalia let out another scream.

"Something's wrong," shouted Federov.

Nikolai dug into his tunic, pulling forth a key that hung from a thin silver chain. Bending over, he inserted it into the lock and turned it, waiting for the telltale click, then straightened his back, looking at his companion.

"Be careful," he warned. "Natalia is highly resistant to magebane, so she might try to use a spell."

Pushing the door open, he let the light flood into the small cellar before entering. There, on the floor, Natalia lay writhing as groans escaped her lips. Nikolai quickly looked over at Stanislav, but the old fool was against the wall, well out of reach. Moving towards the woman, with Federov at his side, he knelt, placing his hand on her back, trying to steady her.

"What is it?" he said.

In answer, she let out a terrible wail that echoed off the walls. Nikolai backed up from the sheer ferocity of it, and suddenly a chain was around his neck, pulled tight by the firm hand of Stanislav. Nikolai reached for his dagger, but the chain tightened.

"Don't even think of it!" ordered Stanislav.

The wail abruptly ended, and then Natalia stood, brushing off her dress. Federov moved towards her, a dagger in hand.

"I wouldn't if I were you," suggested Stanislav. "One more step towards her, and I'll end your master's life."

Natalia moved over to Nikolai and began searching his clothes. Moments later, she pulled a key ring from his belt.

"You won't get away with this," warned Nikolai.

"We'll see about that," said Stanislav.

Natalia flipped through the keys, trying each one until she unlocked the chains on her legs, then moved cautiously around Stanislav, undoing his shackles as well. Moving back to Nikolai, she quickly retrieved his dagger and turned to his henchman.

"Toss over yours," she ordered.

Federov, fearing for his master's life, did as he was bid, watching helplessly as the mage picked it up.

"Into the corner," said Stanislav. "Quickly now."

The old mage hunter began moving towards the door, keeping his front to Nikolai's accomplice as he moved into the room. Natalia backed out, followed by Stanislav, who took only a moment to push Nikolai onto the floor before slamming the door shut. Natalia pulled forth the keys, but none was the right size for the door.

Stanislav cursed. "Leave it," he called out. "We have no time, we must flee while we can!"

They ran through the room, Natalia pausing as she saw her ring sitting on the table. Scooping it up, she held it firmly in her hand as they hurried on their way.

Athgar awoke to see a ceiling above, covered in peeling paint, and quickly realized he was lying in a bed.

A figure shifted to his right. "He's awake," said Sir Raynald.

Turning his head, Athgar tried to shield his eyes from the light streaming through the window. "What time is it?"

"Just past sun-up," said the knight. "Brother Rickard says you were in pretty bad shape when he got to you. What happened?"

"Where's Natalia?"

"We were hoping YOU could tell US," said Sir Raynald. "What happened? Last time I saw you was at the father general's place."

"Natalia saw someone from her past, a man named Nikolai. We followed him to an old theatre, but it was an ambush." His voice choked up. "I tried to save her, but there were too many of them."

Brother Rickard placed his hand on Athgar's arm. "I'm sure you did your best. It's remarkable you managed to escape, considering your wound."

"It was bleeding pretty badly," admitted Athgar. "I barely made it back."

"I have bound it," the Mathewite continued, "but you've lost a fair amount of blood. You shall have to rest for a few days."

"I can't," declared Athgar, sitting up suddenly. "I have to find Natalia!"

"I'll send some knights," said Sir Raynald, "but from your description, I doubt they'll find anything. Whoever sprang this ambush is likely long gone by now."

Athgar sank back down, a look of defeat on his face. "Then it's over. She's dead."

"Have faith," said Brother Rickard. "That may not be the case. Wouldn't they want her alive?"

"If you had asked me last summer," said Athgar, "I would have agreed, but I've become convinced they want her dead."

The room fell silent.

"She was a remarkable woman," said Sir Raynald. "Possibly the most intelligent person I've ever met."

"Hang on," said Athgar, "I just had a thought."

"Which is?"

"He could have killed her right away, but she fell prone. She's been having problems with her magic, you see, due to the child."

"The child?" said Brother Rickard.

"Yes, OUR child. I imagine the Volstrum would want to get their hands on it. I'm told they pay a hefty bounty for gifted individuals, and our child would be powerful, too, wouldn't it?"

"I'm afraid magic is far out of my area of expertise, but it certainly sounds reasonable."

"They would have ridden out of town by now," Athgar said, his face falling.

"Not likely," said Sir Raynald. "Every spare horse in the city has been taken by the Church. Even merchants have had to give up their mounts. They're all needed for the supply wagons."

"So they're still here, somewhere," said Athgar.

"You said you spotted him at the father general's?"

"We did. Oh, and the master of the Temple Knights is a Stormwind."

"A Stormwind? Impossible," said Brother Rickard. "It takes years to become a member of that august family, doesn't it? How could he then also be a Temple Knight? How did you come to this conclusion?"

"He wore a ring that identified him as such," said Athgar.

"Come now, how could you possibly know that?"

Athgar looked the Mathewite in the eyes. "Because my wife's real name is Natalia Stormwind. Let me explain..."

THE WOLF

Autumn 1104 SR

S tanislav peered across the street. "I see some movement in the window."

"That will be Athgar," said Natalia, relief in her voice. "He must have made it back to the room."

"There's always the possibility it's someone from the family. I'll go up there and check it out while you stay here. I'll come and get you if it's safe."

"He won't know you," she protested. "It should be me who goes."

"And risk capture a second time? No, it's better if I go. Your magic isn't working right now, remember?"

"Very well, but be careful."

"I will," he said, pausing for a moment. "Athgar doesn't know me. I'll need something to convince him I'm a friend, something only you would know."

"Ask him if he enjoys bathing," she said.

He scrunched up his face. "What will be his answer?"

"I doubt he'll have one, but he'll know it's from me."

Stanislav nodded. "Very well, now stay here and keep out of sight. I shouldn't be long."

He crossed the road, disappearing into the Wolf of Adenburg.

Athgar sat up, wincing as his leg twinged.

"You must stay still," warned Brother Rickard. "You're in no shape for exertions."

"I can't just sit here waiting," the Therengian replied. "It's killing me."

"You have little choice. If you were to set off after her now, you likely wouldn't reach the end of the block, and then where would you be?"

"He's right, you know," added Sir Raynald. "I've sent Sir Humphrey to the theatre to look things over, but until we hear back, there's little that can be done." He looked out the window, watching people below as they walked by the inn.

A soft knock drew their attention. Brother Rickard looked at Sir Raynald, and the knight nodded, moving to the door and pausing a moment. "Who is it?" he called out.

"A friend," came the reply. "I have a message for Athgar."

Raynald looked at the Therengian, who merely shrugged in response.

"I don't recognize the voice," said Athgar.

Sir Raynald drew a dagger, holding it behind his back as he opened the door. There stood an average-sized man, his dark brown hair liberally sprinkled with grey.

"Can I help you?" asked the knight.

Stanislav peered into the room, relaxing as he saw the brown cassock of Brother Rickard. "I'm looking for a man named Athgar," he said. "I bring news."

"Oh yes?" said Sir Raynald. "And how do I know you mean him no harm?"

"I am here at the behest of Natalia."

"She's been kidnapped," said the knight.

"No longer. We were able to escape."

Athgar sat up once more despite the pain. "Where is she?"

"Hold on a moment," warned Sir Raynald. "How do we know this isn't some sort of trap?"

"I carry a message from Natalia," said Stanislav. "It's for Athgar's ears."

"That's me," said Athgar.

Sir Raynald backed up, allowing the visitor entry.

Stanislav looked at the Therengian, noting his grey eyes and brown hair. "My name is Stanislav Voronsky," he said. "I believe you may have heard of me?"

"I have," said Athgar, "but how do I know you're really who you say?"

"State your message," interrupted Sir Raynald, "and be quick about it."

"Very well. Natalia told me to ask when was the last time you bathed?"

Sir Raynald's hand produced the dagger from behind his back, but

Athgar forestalled him. "It's all right. He's who he says he is." His gaze shifted back to Stanislav. "Where is she?"

"Very close," the mage hunter replied. "We saw movement through the windows, but I thought it best to investigate first. I can summon her if you wish."

"I'll get her," said Athgar, lifting the blanket from his legs.

"No," said Sir Raynald. "You are far too injured, my friend. Let me."

"Very well," said Athgar.

Sir Raynald put away his dagger, then disappeared into the hallway, closing the door behind him.

"So, tell me, Stanislav," said Athgar, "how is it you came to Ebenstadt?"

"I came here looking for Natalia."

"To what end?"

"To warn her. The forces of the family are being bent to her discovery."

"And how is it you knew you'd find us here?"

"I didn't," the old man confessed. "If truth be told, it was a bit of a gamble. Illiana Stormwind sent me here, but I thought it a fool's errand."

"And yet here we are."

"Indeed," said Stanislav. He shifted his gaze to Brother Rickard. "There's more to it, but the rest is best left till we're alone."

"You said you escaped together? The last time I saw you was in the theatre."

"Yes, unfortunately I was followed to Ebenstadt by an old enemy, a man named Nikolai."

"Yes," agreed Athgar. "He was the one who led us into the trap. I thought he wanted Natalia dead?"

"He did," said Stanislav, "until he learned she was carrying your child."

Athgar frowned. "No doubt he wants a reward for taking them both back to the Volstrum. Did he hurt her?"

"No, though I should tell you she is still without her powers." Stanislav noted the look of concern on the fellow's face. "I can assure you," he quickly added, "such a loss is typical for spell casters. It's all quite normal."

"It is?" Relief flooded Athgar's countenance. "Thank the Gods for that."

"The Gods?" said Stanislav. "Oh yes, that's right. Your people follow the old ways, don't they?"

Footsteps approached, and Brother Rickard opened the door to reveal two visitors.

"Look who I found," said Sir Raynald.

Natalia entered the room, smiling as she spotted Athgar. Her face soon changed to a look of concern as she took in the paleness of his features. "Are you injured?" she asked.

"Only a scratch," he answered.

"It's a bit more than that," added Brother Rickard. "He's been told he has to rest."

She moved closer, sitting on the edge of the bed and placing her hand on his arm. "I was afraid they'd killed you," she said.

"He's a tough one," said Sir Raynald, moving to the window and peering out. "It would take more than a few thugs to stop him, I'd warrant."

"What now?" asked Athgar.

"Simple," said Brother Rickard. "You two will stay here and follow my instructions for Athgar's recovery.

"I'm afraid that likely won't be possible," said Stanislav. "News of our escape will have reached our enemies. I'm sure they're already out looking for you."

Sir Raynald stiffened. "I think they've already found us." He was staring below, his eyes focused on movement in the street.

"Get Athgar out of that bed," said Stanislav. "We shall see if we can't buy you the time you need to make your escape. Have you somewhere you can go?"

"Yes," said Natalia. "Back to Runewald."

"Where's that?" asked Sir Raynald.

"Never mind," said Stanislav. "I've heard of it. Now, here's what we're going to do…"

Nikolai gazed up at the windows. "And you're sure that's where they are?"

The man before him nodded, his hand out, waiting for payment. "That's right. The old man and the woman, the one with the pale skin, they entered just a moment ago."

Nikolai dropped a gold coin into the man's hand and sent him on his way. He turned to Federov.

"We'll take them in a rush," he said. "Everyone with me."

He drew his sword while his lieutenant sorted out the order of entry. Nikolai looked at his men. "Remember now, they're casters, so be careful. We need the woman alive, but the rest you can dispatch as quickly as possible. Understood?"

They all nodded, their faces settling into grim determination. Nikolai led them across the street at a run, then burst through the doors. Up the stairs they went until they came to the second floor. Here, there was a short hallway, flanked by some decidedly rough-looking doors. At the other end of the corridor were more stairs going up, but the way was blocked by two men.

"Stanislav," said Nikolai. "We meet again!"

"You shall not have her, Nikolai, not this time!"

"Move out of the way, you old fool. I'm on the family's business."

Stanislav answered by revealing the sword he had held behind his back. Beside him was a particularly well-dressed man, a knight by the looks of him, holding a well-worn dagger.

"And who's this?" said Nikolai.

"I am Sir Raynald," the man replied, "in service to His Grace, the Duke of Erlingen."

"Move aside, Sir Knight. This need not concern you."

"Oh, but it does," Raynald replied. "I'm afraid I cannot allow you to proceed."

"So be it," said Nikolai, waving his hand to bring his men closer. "Kill them!"

A crossbow bolt sailed down the corridor, narrowly missing Stanislav. He countered by rushing forward, his sword striking out with precision, taking a man in the leg.

Sir Raynald, who had given his sword to his comrade, stomped forward, parrying a blow with a deft move, then stabbing forward with his dagger, sinking the blade into the stomach of his opponent.

Nikolai backed up, letting his men do the dirty work. He watched the swordplay for a while, but when two more of his men staggered back, he took up the cause, launching himself towards his nemesis.

Sir Raynald struck down a henchman, slicing across the man's forearm with a wicked stroke of his dagger. Another appeared before him, and he stabbed at his foe's face, causing his opponent to flinch. The knight followed up with his fists, disarming his opponent and grasping the wayward sword as the man fell back, flailing about. Now armed with a more formidable weapon, he struck out, stabbing and slicing with great skill.

More men piled in behind the first wave of attackers, and Sir Raynald pulled back, Stanislav at his side. The knight struggled to keep them at bay and then felt the back of his boot strike the stair behind him.

"Now!" he yelled, taking a step upward.

Stanislav performed the same manoeuvre, even as his blade struck true, puncturing the arm of Nikolai.

A door opened, off to the side, revealing the startled countenance of a Holy Brother. He stepped into the corridor, watching the backs of Nikolai's men, then waved his hand. Athgar and Natalia exited the door, moving slowly, making their way to the stairs that led down to the main floor.

Federov was the one who noticed them, spotting them out of the corner of his eye. He wheeled around to face them, but the Holy Brother ran forward, tackling the henchman and driving him to the floor. Federov rolled to the side, desperate to get the man off him, but by the time he managed to push Brother Rickard out of his way, it was too late; the fugitives had fled.

He tried to yell out, but the clatter of steel, mixed with the shouts of the combatants, drowned out his words. Rising, Federov prepared to run after them, but the cursed brother clung to his feet, and he fell to the floor, sprawling once more.

Sir Raynald struck down another man, his chest heaving with the effort. Beside him, Stanislav parried Nikolai's blow, the two men coming face to face, a mere sword blade between them.

"I should have killed you when I had the chance," said Nikolai.

"You've tried that before," said Stanislav. Taking a step forward, he struck out with a series of wicked slashes. Nikolai backed up, overwhelmed by the sheer ferocity of the attack.

Stanislav was breathing heavily now as were they all. The wounded men cried out in agony, their lifeblood dripping from their veins. He took one more step, driving the tip of his sword deep into Nikolai's chest.

"That," he said, "is for Viktor!"

Nikolai staggered back, gasping for air. He looked down at his chest, noting the gaping wound, then fell to his knees amongst the wounded.

"It's too late," he said, a defiant tone to his voice. "I sent word to the family. They'll never stop looking for that child." His eyes rolled up into his head, and he fell face-first onto the floor, forever silenced.

Sir Raynald stomped forward, but there was little fight left in their opponents. Those who remained on their feet turned and fled, leaving the knight with Stanislav and a handful of wounded men lying in agony.

The knight watched as they streamed down the stairs, too exhausted to follow. A muffled sound came from the wounded, and then Brother Rickard sat upright, his cassock covered in blood.

"Don't worry," the Mathewite said, "it's not mine."

Sir Raynald surveyed the carnage. "This is quite the effort they put into finding those two."

"Indeed," said Stanislav, "but it looks like we got the better of them."

"We did," the knight agreed, "but did you have to go and kill that fellow? I would have liked to have gotten some answers."

Stanislav frowned. "It couldn't be helped. He was trying to kill me."

"I take it you've met before?"

"Oh, yes. He used to work for me many years ago but then betrayed me and murdered one of my friends."

Sir Raynald looked down at the corpse. "Well, I think it's safe to say his murdering days are over."

"This fellow here looks like someone important," called out Brother Rickard.

The knight advanced, staring down at a man sprawled on the floor. There was very little blood, and yet he remained motionless. "What happened here?"

"I tripped him," explained the lay brother. "He was trying to follow Athgar and Natalia."

Sir Raynald knelt by the body. "And what makes you think he's important?"

"The cut of his clothes for one thing. He was also trying to yell orders, or so I thought. It was considerably noisy in here at the time."

"Is he still alive?"

Brother Rickard moved closer, looking for a pulse. "Yes, though he's taken a nasty bump to the head. He must have hit it on the floor when he fell."

Sir Raynald eyed the lay brother. "Are you sure you're not a Temple Knight?"

"Saints, no. Why would you even suggest such a thing?"

"You handled yourself quite nicely in the fight."

"I was merely doing Saint Mathew's work. Now, help with the wounded, will you? There's more work yet to be done."

"Help them?" said Sir Raynald. "Definitely not. They attacked us for Saint's sake!"

"We must be charitable to the defeated," insisted Brother Rickard.

"If you say so."

They began moving the bodies, separating the wounded from the dead. The commotion had been loud, but no one from downstairs had dared to intervene during the fight. Now, with the noise abated, a few patrons took tentative steps up the stairs to see what had transpired.

"Send someone to the duke," Sir Raynald called down. "Tell him one of his knights was attacked."

His task complete, he took a seat on the top stair, blocking anyone else from getting into the hallway.

"What will you do now?" asked Stanislav.

"Do?" said Sir Raynald. "What can I do? The enemy is dead or fled."

"Yes, but there is a connection with the Church. Shouldn't you look into it?"

"There is little I can do, and besides, the army will soon be marching. My place is by the duke's side."

"You must tell him what has transpired."

"To what end? Do you really think His Grace will take such accusations seriously? He can't just storm up to the father general and accuse the master of his order of being a... I don't even know what he would be."

"A spy?" offered Stanislav.

"Call it what you like, but if his control over his knights is as strong as I suspect, it will make little difference. What it all comes down to is that the Church must look after its own. It's not for outsiders to interfere. Athgar and Natalia are safe for now, and that's all we can hope for."

"What of you, Brother Rickard?" asked the mage hunter. "What are your thoughts on the matter?"

"The reports are troubling, to say the least," responded the lay brother, "but what choice do we have? There is no real evidence of this conspiracy. Only the word of two people who we are unable to call as witnesses. It ultimately comes down to mere accusations, for we have no proof."

"There must be something we can do?" insisted Stanislav.

Brother Rickard opened his mouth to speak but fell silent, considering his words.

Sir Raynald, however, had other ideas. "Well I, for one, will keep vigilant lest these fellows strike once more. Never again will I trust a Temple Knight."

"I might remind you," said Brother Rickard, "it is only one order who is involved here. I can't believe the Brothers of Saint Mathew would condone such actions nor the Sisters of Saint Agnes if it came right down to it."

Sir Raynald sighed. "You are correct, of course. But we must take solace that we have defeated the plans of whoever is behind all of this."

"I very much doubt that," said Stanislav. "This whole affair with Natalia and Athgar was a sideshow."

"What makes you say that?" asked Brother Rickard.

"Think about it. It would have taken years for Talivardas to reach the level of a Temple Knight Master. He would have started long before Natalia graduated from the Volstrum, possibly even before she was inducted."

"Then what is their ultimate plan?" asked Sir Raynald.

"I have no idea," replied Stanislav, "but one thing's for sure, I can't go back to Karslev. Nikolai would have seen to that."

"What will you do?" asked Brother Rickard.

"I don't know yet," the mage hunter replied. "I may stick around Ebenstadt awhile. See what comes up."

"You could always work for the duke," suggested Sir Raynald. "The pay's good, and he could use a man like you."

"Like me? A mage hunter? Don't be ridiculous."

"I saw you fight," said the knight. "You know how to handle a sword."

The old man shrugged it off. "No, my fighting days are over. I'd much prefer to spend my time in leisure. Perhaps I'll slow down a little and learn to appreciate life."

"With no coins?" said Sir Raynald.

"Don't trouble yourself on my account," said Stanislav. "I have plenty of friends around the Continent who owe me a favour or two."

"And until you locate them?"

Stanislav knelt by a body, rooting through its pockets. He smiled, holding up a small collection of coins. "I'll make do."

ESCAPE

Autumn 1104 SR

Athgar sat, taking the weight off his leg. They were finally free of Ebenstadt, its grey walls now out of sight, but the spectre of pursuit loomed heavily on both their minds.

"You can't go on using your bow as a cane," said Natalia. "We need to get you a proper crutch."

Athgar looked around. "What would that entail?"

"Have you never used a crutch before?"

"No, can't say that I have. Do you know how to make one?"

"Of course. Helping the wounded was part of my training."

"What do we need?" he asked.

"A branch or stick of suitable size."

Athgar hefted his axe. "You pick out a branch, and I'll cut it down."

She smiled. "It's good you don't use a sword, it wouldn't be half as handy. You wait here, and I'll have a quick look around. I'll come find you once I've got what we need."

He watched her wander around, the sun glinting off her black hair. The day was hot, surprising considering the time of year, and he wondered how many more days like this they would have before winter raised its icy head.

It didn't take long for Natalia to find what she wanted: a 'Y' shaped branch that had long since fallen to the ground.

"This ought to do," she said, "though, of course, you'll need to adjust its height."

"Bring it closer, and let me take a look."

She dragged it towards him, then halted, a pained look coming to her face.

He stood up in alarm, instantly regretting his decision as his leg faltered. "Are you all right?"

She held up her hand, taking a deep breath before continuing. "Only a twinge," she replied. "This baby of ours is determined to make its presence known. Is that a Therengian trait?"

"I have no idea. The truth is, I never paid much attention to such things back in Athelwald, but Skora would know. She's delivered lots of babies in her time."

"I wish she was here now," said Natalia.

"I never thought I'd say it," said Athgar, "but right now, I'd love to have a horse."

"You? The confirmed walker? I thought you hated the things."

"Hate's a strong word, but anything would be better than walking right now. And, let's face it, you're not in much better shape yourself." He limped over to where she crouched, examining the branch.

Natalia sat, pointing at the base of the 'Y'. "Chop off the bottom, right about here. The top you should trim so it fits under your armpit. It'll be awkward to use but much better than your bow."

Trimming it to size was easy enough, but the crook of the crutch took much more work. Luckily, Athgar had his knife with him. Years of crafting bows had given him an excellent feel for wood, and after a few adjustments, he had a finished product. Setting it under his arm, he took a few tentative steps.

"Not too bad," he said. "It lends a lot more support than I would have thought."

"Ready to resume our trek?" she asked.

"As ready as I'll ever be."

They started moving eastward, making good time over the relatively flat terrain. By late afternoon the sun had disappeared behind dark clouds, a sure sign that a storm was brewing.

Natalia cursed. "Just our luck, we'll be caught in a downpour. How can the weather change so quickly?"

"It's the mountains, they mess about with the weather. We need to seek shelter."

"There's a cluster of trees up ahead. Will that do?"

"It'll have to," said Athgar. "Come on, let's hurry before the rain closes in."

They reached the boughs just as it started spitting.

"Look for a fallen branch," suggested Athgar, "about twice my height in length."

"Here's one," she called out.

He moved closer, examining her find. "Good. Now we need to prop it against the trunk of a tree. While I do that, you find as many branches as you can, then we'll lean them up against the side like ribs."

Athgar dragged the fallen branch to a likely target, then set about raising its end, placing it against a large maple. By this time, Natalia was ready with the first group of sticks, piling them at the base and returning to the forest floor to look for more.

Larger drops of rain began to fall, but the overhead branches gave them some cover. Occasionally the water would make its way through, much to Athgar's annoyance. With the ribs finally in place, they began gathering vegetation; a collection of pine boughs, ferns, and moss. To this, they added fallen leaves, the better to insulate against the cold of the coming storm.

Their small cover complete, they crawled inside, pulling a spare branch behind to cover the opening. Athgar conjured a small flame to light the interior, careful to avoid letting the fire touch anything combustible.

"This is quite cozy," said Natalia.

"It'll do for now, though I wouldn't expect it to last forever."

"One night is all we need, then we must be on our way."

"You think the army has marched?"

"No," she said. "We still have a day or two by my reckoning. Remember, the father general called for the army to march in two days, and that was only yesterday."

"So they'll march tomorrow?"

"Maybe even the day after if this storm is bad enough. A large storm can play havoc with the route of march, turning it into a quagmire if it's wet enough."

Athgar smiled. "So the rain could actually be an ally?"

"I suppose that's true. I hadn't thought of it that way."

"Hopefully Kargen was successful in uniting the tribes. I'd hate to think about fighting off the Church without the Orcs."

"You should be more worried about the Therengians," said Natalia. "King Eadred tried to kill us. He won't be happy to see our return."

"One more thing we have to worry about," said Athgar. "I swear the list grows longer every day. Is there no end to it?"

"We shall get through this together, my love. You will see."

"And what do we do in the meantime while we wait for the storm to pass?"

"Sleep," said Natalia. "Now, come over here and keep the cold from me."

"Shall I use my spell of warmth?"

She grinned. "I can think of a more old-fashioned method that would be just as effective."

Long into the night, the storm raged. Athgar and Natalia remained in their shelter, listening to the peal of thunder as it echoed off the distant mountains.

Sometime in the early hours of the morning, their shelter began to leak. They countered this by using Athgar's tunic to act as a makeshift cover while they huddled together in the cold air of the night.

By sunrise, the storm had finally abated. Athgar pushed the branches from the opening and crawled out, the damp leaves of the forest floor sticking to him. Gathering some firewood, he then used his magic to call forth fire, too tired to attempt it the traditional way.

Natalia crawled out, looking exhausted. She tossed him the soaked tunic, which he arranged near the fire, the better to dry it out.

"Hungry?" he asked.

"Starving, but what have we to eat?"

"There's all sorts of things in these parts. It shouldn't be too difficult to find something."

"But you can't hunt, you're injured."

"There's more to surviving in the woods than hunting," said Athgar.

"Like what?"

"Plants. Take that bush over there, it's edible."

She looked in the direction indicated, surprise on her face as she stared at the small yellow petals. "So we just eat the flowers?"

"Gods, no, but the roots are quite tasty."

She wandered over, looking down on the small, leafy plant. "Do I dig down?"

"No, just grab the branches and pull. It should come up fairly easily."

Natalia grasped the stem of the plant, pulling with all her might. The plant gave way easily, sending dirt flying everywhere as she fell backwards. Spitting out some dirt, she looked down at the exposed roots in her hands. Attached were small white bulbs that somehow seemed familiar.

"Have you never seen a turnip before?" asked Athgar.

"Of course. We ate them all the time back in the Volstrum, but I've never seen the plant they come from."

"The yellow flower is quite distinctive," he continued. "And we can eat them raw if we have to, though I much prefer to cook them, given a choice. There's some more to your left."

"I'll gather what I can, while you cook this lot. We can take the rest with us."

By noon the sun was out again, drying the ground, but the air had turned cooler since the storm, threatening flakes of snow. Athgar decided to use his spell of warmth to ward off the chilly air. They made good progress, and by late afternoon they again searched for a decent place to camp.

The first sign of the village was when Natalia tripped, her foot catching on something beneath the long grass. Further investigations soon revealed burned-out timbers, the remnants of a hut that had since been overgrown with weeds. As they moved eastward, the evidence of a lost settlement became more unmistakable with entire wall sections coming into sight.

"We're in a village," said Natalia. "At least it used to be one."

"This must be Ashborne," said Athgar. "Raleth talked of it if you recall. It was burned down five years ago."

"That puts us close to Runewald, doesn't it? Why didn't we notice this on the way to Ebenstadt?"

"We must have been farther north when we passed by. Let's have a quick look around, shall we?"

Natalia halted. "Over here," she called out. "I found something."

Athgar hobbled over to her, casting his eyes down as he approached. Skeletal remains lay at her feet, the shattered skull evidence of its manner of death. He fought back his disgust. "What kind of person leaves the dead unburied?"

Natalia was looking at the distant timbers of the burned-out huts. "This was no battle," she said. "It was a massacre."

"How can you be so sure?"

"There's another body over there," she said, "as if they were running to escape." She moved closer, nodding her head, Athgar soon joining her.

"Look at the skull," she continued. "What do you notice?"

"It's damaged, much like the other one. What of it?"

"If you look closer, you'll see the head was hit from behind, much like the first remains we found. This body looks smaller, likely a woman in her younger years. If I'm right, we'll find others in the same condition."

"So someone chased them away?"

"I imagine there was a fight somewhere, likely on the outskirts of the village. Their defence probably crumbled, and a general rout commenced. It appears horsemen picked off these people. See how the wound is high up on the back of the head?"

"The work of Temple Knights?" said Athgar.

"Either that or the auxiliaries. Did you say it was burned five years ago?"

"That's what Raleth said, why?"

"That would coincide with the second crusade. The Church proclaimed it a great victory, but I don't remember hearing of this type of thing. In any event, there's little we can do about it now. We must find somewhere to settle down for the night."

The farther east they went, the better the condition of the ruins until they found what could only have been the chieftain's hall. The roof was missing, the very tops of the walls showing burned timbers, but the walls themselves were mostly intact, offering shelter from the wind, if not the sky.

"This looks as good a place as any," said Athgar. "We'll build a camp against the north wall. That seems to be the dominant direction from which the wind is coming."

They gathered firewood, ignoring the need for kindling. Soon, the fire was ablaze, started by Athgar's magic. A small pile of logs sat nearby, ready to feed the flames when needed.

Athgar buried the turnips into the ash to cook them as the logs burned down. Soon, they were once more biting into the soft white flesh, careful not to burn themselves. Athgar was just about to finish off his first bulb when he paused.

"What's the matter?" asked Natalia.

"I think I heard something," he replied. They both sat in silence, straining to discern what might be moving about.

"I don't hear anything," whispered Natalia.

"Nor do I, and that worries me. Even the insects are quiet. Someone, or something, is out there." He waved his hand at the fire, using words of power to plunge them into darkness.

"Here, take my knife," he whispered, handing it to her. He then picked up his bow, standing to string it, his back leaning against the north wall.

The snap of a twig off to the east echoed throughout the ruins. Athgar quickly nocked an arrow. He could definitely hear more movement now, skirting the edge of the ruins. Could the army have caught up to them? He chided himself for the thought, for if it were true, they would have been making far more noise. Who then, or better yet, what was making those sounds?

He moved to the east wall, peering through a crack to look beyond.

There must have been a small clearing on the other side of the trees, for a faint light illuminated the area.

"Stay here," he whispered.

"I don't think so," Natalia replied. "You're the injured one, remember? You need me."

"Very well, follow me."

He made his way back out of the ruined hut, Natalia following, and then they turned south, skirting the edge of the ruins, heading towards the light.

In the dark of the night, the campfire stood out like a beacon. All they needed to do was look upward to where the tall pines were lit from beneath. As they drew closer, noises drifted towards them, sounds that made Athgar sigh in relief.

"What is it?" she asked, her voice low.

"Orcs," said Athgar. "A hunting party by the sounds of it." He rose from his crouch, calling out in the tongue of the Orcs. *"Hello?"*

They were greeted by the scurrying of feet, and then an arrow whipped past, burying its head into a nearby tree.

"Who goes there?" called out a familiar voice.

"Kragor, is that you? It's me, Athgar!"

An Orc stood, revealing himself, a powerful warbow held in his mighty grip. Athgar held out his hand, conjuring a green flame to light the area.

"It is good to see you, my friend," the Orc replied. *"We had not expected you back so soon."*

"What are you doing here?" asked Natalia.

"We are keeping watch," said Kragor, switching to the common tongue, "to warn the others when the army is spotted. Have you brought us news?"

They moved forward, Natalia leading. The group of Orc hunters returned to their fire, no longer on the alert.

"The army is moving"—she shifted to a spot in front of the flames—"and is no more than two or three days behind us."

"Was Kargen successful?" asked Athgar.

"I do not know," said Kragor. "I, and my hunters, have been out here for the last three days. When we left Ord-Ghadrak, he and Shaluhk had not yet returned." He watched as Athgar lowered himself to the ground. "You are injured. We must get you to Laghul."

"No," said Athgar. "We need to return to Runewald first. I have to convince King Eadred to stand and fight."

"That will be difficult to do from what I have heard."

"Why?"

"He has gathered the fyrd," replied the Orc.

"Surely that means he intends to fight?"

"I think not, my friend. He means only to guard the way eastward, crossing into Orc lands."

"Then we shall have to convince him otherwise."

"How do we do that?" asked Natalia. "He already tried to kill us once. Who's to say he won't try again?"

"He tried to kill you?" asked Kragor.

"Yes, did Kargen not tell you? He sent his men to murder us in our sleep, but we got wind of it and set up our own ambush."

"Then perhaps it is best if we accompany you back to Runewald. Your words will have more sway with the power of the tribes behind you."

"I can't ask that of you. This is my fight."

"No," said Kragor. "You and Nat-Alia are part of the Red Hand. A fight for one is a fight for all. Let us stand beside you in your time of need."

"It couldn't hurt," offered Natalia.

"I suppose you're right," said Athgar. "Very well, we shall strike out for Runewald at first light."

"A good decision," said the Orc, "and one which I know Kargen would approve of."

"What of your responsibilities here?" asked Natalia. "Didn't you say you were sent to watch for the army?"

"I did, but I did not mention there are others like us in the area. Both our tribe and the Black Axe are watching for the enemy. Do not fear. I shall inform them of our imminent departure, and they will cover this stretch of ground in our absence. In the meantime, you should get some rest. Have you eaten?"

"Only turnips," said Natalia.

Kragor laughed in the low rumble of his people. "Then you shall have meat. I can not have you travel to Runewald on an empty stomach. Now, what of your wound, Athgar? Does it pain you?"

"It does," the Therengian replied. "And my armpit is sore from using this crutch."

The Orc moved closer, examining the bandages. "Is the wound clean?"

"Yes, according to Brother Rickard," said Athgar.

"A name I am not familiar with. Is he a shaman?"

"He has no magic, if that's what you mean, but he knows how to treat a wound."

"Then it is best we do not disturb it. Once we return, Shaluhk can take care of it."

"If she's back," reminded Natalia.

"You should have more faith in the Ancestors, Nat-Alia. Kargen and Shaluhk will return to us, I am certain of it."

THE RECKONING

Autumn 1104 SR

Athgar peered through the trees. "It appears King Eadred has raised the fyrd and brought them all here, to Runewald."

"How many?" asked Natalia.

"Several hundred, by the looks of it."

"Does that mean your king means to stand and fight?" asked Kragor.

"I doubt it," said Athgar. "More likely he's going to push eastward. I think he means to fight the Orc tribes."

"We must stop him," insisted Kragor.

"My thoughts exactly."

"How do you want to proceed?" asked Natalia.

"We'll head directly towards the great hall," said Athgar, "and confront Eadred."

"Are you sure that is wise, Athgar?" said the Orc. "He may not take kindly to your return."

"We haven't time to waste. The army is likely marching, even as we speak."

"Then I, and my hunters, will accompany you."

"Very well," said Athgar. He stood, brushing the leaves from his tunic. The village lay only a short distance away, and so he stepped from the cover of the trees, moving slowly so as not to trip up his crutch. Natalia took her place at his side, Kragor and his half-dozen Orcs following along behind.

As Athgar drew closer, he noticed several wagons gathered before the king's hall. A small group of chainmail-clad warriors loaded wooden chests, heavy ones by the look of them, into the back of one such wagon.

A number of warriors to Athgar's left hailed him. He turned, seeing Raleth and his brother, Harwath, leading a collection of familiar-looking faces, local villagers all.

"How did things go in Ebenstadt?" asked Raleth.

"Not as well as I would have liked," said Athgar. "But you have to excuse me, I must see the king on a matter of great urgency." He pushed on, his target in sight. The members of the fyrd, led by Raleth, began to follow, ignoring the presence of the Orcs in their rush to see what would transpire.

"What's going on here?" Athgar called out as they drew nearer the great hall.

One of the warriors turned, noting the approach of the new arrivals. "The king has ordered the evacuation of the village," the man said. "We are marching eastward."

"But that will take you into Orc lands," said Athgar.

The warrior shrugged. "Better to fight the greenskins than match arms against the skrollings." He was about to say more, but then his vision fell upon Kragor. "What is this?" he said, reaching for his sword.

"Stay your hand," said Athgar. "He is an ally."

"An ally?"

"Yes," said Kragor. "We have come to stand with you in your time of need."

The warrior paused, the words sinking in. "That is good news, but I'm afraid it's too late. King Eadred has commanded us to move eastward, and we must obey."

The Orc was about to protest, but Natalia stilled his voice by placing her hand on his arm. She turned to face the warrior. "I think this is a matter best discussed with King Eadred."

He nodded, moving aside to let them pass. By now, word of their arrival had spread, and more villagers were gathering by the entrance to the king's hall.

Athgar halted as a man exited the structure, struggling with the weight of a small chest.

"What have you there?" asked Athgar.

"One of the king's personal chests," the man said, setting it down.

Athgar moved closer, struggling with his injured leg to kneel to examine the chest in more detail. The labourer, now free of his burden, simply backed up, allowing him access.

The wooden chest, reinforced with iron bands, was held closed by a clasp but with no lock to secure it. Athgar undid the clasp, lifting the lid to expose its contents. Inside were gold and silver coins in abundance, with an occasional ring mixed in.

"Has he many such as this?" he asked.

"This is the third chest I have retrieved," the man replied, "and there's two more inside."

Athgar stood and looked at Natalia. "I think it time we went inside, don't you?"

He pushed open the door to reveal several open chests, half filled with clothing and furs, while two others, similar to the one he had examined, stood off to the side. King Eadred was kneeling before one, placing something inside when the door swung open, striking the wall.

"What is it?" he called out, turning towards the entrance. Equipped for battle, he wore a once ornate chainmail shirt, its links now rusty and damaged. On his hip hung a jewelled scabbard, easily the most expensive item in the village.

Eadred rose to his feet, words failing him as his gaze took in the form of Athgar. His look of surprise soon turned to hatred. "This is all your fault," accused the king.

Athgar remained calm. "My fault? Why do you say that? The outsiders were a threat long before I came along!"

"A threat, most assuredly, but you made it much worse by going to Ebenstadt. You have brought the enemy to the very gates of our land!"

"Is that why you tried to have me killed?"

In answer, King Eadred simply pointed at him. "Arrest that man!"

Natalia was about to speak, but this time it was Kragor who stopped her.

"Let this play out," the Orc said.

Two of Eadred's guards moved into the hall, grasping Athgar by the arms. Rather than struggle, Athgar allowed them to lead him from the building. As soon as they stepped outside, the guards were confronted by an angry mob.

"Release him," called out Raleth. "You know it's the right thing to do."

The guards looked around at the crowd, seeing the determination in their eyes. After only a moment's hesitation, they both released their grips, standing back to allow room for Athgar to be seen clearly.

"You have failed, Eadred," Athgar called out. "Come and face me if you dare." He backed away from the door, allowing room for his foe. In response, the gathering of villagers began spreading out to form a rough circle.

Finally, Eadred emerged, bowing his armoured head to clear the doorway as the bare steel of his sword glinted in his hand.

"We are making a stand against the invaders," declared Athgar. "Join us."

"I am king here, not you," countered Eadred. "This is my decision to make."

"Then make the right one. If we don't fight now, we'll be on the run for the rest of our lives. Is that what you want for your people?"

"You say you want to fight for your people," said Eadred, "but it is not the villagers of Runewald for whom you fight. You can't fool me, Athgar of Athelwald, for I know the truth. You would replace me and rule as king."

"No, I wish only to bring peace to our people."

"There cannot be two leaders," said Eadred. "We must settle this once and for all, you and I."

Athgar sighed. "If that is your wish."

"Take a shield," said Eadred, "and let us settle this as true warriors." The king waited as a member of the fyrd handed over a shield, then taking one for himself, he advanced into the impromptu circle.

Eadred moved into a slight crouch, banging his sword against his shield. "Hear this, Athgar? It's the sound of your doom."

"You don't scare me, Eadred. I've faced worse foes."

The king merely smiled in response, shifting to his right. Athgar tried to mimic Eadred, but with his injured leg, his movements were clumsy, his pacing weak.

The king, noticing his opponent's discomfort, lunged forward, the tip of his sword striking out at Athgar's face. The Fire Mage stumbled back, giving ground.

Feinting, the king watched with a smirk as Athgar awkwardly tried to manoeuvre. With his suspicions now confirmed, Eadred moved forward, using a series of blows to force Athgar farther back, not worrying about actually striking his target. When Athgar stumbled, Eadred used the edge of his shield to smash into the wounded leg, laughing as he watched fresh blood seep to the surface.

Athgar thought to use his magic, but the king attacked with such speed, he had little time to cast. He needed to put some space between them, but with his wounded leg, he was unable to increase the distance.

Eadred struck again, and Athgar parried, then countered with a swing to the chest. He could feel the blade of his axe dig into chainmail, but the blow was short, missing flesh. Instead, it tore into the old-and-worn links, bursting at least half a dozen.

The king backed up, looking down at his chest. "You'll have to do better than that," he sneered. He struck again, this time swinging his sword from the right to glance off of Athgar's shield, making a loud thud.

In answer, Athgar thrust forward with his axe, only to pull it short on purpose. The king, reacting to the expected attack, drew his head back, out of range, and that's when Athgar attacked, hooking the edge of Eadred's shield with his axe and pulling him forward. Unbalanced, the king stumbled, and Athgar thrust again, the top of his weapon crashing against his foe's helmet, the clang of metal on metal ringing out. Pulling back, he noted the dent he had created on the helm's rim, and beneath it, he saw where the edge of the helmet, deformed by the blow, had sliced into Eadred's forehead.

"Enjoy it while you can, Athgar of Athelwald," shouted Eadred as blood poured down his face. Using his shield, he pushed Athgar back. The unsteady bowyer's feet caught on some uneven ground, and he tumbled to the dirt with Eadred now looming over him.

The king struck, again and again, forcing Athgar to hold up his shield in an effort to stem the endless flow of blows, until he felt a tugging, and then the shield flew from his hands, tossed into the crowd.

Eadred, who had discarded his own shield, stood over the Fire Mage, his sword held above Athgar's face, both hands firmly on the hilt ready for the killing blow.

"It's time to put an end to this!" Eadred shouted for all to hear.

Athgar, seeing the sword hovering in front of his face, uttered a spell, the only one he could cast in so short a time. A small green flame leaped to life, and he thrust out his hand in desperation. The effect on Eadred was instantaneous; he cringed, fear filling his face. Even the spectators were shocked, many backing up, making more room for the combatants.

Athgar rose to his feet, allowing the flame to die. "I don't need my magic to defeat you, Eadred."

The king's face grew red. "I am your king!"

"You are no king!" shouted Athgar. "A true king looks after his people. All you've done is hoard wealth and see to your own comfort."

The crowd started murmuring, and Eadred looked around as if seeing them for the first time. "This is unconscionable," he shouted. "You are the one who is a traitor to your people. You have sided with the Orcs."

Athgar shifted, taking the weight off his wounded leg. "It is the Orcs who will help us win, Eadred. Can't you see that?"

"You cannot talk to me like that." The king's eyes sought out his guards. "Kill him!" he ordered.

One bodyguard stepped forward, drawing his sword, but then an arrow took him in the chest. He staggered back, gaping at his wound as he collapsed. Witnessing this, the others backed up, holding their hands away from their weapons.

Eadred cursed, then rushed forward, taking Athgar by surprise to slam into him, driving them both to the ground. They kicked up dead sticks and leaves as they rolled about, the crowd parting to allow them through. When the tumbling ceased, Athgar was once again on his back with Eadred straddling his legs, pinning him in place as he placed his sword over the heart.

Athgar, still holding his axe, moved it up, striking the king's sword, but Eadred's grip was solid, and the blade didn't waver. With nothing else to do, Athgar gripped his axe by the head, pushing up with all his might. The blade of his weapon struck upward, through the broken links of chain to sink into the king's chest, catching for a moment as it struck bone, and then he pushed harder, feeling the splatter of blood as the axe dug into flesh.

Eadred's eyes went wide in surprise, his grip weakening until the sword fell from his hands. His eyes rolled up into his head, then he slumped forward onto Athgar's prone form.

Athgar was struggling to breathe under the crushing weight until a pair of Orcs pulled the king's body off of him, and then Natalia was beside him, examining his wound. Many gathered around the couple, their voices cheering his victory.

"I'm fine," he said to her, his voice breathless.

She helped him to his feet while others crowded in, congratulating him on his victory. Somebody called out in alarm, and hands went to weapons. Moments later, the voice of Kargen boomed out across the village, "What have we here?"

"Athgar has beaten Eadred," said Raleth. "He is now our king."

"I am no king," said Athgar. "Merely a fellow Therengian who wishes to see his people safe."

Kargen pushed through the onlookers, Shaluhk by his side. It only took a moment for the shamaness to notice Athgar's wounds, and then she was moving in closer, conjuring forth her magic. The flesh knit as the magic took hold, and a sense of relief fell over Athgar. He looked up from his newly repaired wound to see expectant faces staring down at him.

"The enemy is coming," he declared. "They won't be satisfied until the last of our people lies dead. If we flee, they will only follow, chasing us down to the ends of the Continent. The time for action is now, while we are still strong! We must stand with our Orc allies and rid ourselves of this threat once and for all."

The crowd was enthusiastic, but one of Eadred's guards spat on the ground. "They are led by Temple Knights," the man said. "How can we hope to defeat such men?"

Athgar looked at Natalia. "Will you lead us?"

"Me?" she replied.

"You're the battle mage. You're trained in such things."

"Very well, but only if you command the Therengians."

"Me?" said Athgar. "I'm no leader."

"Yes you are. You just haven't realized it yet. These people, YOUR people, look to you for inspiration."

"Very well," he said, "but they are OUR people, not mine alone." He returned his attention to the villagers. "As many of you know, Natalia is a battle mage, trained in the art of war since childhood. It is she who will lead us to victory."

Those assembled erupted into cheers, drowning out any further objections.

Kargen moved closer, leaning in to be heard over the noise. "We must talk, my friend. There is much to discuss."

Athgar looked around, spotting some familiar faces. "Harwath, secure those chests while we retire to plot our strategies."

"Yes, Athgar," the man replied.

"The wound is healed," said Shaluhk, "but you still suffer from blood loss. You will be weak for some time."

Kargen passed a cup across the fire to Athgar, who drank thirstily.

"I wish we had more time," said Natalia.

"So do I," said Kargen, "but the enemy is approaching. They will be upon us in a few days. We must hasten to prepare our defences."

"We must choose where to fight," said Natalia. "This village is too open."

"Zahruhl knows of a place," said Shaluhk. "A place of great magic."

"Tell us what you know," said Athgar.

"It is an ancient stone construction. Zahruhl referred to it as a gateway, but the secret of its use has been lost to the ages."

"Then how can it help us?"

"It enhances the power of magic used in its vicinity," said Shaluhk.

"All magic?"

"Primarily that of the earth," she continued. "I have heard of such things before, but never have I experienced one myself."

"What of the land thereabouts?" asked Natalia.

"That I can not say, for I have not yet seen it."

"How far to these standing stones?" asked Athgar.

"Two days," said Kargen, "maybe less."

"And the other tribes?"

"They are gathering even as we speak. Zahruhl and Kirak will join forces with us at the stones."

"You have hunters near the ruins of Ashborne," said Natalia. "Have them withdraw towards the stones only after the enemy has seen them. We must draw them into our net."

"It shall be as you wish," said Kargen. His eyes fell onto the chests that King Eadred had hoarded. "What of those?"

"I would suggest we send them to Ord-Ghadrak for safekeeping, at least for the moment."

"And if we win?"

"WHEN we win," corrected Natalia, "it will be Athgar's decision as to what we do with them."

"It belongs to the people," said Athgar. "Let it be used to purchase better weapons and armour for us all."

"All well and good for the long term," said Kargen, "but let us concentrate on the situation at hand. Such wealth will not help us at present."

"Wise words," said Natalia, "during this time of strife."

"He is always at his best during times of conflict," said Shaluhk. "He thrives on it."

"Where is Laruhk?" asked Athgar. "I thought he'd be with you."

Kargen smiled. "He is looking into something for us. A little surprise if you like."

"Are you going to tell us what it is?"

"Not until we know if it is successful. I would not like to get your hopes up. Suffice it to say that it might give us an edge."

"Of course we're talking about my brother," said Shaluhk. "It could just as easily turn out to be nothing."

CONTACT

Autumn 1104 SR

U rughar pushed aside the long grass, peering into the mist. In the early morning, small patches of it clung to the lower parts of the land, giving the place an eerie feeling. Off in the distance, men came into view, heading eastward at a speed that would see them soon cross in front of the Orcs' position, which lay just to their south.

"They have quite a few archers," noted his fellow Orc.

Urughar turned to his sizable companion. Ogda was a relatively heavy individual but surprisingly agile on his feet. At the moment, his attention was on the distant warriors, but Urughar knew he feared the horsemen more than anything on foot. *"We have yet to see their knights."*

"I wish we had the warbows of the Red Hand," said Ogda.

"We shall, eventually. In the meantime, we will make do with what we have. It is no worse than our enemies. The archers are not our concern. Let them continue unhindered."

They watched in silence as the archers marched past.

"Why do they not send skirmishers to the side?" asked Ogda. *"Do they not think us cunning?"*

"They do not even know we are here," replied Urughar. *"They think they are only fighting the Therengians."*

His companion snorted. *"It will be a big surprise to them when we strike."*

"So it will, but remember, our task here is not to fight a battle, merely to strike where they are weak and then withdraw, tempting them to follow."

"But their horses can outpace us! Are we then to sacrifice ourselves?"

"Fear not, old friend, for our allies, the Stone Crushers, will keep the horses occupied elsewhere. By the time they realize what we are doing, it will be too late. We will be safely away from this place."

Urughar advanced at a crouch, moving slowly to preserve the tall grass. Ogda followed, the rest of the party strung out evenly behind them, each five paces from the last. They had thought to move forward in a line, but the risk of discovery was increased significantly with such a manoeuvre, so they decided on this simpler approach.

As he drew nearer to the edge of the grass, Urughar went prone, keeping his eyes on the distant target. This was, perhaps, the most dangerous part of the plan, but they needed an accurate count of what they faced, and so he and his hunters had been sent to gather what information they could. Lying in silence, he watched as the enemy moved past less than ten paces away.

Behind the archers walked footmen wearing light grey tabards. The significance of this garb was lost on Urughar, but he made a mental note to bring it to the attention of others. Whoever they were, they were well-armoured, wearing the metal plates typical of knights, though they lacked the horses.

He counted more than two hundred of these warriors as they filed past, then smiled at the distant sound of approaching horses. All his life, he had been told of the Human knights. To him, they were like mythical creatures, covered in metal, and riding great beasts that fought as ferociously as the best warriors of antiquity.

The Temple Knights, when they finally came into view, were as awe-inspiring as the tales. From his vantage point on the ground, they looked massive, their great horses towering over everyone else. Their silver-plated armour gleamed in the sun while their dark grey tabards gave them a uniform appearance. The very ground seemed to shake as they rode by, leading Urughar to contemplate what it would be like to face them in battle. He had spent years confronting wild beasts on the hunt, but the thought of such adversaries chilled him.

Ogda, on the other hand, merely grunted.

"You are not impressed?" asked Urughar.

"They are not as imposing as I would have thought," the large Orc replied.

"And yet I would not wish to face them in battle."

"Nor I, but they are useless in the forest."

Urughar nodded. *"So they are, but out in the open, they would be our match."*

"*By the Ancestors,*" said Ogda, "*there are a lot of them. I count more than four hundred so far, and still, they come. Will there be no end to it?*"

Finally, the last of the Temple Knights rode into view. Behind them marched more footmen, this group looking far less uniform in their garb.

"*These are not knights,*" said Ogda.

"*True,*" replied Urughar, "*but they wear more armour than us.*"

"*Do you think any of that armour would fit an Orc?*"

"*I doubt it. The Humans are far thinner than we are. Note their weapons.*"

"*They appear to favour spears,*" said Ogda. "*An advantage to us once we are inside of their reach.*"

"*Yes, but to THEIR advantage when approaching. They will be able to strike first.*"

Following the spear wielders came yet more footmen, these more heavily armoured, with many in chainmail and sporting a variety of swords, axes, and even hammers.

"*These are the ones who will cause the most problems,*" said Urughar, "*for they walk with purpose.*"

"*Meaning?*"

"*They are more experienced warriors. That is what makes them dangerous.*"

A small group of mounted knights came next, then the endless stream of wagons.

"*At last,*" said Urughar, "*our targets are in sight.*"

He nodded to Ogda who, in turn, waved the hunters forward. They took up positions along the edge of the grass, rising as Urughar called out the command.

The first volley peppered the wagons, knocking down two men but doing little else. They held their next barrage until all were ready, then sent a hail of arrows sailing forth. This time the damage was more readily apparent, with five men taking hits.

The enemy shouted in alarm, many taking cover behind the wagons. To the east, the knights were turning around, no doubt roused by the pleas for help.

Urughar ordered one more volley, though it did little other than sink into the wood-sided wagons.

"*Back,*" he called out.

Gahruhl knelt at the base of the huge pine to watch northward as the archers began passing her position. She looked at Karag, who sat to her right. "*What do you think?*"

"They have many archers," he replied, "but some of them carry strange weapons."

"Those are crossbows," said Gahruhl. "Kargen spoke of them. They are common amongst the Humans."

"Why is that?"

"It is said they are easier to use, requiring little training to master."

"Do the Humans care so little for the hunt?"

"It is not about the hunt," explained Gahruhl, "but such a weapon could be used by a man on a horse."

"Yet these men are all on foot."

"Let us be thankful. It will help us achieve our objective this day." She glanced left to where her hunters crouched, spears in hand. The Humans were less than a stone's throw away, unaware of the presence of the Orcs.

Gahruhl was thinking over her options when a lone soldier split from the rest of his cohorts, jogging towards their place of concealment.

"What is this?" asked Karag, gripping his spear tightly.

"Let us wait and see what he does," she cautioned.

The man drew closer to the trees, then slowed, fumbling with his clothes. Moments later, he halted, undoing his belt, and letting out a sigh as he relieved himself of a full bladder.

The smell of urine drifted towards the Orcs. Gahruhl looked at Karag, simply nodding. In answer, the Orc hunter crept forward, drawing his long knife and leaving his spear behind.

Gahruhl shifted her attention to the archers in the distance, but they continued on their way, unfazed by their companion's absence.

Karag returned, crossbow in one hand, a quiver of bolts in the other. "It is done," he said.

"What is this?"

"I thought you might want to look at the crossbow you spoke of. These are the small arrows that it uses."

"How does one load such a weapon?"

"I have no idea," said Karag, "but maybe our Therengian friends can tell us more."

"The Therengians do not use crossbows."

"True, but the battle mage, Nat-Alia, is surely familiar with such things."

"I would think so, yes."

"Look," said Karag. "A small group of archers are heading our way."

"They have likely noted the absence of their comrade. I was hoping to hold the moment of our attack for a more suitable target, but it appears our plans will have to be adjusted."

"You mean to attack so soon?"

"An attack on the archers would suit our purposes just as well as others. Prepare the hunters. You may strike when ready."

Karag grinned, retrieving his spear. He turned to his fellow tribe members and waved them forward. They rose silently, moving north to the very edge of the trees, each with a spear in hand.

Gahruhl watched with an appreciative eye as the mighty hunter waited for just the right moment. She gave the command, and then they all stepped into the grassy field, hefting their spears in unison. The projectiles sailed through the air, unseen until the moment before impact. With a startled yell, they struck home, taking down five men and scattering the rest.

Karag kept his hunters where they were, waiting for the enemy to see them before ordering the withdrawal. They fell back into the woods, hardly making a sound.

The Humans, meanwhile, were yelling in alarm, drawing the attention of the main army. The rest of the archers, though slow to react, were soon swarming south to help repel the enemy.

Karag and the others streamed past Gahruhl, but the master of earth remained, her eyes locked on the Humans. The archers formed into a ragged line and began peppering the treeline with arrows. As more men joined them, they became emboldened, several advancing to get closer to their targets.

Gahruhl ignored the arrows that flew overhead, her attention firmly on those in the front. She waited until they were less than ten paces ahead, then began casting. Words of power began to issue from her lips, the air buzzing with the buildup of magical energy. Small wisps of grey flew from her fingers, sinking into the ground in front of the advancing enemy.

She could almost feel the ground moving, and then small sprouts erupted from the dirt. They grew quickly, the branches intertwining as thorns sprouted, completing the effect. Gahruhl kept up her concentration until the wall of thorns was taller than an Orc.

Rising, she listened for the enemy's response, for their army was now hidden from sight. Hearing arrows strike the hedge, she knew it was time to leave. She turned her back on the thorns and began moving south to rejoin the other members of her tribe.

Father General Hargild sat on his horse watching the Temple Knights ride by. They were a formidable force, the largest concentration of such troops in years, and he took pride in knowing they were the finest soldiers on the Continent. His moment of reflection was interrupted by the arrival of Captain Hadmar. The father general struggled to hide his irritation.

"Yes, Captain?" he said.

"We are under attack, Your Grace."

Hargild looked east and west. The column spread in both directions, but where the road was curved, the trees hid much of his troops. "Where?" he demanded.

"To the rear, Your Grace. It appears the enemy has employed mercenaries. Greenskins, to be exact."

"Orcs? Here? Are you sure?"

"There is no doubt, Lord. They struck at the wagons, then fled south, back into the woods."

"Casualties?"

"Light, Your Grace, but panic is spreading amongst the supply lines. I fear there are not enough troops to keep them secure."

"Tell the Duke of Erlingen to send more troops to the rear. That ought to keep the Orcs at bay."

"Do you think they mean to attack in force, Your Grace?"

"I doubt it," said Hargild. "They are skirmishers. Orcs don't fight using traditional tactics; they mainly play at hit and run. They are a nuisance, to be sure, but pose little real threat to us if we keep our heads."

Captain Hadmar turned his horse around, eager to ride off.

"Captain?" called out the father general.

Hadmar snapped his head around. "Yes, Your Grace?"

"You are a Temple Knight of Saint Cunar. As such, I expect you to act the part. There will be no rushing this day. To do so gives the impression of fear. Is that clear?"

Hadmar, duly chastised, nodded his head. "Yes, Your Grace." He rode off at a very slow trot.

Hargild returned his attention to the Temple Knights. They were five hundred strong, the best of the Holy Army. A group of them turned their heads towards him, raising their swords in salute. He acknowledged their attention with a wave of his hand, pride swelling in his chest.

A call from his left drew his attention, and he looked to see Brother Lungren, commander of the initiates, approaching on foot. The man wore the same light grey tabard as his charges, but the edges of his were trimmed in white. Easy to spot amongst the darker grey of the full-fledged knights of the order.

"Something troubling you, Brother?" asked the father general.

"The front of the column is under attack, Your Grace."

"Let me guess. Orcs?"

The commander's startled look betrayed his surprise. "Yes, my lord, how did you know?"

"They have also been harrying the rear of the column. Do not fear, they will do little damage."

"Yes, sir." The commander stood, waiting.

"Is there something else?"

"Yes, Your Grace," admitted Lungren. "Allow me the honour of sending the initiates into battle. Let us drive the enemy from their place of concealment."

Father General Hargild thought it over. They were all knights, trained before entering the order, but each must serve for one year as an initiate, little more than armoured footmen, before they were allowed to wear the full trappings of the order. As such, they were all eager to show their devotion.

"Very well," he finally said. "You may take the initiates and push into the woods. Do not stray too far, however. We must not be distracted by these greenskins. It is the Human death worshippers we are after."

"Yes, Your Grace." Brother Lungren turned, making his way back to his men.

Hargild looked eastward once more. How much longer would it be until they found their objective?

Athgar glanced left and right, noting how straight the line of warriors was. He had taken a hundred of the youngest, fittest members of the Therengian fyrd and arrayed them across a small clearing as if they were intent on making a stand. They were positioned with spears and shields but little else in the way of protection, something that troubled him deeply. The enemy, he knew, had armour, even the newest recruits, and he wondered, not for the first time, if making this stand was sheer folly.

The woods to his front erupted with activity as Orcs streamed back towards his lines. As they drew closer, they took up positions on either flank, swelling their numbers.

Gahruhl was the last to emerge, sprinting across the field to halt before him, barely out of breath. *"They are coming,"* she said, using the Orcish tongue. *"My magic has slowed them, but there is no mistaking the noise of their approach."*

"Any idea of numbers?" Athgar asked.

"The archers are in the hundreds, but I fear it is the footmen who are coming through the woods. I can not say for certain how many."

"Then we shall just have to wait and see."

"I will take up my position on the flank."

"*Very well,*" the Fire Mage said, "*but remember, our only purpose here is to draw them south, not engage in a melee.*"

"*Understood,*" said Gahruhl. She ran off to Athgar's right, squeezing into the line beside Karag.

"Are you sure you're ready for this?" asked Raleth.

"It's a bit late asking now, isn't it?" Athgar replied. "In any event, we have little choice. Here they come."

Athgar was expecting the enemy to charge forward, but instead, they showed remarkable discipline, halting at the edge of the forest to form up into a solid line, their light grey tunics making them look like ghosts.

He waited, watching them as they finally began their advance. They wore heavy armour, much like full Temple Knights, but the uneven ground kept them at a slow pace. They struggled to keep their lines straight.

Athgar drew his axe and raised it high, a signal that things were about to begin. All along the line, men tightened the grip on their shields. On the flanks, the Orcs readied axes.

The enemy drew closer until Athgar could make out the differences in each one's armour. It was a frightening sight as the knight's metal armour made them look as if they were some strange conjuration from the Underworld. He had fought Temple Knights before, but that had been from behind the palisaded walls of Ord-Kurgad. Here, the stakes were much higher, for there were no walls to seek refuge behind.

He glanced at the ground seeking his markers. Before forming the line, he had paced off the range of his magic. Now the enemy was passing his carefully placed stones, marking the point of no return.

Athgar brought the axe down, signalling the battle to commence. On the flank, Gahruhl began casting, and then a small sliver of grey raced across to sink into the dirt. The ground rumbled as small spikes of rock burst upward, each no more than the length of a forearm. The effect on the enemy was immediate, causing them to falter.

As orders were called out trying to straighten their line, Athgar sent forth a streak of fire, striking the centre of the enemy formation. The plate armour of the knights protected them, but their grey tabards, in which they took so much pride, burst into flames. The initiates, not as hardened to magic as they were to regular combat, began to waver.

Another spell flew from Gahruhl's hands, and then the ground opened up, revealing a small trench before the enemy. The front rank panicked, halting far too quickly for those behind to understand what was happening. Men fell forward, mostly uninjured, but exposing the second rank rather unexpectedly.

On Athgar's left, Urughar's archers let loose with their volley. The arrows did little actual damage, but the effect on their morale was marked. Athgar called on his inner spark once more, and a wall of fire leaped up before the enemy. They backed up in fear as officers struggled to regain control over their charges.

"Now!" ordered Athgar. His men about-faced, placing their backs to the enemy, and started running. This was the most dangerous part of the battle, for their withdrawal could quickly turn into a rout.

They raced back across the field to the safety of the trees. The Orcs, who were fleeter of foot, had already formed back up at the treeline and were standing ready, covering the Therengians as they made their withdrawal. Athgar halted by Gahruhl, his breath coming in ragged gasps.

"It has worked," said the Orc. "The enemy has stalled for now. No doubt they will send for help, then the entire army will pursue. I hope Nat-Alia knows what she is doing."

"So do I," said Athgar. "So do I."

OPENING MOVES

Autumn 1104 SR

Athgar looked north, watching for the approach of the enemy. The Therengian line stretched to his left and right, a solid mass of men and women willing to sacrifice their lives to protect their families. The hill they stood on overlooked a flat plain, flanked on either side by dense woods. Three hundred and fifty of his spearmen formed the front rank while his archers, meagre as they were, were farther up the hill. They would use their advantage to loose volleys over their comrades' heads as the enemy approached. Most of his warriors had little in the way of protection, save for their shields. A small group was blessed with chain shirts, and these he kept as a reserve, able to reinforce the line when needed.

He glanced farther up the hill to where Natalia stood surveying the area. She would be commanding the battle, standing beneath the stone gate the Orcs had spoken of. Around her were Zahruhl and the Stone Crushers, ready to wield the magic of the earth, taking full advantage of the powers of the strange stones. Of the other tribes, he saw no sign but knew they were waiting on either side of the field, their hunters ready to harass the enemy as they approached.

The early morning mist was just burning off, revealing the small stream that meandered across the plain. The sight somehow reminded him of home, and he was suddenly struck by the memory of his father teaching him how to fish. His recollections were soon cut short by the sight of a lone rider appearing out of the mist. The horseman halted just shy of the water and stood in his saddle straining to make out the Therengian line. Whoever it was didn't wait long before turning around and riding north. It appeared the enemy had finally arrived.

———

Father General Hargild watched Duke Heinrich's approach with a smile. "We have them," he called out.

"At last," called back the duke. "Are they close?"

"Just to the south, in fact. They've finally decided to make a stand."

"Any idea of numbers?"

"About five hundred," replied the father general. "I'm surprised they chose to fight."

"Perhaps they have no choice. Their village may be nearby."

"If it is, we shall find it soon enough. In the meantime, we shall destroy this ragtag army of theirs once and for all."

"What is our plan?" asked the duke. "Shall we rush them in one large mass?"

"Tempting though it is, I'm inclined to be more cautious. They may have more warriors in the woods. We'll split your forces up. I want your lighter troops on either side, and we'll use them to flush out the woods. Concurrent with that, your more experienced men will conduct a frontal assault."

"And your Temple Knights?"

"I shall use the initiates to reinforce the flanks. The rest I will hold in reserve until you've weakened the enemy line."

"You surprise me," said the duke.

"Oh? How so?"

"Your initiates are all trained knights. Why do you have them serve on foot?"

The father general smiled. "Unlike the other orders, warriors come to our order already trained in the art of combat, but they often lack the experience of our seasoned knights. As such, we have them serve on foot for the first year of their service. It teaches them humility."

"Seems like a waste to me," said Heinrich. "The very idea of knights fighting on foot is counterproductive."

"I might remind you the Temple Knights of Saint Cunar are the premiere fighting force on the Continent," said the father general. "Our methods have been developed over centuries."

"I trust you won't be insulted if I lead my own knights into the fray?"

Hargild smiled. "Of course not. Our objective here is to defeat the enemy. Whether that's done by your forces or mine is of little consequence." He looked at the sun briefly before returning his gaze to the duke. "How long to get into position, do you think?"

"In a hurry, are we?"

"It would be convenient if we could wrap this up before noon," said the father general. "We still have a village to find after all."

"I should have the men in position by mid-morning. Will that be sufficient?"

"It would indeed."

"Then I shall be off," said Duke Heinrich. "There is more work yet to be done."

"The Saints be with you," said the father general.

Natalia stifled a yawn. She had not slept well last night, the burden of command weighing heavily upon her shoulders. In her heart, she knew making a stand was the best option, but looking around at the men and women gathered here, she began to have doubts. How many would die this day?

Off in the distance, she could make out individuals riding back and forth, cajoling the enemy warriors into position. Natalia knew this was typical for an army, her training had included such knowledge, but to actually see it was still intriguing. Looking at her own troops positioned before her, she saw a solid line of Therengians under Athgar's command. They were relaxed at the moment, the enemy still distant, but she sensed their unease as the full strength of the Holy Army unfolded before them.

Feeling the presence of an Orc at her side, she turned, expecting to see Shaluhk. Instead, she looked into the stern countenance of Voruhn. Kargen had told Natalia of their experiences in Khasrahk, leading them all to wonder about Voruhn's loyalty.

"Fear not," said Voruhn as if sensing the unease. "I shall do all I can today to ease the misgivings you have about me."

"You speak the common tongue?" said Natalia.

"I suppose I do," replied the shamaness, "though it is a surprise to me."

"You were unaware you spoke another language?"

"My mind is full of strange memories of late. I wonder if the Ancestors are speaking to me?"

"And what of Zahruhl?" asked Natalia.

"He, too, is eager to make amends. We shall both do our best this day. I promise you."

They stood in silence, mesmerized by the sight of their enemy.

"Such large numbers," said Voruhn. "How shall we defeat them?"

Natalia set her mind to work, burying her doubts. "They mean to push up to either flank. You can see by the way they're deploying their troops."

"Surely the centre is the most dangerous?"

"True, but their commander is cautious. He won't move up until either side is secure. He's worried about being attacked from the sides."

"And are we doing so?"

"No," said Natalia. "We have hunters on both sides, but their job is only to skirmish."

"To what end?"

"Fighting a battle is about stamina and courage. Break either, and we shall have a victory, but if we fail, we'll have no second chance."

"And so you mean to wear them down?"

"If we can."

"How do we do that against so many warriors?" asked Voruhn.

"By using the one advantage we have, magic."

"Magic is powerful against an individual, I will grant you that, but against an army?"

"Battle magic is not always about killing," said Natalia. "It is about destroying the enemy's will to fight. Mages are not common amongst Humans, and we know the enemy we face today has none. That also means they likely lack experience facing such foes. We can use that to our advantage."

"But surely they have mages in the Human kingdoms?"

"They do," agreed Natalia, "but seldom are they trained in the battlefield employment of magic. There is much more to becoming a battle mage than learning spells."

"So you are saying not all Human casters are battle mages?"

"Very few, if the truth be known. Only the family is said to provide such training."

"Then it is good you are on our side. We shall attempt to live up to your training."

Kargen stared out from amongst the trees at the distant warriors. Even as he watched, enemy archers were advancing towards the forest to his north.

"They mean to flush us out," he remarked. *"I think it is time you strung your bows."*

Kragor laughed. *"We have plenty of time for that. At this speed, it will take them half the morning to get to us."*

"Very well, but keep your eyes on them. We do not want to be taken by surprise."

"Do not worry, we will not fail you."

Kargen looked at the archer. *"I have complete trust in you, my friend."*

"And I, you," Kragor replied, *"but I wish Laruhk were here."*

"As do I, but it could not be helped. He and the others were needed elsewhere."

"Where are they?"

Kargen grinned. *"You shall see, in time. It is best you do not know just yet. It might unsettle you."*

"I am afraid of nothing," protested Kragor.

"So I see, and yet you should be. A little fear keeps an Orc alive."

"You are hiding something," his companion accused, *"but I shall pry no further. It is not a hunter's place to question the acts of his chieftain."*

"You are wrong," said Kargen. *"It is quite within a hunter's right to question authority, but in this case, I shall not answer. Laruhk, Durgash, and the others are trying something new, something no Orc has ever before attempted, at least as far as we know."*

"Now you have me intrigued. How am I to concentrate on the task at hand?"

Kargen laughed. *"I tell you this only to give you hope, my friend, not to distract you."*

"Where is Shaluhk?"

"Behind us," said Kargen, *"with the other hunters. As our hunters are wounded, they shall fall back to her position, allowing her to heal them. They, in turn, will take the place of the injured, ensuring our strength is maintained."*

"It would be easier if we had more bows," suggested Kragor.

"So it would," agreed Kargen, *"but we had scant time to prepare for battle, and our warbows are difficult to make. In time, the entire tribe will be so equipped, but for now, we must make do with what few we have. Now remember, do not use them until the enemy is close. We must make every arrow count."*

To the west, Mortag shifted his feet, trying to ease the strain on his back. He moved his left arm, the withered appendage in a sling, a constant reminder of his difficult birthing. He was old by Orc standards, and yet his mastery of fire was well developed. He cast his eyes to the trees above, noting their condition. It had been a dry summer, and the winter snow had yet to arrive. The trees in this part of the woods were pine, littering the ground with their needles, leaving the forest floor bare of undergrowth. It meant the Orcs could use their bows with ease, but the same could be said of the enemy.

He glanced to his rear, where Laghul was waiting with a small group of attendants. The shamaness would heal the wounded, as was the custom, while beside her stood Kirak, perched at the edge of the woods, his eyes focused on the enemy.

The Humans had begun their advance, a long line of footmen interspersed with archers. Behind them came the foot troops of the Church, easy to spot in their light grey tabards. The edge of the woods was a slightly higher elevation, giving Mortag a good view of the enemy as they approached. He marvelled at the Human fascination for forming their men into tight groups. This was certainly not the Orcish way, and yet who was he to complain when it gave his hunters such easy targets?

Mortag waited until the rear rank of Humans entered the stream, then gave the command to attack.

Natalia watched as a cloud of arrows appeared to the west, marking the start of hostilities. She thought back to her training at the Volstrum. Strategy and tactics had always been of interest to her. But now, at this moment, she wished she'd paid even more attention to the little details.

To her front came the enemy foot soldiers, their metal armour gleaming under the banner of the duke. They carried a variety of weapons, ranging from hammers to axes and even swords as they advanced against the unarmoured Therengians, confident in their victory and spoiling for a fight.

The footmen were flanked by crossbowmen, an excellent choice when confronting armoured opponents, but their slow rate of fire would prove advantageous to her side, of that she was sure. So far, the enemy had done precisely what she had expected, but she wasn't fooling herself; she knew plans seldom survived initial contact. As they began crossing the stream, she could finally make out the duke's knights.

For a fleeting moment, she wondered where Sir Raynald was but quickly put such thoughts from her mind. There was a battle to be won, and he was an enemy combatant after all.

In front of her, the Therengians stirred, checking shields and weapons as they finally prepared for the impending assault. She saw Athgar look her way and smile, bringing a warmth to her heart. The thought of losing him closed in on her mind, and she struggled to fight down the panic.

A hand rested on her shoulder. "He will survive," said Voruhn. "Of that, you must have no doubt."

"How can you be so sure?" Natalia asked.

"I can not believe fate has brought him here to die. Think of all you have been through already."

She looked at the Orc, seeing the determination in her eyes. "I suppose you're right."

"Now," continued Voruhn, "you must put such thoughts from your mind. You have a battle to manage."

Shouting echoed across the field, drawing Natalia's gaze westward. The Orcs of the Black Axe had begun their skirmishing, catching their foes by surprise. The Humans, after their initial shock, soon recovered, and their archers began sending volley after volley into the woods while their footmen drew closer. Soon they were well into the trees themselves, making it impossible for their own archers to assist.

Natalia smiled. This was an unexpected twist, for it appeared the duke had not foreseen this complication. From her angle, she could see little, save for the enemy pushing farther into the treeline, but the sounds of battle certainly told the story of an intense struggle. The enemy archers soon disappeared into the trees, following their compatriots, while the temple footmen brought up the rear.

She forced herself to look eastward to where a similar force was advancing. The commander on that side, however, had wisely kept his archers in the open, where they might best use the power of their volleys. The footmen were in amongst the trees, but Kargen and the Orcs of the Red Hand were farther south, waiting for the best moment to strike.

To her front, the duke's men pushed closer, picking up their pace now that the enemy was almost within their grasp.

"Archers may begin," she called out. Her orders were echoed down the line, and then the onslaught of arrows began. The first volley fell short, but it didn't take long to find the range. Soon the Stone Crusher Orcs were joining in, sending a hail of projectiles towards the enemy.

Arrows clattered on armour, causing the advancing enemy to waver under the ferocity of the attack. They soon regained their momentum as sergeants and officers urged them on. Closer they drew until even spears were within range.

Gahruhl moved up, beginning her first spell. Shards of stone erupted from the ground, penetrating boots and throwing the enemy into disarray. The master of earth held back her power, knowing she must conserve her strength, but even so, the result was impressive. Amplified by the magic of the stone gate, the shards grew larger, forming into great spears that interfered with the enemy formation, forcing them to bunch up to thread their way through the new obstacles.

The archers redoubled their efforts, concentrating on the points of convergence. Once more, Gahruhl called forth the power of the earth, and a tiny spark sailed forth, striking the ground before the enemy's advance. The ground rumbled, and then the earth split, causing a small fissure to appear, no deeper than a man's shin. She kept concentrating as it elongated, spreading across the front of the enemy, causing further mayhem.

Athgar stood his ground. The enemy was merely a spear's throw away, their attack slowed by the obstacles, but it was still only a matter of time until they broke through. Out of the corner of his eye, he noticed a man go down, a crossbow through his neck. Another bolt whistled overhead, but he ignored it. "Shields up!" he ordered.

The fyrd raised shields, overlapping their edges, their spears prepared to strike. It would be one initial thrust, then the enemy would be upon them, and it would become the work of axes and long knives to deal out the damage.

He briefly worried for Natalia's safety and then shook his head. He must concentrate on his own battle this day. She was more than capable of looking after herself.

A roar of defiance arose from the enemy troops, and then they launched themselves forward, covering the last few yards at a run. The Therengian spears came down, thrust into the first wave of warriors. A clash of arms soon followed as swords beat on shields, and axes rang out against armour.

The Therengian in front of Athgar fell, a vicious cut to the face. Thinking quickly, the Fire Mage cast, thrusting out his hands and sending a stream of fire through the gap. The enemy warriors paused for a moment, steeling themselves to face the wielder of fire, allowing Athgar to grasp the injured man's arm and pull him back to safety. He stepped into the gap, raising his shield just in time to deflect a blow.

A titanic struggle now erupted as the duke's footmen attempted to smash through the shield wall of the fyrd. A few enterprising individuals tried slashing low at the Therengians' legs, but this was soon countered by the quick thinking of those in the second row, who stabbed out with knives and short spears.

Athgar, feeling the press of the enemy on his shield, planted his legs to give him more stability. Pulling forth his axe, he called on his inner spark, and the head ignited, green flames licking along its edge. He struck out, feeling his weapon cut into metal. As he wrenched his weapon free, his opponent fell, lost to sight amongst the press of men.

Suddenly the man beside Athgar went down, a sword to the chest, and the enemy, sensing their moment was upon them, redoubled their efforts.

BATTLE OF THE STANDING STONES

Autumn 1104 SR

The line began to break. Natalia gave the order, and the reserve moved up, experienced Therengian warriors ready to push back the enemy. They rushed down the hill straight into the melee with a mighty clash of arms. So ferocious was their advance that she watched as the enemy was driven back, rushing downhill to escape the slaughter.

The counterattack had done its job, halting the enemy's advance. But now the Therengians, flush with victory, ran past their initial position, and the enemy responded with a fury, sending in fresh troops to trap them.

She watched in fear as Athgar struggled to bring order to chaos as the duke's men renewed their attack. He was in the thick of it now, hacking away with his axe, a line no longer even a possibility. The battle had degenerated into one big mass of warriors, each fighting for their lives.

The Orcs of the Black Axe fell back as the enemy warriors streamed through the forest. The western flank was collapsing quickly, and Mortag, master of flame, knew it was up to him to put an end to it. Hearing the call from his chieftain, he began casting. All around the woods, they had prepared bundles of sticks at the base of many trees. Mortag closed his eyes, digging deep to conjure forth his spark.

Smoke began billowing from three of the pyres, then they burst into flames. He cast again, igniting two more stacks of wood. The dry trees of the forest crackled and popped as bark caught fire, then flames began climbing up the heights.

The fire spread quickly, soon covering the ground in dense grey smoke. Mortag slowed his breathing as he prayed to the Ancestors, but as fate would have it, it was unnecessary, for the prevailing wind blew the smoke northeastward, directly into the enemy's faces.

The master of flame waited just long enough to see the enemy begin to panic, then turned and sprinted to rejoin his companions.

"They will be hard-pressed to stand," noted Kirak, *"but how will we extinguish the flame once the battle is over?"*

"It will be difficult," noted Mortag, *"but worth the sacrifice to defeat the enemy."*

Kirak smiled as Laghul appeared beside her bondmate. *"How are the casualties?"*

"Light," she replied. *"It seems the Humans are not used to our style of fighting. It is but a simple matter to duck behind the trees when they use their volleys."*

"Volleys?" said Kirak. *"They use such tactics even in the woods?"*

"I doubt they know any different," observed Mortag. *"They are warriors, not hunters. Such ideas have likely never crossed their minds."*

"It is to our advantage," said Laghul. *"Let us not complain. What is our next step?"*

"We shall give them a chance to burn for a little longer," noted Kirak. *"Mortag, can you extinguish a corridor of fire?"*

"I can," the old Orc replied, *"but it will not last long. You mean to counterattack?"*

Kirak nodded. *"I do. If we strike at the right time, I think they will break."*

The smoke began to thicken as the flames reached the upper boughs. There was a crack as a large branch fell, sending sparks high into the air where they swirled around, caught up the strange wind that swept through the woods.

Kirak called his hunters forward, each of them with an eager look upon their faces. *"Prepare yourselves,"* he began, *"for when Mortag casts his spell, I shall lead you through the fire."*

He recognized the look of fear on their faces but also the look of determination. They would follow him into the spirit realm if he asked them, of that he was sure, but at what cost?

Laghul touched his shoulder. *"I pray the Ancestors will look over you."*

Kirak took a deep breath, steadying his nerves. *"And you,"* he replied. The fire was spreading quickly now, and he knew the moment was at hand.

Nodding at his master of flame, he gripped his axe, steeling himself for what was to come.

Mortag held his arms out to the side as words of power flowed from his lips. Smoke swirled around almost blinding everyone's view of him, and then he thrust his hands forward, sending a vortex of smoke northward. Along the indicated path, flames became more subdued, soon little more than small sporadic wisps of soot and smoke.

Kirak gave a yell and launched himself down the corridor, the brave hunters of the Black Axe following.

In the east, Kargen watched the fierce melee going on at the centre of the line, but his task was here, on the flank. He waited as the enemy footmen emerged from a thicket of trees. Here, the forest was more sparse than to the west, with many small clearings to break up the woods. He had picked his place of concealment carefully and was now rewarded by the sight before him.

"*Now,*" he roared.

Kragor was the first to let loose his arrow. It struck a footman, a sergeant by the looks of him, just as he was trying to issue an order. Others soon followed, the mighty warbows of the Red Hand making short work of the light armour of their enemy.

Three more volleys sailed forth, sending the enemy into chaos, and then Kargen rose, calling out a challenge that echoed off the trees. Kragor's warbows shifted targets to the archers along their flank as the hunters rushed past in a blur, axes seeking blood.

Kargen hit the line in a fury, striking out with his axe, taking an arm clean off at the elbow. He kicked his opponent aside, striking out again, using his massive strength to move the blade with lightning speed. It scraped across a warrior's chest, cutting leather but doing little else. A spear came towards his face, and he ducked, the point going just over his head. Grasping the offending weapon in his left hand, he pulled, watching in satisfaction as his foe was pulled off balance. The great Orc followed up with an overhead blow that split the man's skull open, but when he yanked back on the weapon, he discovered the blade had become caught in his opponent's helmet, leaving him vulnerable. A sword jabbed out, catching him in the forearm, and black blood trickled down his arm as he gave a massive tug on his axe, freeing it from the grip of the metal.

All around him, Orcs pressed forward, the enemy stunned by the suddenness of the attack. Beside him, a fellow hunter struck out, slicing into the leg of a Human. Then a spear came out of nowhere, digging into the hunter's stomach and driving him to the ground. A Human stepped up, driving his sword into the hunter's brain with a clean, swift motion.

Kargen bellowed in rage and struck out, but the man shifted his stance, avoiding the blow. The warrior's blade sliced forward yet again, stabbing into the chieftain's thigh, penetrating the leg muscle. Kargen gave a thunderous roar of pain as the blade came out the other side, tearing through flesh.

Pivoting on his uninjured leg, he ripped the sword from the man's grip. The warrior tried to back up, but Kargen was soon upon him, driving him to the ground. Moments later, his axe dug into the Human's chest, sending a crimson spray into the air.

***

Athgar walked forward, slipping as he stepped over bodies. All around him was death and destruction. The moaning of the wounded was overshadowed only by the sounds of the living, struggling as they were to destroy their enemies.

A sword glanced off the Fire Mage's helmet, and he staggered back from the force of the blow. Thrusting his hands out, he sent forth a streak of flames but missed his target in the confusion of battle. When an axe dug into his shield, he felt the wood give way, splintering as it fell apart. He struck back with his own axe, feeling it bite into metal, and then pulled back, grunting with the effort.

He caught a glimpse of Harwath, his arm covered in blood, though whether it was his own or someone else's, Athgar had no idea. The fighting seemed to go on until he felt as though he had no strength left.

The duke's men were pushing hard despite their losses, desperate to gain the heights. Athgar lashed out at a foe, driving the axe blade into a leg, but before he could withdraw it, a horse slammed into him, knocking him to the ground. The mount rode past, stirrups rattling as the duke's knights pushed up the hill.

***

Natalia saw Athgar go down, disappearing beneath the hooves of the enemy as the knights surged up the hill, with little left to stop them. She ordered the Orcs forward, and the Stone Crushers rushed ahead, heedless of the danger that awaited them.

Without warning, a horse reared up in front of her, and she dove out of the way. Moments later, a shard of stone shattered against the rider, knocking him from the saddle. Orcs swarmed him, hacking away with their axes.

She felt anger building as she thought of Athgar lying dead on the battlefield. Focusing on the closest group of riders, she began concentrating on drawing out her power despite the pain. Her stomach went cold. A tight knot made breathing difficult, but she held on, gritting her teeth even as the words of power spilled from her lips. Streaks of ice flew from her hands, a massive volley that turned the air cold. They clattered against armour and stabbed into horses, cutting them down as they struggled against the hill.

Still, she kept up the spell, with more and more ice flying through the air, the impact rattling as it struck helmets, shields, and breastplates. Her vision began to blur, and she collapsed, gasping for air, her stomach no longer cold, but burning with a fierce, fiery agony.

Voruhn appeared beside her, working her magic to stem the pain. Natalia thought her stomach was about to explode, so intense was the feeling, and then the magic began to flow from the Orc, seeping into Natalia and giving her strength. She staggered to her feet.

"What happened?" asked Voruhn.

"I don't know. It felt as though my stomach was on fire." She wanted to say more, but at that precise moment, the enemy was gathering for another charge. Natalia sought out the duke, easily identifiable beneath the banner that bore his coat of arms. From her vantage point, it was a tricky shot, but she knew it was now or never. She took a breath, summoning all that remained of her reserves.

The blast of ice that emanated from her hands was not so much a group of shards as it was a giant, single spike. It raced across the distance like a thunderbolt of the Saints, crashing into the duke and punching clean through his breastplate. For a moment, Natalia thought she had missed, but then the man swayed, leaning to the right until he finally toppled to the ground amid the carnage.

Natalia watched, knowing she had pushed herself beyond her limits. She felt moisture pooling in the corner of her eye and wiped it, only to notice it was blood. Feeling light-headed, she staggered back, desperate to remain on her feet.

Kargen rushed to the cover of the trees. The warbows were still doing their damage, driving the enemy archers back, but he knew they would soon return. Even as he gasped for breath, the temple footmen set about clearing the woods. These were heavily armoured warriors; they would not be so easily defeated.

He looked across to where Shaluhk was tending to the wounded, her magic in almost continuous use. *"It is time,"* he said.

She finished her spell, watching as the flesh mended. The Orc warrior rose, testing his leg, then ran back to the front lines.

"Are you sure?" she asked. *"The enemy still has not committed their Temple Knights."*

Kargen stared off into the distance where the Temple Knights remained formed up behind the duke's forces, more than five hundred strong. He would have liked to wait, but the situation in the centre of the line was deteriorating rapidly. *"We have little choice,"* he said. *"It is now or never."*

Shaluhk knelt, digging deep into her repertoire of spells. Words began to tumble from her lips as the magic enveloped her. Moments later, she saw the ghostly form of Laruhk before her. *"It is time,"* she said. *"You must act now before it is too late."*

Laruhk nodded, then looked at someone out of Shaluhk's sight. She broke the spell, returning her gaze to the battle unfolding before her eyes.

Laruhk turned to Rugg. *"Are you sure this will work?"*

"The magic of the earth is not just about working stone," the shaman replied. *"Now come, all is as I have foretold. It is time for us to begin."* He urged his mount forward, the great beast responding instantly.

Laruhk held his spear tightly, his legs wrapped around the beast's ribs. The line of mounted Orcs began moving as one, crossing the ground quickly, hooves thundering as they went.

The Orc riders broke from the woods in time to see the Cunar footmen getting ready to advance. The enemy had formed up, presenting a solid wall of steel, but it made little difference to Laruhk's Orcs. He led his band straight into the enemy, the tuskers ripping through armour and tearing flesh as if they were paper.

Laruhk fought to keep his seat. They were riding bareback, holding on by little more than the tuft of hair that ran down the creatures' backs. Stabbing out with his right hand, his spear took a man in the shoulder as his mount roared past, bowling over five more before Laruhk could even draw a breath. He caught a glimpse of Durgash, firing off a bow and wondered how his comrade was able to maintain his balance on such a wild beast.

There were nearly two dozen tuskers, each ridden by an Orc. It had been Rugg's idea to utilize them as cavalry, and Laruhk had quickly agreed. It only took the magic of the master of earth to communicate with them, and the fearsome beasts had readily agreed. Now they tore through the enemy without so much as a blink.

A few brave men tried to make a stand, but the thick hide of the tuskers proved immune to their weapons. They were quickly knocked aside or driven beneath the hooves of the giant beasts.

Through the Cunar footmen they rode, doing immense damage. These men were all knights, a requirement for joining the order, but the helplessness of their position soon overwhelmed them. They broke, rushing for the safety of the woods.

The Orc riders, now with their blood up, turned west, heading directly for the mass of troops threatening the centre.

Athgar staggered to his feet, pulling off his helmet to wipe blood from his eyes. Looking up, he noticed a horseman bearing down on him, and he threw himself to the ground just as the hooves thundered past. The horse slowed, and the rider turning in place, his sword already bloodied. Athgar stared, stunned to see Sir Raynald, but the duke's man didn't recognize him beneath the mud and blood.

"Stand down," he roared.

Sir Raynald halted his advance. "Athgar? Is that you? What are you doing here?"

"These are my people," he replied, "and I will fight to the end to save them."

"They are death worshippers," insisted the knight, "and must be destroyed."

"No!" Athgar shouted. "They are people, just like you. You've been lied to, Raynald, as has everyone else. These are not worshippers of death! They never have been. Put down your weapons, and let us end this."

Sir Raynald raised his sword. "I'm afraid I can't do that, my friend. I have given my oath to the duke. To surrender now would be to face dishonour."

"Then I'm afraid I shall have to kill you."

Sir Raynald saluted Athgar with his sword. "So be it. Let us fight to the death." He lowered his visor and kicked back on his spurs, charging forward with his sword extended.

Athgar called forth a blast of fire that smashed into the knight's horse. The beast reared up, its hair on fire. Sir Raynald leaped from the saddle at the last moment, avoiding damage as his mount fell, crashing to the ground. The horse cried out in pain, but the knight ignored it, racing towards his prey on foot, still gripping his sword.

Athgar picked up a discarded shield and advanced, ready to fight to his last breath. Around them, the fighting had devolved into individual clashes almost as if the Gods themselves had selected pairs of enemies to settle their scores.

Sir Raynald attacked first, a powerful strike that smashed against Athgar's shield with a dull thud. Athgar countered with a blow of his flaming axe, taking the knight on his plate-covered arm, but it merely glanced off and sent sparks flying.

Raynald countered, stabbing out with the tip of his sword. The Therengian jumped back, but still, the blade bit, drawing blood, yet thankfully doing little real damage. The knight pressed his attack, stamping forward and slashing at his opponent's legs.

Athgar continued backing up, overwhelmed by the onslaught. Sir Raynald was a knight, with a lifetime of training to back up his assault. What did Athgar have? Momentarily distracted by his doubts, he tripped over a body and fell to the ground.

Sir Raynald loomed over him. Athgar thrust out his hand, frantically sending out a streak of fire that missed his target but caused the knight to back up, giving the Fire Mage time to recover.

"Give up," called out Sir Raynald. "You know you won't defeat me."

"I can't," replied Athgar. "To do so would sacrifice my people. Would you do any less for yours?"

Raynald paused, looking at the battle raging around them. Without their leader, the fight had gone out of the duke's men. First, it was only a few, those nearest to their fallen lord, but as word spread, so, too, did their panic. Men began running away, clearing the way for the Therengians to advance.

Athgar stood, waiting for Raynald's attack. The knight stared back, indecision on his face, for it was now clear that the army was disintegrating. He was struggling to come to grips with this when an arrow flew out of nowhere, taking him in the arm, then Athgar was there knocking his sword aside. Raynald tried to draw his dagger, but a kick from his adversary sent him onto his back.

Athgar stood over him, his axe raised for the killing blow.

"I surrender," called out Sir Raynald. "I ask for quarter."

"Why should I let you live?" demanded Athgar. "You have come to destroy us."

Sir Raynald released his dagger. "Do as you must," he said, "but know if you let me live, I shall never again take up arms against your people."

"What of your oath to your duke?"

"Look around you," said the knight. "You have destroyed his army. Only the Church stands in your way of total victory."

COUNTERATTACK

Autumn 1104 SR

The duke's forces had begun their rout, fleeing the scene of carnage. Had they known how weak their foe was, they could have easily smashed them, but with the death of their leader, the fight went out of them. They raced north in a panic, their enemy at their heels.

Father General Hargild was waiting, ready to release the superior power of the Temple Knights, but with his overconfidence, he had brought them up close to the lines of battle. Now, with the army retreating, men were streaming past the horsemen, clogging the field, and making a charge impossible. He looked west with the idea of flanking the masses before him, but a large number of Orcs emerged from the trees, driving even more of the duke's men before them.

East looked promising, but then another horde of greenskins rushed forth, stopping to loose arrows as they ran. The armour of the Temple Knights was the best on the Continent, but the enemy targeted their horses, the arrows digging deep into flesh.

Then his eyes caught a glimpse of the great beasts heading his way. Father General Hargild was a brave man, but the sight of these unnatural brutes charging towards him turned him pale. They closed at an impossible speed, crashing into his men with a booming crescendo.

The Temple Knights of Saint Cunar were the finest warriors in the civilized world. They could be counted on to defeat any enemy in the Petty

Kingdoms, yet these strange creatures were more than just mounts; they dug in with tusks and razor-sharp teeth, tearing their way through the Church lines.

With many of their horses down and caught in the press of a retreating army, there was little they could do. They fought back as best they could, but the swords and axes of knights were of little use against the thick hides of the tuskers.

Laruhk struck out with his spear, taking a knight in the chest. With the added force of his tusker behind his thrust, the tip easily penetrated the plate armour, but as he rode past, he was forced to release his grip or be pulled from the beast's back.

His eyes darted around, spotting the other riders. The tuskers ran as a herd, plowing through the knights as if they were little more than blades of grass. Those who weren't trampled to death were torn asunder by the massive teeth of the creatures.

Laruhk watched as one of his riders went down, his mount punctured by a well-placed lance. A knight rushed forward ready to finish off his foe, but an arrow from Durgash took him in the neck, and he fell to the ground, unmoving.

Shaluhk spotted her chance. In the wake of the tusker charge, the Temple Knights were staggering around, disoriented by the fury of the impact. Closing her eyes, she called upon all the power she could summon. It was a difficult spell, one she had never before attempted, but she knew, in her heart, now was the time to act. The magic surged through her as she intoned the words, struggling to maintain her balance under the onslaught of mystical forces. As she released the spell, small white particles shot from her hands to land just a stone's throw in front of her, quickly sinking into the ground.

Moments later, the particles expanded, growing into columns of mist before they slowly coalesced, forming into images of Orcs. These were no hunters, but Orc warriors, armed in ancient armour, the likes of which the world had not seen for centuries. When they looked at her with lifeless eyes, she pointed at the great battle before her.

As one, they turned, letting loose with a keening sound that shook her to her very bones, and then they were rushing forward with spears and swords, tearing across the ground in a mad dash to engage the enemy.

The warhorses of the knights, caught between the vicious tuskers and the otherworldly images of the spirit warriors, panicked. The fear spread like a wildfire, and it was all the knights could do to save themselves from being trampled to death by their own horses. Many of the Temple Knights abandoned their mounts, eager to take up arms against their foe, while others were carried from the field as their horses bolted off in terror.

Kargen blocked a sword, then struck out in retaliation, his axe biting deeply into the knight's forearm, cutting through the metal and down into the bone. The man screamed out in pain, but the Orc just pushed him out of the way with his shield. Kargen took another step, calling out a challenge, but the enemy was retreating. The great chief could not understand why, and then a chill fell over him as wispy shapes surged past. He had a brief glimpse of the ghostly figure of an Orc warrior dressed in some type of scale armour, and then more appeared. All he could do was watch in fascination as these ancient warriors smashed into the enemy, leaving a trail of death and destruction in their wake.

Kargen looked around, orienting himself, only to spot Shaluhk amongst the wounded, barely able to stand. He rushed to her, catching her just as she fell.

"*Shaluhk!*" he called out. "*Are you hurt?*"

"*No,*" she replied, "*but I have exhausted my strength. It took all I had to cast that spell.*"

He looked into the distance where the melee still raged. "*What did you do?*"

"*I summoned ancient warriors to do my bidding.*"

"*Wherever did you learn such a thing?*"

"*I did not,*" Shaluhk replied, "*but Khurlig used her powers to possess me back in Ord-Kurgad. It seems when Uhdrig drove her from my body, some of her memories remained.*"

"*You must rest.*"

"*I can not, for to do so would release the conjured warriors from the physical world.*"

"*Release them, how?*" asked Kargen.

"*They would return to the realm of spirits. I must remain awake long enough to keep them here, but I am exhausted.*"

"*Then let me share your burden.*"

"That is very sweet of you," said Shaluhk, *"but how would you do such a thing? You are no shaman."*

"No," he agreed, *"but while I still have strength, I will not see you struggle. I shall carry you."*

Kargen lifted her, his arms beneath her knees and back. He took a couple of steps, then adjusted his hold slightly. *"There,"* he said. *"Now we are together once again."*

"As we should be."

Natalia watched Laruhk's forces as they tore through the enemy formation. From her vantage point, it was a remarkable sight as if a shark had just swum through a school of fish. Riderless horses began rushing northward, eager to escape the ferocious tusks of the great beasts.

She looked to the east where the warbows of the Red Hand were keeping up a steady stream of arrows, picking off those who survived the initial onslaught. Even from this distance, she could make out Shaluhk. The Orc was invoking her magic, and Natalia briefly wondered what spell she might be utilizing, for the shamaness was a healer, not a warrior. To the Water Mage's surprise, ghostly warriors materialized out of thin air.

She looked at Voruhn, to see her staring off in the same direction. "What spell is that?" Natalia asked.

"Warriors of the past," replied the shamaness, "though she must be powerful indeed to call on such spirits."

"I've never heard of it."

"Nor should you have," said the Orc. "It is an ancient spell, calling forth our Ancestors from the times of the great cities."

"I thought Orcs were hunters, not warriors."

"And so we are, these days, but in ancient times, we prided ourselves on our martial prowess. It remained so for many generations until the Elves put an end to such things."

"How long will they remain amongst the living?" asked Natalia.

"Only as long as Shaluhk can maintain her concentration. It takes great effort."

They watched in silence as the spirits raced into battle, sweeping aside their foes. Natalia saw an ancient warrior destroyed, its physical form dissipating like so much dust.

"I don't understand," she said. "How can a spirit die?"

"The magic gives them a physical form. If that form is disrupted, then the spirit is freed. They are not ghosts, at least not in the traditional sense, but rather a physical manifestation of their original life. How else would they be able to fight?"

"I hadn't thought of it that way. Is this a common tactic amongst your people?"

Voruhn turned to look at her. "They are your people too, Nat-Alia, for you are a member of the Red Hand, are you not?"

"I am, and proud to be so, but you still haven't answered my question."

Voruhn smiled. "I have never heard of such a spell being used before."

"And yet you know of it."

"I do, but I suspect that has more to do with my possession at the hands of Khurlig. It looks like we may have unlocked ancient knowledge as a result of her interference. Perhaps it is the will of the Ancestors."

"The Ancestors advise," cautioned Natalia. "They do not control."

"You are right, but you can not deny it is to our advantage."

"Do you think that's why you can speak our tongue?"

"I had not thought of that," answered Voruhn. "It is a gift that keeps on giving."

They turned their attention to the north once more, where the rest of the duke's warriors were now surrendering, throwing down their weapons, and begging for mercy. When Natalia finally spotted Athgar, her heart skipped a beat for he was up and walking amongst the wounded, alongside a familiar looking face, that of Sir Raynald.

She made her way down the hill, picking her way through the field of battle, Voruhn following. Athgar smiled at her approach, his white teeth in stark contrast to his bloody countenance.

"Are you hurt?" she called out.

"Only sore," he replied. "It has been a busy morning."

She moved closer, embracing him. He returned the gesture, crushing her against him. They stared into each other's eyes for a long moment, then kissed, lingering on the act until Sir Raynald coughed.

"Might I suggest," said the knight, "you ask the Temple Knights to surrender?"

"You think they might?" asked Athgar.

"They are honourable men. I know that's hard to believe under the circumstances, but I think they truly believed they were here to fight a death cult, as did I."

"That being so," said Natalia, "would they even be willing to listen to us?"

"Let me speak on your behalf," offered Sir Raynald. "I'm sure I can convince them of the error of their ways."

"It's worth a try," said Athgar, "but Natalia's the one in charge. It's her decision."

"Very well," said Natalia, "but how do we pull back our forces? We can't very well ask for their surrender with our army tearing through them."

"Leave that to me," said Voruhn.

Athgar looked at the Orc in wonder. "You speak our language?"

Natalia smiled. "She does."

"This day is just full of surprises," he said.

Voruhn lifted a horn to her lips, blowing three clear notes. The call was taken up by others, and soon the Orcs began to withdraw from the melee. The Temple Knights, now bereft of the majority of their horses, moved closer together, forming into a hollow circle, their few remaining mounts in the centre.

Now that the fighting had ceased, only the cries of the wounded echoed across the bloody field. Sir Raynald stepped through the carnage, Athgar at his side while Natalia watched from a distance, her position as commander too important to be risked in such a role.

The knight halted, pulling off his helmet. "I would speak to whoever commands," he called out.

"I am in charge here," called back Father General Hargild. "What do you want?"

"I call on you to give up this fight. You have been misled, Your Grace, as we all have. There are no worshippers of death here. These are ordinary folk."

"You lie!" insisted the father general. "Our grand master has ordained that ours is a just and holy cause. We will not submit to you. You have been tainted by their magic!"

"Please, you must believe me. There is no worship of death here. Do not let your knights die in vain."

"My men will die serving their Saint. Temple Knights do not surrender, nor do they treat with the enemy. Now begone, and let us settle the matter once and for all."

Sir Raynald turned to Athgar. "I'm sorry," he said. "It appears they are determined to fight to the bitter end."

"Do you believe he'll change his mind if we give him some time to think on it?"

"No, they're strong in their beliefs. I doubt they would waver in their resolve."

"Let's see what Natalia thinks," said Athgar. He turned, leading them back through the debris of the battlefield to where the others waited.

"Their answer?" asked Natalia.

"They refuse to surrender," said Athgar.

"I was afraid of that. I've ordered the Orcs to encircle what's left of them. They won't get very far if they try to flee."

"They won't run," insisted Sir Raynald. "They're Temple Knights. They can be stubborn that way."

"And so instead they'll stand and die?" said Natalia.

"It's part of their training. Temple Knights don't retreat."

"That's not true," said Athgar. "We learned that at Ord-Kurgad."

"Yes," added Natalia, "but that was only after the Sisters of Saint Agnes arrived to place their leader under arrest."

"You defeated Temple Knights?" said Sir Raynald. "I've never heard of such a thing."

"Hardly surprising when you think about it," offered Natalia. "If your men lost a battle, would you talk of it?"

The knight blushed. "No, I suppose not. Did you say they gave up when their leader was arrested?"

"They did. He was a father general, much like Hargild is here."

"Perhaps his death would end the fight," mused Athgar.

"It certainly took the fight out of the duke's men when he went down," said Raynald. "Are you suggesting you just kill him?"

"Too difficult when he is amongst his men," said Natalia. "And in any case, command would fall to someone just as zealous. They are a dedicated group, these Cunars."

"Then what do we do?" asked the knight.

"We heal our wounded as best we can and wait, hoping time will convince them of the error of their ways."

"That's it?" said Raynald. "All you're going to do is wait?"

"No, not all," said Natalia, "but I might remind you that you are a prisoner, Sir Raynald. I will not divulge all our plans to you."

"Of course," said the knight, bowing respectfully. "I should know my place."

"Take him back to the stone gate," said Natalia, looking at Athgar, "and have his wounds treated. Then I'll need you back here, with me. We have work to do."

"I can take him," offered Voruhn.

"Very well. We shall leave him in your care."

The Orc shaman escorted the prisoner away, leaving the two mages to continue their discussion.

"How many warriors do you have left?" asked Natalia.

"Not many, I'm afraid," admitted Athgar. "We took heavy casualties.

Many of them will recover, thanks to the Orc shamans, but they won't be of any further use today. I might be able to muster about a hundred."

"And the archers?"

"Relatively unscathed. They were held back during the melee. I thought that a wiser use of their skills."

"We'll bring them up here," she decided. "Have them gather what arrows they can from the battlefield. I fear they shall need them."

"Even so, it won't be enough to defeat the Temple Knights."

"True, but time is on our side."

"How so?" he asked.

"Shaluhk needs rest," Natalia said, "but by late this afternoon, she should be able to cast again. We'll bring the Stone Crushers up as well. Their mastery of Earth Magic should prove devastating to a stationary enemy."

Athgar shuddered. "Those spirits were terrifying. I'm glad they're on our side."

"They will not be as effective a second time. The enemy now knows of their existence. Still, if it saves the lives of the living, it's worthwhile employing them."

A call drew their attention. They both turned, seeing Kargen coming from the east, his bondmate held in his arms.

Athgar smiled. "Glad to see you two made it through in one piece."

"As are we," said Kargen, "but it looks like the battle is not yet over."

"Are you injured, Shaluhk?" asked Natalia.

"No, Sister," the Orc replied. "Only tired from casting. Do not worry, my strength will recover soon enough. What of you? Have you emerged unscathed?"

A look of doubt crossed Natalia's face.

"What is it?" urged Shaluhk.

"I used my magic, despite the pain. The results were not what I expected."

"How so? Did you feel the ice in your stomach again?"

"I did," Natalia confessed, "but I fought through it. I managed to cast, but then a great fire erupted in my belly. It was quite painful."

"A flame, you say?" said Kargen.

"Yes, that's right. Why?"

Kargen looked at Athgar. "That is the mark of a master of flame."

"That's impossible," said Natalia. "My child bears all the telltale signs of Water Magic, hence the cold feeling."

"Could it be twins?" asked Athgar.

"Put me down, Kargen. I must examine Nat-Alia."

Kargen let his bondmate get to her feet. She moved closer, casting a spell as she reached out to place a hand on Natalia's stomach. Black blood ran from her nose.

"You mustn't," said Natalia. "You're pushing yourself beyond your limits."

"Hush now, Sister mine. It will take but a moment." They all held their breath as the shamaness concentrated. Her eyes lit up with an inner light, and then she finally withdrew her hand, wiping the blood from her nose. "There is only one life within you."

"What does that mean?" asked Natalia. "Have I lost a child?"

"No," said Shaluhk, "even in death, I would detect the presence of a body. There has only ever been one child in you, Nat-Alia."

"But the magic of fire and water are opposites. They cannot exist in one person!"

"So we have always thought. But perhaps there is another explanation."

"Go on," urged Natalia.

"You were captured back in Ebenstadt, were you not?"

"I was, why? What has that to do with my baby?"

"Did they use magebane?"

Natalia's eyes went wide. "They did, as a matter of fact. Are you saying it harmed my child?"

"No, at least not in any way I can see, but we have always been taught magic is passed down from parents to children. You, Nat-Alia, are a very powerful Water Mage, so it is only natural your magic would be passed down to your child."

"Then what was the intense heat I felt?"

Shaluhk smiled. "I think your child will one day master both fire and water."

"But that's impossible!"

"Is it? I think the magebane suppressed the Water Magic within your child long enough for the spark to be born within her."

"Are you saying it's a girl?" asked Athgar.

"It is merely a turn of phrase," said Shaluhk. "I have no idea what your child will be."

"And this spark," pressed Athgar, "will she be able to harness it?"

"Her twin powers might simply cancel each other out, but I do not know for sure. I have never heard of both existing in harmony. Other than that, the life within you is strong and healthy, though I am surprised you are not bigger. Are all Human babies so small?"

"I have no idea," said Natalia. "This is my first."

"Skora would know," offered Athgar, "but that is, I think, something left for discussion later. We still have an enemy to defeat."

THE LAST STAND

Autumn 1104 SR

A s the afternoon wore on, the dead were collected while the wounded were helped where possible. What was left of the duke's knights were all granted quarter and took an oath to never again take up arms against the Therengians or the Orcs. Sir Raynald led a small group northward, recovering stray mounts and returning by late afternoon. Shaluhk and the other mages rested, regaining their strength for the coming fight.

Athgar tried once more to convince the Temple Knights to surrender but to no avail. Stubborn as ever, they stood, shoulder to shoulder, ready to make a final stand.

The sun was just getting low when Natalia made the decision to act. Archers came forward, arrows nocked, prepared to rain death upon the enemy. The Temple Knights stood ready, confident their armour would protect them, their courage bolstered by their faith.

Natalia reluctantly gave the order, and the volleys began. They did little damage at first, most merely bouncing off armour, but then Kragor brought up his warbows. As the rest of the archers kept up a steady stream, the hunters of the Red Hand took careful aim. One by one, the enemy fell, their armour punctured by the great bows.

Sir Raynald, unable to watch the carnage, turned his back on them, his stomach releasing its contents to spill onto the ground.

Next came Shaluhk. Once more, she called forth warrior spirits, though this time fewer in number. They swarmed across the open ground, crashing into the enemy formation, bringing death and destruction to the holy warriors.

Still, the Temple Knights fought on, their casualties mounting. Shaluhk's power began to wane, and then Voruhn did something Natalia had never seen before. She walked up to her sister Orc, casting a spell, and placing her hand upon Shaluhk's shoulder. She glowed a vibrant white, and then the colour seeped into her fellow shamaness, filling her depleted reserves of magical energy. The spirits fought on even as the sun began to set.

Mortag had moved up, watching with keen interest as the fight played out before him. The last of the spirit warriors finally faded, their time amongst the living at an end, and then he cast his spell, sending a rolling ball of flame into what was left of the enemy. The smell of scorched flesh drifted back across the field as warriors burned. The devastation was immense, but still they refused calls for surrender.

The Stone Crushers moved closer, and Rugg and Gahruhl sent spikes of stone racing towards the enemy. They punched through armour, but the iron plates lessened the blow, and the Temple Knights fought on.

With darkness came a short respite. Torches were lit, forming a ring around the enemy while the tuskers moved into position. One more call for surrender echoed in the night air, but their foe was stubborn. For a final time, the refusal came back.

Natalia looked at her mages, and she was suddenly struck by their presence. A typical kingdom might boast a single mage, maybe even two if they were wealthy, but here she was blessed by more than half a dozen, likely the largest grouping of mages in ages. Their alliance had pulled together shamans from three tribes, amongst them healers, masters of flame and of earth. Now they gathered, all united in their effort to bring destruction to their enemy.

An initial volley of warbows announced the final assault. Magic was conjured in such volume that the hair on everyone's necks stood on end. Natalia was used to the familiar tingle of magic being cast, but this time it was different. She felt a deeper vibration, a rumble, if you will, that echoed across the field, originating from the stone gate which stood atop the hill. She remembered the gate's amplifying effect, glancing at it only a moment as her thoughts drifted back to what she had been told.

The stone gate consisted of two vertical stones, over which a third rested, forming a doorway of sorts. Now, as she looked, the centre of the door rippled, distorting the view for just a moment.

Her concentration was broken as the spells went off, dragging her attention back to the battle. Fire leaped from Mortag's hands, lighting up the night sky, while beside him, Athgar added his own contribution, a thick smoke to blind their enemies. Even Urumar was there, the apprentice mimicking his master's spell. Rugg and Gahruhl sent forth shards of stone, striking the metal-clad warriors and causing a tremendous clamour.

Natalia watched the display of raw power with a sense of awe. All of her training had taught her how to utilize magic on the battlefield, but no one, not even the instructors at the Volstrum, could have foreseen it being used on such a scale. She felt the flow of magic even though she herself was not casting. It was a feeling of euphoria.

Fire and stone continued to pour forth, dealing horrific damage, and soon a hole opened up in the tightly packed enemy formation. The Temple Knights staggered under the impact, trying to fill in the empty spaces, and then Laruhk led his tuskers through the gap.

The ground reverberated as hooves dug in, the great beasts closing the range quickly, and then they were in amongst their prey, tearing and biting while their riders struck out. Many of the witnesses to this destruction turned away, avoiding the scene. Even hardened warriors found it difficult to watch the slaughter as knight after knight fell beneath the savage attack.

Thankfully, it didn't last long. The Temple Knights, their formation broken, began to fall in great numbers. Some tried to flee, only to be trampled to death or torn to pieces by the vicious teeth of the tuskers.

A great stillness fell over the field, broken only by the laboured breathing of the tuskers as they rooted around, looking for something to kill. The masters of earth moved forward, using their magic to calm the creatures, while others entered the blood-soaked field searching for survivors.

Even in their final moments, the remaining knights chose to fight, reaching out in death to strike back at their enemy. Shaluhk was kneeling, ready to use her magic to help a fallen warrior when the man struck out with a broken sword. The blade scraped along the Orc's forearm, drawing blood. Her response was quick as she drew her long knife and slashed down, ending his defiance forever.

Kargen rushed forward, concerned for his bondemate's safety, but she was already using her magic to knit her flesh. She continued on, forgetting the attack, but grateful for the presence of her bondmate by her side.

Natalia stared at Athgar's face. He was pale, and for a moment, she wondered if he had been injured somehow. Sensing her, he turned, looking at her with dull eyes.

"It's done," he said, "though there was no pleasure in it."

She nodded. "Battle is not something to take pleasure in. It's a dirty thing, to be avoided whenever possible."

"All this death," he added. "Why couldn't they have simply accepted defeat?"

"To some, honour is more important than life itself."

"Honour?" said Athgar. "Hundreds of them gave their lives because of honour. It's a hollow word."

"Do not discount the beliefs of others, my love."

"Is that what the Saints say?"

"It is a universal truth," Natalia replied. "It doesn't matter whether you worship the Saints, the old Gods, or even the Ancestors. What matters is that you hold on to your beliefs; it's what gives you strength. Would you think any less of your own if you died fighting for them?"

"If I was dead, I couldn't think."

"And yet we know that's not true," said Natalia. "The magic of the Orcs has proven that. If the dead do not speak, who are the Ancestors?"

He nodded, then began to sway on his feet.

"Athgar? What is it?"

His eyes rolled up into his head, and he dropped to his knees. Natalia rushed forward, cradling him as he fell backwards.

"Shaluhk!" she called out, but her tribe sister was out of sight. Others gathered around, and she sought out a familiar face, soon finding it in the form of Rugg.

"Something's wrong!" she pleaded.

The old Orc knelt, forcing back Athgar's eyelids to peer within. "He is exhausted," Rugg announced, "nothing more. The battle has been hard on him. I should not have allowed him to cast in such a state."

"Stand back," roared Kargen, pushing his way through the crowd. In his wake followed Shaluhk, concern on her face.

"What has happened?" she asked.

"He collapsed," said Natalia.

Shaluhk reached forward, feeling Athgar's forehead. She knit her brows, then reached out to Natalia, feeling hers as well. "For comparison," she explained. "You Humans are far different than Orcs."

Natalia tried to calm herself, but her mind wouldn't settle. Time seemed to stretch out for an eternity as her tribe-sister cast a spell, and then her eyes began to glow. They all waited with bated breath as Shaluhk withdrew her hand, her magic complete.

"Well?" said Kargen.

"His life force is weak," she said, "but there is no physical injury. I suspect he is suffering from magic fatigue."

"Magic fatigue?" said Natalia. "How can that be? He's used his magic before without such effects?"

"Those who use magic seldom fight with weapons. It is the combination of physical exhaustion together with the depletion of his magical reserves. To put it another way, the spark within him is reduced."

"Is that dangerous?"

"No. So long as he rests, he will recover fully."

"I've heard of this before," added Rugg. "It is very likely that when it returns, he will be even more powerful."

"I don't understand," said Natalia. "I was taught nothing of this at the Volstrum."

"Athgar was not born a mage," Rugg continued, "rather his spark was born through great suffering. There are some who believe such inner fires grow in times of great distress."

"Are you saying he's a wild mage?"

"No," said Shaluhk. "However, had it not been for Master Artoch, his spark would have consumed him. His teachings have given Athgar the discipline needed to keep the spark at bay."

"That's contrary to everything I've ever learned," said Natalia.

Shaluhk looked at her square in the eyes. "Can you be so foolish as to believe this Volstrum of yours knows everything about magic? Magic is a powerful force, Nat-Alia. We can harness it, but we can not control it. That is why discipline is so important."

"And why wild mages are so dangerous," said Natalia. "I understand now. I'm sorry, Shaluhk. I meant no offence."

Shaluhk smiled. "And I take none, Sister mine. Now, I suggest we get Athgar to somewhere that he can rest. You must go with him, Nat-Alia."

"But there's so much to do here."

"I can take care of that," said Kargen. "Or do you doubt the word of a chieftain?"

"No, of course not. Thank you, all of you. You'll never know how much this means to me."

Sir Raynald knelt by the body of the father general. "Such a waste," he said.

"This Human," said Voruhn, "he was their leader?"

The knight nodded. "Yes, but he was following the orders of his superior, Master Talivardas." A sudden thought struck the knight, and he began searching the body.

"You think he will have something of worth?" asked the Orc.

"No. I search for his orders," said Sir Raynald. "He likely kept them with him as a reminder of his duty." He smiled as he withdrew a folded paper. "Here they are."

"What do they say?"

The knight unfolded the package to reveal a neatly penned letter. He scanned its contents, then looked towards the Orc. "As I thought. It's a letter from the grand master."

"How does that help us?" asked Voruhn.

"I'm not sure it does," said Raynald. "But..." His voice trailed off.

"What is it?"

"There's something here I can't explain."

"Perhaps I can help?"

"This letter is dated only three weeks ago."

"And?"

"It was written in Corassus, or so it claims."

"And of what consequence is that?" asked Voruhn.

"There's no way a letter could have travelled from Corassus all the way to Ebenstadt in only three weeks."

"Could it have come by mage?" suggested the shamaness. "It is said that some can use magic to travel great distances."

"The only users of magic in the Church are Life Mages," noted Sir Raynald, "and even they are few and far between."

"Then how do you account for the error?"

"There is only one answer; it's counterfeit. It appears someone went to great pains to legitimize the crusade."

HOME

Winter 1104 SR

Athgar took a sip of the milky-white liquid, passing it to Kargen. The Orc chieftain drank deeply, draining the bowl.

"Kargen," said Shaluhk. "You're supposed to sip it, not drink it dry."

"Then it should not taste so good," he said.

A shout erupted from the doorway, and then Agar ran through the hall, his wooden axe held high. He pounced on Laruhk, who fell back, holding the young Orc above him.

"He has quite the spirit," said Athgar. "He'll make a great hunter someday."

"Perhaps he will become a shaman," suggested Shaluhk.

"It matters not," said Kargen, "so long as he is happy." He turned his attention to Natalia. "And what of you? How much longer must you carry this youngling?"

Natalia rubbed her swollen belly. "Not much longer, I hope. Skora thinks it will only be a few more weeks, and I must admit I'm eager to get her out. She's making me quite uncomfortable with all her shifting about. I think she takes after her father."

"I don't make you uncomfortable, do I?" asked Athgar.

"Uncomfortable, no, but you do shift around a lot. I don't think you've sat still since I started to show."

"You Humans are a curious race," said Shaluhk. "I could have birthed two younglings in the time it takes for you to have one. How did your people ever come to dominate the Continent?"

"Beats me," Natalia replied, "but I'm with you. I wish we had a shorter gestation period."

"More ale?" asked Athgar.

Kargen grinned. "Need you ask?"

Athgar poured the drink, filling the tankard to the brim.

"This is an excellent brew, my friend," said Kargen. "You have quite a gift for making it."

"It's Skora you must thank," the Therengian replied. "It's her recipe."

"Where is she?" asked Shaluhk.

"There were many spare huts after the battle," said Natalia. "She chose to take one for herself, though she still drops by every day to check up on us."

"Yes," added Athgar. "She's become quite the popular person now, with all her wealth of experience. Many's the young villager who looks to her for guidance."

"And you?" said Kargen. "How have you been?"

"I've been well. We both have, aside from the whole pregnancy thing, that is."

"And now you live in the chieftain's hut."

"We do, but that wasn't my idea."

"Then whose?" said Kargen.

"Don't look at me," said Natalia. "That was all decided by the villagers. They officially elected Athgar as their thane."

"What of the tribe?" said Athgar. "Have you finally decided where to build your new village?"

"We have," the chieftain replied. "We sent hunters far and wide, seeking the best location in which to build. Such a place must have fresh water and wood in abundance."

"That sums up the entire area," said Athgar. "There must be more to it than that?"

Kargen grinned. "There was indeed. We also needed a place in close proximity to our allies, so we could come to their assistance if needed."

"And what was your conclusion?"

"I think we have found the perfect spot."

"Go on," urged Athgar.

"Yes," insisted Natalia, "don't keep us in suspense. Where will you rebuild?"

Kargen looked at Shaluhk. "That depends," she said.

"On what?" asked Athgar.

"On what you might think," added Kargen. "We would not want to upset you."

"Are you going to tell us where you will settle or not?"

"Well," said Kargen, drawing out the conversation as long as possible, "we thought we might build here, right beside Runewald."

"Beside us?"

"Yes. Naturally we would have to coordinate such a thing. The palisade, for instance, would have to incorporate your village as well as ours."

Athgar broke out into a grin. "That's a marvellous idea."

"Yes," added Natalia, "and you can use our great hall."

"Or better yet," said Athgar, "we'll build a new one, of stone, with rooms off either end, one for us and one for you. What do you think, Shaluhk?"

"I think it a grand idea," replied the shamaness. "It will bring our people even closer together."

"And we shall continue this great alliance," added Kargen. "We will meet regularly with the other chieftains and thanes to better us all."

"Yes," agreed Shaluhk, "but we must find a better name for our land."

"I have it," called out Laruhk. "The Great Alliance!"

"I think you should stick to hunting," said Shaluhk, "and leave the naming to others."

They all laughed, little Agar joining in despite his lack of understanding.

Natalia leaned back against the furs, soaking in the look of merriment on the faces of her friends and realized she and Athgar had finally found a home.

EPILOGUE

Winter 1104 SR

Illiana Stormwind was laid out in her formal attire as people shuffled past, paying their last respects. She had been head of the family for years, keeping an iron grip on the reins of power until age had finally claimed her. Now, with her death, the struggle for control of the vast influence of the family was set to commence.

Marakhova Stormwind gazed down at the body of the matriarch, a smile crossing her lips. There had been a bitter feud between them these last few years, fuelled by the matriarch's strange obsession with one of her students, Natalia Stormwind. The girl was a powerful mage, likely the most gifted student of the last decade. And yet there was something else to this graduate of the Volstrum aside from her power, something that took hold of Illiana's interest, and Marakhova was determined to discover what it was.

She moved away from the body, finding a window to gaze out as she struggled to come to grips with the ramifications of the matriarch's death. Outside, the winter winds howled across the courtyard, sending flakes of snow swirling in the air, but Mistress Marakhova had far more important things on her mind.

Malvar Stormwind, one of their most powerful Water Mages, cleared his throat. She turned, giving him a stern look. It was a well-known fact that the Grand Mistress of the Volstrum disliked interruptions, something of which he must surely be aware. This intrusion into her thoughts must indeed be important.

"What is it?" she snapped.

"We have news," he said, "from Ebenstadt."

"Go on."

"There has been a great battle, east of the city," he reported. "The Army of the Church has been defeated, exactly as you predicted."

A ghost of a smile flickered across her face. "It would appear that our Cunar Master, Talivardas, has been much more successful than we had hoped. How did he accomplish such a thing?"

"You can ask him yourself if you like. He's here, paying his respects."

Marakhova's eyes roamed the crowd, focusing on the dark grey mantle of Master Talivardas.

"Fetch him," she commanded. "I would have words."

Malvar bowed, then turned, making his way through the crowd.

Marakhova returned her gaze to the window. Malvar was a trusted ally, she reminded herself, and such allies would be scarce in the coming power struggle. She must remember to curb her temper.

"Grand Mistress," came a deep voice.

"Master Talivardas," she said, turning her head. "I hear things have gone well."

He bowed, a rather formal action easily noticed by those in the room. "They have," he said.

"And what are the losses?"

"The order has lost close to seven hundred knights, including more than two hundred initiates. The strength of the Temple Knights of Saint Cunar is now greatly diminished."

"This is excellent news. Is your own position safe?"

"Indeed it is, Grand Mistress. I took pains to pass the blame onto the grand master himself. He shall be hard-pressed to explain his actions. I have also sown the seeds of discontent within the rest of the order's hierarchy. I have no doubt that a review of the events leading up to the campaign will result in the election of a new grand master."

"I take it you are ready to take up this mantle, should it be offered?"

"I am indeed, Grand Mistress."

"Then it seems our plans are nearing fruition," said Marakhova.

Talivardas cast a glance at the gathering. "And this? Will it change things?"

"This is merely an interruption," she replied. "A distraction that should be sorted by spring. You, on the other hand, must return to the task at hand. I wouldn't want your absence to be noted."

"My magic will have me back before they know I'm gone."

She was about to dismiss him but noticed the indecision on his face. "Something is bothering you," she said. "Out with it."

"I heard rumours in Ebenstadt," he said.

"What kind of rumours?"

"There are reports that the renegade, Natalia, was spotted within the city limits."

Marakhova moved closer, lowering her voice. "Go on."

"Nikolai had her in custody, but then she escaped. He asked for extra troops to hunt her down, but the army had already begun assembling. There was little I could do."

"It is an irritation, to be sure," she said, "but understandable under the circumstances. Why bring this to me now?"

"Before he tracked her down, he told me something, something I think would be of interest to you. It seems she was carrying a child."

Marakhova's eyes went wide. "A child, you say? Are you sure?"

"Nikolai was adamant."

"Where is he now?"

"Unfortunately, his body was found the next day, along with those of his men. I'm afraid she slipped through his grasp. Why? Is it important?"

"Important?" said Marakhova. "Natalia is a powerful mage, one of the most powerful we have ever produced. If what we have heard is true, she has taken up with a relatively potent Fire Mage. We have waited generations for this. That child is the future of this family!"

<<<<>>>>

If you enjoyed this book, please share your favourite parts! These positive reviews encourage other potential readers to give the series a try and help the book to populate when others are searching for a new fantasy series. And the best part is, each review I receive inspires me to write more in the World of Eiddenwerthe and beyond. Thank you!

REVIEW FLAMES TODAY

If you liked Flames, then TEMPLE KNIGHT, the first book of the Power Ascending series, is a great book to add to your to be read pile!

SERVANT OF THE CROWN - PROLOGUE

HEIR TO THE CROWN: BOOK ONE

Walpole Street

Summer 953 MC*
(*Mercerian Calendar)

T HE sun was hot, and for what felt like the tenth time that morning, he removed his helmet to wipe the sweat from his brow, absently flinging the moisture from his hand. He cursed the heat yet again as the stink of the slums curled around his nostrils, causing him to gag. Even as he stood, someone emptied a chamber bucket from a second-storey window, the contents splattering to the ground. The waiting was agonizing, particularly with his old leg wound throbbing painfully. The men stood with their backs to him, waiting for the mob to appear, while beside him, the captain, Lord Walters, sat upon his steed surveying the street, as if it held some hidden secret. The line of men stretched across the road from the tavern on the right, to the general goods store on the left. The shopkeepers had already barricaded their doors by the time the troops had taken up their station, fearful of the coming bloodshed.

It had been a harsh winter, and the last harvest had been one of the worst in years. The city was starving, and the poorer sections of town had risen up in protest. This morning, word had come from the Palace ordering the troops to prevent any rioting from making its way into the more prosperous areas of the capital, Wincaster.

The soldiers stood with weapons drawn, relaxed but alert. Sergeant Matheson wiped the sweat from his forehead again. It was far too hot. Tempers would flare; there would be trouble, he could feel it in his bones.

The captain, tired of watching the street, looked down at his sergeant.

"Sergeant Matheson!" he yelled in an overly loud voice.

The sergeant looked up at the lord and noticed he was nervous; the man's eyes shifted back and forth. He was trying to sound confident, but the cracked voice betrayed his fear.

"Have the soldiers move closer together!"

Gerald Matheson had been a soldier almost his entire life. For more than twenty years he had served his country, mostly in the Northern Wars. Now, he was here, on the street, being told by an untried officer how to conduct his men.

"Yes, my lord!" he replied back.

He knew there was no use in arguing, so he gave the command and the soldiers moved together. After carrying out the manoeuvre, they did not entirely cover the width of the street, leaving their flanks exposed. Gerald had thought of forming a single line, but a shield wall needed men in a second rank to help support it. Here he was with only twenty men, stretched across the road in a sparse double line. A company was fifty soldiers on paper, but the realities were far different here in the capital. With the crown holding the purse strings, most were lucky to have thirty men. On top of that, with sick and wounded, his company could barely scrape together twenty at any one time. He looked up at the officer and knew that Lord Walters failed to grasp the danger of their situation.

He glanced over at the far end of the line and immediately realized it was sloppy. He cursed under his breath, now he would have to walk over there to see to it himself. He wondered if he should take his numbleaf, but decided against it; better to be in discomfort and alert than to have his senses dulled. With the first step forward, his leg threatened to buckle as the unwelcome, but familiar shooting pain returned. He stopped to catch his breath as he examined the line, trying to hide his weakness. His hand instinctively sought out his belt pouch, and he withdrew a small, pale green leaf. The line was still facing forward; no one was watching him. He looked at the small leaf in his hand and was overcome with guilt knowing that each one cost him dearly. The bulk of his pay funded the relief he now sought. He was tempted to put it away, but he knew he would welcome the relief the leaf would bring. He popped it in his mouth, looking around conspiratorially, lest anyone see his actions.

He quickly chewed the leaf, and as soon as the skin was broken, he felt the effects. The slightly minty taste enveloped his mouth and then the blessed numbness soaked into his limbs. His leg no longer pained him, but he knew his senses were dulled. He cursed the Norland blade that had wreaked so much damage. Looking back toward the line, he saw that Henderson was still out of place, and he began moving again, hobbling down the line to stand behind the man.

"Henderson," he said, "move forward, you're in a battle line, not a brothel."

The man moved forward, and the sergeant stared at him a moment.

"Where's your helmet man?" he yelled.

Henderson looked back at him and blushed, "Left it in the brothel, Sergeant."

The soldiers around him laughed at the joke. The man had likely sold it for some coins to buy drink, but now the mistake could very well cost him his life. The laughter died down. They were good men, but inexperienced in combat, and he wondered, not for the first time today, if they would do their duty. He knew they were nervous; he must keep them occupied so they wouldn't focus on their fears.

In an undertone, he uttered, "All right lads, when you see the mob, I want you to spread out to your left. Never mind what his lordship says."

The muttered response indicated they understood. He casually strolled over to the other end of the line and repeated the same command. Confident that everything was taken care of, he marched back to the captain and stood beside him. The officer's horse, already skittish, shied away from him, while the rider tried to maintain control over his mount.

"It's cursed hot out here today Sergeant!" his lordship exclaimed, trying to sound calm.

"Yes, my lord," he answered.

The officer was nervous; he was trying too hard to appear nonchalant. For a captain who barely spoke to his social inferiors, he was positively chatty. Gerald had stood with officers behind a line before. Lord Fitzwilliam of Bodden had an easygoing attitude toward his men. His capacity to entrust his sergeants to carry out orders had inspired their loyalty, but that was the frontier. Here, in the cesspit of the kingdom, the quality of officers was limited to those who spent most of their time socializing with the elite rather than training.

He stood still and waited as the sun grew hotter. Noon was approaching, and his right leg began to ache again. Had the numbleaf worn off already? Each time he sought relief with the remedy, it was less effective, and now he could barely get a morning out of a single leaf. He hobbled back and forth behind the men to try to hide his unease, knowing the pain would return shortly. He had reached the end of the line and turned, beginning to retrace his steps when he heard a noise in the distance. He stopped to listen; a dull roar echoed through the streets.

"Shields!" he yelled as he made his way back to the captain. "They're approaching, my lord!"

"Steady men," the officer yelled, rather unnecessarily. The soldiers stood at the ready, shields to the front, swords held up, braced to receive the enemy. Gerald would have hoped to form a proper shield wall with their shields interlocked, but the men here had no such training.

Two blocks down, a swarm of people rounded the corner. They strode confidently, brandishing clubs, daggers, and even broken bottles. There were old men, young men, women, even children in the crowd yelling and screaming. When they saw the soldiers lined up across the street, it was as if a tidal wave was released. The mob surged forward, increasing their speed. He saw the soldiers begin to shift.

"Hold your positions!" he yelled.

The last thing he needed was the soldiers to break and run. He drew his sword and walked behind the line, peering over his men's shoulders to see the oncoming mass of humanity. It was the job of the sergeant to make sure soldiers didn't run from battle. In the North, he was confident that every man would do his duty, but here, there was not the same level of dedication.

"Wilkins, lift up that sword!" Gerald yelled. "Smith, plant your feet properly, or you'll be knocked down."

He distracted the men, made them think about what they were doing rather than focusing on the mob. The officer was yelling something, but he didn't give a damn.

"Here they come, steady... steady... hold your ground!"

The mob slowed, then stopped short of the line, jeering at the soldiers that barred their way. He couldn't blame them. The king had been brutal in his suppression of past riots. The crowd was hungry and desperate, and he knew desperate people would do desperate things. Somewhere in the throng, yelling started; he watched people trying to gather the courage to attack.

"Don't do it," he said under his breath, "don't throw your lives away."

"What was that Sergeant?" said the captain.

"Nothing, my lord, just keeping the men in line," he lied.

The noise in front grew more intense, and then suddenly, bottles and rocks were being thrown. Most hit the shields doing no damage, but Gerald saw the poor bloody fool Henderson take a hit to the head. The man collapsed like a rag doll, and then the anchor at the end of the line was gone. The yelling intensified. He knew it was only a moment before the crowd attacked. He moved as quickly as he could to Henderson's position and dragged the fallen man back from the impending onslaught. A sudden primal scream emanated from the middle of the press of people, giving them the courage to surge forward. He stepped over Henderson's body quickly, grabbing the man's shield as he drew his own sword just in time.

The rioters hit the wall like water breaking against rocks. A thunderous sound erupted as bodies slammed into the wall of soldiers. The line moved back at least a foot and a half, but it held. He knew that if they could only continue to hold, the crowd would give up. He didn't want to have to kill these people. He silently prayed for them to retreat, but they clawed and stabbed with their makeshift weapons. The soldiers occasionally struck back with their swords, but mostly they hid behind their shields, trying not to be hit themselves. During the war, a soldier who didn't fight back was considered cowardly. Here, he was thankful, for perhaps blood on both sides would be spared because of their inexperience.

Sure enough, after the initial surge, the mob, resembling some obscene monster, backed away from the line, and the confidence that they had displayed began to be replaced with fear. The grim reality of swords versus clubs, of bottles versus shields and armour, began to sink in. You could see it in the face of the townsfolk; the sudden look of terror as they realized what was about to happen. Gerald was glad. They would retreat, and the already tense situation would be over. The troops would have stopped the mob, and things would return to normal. All that changed in an instant.

As the crowd began to cautiously back away, the captain found his voice. "Kill them!" he screamed. "Kill them all!"

Gerald looked up with horror at the captain's orders, "My lord, the people are dispersing, we should hold the line!"

Captain Walters had a wild look in his eyes. His fear had overcome him, and he looked down with rage at his sergeant.

"Do as I say, Sergeant! Kill the stinking peasants!"

Gerald heard a yell come from the soldiers, and suddenly the terror they had held in for so long was unleashed, and they surged forward. This was no organized manoeuvre, but a mad rush at the enemy, many of whom had turned their backs to run. It was too late to stop it. The captain was yelling and screaming incoherently at the men.

The sergeant stepped forward, determined to stop the madness, but collapsed to the ground, his leg giving out beneath him. He sat, stunned for a moment, staring at the pool of blood forming around him. He'd been cut in the assault, but the numbleaf and adrenaline had prevented him from feeling it. Now, he was bleeding out, too weak to do anything but look on in horror as his life ebbed out of him.

"How did I get here?" he wondered. "How did my life culminate in bleeding to death in this stinking street, of all places?"

CONTINUE SERVANT OF THE CROWN

A FEW WORDS FROM PAUL

Flames is, at its heart, about people, be they Orcs or Humans. It is the friendships they make along the way that prove to be of the greatest benefit in their quest for a home. Indeed, they are the very thing that makes their victory over the Holy Army even possible.

As Athgar and Natalia finally find a place they can call home, their two greatest foes, the Church and the family, seem to be in conflict. What is the family up to, and why have they taken steps to weaken the Temple Knights, the most powerful military force on the continent? The bigger picture is just starting to emerge.

The fragile peace sees Athgar's people claiming the land for their own, alongside their stalwart allies, the Orcs, but this new alliance may very well threaten the Petty Kingdoms' fragile peace.

Flames marks the third book in The Frozen Flame series and was definitely a joy to write. These characters have grown so much since we first met them, yet there is so much more I have to reveal, beginning in the next installment, Inferno.

This work, like all my other stories, relies on the support of many people. At the top of the list, I must thank Carol Bennett, without whom these tales would never see the light of day. It is her encouragement and enthusiasm that keeps me going. I should also thank Christie Kramburger, Stephanie Sandrock and Amanda Bennett for their support and interest.

Thank you also to my fantastic Beta Team: Rachel Deibler, Michael Rhew, Phyllis Simpson, Don Hinckley, James McGinnis, Charles Mohapel, and Debra Reeves.

Finally, a big THANK YOU to you, my readers, for encouraging me with your reviews and comments. If it wasn't for your interest in reading my stories, I wouldn't be writing these tales, so please take a moment and let me know what you thought of Flames.

ABOUT THE AUTHOR

Paul J Bennett (b. 1961) emigrated from England to Canada in 1967. His father served in the British Royal Navy, and his mother worked for the BBC in London. As a young man, Paul followed in his father's footsteps, joining the Canadian Armed Forces in 1983. He is married to Carol Bennett and has three daughters who are all creative in their own right.

Paul's interest in writing started in his teen years when he discovered the roleplaying game, Dungeons & Dragons (D & D). What attracted him to this new hobby was the creativity it required; the need to create realms, worlds and adventures that pulled the gamers into his stories.

In his 30's, Paul started to dabble in designing his own roleplaying system, using the Peninsular War in Portugal as his backdrop. His regular gaming group were willing victims, er, participants in helping to playtest this new system. A few years later, he added additional settings to his game, including Science Fiction, Post-Apocalyptic, World War II, and the all-important Fantasy Realm where his stories take place.

The beginnings of his first book 'Servant to the Crown' originated over five years ago when he began a new fantasy campaign. For the world that the Kingdom of Merceria is in, he ran his adventures like a TV show, with seasons that each had twelve episodes, and an overarching plot. When the campaign ended, he knew all the characters, what they had to accomplish, what needed to happen to move the plot along, and it was this that inspired to sit down to write his first novel.

Paul now has four series based in his fantasy world of Eiddenwerthe and is looking forward to sharing many more books with his readers over the coming years.